THE BEST OF
PAMELA SARGENT

Also by Pamela Sargent

Fiction

Cloned Lives
Starshadows
The Sudden Star
Watchstar
The Golden Space
The Alien Upstairs
Earthseed
Eye of the Comet
Homesmind
Venus of Dreams
The Shore of Women

Anthologies

Women of Wonder
Bio-Futures
More Women of Wonder
The New Women of Wonder

with Ian Watson
Afterlives

THE BEST OF
PAMELA SARGENT

Edited by
Martin H. Greenberg

Published in 1987 by
Academy Chicago Publishers
425 North Michigan Avenue
Chicago, Illinois 60611

Copyright © 1987 by Pamela Sargent

Foreword Copyright © 1987 by Michael Bishop

Printed and bound in the USA

Library of Congress Cataloging-in-Publication Data

Sargent, Pamela
    The best of Pamela Sargent.

    1. Science fiction, American. I. Greenberg, Martin
Harry. II. Title.
PS3569.A6887A6   1987   813'.54   86-32280
ISBN 0-89733-242-3
ISBN 0-89733-241-5 (pbk.)

Contents

Foreword by Michael Bishop ix
Introduction by Pamela Sargent xxi
Gather Blue Roses 1
Clone Sister 8
If Ever I Should Leave You 37
Bond and Free 54
Shadows 82
The Novella Race 130
The Summer's Dust 148
Out of Place 197
The Broken Hoop 214
The Shrine 233
The Old Darkness 248
The Mountain Cage 268
Heavenly Flowers 290
Fears 306

Foreword
by Michael Bishop

Singers sing, dancers dance, actors act, and tuba-players . . . well, they *tuba*. These truisms surprise almost no one. However, if you add to this unremarkable list the parallel observation that "writers write," some people demur. Writers (they ignorantly beg to differ) take business lunches with editors, pontificate on talk shows, hold signing sessions in the book departments of glamorous retail emporia, collect royalty checks, negotiate with Spielberg or Coppola for movie rights, vacation in the south of France, win the Nobel Prize for Literature, and—fulfilled, honored, wealthy—shuffle off this mortal coil at age ninety-three only to pass into the Undying Collective Memory of Posterity.

Writing (such people self-delusively declare) has nothing, or almost nothing, to do with it.

And, of course, when we confront the writer-celebrities whose stock-in-trade is self-promotion and high profile public strutting, these people (the ones who want to be writers, too, but who don't care to put their fannies to a chair bottom and their fingers atop a keyboard or around a pencil to earn that title) may appear to be on to something.

Obviously, however, the key word here is *appear*. The celebrity writers who may first come to mind— Norman Mailer, Gore Vidal, and Garrison Keillor from the literary mainstream; Isaac Asimov, Harlan Ellison, and Stephen King from the sf and horror fields—have all gained access to media attention, for good or for ill, by virtue of a firm commitment to the written word. More simply put, it was their *writing*, not their engaging and/or infuriating public personalities, that first opened the doors for them to reveal their talents for telegenic soliloquy and showmanship.

"For Pete's sake," I can hear the reader impatiently grumbling, "what has all this got to do with Pamela Sargent?"

Mostly this: Writers write, and truly dedicated writers write whether their reward is adulation or adversity, fame or obscurity, prizes for misfires or peanuts for masterpieces. Pamela Sargent is a writer dedicated to her profession, but also one who apparently has no proclivity at all for gregarious self-touting. She lets the work that she produces at the typewriter speak for her. Over the past sixteen years, it has spoken eloquently enough that she has won an enviable following and the admiration of many of her most perceptive and hard-to-please colleagues, including Algis Budrys, Gregory Benford, James Gunn, and (if I may immodestly lay claim to at least a degree of perception) the undersigned. And, to repeat, Sargent has achieved this success by giving herself almost wholly to the primary task of any writer, *writing*.

Her novels include *Cloned Lives*, an impressive seminal work on the human impact of new biological technologies; *The Sudden Star*, a scary disaster novel done with the hard-boiled panache of Dashiell Hammett; *Watchstar*, a lyrical adventure and a far-future quest for knowledge; *The Golden Space*, which Algis Budrys has legitimately cited as a benchmark achievement in sf speculation about human immortality; *The Alien Upstairs*, whose title hints provocatively at its subject matter; a trio of admirable novels for younger readers, from which adults can also take much pleasure (*Earthseed*, *Eye of the Comet*, and

Homesmind); and two formidable but quietly elegant "blockbusters," *Venus of Dreams* and *The Shore of Women*, both of which appeared in 1986. *Venus of Dreams*, the first novel in a trilogy, convincingly details the transformation of Venus into a livable human world; while *The Shore of Women*, a love story set against the postnuclear backdrop of a society fashioned by and for women, elicited enthusiastic responses from France and England even before its appearance in the United States.

Further, Pamela Sargent has published a collection of her early stories, *Starshadows*, and has edited three noteworthy anthologies of science fiction by women: *Women of Wonder*, *More Women of Wonder*, and *The New Women of Wonder*. *Bio-Futures* is yet another editorial effort accomplished solo; and she has co-edited with England's Ian Watson what I regard as the best one-shot sf anthology of 1986, the intelligently compiled *Afterlives*, with more than a dozen new tales (by James Gunn, Leigh Kennedy, Gene Wolfe, Jody Scott, Rudy Rucker, Howard Waldrop, and others) and seven reprints by such inimitable talents as J.G. Ballard, James Blish, Ursula K. Le Guin, and Pamela Sargent herself—with a well-considered revision of a story that you will discover in its revised form in this collection, "If Ever I Should Leave You."

What amazes about this undeniably remarkable accomplishment is not the accolades that Sargent has won (for she deserves them), but the fact that in some quarters she remains either an unpraised or a ludicrously unacknowledged force in the fields of science-fiction and fantasy letters.

For instance?

Attend: Neither the collective readership known as fandom nor the Science Fiction Writers of America

(SFWA) have found the grace or demonstrated the perspicacity to honor Sargent's contributions with an award. No Lucite blocks (Nebulas) or silver rocketships (Hugos) sit on her shelves; and her quiet but probing fiction has rarely—indeed, *if ever*—landed on the final ballots of either of these purported indices of quality in the sf and fantasy fields, an oversight that after only a moment's consideration boggles the mind. Sargent has somewhat wistfully joked that she does not even qualify for the lugubrious camaraderie of the Hugo & Nebula Losers Club, membership in which provides a glum sort of consolation to writers who have just seen luckier and often more visible—though not always more talented—fellow storytellers walk away with the aforementioned doorstops and desk ornaments.

But, of course, awards in any field of endeavor—television, film, theatre, postal delivery—are iffy commodities at best, and it would be foolish to make too much of the fact that fandom and the SFWA have alike fallen down in failing to give closer attention to the invention and integrity of Pamela Sargent's oeuvre.

However, attend again: At this writing, a Major Figure in the science-fiction world, and one of Great Britain's foremost Literary Lions, has just permitted the publication of a book, the revision of a 1973 tome, purporting to be "The History of Science Fiction." He has updated this earlier effort to include "timely" references to such hot-off-the-presses talents as James Morrow, Mary Gentle, and Bruce Sterling. Unbelievably, and inexcusably, this same book contains not a single word about the longstanding achievement of Pamela Sargent, whose name—were justice served—should appear in the index between "'Sandman, The', see E. T. A. Hoffman" and "*Saturn 3* (1980), 274" and whose contributions to the field should

occupy at least as many pages of text as the Lion gener-
ously allots to, say, Michael Bishop. (An example I em-
ploy not for purposes of self-puffery, but to deflect the
suspicion that I have a private ax to grind. I don't. I have
only minor nits to pick with the Lion's relatively gener-
ous assessment of my work.) What Pamela Sargent herself must think of this latest oversight, I have no idea. But
I believe that, almost by itself, it sabotages a major por-
tion of the credibility of an otherwise comprehensive and
valuable history; and I pray that the Maned Authority
survives long enough to rectify his mistake in a third
revision. To be on the safe side, I advise him to begin
work at once.

"Why these oversights?" some readers might begin
to ask. "Is it conceivably because Ms. Sargent lacks the
ability of the award winners? Is it conceivably because
she lacks the hipness of these with-it new writers who call
themselves, or who happily suffer the label, 'cyberpunks'?"

The answer to the first question is "No, it isn't
conceivable"; the answer to the second is "*Are you kid-
ding?*"

I have my own theories about Pamela Sargent's failure to knock fandom and the unwashed masses of her
fellow writers dead, theories that likewise explain—or go
a small way toward explaining—the inability, or the un-
willingness, of a Major Figure like the author of this
recent (inevitably flawed) "History of Science Fiction" to
recognize the breadth and depth of her contributions.

First, Pamela Sargent eschews self-promotion. She
has neither the disposition nor the taste for it. In one of
this collection's wittiest stories, "The Novella Race," she
postulates a tomorrow in which writing becomes an
Olympic event, with all the cachet of pole-vaulting and

luging. The story brims with inside jokes about the craft and profession of writing, but it also offers a poignant character study of the narrator, whom—throwing not only caution but also academic critical orthodoxy to the winds—I cannot help identifying with Sargent herself:

> My stock-in-trade was unobtrusiveness and self-doubt. I would have preferred being a colorful character like Karath [something of a Harlan Ellison figure in this story], but I could never have carried that off. Being quiet might not win many points, but there was always a chance the judges would react unfavorably to histrionics and give points to a shy writer.

Later, the narrator ponders another writer's observation that Huong, who has never won a medal, may be the best of them all:

> If she was the best, it meant that inferior writers defeated her regularly. And if that was true, it might mean that inferior writers beat better ones in all contests. MacStiofain, I recalled uncomfortably, believed that APOLLO [the computer judge] picked the winners at random, although the human judges might give you an edge. The Olympic committee denied this, but we all knew that MacStiofain's sister had taken a gold in cybernetics. She might have told him something.

Sargent attends few conventions. By her own self-confession, she is uncomfortable speaking to groups. Therefore, she stays home and does what she does best: write. Unfortunately, the failure to self-promote—in a field conspicuously geared to that activity—too often renders one invisible, or nearly so; and this translates into the general perception, especially among fans, writers, and academics who enjoy the social aspects of their sf involvement more than they do reading, that you Do Not Exist.

Second, Pamela Sargent's editorship of the afore-mentioned *Women of Wonder* anthologies—containing stories exclusively by women, and frequently about women as well—gave her a reputation as a feminist (which she unapologetically is) that did not go down well in some quarters. I feel sure that certain male writers resented the compilation of books, even as correctives to the male-oriented stories and anthologies of earlier eras, that deliberately excluded their work on the basis of gender. Some used the premises of these anthologies to cry, rather blindly, "Foul!" and some may well have dismissed Sargent's own fiction as that of an ideologue, when the truth—as *The Best of Pamela Sargent* demonstrates—is that she is a humanist after the fashion of Ursula K. Le Guin, Kate Wilhelm, and such relative newcomers as Connie Willis and Nancy Kress. Even the story "Fears," which posits an all-male dystopia while limning the fears of its outcast narrator-protagonist, never loses sight of the damaged humanity of *all* its characters.

Third, Pamela Sargent has as capable a command of fantasy as she does of science fiction. This would seem to be a virtue, but often the ability to straddle, yoke, or mix-and-match categories diffuses rather than solidifies a writer's audience. Critics who confine themselves to horror miss your sf while those who debunk or extoll the latest space opera miss your idiosyncratic dark fantasy, with the unhappy result that you fall between stools and go down to dismaying anonymity wondering what the hell happened. Sargent has not quite suffered *this* fate, but it may be the case that her range has occasionally played against her.

Consider this collection. Each of these fourteen stories is an exemplar of "imaginative fiction," by which I mean either science fiction, horror, or fantasy. Nine, by my reckoning, qualify as sf, while the other five strike me as stories in which fantasy elements predominate. These latter five include "Out of Place," a funny story in which people suddenly find themselves able to eavesdrop on the thoughts of animals; "The Broken Hoop," a persuasive historical tale about an Indian woman caught between two worlds; "The Shrine," a contemporary horror story that recently came to our nation's TV screens on the syndicated series *Tales from the Darkside*; "The Old Darkness," another horror story but one in which the gothic element derives from a quintessentially modern phenomenon, a power failure; and "The Mountain Cage," in which the reader gets a glimpse of the Holocaust from the unusual point-of-view of Hrurr, a cat. Indeed, this last story is a kind of cameo *Watership Down* (antedating Tad Williams's *Tailchaser's Song* by a year or two), with felines taking the place of long-eared lagomorphs.

Even within the nine science-fiction stories, Sargent's range is noteworthy and enviable. She treats of many of the classic sf themes and in each case brings something new and pertinent to her use of them. "Shadows" takes an oblique but frightening look at alien invasion. "If Ever I Should Leave You" is a time-travel tale about both death and longing. "Bond and Free" examines a world in which superpowers have become commonplace, but from the perspective of an institutionalized person with the handicap of what you and I would call "normality." "Gather Blue Roses" has as its subject a variety of telepathic talent—universal empathy—that proves, to more than one of its characters, a greater bane than blessing. "Heavenly Flowers" considers a postnuclear world from the hapless vantage of the survivors, who want, above all else, to *remember* the causes and extent of the destruction. "Clone Sister" is a daring, but not tawdry or sensational, study of a new variety of incest; and "The Summer's Dust" gives dramatic impetus to the notion that with the coming of immortality, one thing that *dies* is the prospect for genuine change.

Let me repeat: Sargent's range, her refusal to confine herself to this genre or that, may occasionally work against her when the world starts looking for writers to whom to apply superlatives: the best sf writer, the best modern fantasist, or the best purveyor of contemporary horror. She may not be (even Sargent, I think, would admit this) the mythological "best" in any single one of these sometimes arbitrary categories, but she excels in all of them; and perhaps her doing so has scattered her audience and discombobulated some of our critics and historians.

Fourth, Sargent's style is never flamboyant, and the stories themselves—as already implied—never resort to sensationalism or shoddy melodrama to heighten their impact. A generation raised on the *Star Wars* films, music videos, and the explicit brutalities of most latter-day-horror movies (not to mention the evening news) is often less than well-equipped to cope with thoughtfulness, and Sargent's work almost always reveals that very quality. Her spare, quiet prose—which rarely draws attention to itself, preferring to convey information rather than to jump up and down bleating, "Hey, look at my exotic syntax! Behold my mastery of jargon, neologisms, and pseudo-scientific buzzwords!"—deserves closer attention than anyone has yet given it, particularly when it functions to reveal the mental states of Sargent's characters as well as to advance the forward movement of her stories. Attend this simple but evocative passage from "The Mountain Cage," in which Hrurr sees a "herd" of Nazi limousines arrive at Hitler's headquarters:

> Several two-legged ones in gray skins stood by the gate; two of them walked over to the first metal beast, and peered inside its openings, then stepped back, raising their right arms as others opened the gate and let the first beast pass. The two moved on to the next beast, looking in at the ones inside, then raised their arms again. The flapping arms reminded Hrurr of birds; he imagined the men lifting from the ground, arms flapping as they drifted up in lopsided flight.

Good, clear writing in the service of an allegorical critique of the "attractiveness" of Nazism—the virtues of simplicity and thoughtfulness in the same story, at a time when high-tech glitz—a decadent infatuation with bright or grungy surfaces—has become a hallmark of our most popular mass-culture entertainments, from movies to music videos to sf novels.

Which brings me to my fifth and final point. Pamela Sargent's first story—not included here—appeared in *Fantasy and Science Fiction* in 1970. Throughout that decade and into the early years of the 1980s, she developed and grew as a writer, producing solid and in some cases groundbreaking work as her talent matured. Other writers created more stir and copped more awards, but, although she occasionally and altogether understandably fell prey to self-doubt, she persevered. She kept writing.

She allowed her dedication to the profession to carry her over the rough places, and she bided her time in the expectation—I would imagine—of some belated acknowledgement of her achievement.

In the 1980s, however, a new militancy—a new sense of vision and drive—gripped many of the sf field's younger writers, those variously hailed as everything from cyberpunks to Neuromantics to outlaw technologists; and the noise that their stories and novels made, along with their flair for confrontational self-promotion and proselytizing (some of which was blood-stirring and amusing; a lot of which was adolescent, crass, and needlessly divisive), tended in some cases to drown out the voices of writers who had come to their maturity in the 1970s. The hoopla attending the appearance of such notable talents as William Gibson and Bruce Sterling, for instance, has led some people to the nitwit belief that nothing of importance occurred in the sf field between the demise of the New Wave in the late 60s/early 70s and the appearance of Gibson's first "romantic, cybernetic, radical-hard sf" story in *Omni*.

As much as I like the better efforts of some of these writers—Sterling's novel *Schismatrix* prompted an unabashed fan letter—just that much do I deplore the way in which the attendant hoopla and propaganda has mindlessly overwhelmed the voices of the good writers who preceded them. Notably, Pamela Sargent's. Sterling would undoubtedly reply, "Well, she could get a copying machine and put out a self-promoting agitprop broadsheet of her own, just the way I did," to which the obvious answer is, "Why the hell should she, or anyone else, have to?" Writers, as I said at the opening of this piece, write; and although agitprop is admittedly a variety of that activity (the way that letting wind might be construed as a variety of music-making), that is not the sort of writing to which I am pointing when I say "writers write" and declare Pamela Sargent a praiseworthy example of that dictum.

No Hugo. No Nebula. No mention in a long-awaited history of the field that—in an ill-advised stab at appearing as hip and up-to-the-minute as possible—falls all over itself to comment on some titles from the mid-1980s that may well prove as ephemeral as summer midges. Pamela Sargent deserves far better, and *The Best of Pamela Sargent*, the collection now in your hands, provides tangible proof of the shamefulness of these oversights. It also, to my way of thinking, manages to rectify them to some small extent, for if a writer writes, the most lasting legacy of that honorable activity is not the money that it makes, or the prizes that it accrues, or the critical attention that it commands, but the books and stories that come out of it and the impact that these artifacts have on the people who read them.

If you are sitting down to *re*read a Pamela Sargent story, you already know and value what its impact is likely to be. If you are coming to her work for the first time, get ready to be astonished, amused, provoked, stimulated, and moved. Writers write, of course, so that readers may read, and you are fortunate to find yourself in the capable, caring hands of this capable, caring writer. Indeed, the only literary advice that I can think to tender her is advice designed to prolong her career: "Pam, when the hell are you going to give up those friggin' cigarettes?"

—Michael Bishop
December 10-11, 1986

Introduction
by Pamela Sargent

I threw my first published story away. I'd thrown away stories before, and it was turning into a habit by then. Write them, then chuck them into the wastebasket—that was my *modus operandi*. I could have the pleasure of writing them without the pain of submitting them for judgment.

It's hard to know what I feared more—that I would be told the stories were lousy, or that someone might actually think they were good, in which case I'd have to make some hard decisions.

Obviously, this story didn't stay thrown away, or it wouldn't haven seen print. But I'm getting ahead of myself.

The first story I recall throwing away was written during my teens. The main character was a man who lived in a world where nobody was allowed to be unhappy or to feel pain. To insure this, everybody had to wear a wrist-monitor kind of device; if you were miserable, somebody would show up with tranquilizers, and so forth. My character tries to commit suicide, fails, and then has to flee from the Euthanasia Corps, which has decided that he's too unhappy to live. After lots of thrilling chase sequences, he's captured by the Corps, and, as he dies, he realizes—surprise—*that he wants to live after all*.

This story—my first science-fictional effort, as it turned out—was written for my English class. But what kind of grade was I going to get if I turned in this story? I went to a girls' school where many of us had literary pretensions. My teacher, an extremely intelligent woman who was a published poet herself, had assigned *Brave New World* and *Nineteen Eighty-Four* as readings, and had tolerated a long paper from me on the science fiction of H.G. Wells, but even she, I supposed, had her limits.

"Nah," I said as I threw my story away the night before it was due. I wrote another, a slice-of-life involving kids on a playground, that might have owed something to *Lord of the Flies*. I got my A, and the story later ended up in our school's literary magazine.

I was already learning about both self-censorship and the limits of the marketplace, as it turned out.

I'd learned a little about the limits of the marketplace somewhat earlier, when I didn't always throw stories away. In sixth grade, my teacher came up with the notion of having our class put out a mimeographed collection of our writings. This was around the time of spring vacation (or "Easter vacation," as this public school called it in those days before various Supreme Court rulings), and it occurred to me that a Jesus story might be in order.

This was kind of a strange choice for a professed atheistic non-Christian, but I had my own ideas for the story. I decided to write about Mary Magdalene: She's going to the tomb of Jesus with the other two Marys, and she's feeling pretty bad. In fact, she's kind of annoyed with Jesus for getting himself crucified in the first place instead of leaving town. She's brooding on this when they get to the tomb and find the stone rolled away. Nobody sings hosannas, and nobody goes running to spread the news, because these women are totally mystified and don't know what's going on, but at least Mary

Magdalene isn't mad at Jesus any more.

The story ended on this inconclusive note. I was learning the value of ambiguity when the writer's aim is different from what the audience (in this case, parents of sixth-graders in a conservative community) is expecting.

The first writing I ever did on assignment, outside of school, was also done during childhood. My father was in and out of the hospital for surgery and various diagnostic tests, and I couldn't visit him there because I was under the hospital's minimum age for visitors. My mother suggested that my father might appreciate a written and illustrated record of the family's weekly doings.

There wasn't a whole lot to write about. My brothers, my sister, and I went to school, came home, played with friends, watched television, fed the cats, and went to bed; it wasn't promising material. So I had to heighten and exaggerate. A ride on the school bus became an ominous journey to a dreaded destination; an argument with a brother became a highly-charged prelude to violence and drama; a dinner prepared by my mother was a mighty effort to placate the gang of budding food critics she was rearing; after-school play was fraught with danger and rivalry. When reality failed, I resorted to invention.

I sometimes think my father might have wondered why things weren't so exciting when he was home.

I might not have become a writer without the experience of an eighth-grade English class with a teacher named Mr. Ketchum. The first week we were in his class, he decided that lecturing to us on brain physiology was a lot more interesting than whatever we were supposed to be doing. It made sense; we'd find out how it was possible to learn anything at all before he tried to teach us grammar. Mr. Ketchum covered the blackboards with drawings of cerebrums, cerebellums, medullas, cerebral cortexes, and representations of young neural pathways in which he hoped some of his knowledge would be etched and stored. We loved it; anything beat diagramming sentences. We didn't call his class "English;" we called it "the fun class."

Of course, we had to diagram sentences eventually, and take grammar tests. "Diagramming is fun!" Mr. Ketchum would shout whenever he gave a test. He was the kind of guy who got a workout while teaching, waving his arms and bounding across the room. "Memorizing poetry is fun! Learning the parts of speech is fun! Reading and looking things up is fun!" He'd make you believe it.

He also assigned a lot of themes. Originality was what he was after in these writings. Being a good, conventional student was fine for taking tests, but he expected more on themes—a new insight, a quirkiness in the way you looked at the world, a new idea or way of doing the assignment—something different.

His agenda coincided with mine, and I started getting A's. You could get an A on a theme even if you misspelled or made grammatical errors, as long as you were original and learned from your mistakes. Those of us who were anarchists at heart thrived, but the kids who did everything the way you were supposed to didn't do so well. "It isn't fair," one boy said to me after I turned in a theme with mistakes and got an A, while he did one without a single error and got a B.

Mr. Ketchum taught me that creativity and originality will always be rewarded. Unfortunately, given the way the world works, this isn't a lesson anyone should take to heart.

I threw away my first science fiction story because I was pretty sure, perhaps mistakenly, that it would meet with puzzlement or disapproval. Later, I was throwing away other stories because I'd lost the clear-eyed confidence of childhood and had replaced it with the insecurities and fears of adolescence. I was becoming an adult—a degenerated child, by some definitions—probably the last thing any writer should aspire to be.

It's discouraging to recall your childhood, which is probably why so many people choose not to remember that time. There you are as a child—however miserable you were, or confused, you probably saw a lot of things pretty clearly. You'd see the older people around you making a mess of their lives or compromising all over the place, and you'd find out that they didn't always have a good reason for their actions. You saw how absurd and ridiculous a lot of their behavior was, and probably had a good laugh when they told you what a wonderful time childhood is. You were honest and called a spade a spade, then got lectured about etiquette or were told you were being mean or unfair.

Later on, you look at the pile of cigarette butts in your ashtray and think of how your childhood self was puzzled by this useless habit of adults. You stare at the third drink you shouldn't be having and recall how silly adults acted when they'd had one too many. You hear yourself making a pompous or phony remark to a child or teenager and think of how you've turned into just the kind of horse's ass you once scorned. You realize you've betrayed your childhood self.

Writers are supposed to remember. Sometimes, you'd rather forget.

The year before I went to college, I was taking some advanced placement tests in the hope of avoiding a couple of required freshman courses. My English teacher, Mrs. Collins, happened to ask me what I was considering as a major.

"I don't know," I replied, unwilling to admit that my main reason for going to college at all was that I had a scholarship and couldn't think of anything better to do.

"Are you thinking of English?" she asked. It was a reasonable question, since it was one of my best subjects.

"I don't know," I said.

"You ought to think about it," she said then, "because I don't know if that's really for you."

Mrs. Collins had a good reason for saying this. She suspected that I still wanted to write. If I majored in English, I might leave college with a load of critical tools that would only inhibit me, and I was growing inhibited enough. I took her advice; at least I could eliminate one possible major.

But I was fairly sure by then that I wouldn't be a writer, either. By the time I entered college, I made up my mind never to write any fiction again; there would be enough to do without that distraction. I would bypass the wastebasket, and throw part of myself away instead.

This resolution was soon broken. After I'd been in college for about a year, I found myself writing a piece of fiction again. I still remember the moment—the dream-like state, the pen moving across the paper, the bright sunlight through the dormitory window, the smell of formaldehyde on my hands (I was studying biology and doing a lot of dissection).

The story was a slice-of-life about a college student. I was so taken with the first page that I read it to a classmate who was also an aspiring writer. The verdict was unequivocal; the page stank. My confidence shattered, I tossed the story away before finishing it.

I'd learned a valuable lesson, though it took years to understand it, and that was never to show unfinished work to anybody in the heat of inspiration. Finished stories can take it; unfinished ones can't.

I'd given up writing, but another student I knew hadn't. George Zebrowski was not only writing, but actually submitting stories to editors; this was annoying, especially since rejections only seemed to fuel his determination. It annoyed me more when he managed to sell one effort; that was going too far.

I sat down and wrote a story of my own, "Landed Minority," another tale of a college student, but with a science-fictional setting. Old habits aren't easy to break, though, and this story got chucked into the wastebasket, where it would have remained if George hadn't fished it out.

"Type it up and send it to a magazine," he insisted. I refused at first, then convinced myself that sending it out was simply an extension of throwing it away. There was little chance it would be published, and even my fragile ego would be able to handle a rejection from an editor I'd never met.

The story was rejected by the first editor who saw it, but that pain was dulled because he later decided to buy another story I'd written in the meantime. The second editor who saw "Landed Minority," Edward Ferman of *The Magazine of Fantasy & Science Fiction*, bought it and published it some time later. I had outsmarted myself, and was going to be a published writer after all.

I was gratified—actually, ecstatic—but still didn't think of myself as a writer. I had sold my story not long before my college graduation ceremony; coincidentally, Isaac Asimov was the commencement speaker that year (his first time as such a speaker, although I didn't know that at the time). My father dragged me over to him and introduced me as a colleague, something that must have caused Dr. Asimov some amusement. Fortunately, even his prodigious memory didn't store this encounter for his autobiography.

Had I learned by then not to throw anything away? Not exactly. My first novel was thrown away, too.

I began a novel during the summer after graduation, writing it at night after work. The entire book was a flashback told in first person from the point of view of a prostitute who had plied her trade on spaceships and various planets; I must have thought this would pass as a daring topic. The character began by recalling her child-hood in a Catholic community on a planet near Tau Ceti; her recollections were interspersed with details of her present, unhappy life as the mistress of an alien.

I committed almost two hundred pages of this saga to paper before seeing how hopeless it was. The story was only a series of incidents. The protagonist was an airhead given to purple prose and even I didn't care what happened to her. I tried to imagine this story in published form, had any editor been foolish enough to take it.

I threw it away. Some things need throwing away. I

thought I was doing what I'd always done, but I wasn't; I was learning the difference between a story that could be saved, and an utter failure. I was also learning that you can't often tell whether a story will fail until it's written.

I went to graduate school and became a teaching assistant in philosophy, but kept writing on the side. The wastebasket was no longer necessary; editors with rejection slips could dispose of the stories that needed throwing away.

I wasn't a writer, though, still couldn't admit that to myself. Real writers were into a different head, as we put it in those days. Writers were disciplined and convinced of their works' worth; they learned about contracts and even went to workshops, something I regarded as an exercise in masochism.

I was just a grad student who dabbled. Later, when I left graduate school, I was somebody who was just fooling around with writing until it was time to settle into my real work. Even with copies of published stories on the shelf, I kept thinking it was only a phase, that the stories would cease to inhabit my brain eventually and would take up residence elsewhere. Writing, along with bulimia, experiments with drugs, sleeping until noon, and other youthful disorders, was something that would have to be put aside sooner or later.

I was ignoring most of my work once it came out. I never reread it, never looked back; maybe I was pretending it was in the wastebasket, where I didn't have to worry about what other people thought of it. All of this changed in 1974, when a magazine published my story "If Ever I Should Leave You."

I took a quick glance at the story when it was out, mostly because of curiosity about the accompanying illustration—and immediately saw that something was wrong. Sentences I had never written were set in type under my name; my protagonist had a name I had never given her. I reread the story (the first time I'd ever done so after a story was published) in a state of shock and mounting rage. Someone had rewritten my story without consulting me, and none of the changes was an improvement.

I have a file of correspondence, tens of pages thick, that includes my letters to the editor and to the grievance committee of the writers' organization to which I belonged, various letters to me, and an extremely long and stupid letter from the creature (not the editor, as it turned out) who had rewritten the story, in which he sought to justify the changes. After months of battling, some of it accompanied by threats of action to be taken against me if I didn't stop "shooting off my mouth" about my ravaged story, I managed to get an apology from the editor who had purchased the story and from the magazine's new editor, who published my letter disowning the version of my story in print.

Small consolation, but it was a valuable lesson. No longer was publication an extension of the wastebasket, a way of detaching the story from me and disposing of it. If I didn't care about the work once it was written, why should an editor care? The stories, whatever their worth, were part of me; they had to be tended, and I had to stand behind them. They were not a solitary means of self-expression, or the product of an unfortunate quirk I couldn't get rid of, but a way of communicating to others with my words.

I had to face it at last; I was a writer.

Not long after this dispute was settled, I owned up to what I was out loud—in a shoestore, of all places. The clerk had taken my credit card and asked casually what I did.

"I'm a writer," I blurted out without thinking. Not "I do a little writing," or "Well, I'm sort of writing some stuff until I finish my Ph.D.," or "I'm self-employed in the home," or any of my usual responses, but "I'm a writer."

It was a momentous admission, and even the clerk's next question—"Ever published anything?"—couldn't really dampen my mood.

I had relapses. I still threw some writings away instead of letting them sit until parts of them could be salvaged. I sneaked up on my first published novel by writing it as a series of shorter pieces instead of attacking it head on. I indulged in self-doubt when I should have been sitting at my desk. But I learned that the profession of writing isn't over when the work is finished and you get up from the typewriter.

What you think of yourself sometimes has little to do with what you are. There may be some consolation in knowing that.

Some writers know what they are early, and embrace the work. I had to be dragged into writing by people who saw what I might be before I could see it. George Zebrowski, Jack Dann, and others set the example I needed. Editors Ed Ferman, Terry Carr, David Gerrold, Michael Moorcock, Joseph Elder, Damon Knight, and others encouraged my early work, even when they rejected some of it. Mr. Ketchum and Mrs.

Collins probably had something to do with it, too.

You can blame this collection partly on them, but I'll accept my share of the responsibility.

Even with this book, I had to be persuaded. Marty Greenberg proposed it to me; self-doubt and the specter of the wastebasket again put in an appearance.

"Don't you think it's a little premature?" I asked. Such collections were, I presumed, supposed to come out when a writer was retired, dead, or unlikely ever to improve. The title might jinx my future work, or readers might find it amusing—I was regressing to some of the fears I'd had when I first started to write.

I made similar noises when the publisher, Jordan Miller, called to discuss the book. Mr. Miller, fortunately, is a man with some tact and sensitivity. "Why don't we think of it," he responded, "as *The Best of Pamela Sargent So Far?*"

I guess I can live with that. Here are some of the tales that weren't thrown away.

Gather Blue Roses

I cannot remember ever having asked my mother outright about the tattooed numbers. We must have known very early that we should not ask; perhaps my brother Simon or I had said something inadvertently as very small children and had seen the look of sorrow on her face at the statement; perhaps my father had told us never to ask.

Of course, we were always aware of the numbers. There were those times when the weather was particularly warm, and my mother would not button her blouse at the top, and she would lean over us to hug us or pick us up, and we would see them written across her, an inch above her breasts.

(By the time I reached my adolescence, I had heard all the horror stories about the death camps and the ovens; about those who had to remove gold teeth from the bodies; the women used, despite the Reich's edicts, by the soldiers and guards. I then regarded my mother with ambivalence, saying to myself, I would have died first, I would have found some way rather than suffering such dishonor, wondering what had happened to her and what secret sins she had on her conscience, and what she had done to survive. An old man, a doctor, had said to me once, "The best ones of us died, the most honorable, the most sensitive." And I would thank God I had been born in 1949; there was no chance that I was the daughter of a Nazi rape.)

By the time I was four, we had moved to an old frame house in the country, and my father had taken a job teaching at a small junior college near by, turning down his offers from Columbia and Chicago, knowing how impossible that would be for mother. We had a lot of elms and oaks and a huge weeping willow that hovered sadly over the house. Our pond would be invaded in the early spring and late fall by a few geese, which would usually keep their distance before flying on. ("You can tell those birds are Jewish," my father would say, "they go to Miami in the winter," and Simon and I would imagine them lying on a beach, coating their feathers with Coppertone and ordering lemonades from the waitresses; we hadn't heard of Collinses yet.)

Even out in the country, there were often those times when we would see my mother packing her clothes in a small suitcase, and she would tell us that she was going away for a while, just a week, just to get away, to find solitude. One time it was to an old camp in the Adirondacks that one of my aunts owned, another time to a cabin that a friend of my father's loaned her, always alone, always to an isolated place. Father would say that it was "nerves," although we wondered, since we were so isolated as it was. Simon and I thought she didn't love us, that mother was somehow using this means to tell us that we were being rejected. I would try very hard to behave; when mother was resting, I would tiptoe and whisper. Simon reacted more violently. He could contain himself for a while; but then, in a desperate attempt at drawing attention to himself, would run through the house, screaming horribly, and hurl himself, head first, at one of the radiators. On one occasion, he threw himself through one of the large living room windows, smashing the glass. Fortunately, he was uninjured, except for cuts and bruises, but after that incident, my father put chicken wire over the windows on the inside of the house. Mother was very shaken by that incident, walking around for a couple of days, her body aching all over, then going away to my aunt's place for three weeks this time. Simon's head must have been strong; he never sustained any damage from the radiators worse than a few bumps and a headache, but the headaches would often keep mother in bed for days.

(I pick up my binoculars to check the forest again from my tower, seeing the small lakes like puddles below, using my glasses to focus on a couple in a small boat near one of the islands, and then turn away from them, not wanting to invade their privacy, envying the girl and boy who can so freely, without fear of consequences, exchange and share their feelings, and yet not share them, not at least in the way that would destroy a person such as myself. I do not think anyone will risk climbing my mountain today, as the sky is overcast, cirro-cumulus clouds slowly chasing each other, a large storm cloud in the west. I hope no one will come; the family who picnicked beneath my observation tower yesterday bothered me; one child had a headache and another indigestion, and I lay in my cabin taking aspirins all afternoon and nursing the heaviness in my stomach. I hope no one will come today.)

Mother and father did not send us to school until we were as old as the law would allow. We went to the small public school in town. An old yellow bus would pick us up in front of the house. I was scared the first day and was glad Simon and I were twins so that we could go together. The town had built a new school; it was a small, square brick building, and there were fifteen of us in the first grade. The high school students went to classes in the same building. I was afraid of them and was glad to discover that their classes were all on the second floor; so we rarely saw them during the day except when they had gym classes outside. Sitting at my desk inside, I would watch them, wincing every time someone got hit with a ball, or got bruised. (Only three months in school, thank God, before my father got permission to tutor me at home, three months were too much of the constant pains, the turmoil of emotions; I am sweating now and my hands shake, when I remember it all.)

The first day was boring to me for the most part; Simon and I had been reading and doing arithmetic at home for as long as I could remember. I played dumb and did as I was told; Simon was aggressive, showing off, knowing it all. The other kids giggled, pointing at me, pointing at Simon, whispering. I felt some of it, but not enough to bother me too much; I was not then as I am now, not that first day.

Recess: kids yelling, running, climbing the jungle gym, swinging and chinning themselves on bars, chasing a basketball. I was with two girls and a piece of chalk on the blacktop; they taught me hopscotch, and I did my best to ignore the bruises and bumps of the other students.

(I need the peace, the retreat from easily communicated pain. How strange, I think objectively, that our lives are such that discomfort, pain, sadness and hatred are so easily conveyed and so frequently felt. Love and contentment are only soft veils which do not protect me from bludgeons; and with the strongest loves, one can still sense the more violent undercurrents of fear, hate and jealousy.)

It was at the end of the second week that the incident occurred during recess. I was, again, playing hopscotch, and Simon had come over to look at what we were doing before joining some other boys. Five older kids came over. I guess they were in third or fourth grade, and they began their taunts.

"Greeeenbaum," at Simon and me. We both turned toward them, I balancing on one foot on the hopscotch squares we had drawn, Simon clenching his fists.

"Greeeeenbaum, Esther Greeeeenbaum, Simon Greeeeenbaum," whinnying the green, thundering the baum.

"My father says you're Yids."

"He says you're the Yid's kids." One boy hooted and yelled. "Hey, they're Yid kids." Some giggled, and then they chanted, "Yid kid, Yid kid," as one of them pushed me off my square.

"You leave my sister alone," Simon yelled and went for the boy, fists flying, and knocked him over. The boy sat down suddenly, and I felt pain in my lower back. Another boy ran over and punched Simon. Simon whacked him back, and the boy hit him in the nose, hard. It hurt and I started crying from the pain, holding my nose, pulled away my hand and saw blood. Simon's nose was bleeding, and then the other kids started in, trying to pummel my brother, one guy holding him, another guy punching. "Stop it," I screamed, "stop it," as I curled on the ground, hurting, seeing the teachers run over to pull them apart. Then I fainted, mercifully, and came to in the nurse's office. They kept me there until it was time to go home that day.

Simon was proud of himself, boasting, offering self-congratulations. "Don't tell mother," I said when we got off the bus, "don't, Simon, she'll get upset and go away again, please. Don't make her sad."

(When I was fourteen, during one of the times mother was away, my father got drunk downstairs in the kitchen with Mr. Arnstead, and I could hear them talking, as I hid in my room with my books and records, father speaking softly, Mr. Arnstead bellowing.

"No one, no one, should ever have to go through what Anna did. We're beasts anyway, all of us, Germans, Americans, what's the difference."

Slamming of a glass on the table and a bellow: "God damn it, Sam, you Jews seem to think you have a monopoly on suffering. What about the guy in Harlem? What about some starving guy in Mexico? You think things are any better for them?"

"It was worse for Anna."

"No, not worse, no worse than the guy in some street in Calcutta. Anna could at least hope she would be liberated, but who's gonna free that guy?"

"No one," softly, "no one is ever freed from Anna's kind of suffering."

I listened, hiding in my room, but Mr. Arnstead left after that; and when I came downstairs, father was just sitting there, staring at his glass; and I felt his sadness softly drape itself around me as I stood there, and then the soft veil of love over the sadness, making it bearable.)

I began to miss school at least twice a week, hurting, unable to speak to mother, wanting to say something to father but not having the words. Mother was away a lot then, and this made me more depressed (I'm doing it, I'm sending her away), the depression endurable only because of the blanket of comfort that I felt resting over the house.

They had been worried, of course, but did not have their worst fears confirmed until Thanksgiving was over and December arrived (snow drifting down from a gray sky, father bringing in wood for the fireplace, mother polishing the menorah, Simon and me counting up our saved allowances, plotting what to buy for them when father drove us to town). I had been absent from school for a week by then, vomiting every morning at the thought that I might have to return. Father was reading and Simon was outside trying to climb one of our trees. I was in the kitchen, cutting cookies and decorating them while mother rolled the dough, humming, white flour on her apron, looking away and smiling when I sneaked small pieces of dough and put them in my mouth.

And then I fell off my chair onto the floor, holding my leg, moaning, "Mother, it hurts," blood running from my nose. She picked me up, clutching me to her, and put me on the chair, blotted my nose with a tissue. Then we heard Simon yelling outside, and then his banging on the back door. Mother went and pulled him inside, his nose bleeding. "I fell outa the tree," and, as she picked him up, she looked back at me; and I knew that she understood, and felt her fear and her sorrow as she realized that she and I were the same, that I would always feel the knife thrusts of other people's pain, draw their agonies into myself, and, perhaps, be shattered by them.

(Remembering: Father and mother outside, after a summer storm, standing under the willow, father putting his arm around her, brushing her black hair back and kissing her gently on the forehead. Not for me, too much shared anguish with love for me. I am always alone, with my mountain, my forest, my lakes like puddles. The young couple's boat is moored at the island.)

I hear them downstairs.

"Anna, the poor child, what can we do?"

"It is worse for her, Samuel," sighing, the sadness reaching me and becoming a shroud, "it will be worse with her, I think, than it was for me."

(1972)

Clone Sister

After they made love, Jim Swenson leaned back on his elbows and looked at Moira Buono. She was a slender dark-haired girl with olive skin and large black eyes. Her nose was a bit too large for her delicate face. As she lay at his side, her small breasts seemed flattened almost to nonexistence. Her abdomen was a concavity between two sharp hipbones. Her legs contrasted with the slenderness of her torso; they were short and utilitarian, well-muscled appendages that carried her around efficiently and without much strain. She was beautiful.

She watched him with dark eyes. Her black hair lay carelessly around her head in the green grass and her face bore a calm and peaceful smile. She reached out for his hand and drew it to her belly. In the distance he could hear the high-pitched laugh of Ilyasah Ahmal and the deeper rumblings of Walt Merton. He traced the outline of shadows on her body, shadows created by the summer sun's rays and the leafy branches of the trees overhead. A summer breeze stirred the branches, the shadows drifted and changed shape on Moira's body.

Jim took his hand away from her and got up. His penis felt cold and sticky. He pulled on his shorts and began to walk toward the clearing ahead. He knew Moira was watching him, probably puzzled, perhaps a little angry. He came to the clearing and walked toward the stone wall at its edge. The grass brushed against his feet, tickling his soles. Two grackles perched on the wall, cawing loudly at some sparrows darting overhead. As he approached, the two black birds lifted, cawed at him from above, and were gone.

Jim leaned against the wall and looked down at the automated highway two hundred feet below him. The cars fled along the road in orderly rows, punched into the automatic highway control. He watched them and thought of Moira. She had retreated from him again, hiding even at the moment he had entered her body. She had been an observer, looking on as he held her, sweating and moving to a lonely, sharp spurt of pleasure. She was an onlooker, smiling at him from a distance as he withdrew, her black eyes a shield between their minds.

They stood in a gray formlessness. "Moira," he said, and she looked at him, seeming to be perplexed, seeming to be impatient. She withdrew, and clouds of grayness began to cover her, hiding her legs, then her face and shoulders.

His view of the highway was suddenly obstructed. "Are you trying to ruin today, too?" Moira's voice said. He pulled at the shirt she had draped over his head and put it on. She was sitting on the wall to his right. Her skin looked sallow next to her yellow shorts and shirt. She stared past him at the trees.

"I'm sorry," he said, "it's just a mood." He wanted to take her hand, touch her hair. Instead, he went back to leaning against the wall. He looked up at her face. Her eyes were pieces of onyx, sharp and cold. Her skin was drawn tightly across her cheekbones.

"I'm sorry, it's just a mood," she said. "How many moods do you have? Must be half a million by now. And they're always ones you have to apologize for."

Jim turned and saw Ilyasah coming toward them, black hair a cloud around her dark face. Jim forced himself to smile.

"You were right about this place," Ilyasah said.

"Nice and quiet. Ever since they reclaimed that area up north, you can't go there without falling over bodies. Something wrong, Moira?"

"No," Moira muttered.

"Give us half an hour," Ilyasah went on, "and we'll get the food out."

Jim took the hint. "Sure," he said. Ilyasah left and disappeared among the trees. The black girl had still not shaken off the remnants of her rigid Muslim upbringing and wanted to be sure no one observed her with Walt. Moira had returned to her dormitory room with Jim one evening a little too soon. They had calmly excused themselves and gone to one of the lounges instead, but Ilyasah had been embarrassed for days afterward.

"I guess we'd better watch the path," he said to Moira. "I wouldn't want anyone else to embarrass your roommate." Moira shrugged and continued to sit on the wall.

He tried to fight the tightness in his stomach, the feeling of isolation that was once again wrapping itself around him. *Talk to me, Moira*, he thought, *don't make me stand here guessing and worrying.*

The dark eyes looked at him. "I'm leaving next week," she said quickly. "I'll probably come back in August, but my mother's fixing up her new studio and she needs some help." Her eyes challenged him to respond.

"Why?" he cried, suddenly realizing that he had shouted the word. "Why," he said more quietly, "didn't you tell me this before?"

"I didn't know before."

"Oh, you knew it before. She's been after you for a month about it, and you said she had enough help. Now all of a sudden you have to go home."

Moira hopped off the wall and paced in front of him.

"I suppose," she said, "I have to go through a whole explanation."

"No," he said. *Of course you do.*

"All right," she went on. "I decided to go home a while ago. I would have told you before, but—"

"Why not? Why didn't you tell me before?"

Moira smiled suddenly. "You really don't understand, do you? If I had told you before, you would have gotten upset and tried to talk me out of it, or acted as though I did something terribly wrong. So I tell you now, so you don't have time to talk me out of it. I thought I was doing you a favor. But of course you're going to act the same way anyway."

"I want to be with you, is that so wrong?" Jim swallowed, worried that he had whined the words. "I don't like to be separated from you, that's all," he said in a lower tone.

"No, you'd rather be underfoot all the time," she said. "I can't even meet your brothers and sister. Every time I mention that I might like to talk to them, you evade the whole thing. Why?"

He was silent. He could feel sweat forming on his face and under his beard.

"I guess," she said, "you're jealous of your own family too."

He shrugged and tried to smile. "It isn't so bad," he said. "You'll be back in August, and we can—"

"No." She stopped pacing and stood in front of him, arms folded across her chest. "No, Jim. I don't know yet. I want to think about things. I don't want to make any promises now. I'll just have to see. Maybe that's hard on you, but . . ."

She sighed, then walked over to the trees. She stood there leaning against a trunk, her back to him.

"Moira."

No answer.

"Moira." She was gone again, having said what she had to say. He could stride over to her, grab her by the shoulders, shake the slender body while shouting at her, and she would look at him with empty eyes.

Do I love you, Moira? Do I even know you? He stared at the girl's back, stiff and unyielding under the soft yellow shirt. *Am I too possessive, too demanding? Or is that just an excuse, a way to avoid telling me that you can't love a freak, that it would be as easy for you to love one of my cloned brothers if you knew them, that we're all interchangeable?*

Moira, look at me, try to understand me, he wanted to shout. He walked over to her, afraid to touch her, afraid to reach out and hold her. She was lost in her own world, and seemed unaware of his presence.

It was over. He was sure of that, in spite of Moira's comments about waiting until August.

She turned around and looked at him, black eyes expressionless. "Surely you realize," she said, "that I'm getting a bit sick of the newsfax guys always asking for exclusive interviews on what it's like to be with a clone, that's one thing. The fact is, you're trying to use me to prove something to yourself, to show everyone that you are an individual, that I only love you, that I'm completely yours. Well, I've got better things to do than build up your ego."

She still refused to speak. *You could at least say what you mean,* Jim thought as he looked at her back.

"Hey!" Jim turned and saw Walt Merton on the path leading into the woods. "Come on," Walt said, "we're getting the food out."

"Yeah," said Jim. "We'll be along in a minute."

Walt looked from Jim to Moira. "Sure," he said. His dark face showed concern. He looked doubtfully at Jim, then turned and went back down the path.

"Let's go," Moira said suddenly. "I'm starving." She smiled and took him by the hand. She was hiding behind a shield of cheerfulness now: *Nothing's wrong, Jim; everything's settled.* "Damn it, Moira," he said harshly, "can't you at least talk it over, or let me try to get through to you?"

She ignored his question. "Let's go," she said, still smiling, still holding his hand.

* * *

The rain had started as a summer shower, but was now coming down steadily, forming puddles on the lawn. Jim sat on the front porch of the large house he shared with his brothers and sister. The evening air was cooler and fresher than it had been for several days.

The large house stood at the end of a narrow road amid a grove of trees. Farther down the road, near one of the other houses, Jim could see a group of naked children dancing in the rain. On the lawn in front of him his brothers Al and Mike were throwing a football. Mike was always ready to use any excuse for fooling around and had dragged Al outside almost as soon as the rain began to fall.

Al's thick brown hair was plastered against the back of his neck and shoulders and Mike's mustache drooped on both sides of his mouth. "Whup," yelled Mike as he drew his arm back and made a forward pass. As the ball left Mike's arm, he slipped on the grass and landed on his buttocks, bare muddy feet poking high into the air. Al hooted and caught the ball. He began to run with it, laughing as Mike got up with mud on his shorts.

Jim watched his brothers. They had not insisted that he join them, understanding almost instinctively that he needed some solitude. He had gone to the university early that morning to drive Moira to the monorail that would take her home.

He had tried once again the night before to talk her out of leaving. "I can't believe your mother needs your help with all those others around," he had said. Moira's mother lived with five other women and Moira herself had been raised communally by the group with three other children. She saw her father only rarely. He had retreated to Nepal years before, emerging only occasionally to face a world that frightened him.

Moira shrugged. "She can still use some extra help," she said.

"Come on, Moira," he shouted. "Stop being so evasive and at least be honest about why you're really going."

She was silent as she packed her things. He had finally left her dormitory room, angrily telling her she could take the shuttle from the university to the monorail.

He had relented, of course, driving onto the automated highway, punching a button, leaning back in his seat as the highway took control of his car. He had reached for Moira, pulled her to him. She had watched him, her black eyes seemingly veiled. She unfastened her blue sari and draped it on the back of the seat. Then she unzipped his shorts, crawled onto him, holding his penis firmly with one hand. He was suddenly inside her, clutching her, gazing up at her face. Her eyes were closed.

"Moira," he had whispered to her. "Moira." He came quickly. She withdrew from him and moved back to her side of the seat.

Jim shivered in the air-conditioned car. He zipped up his shorts and looked over at the dark-haired girl. She was fastening her sari while staring out her window at the blurred scenery. *What was it, Moira, a formality because you're leaving? a way of saying you still care? a way of saying, Goodbye, Jim, it's the last time?* She gave him no answer, not even a clue. Once again she had remained unresponsive, giving him no sign that she had taken pleasure in the act.

He grabbed her, pulling her sari from her and pushed her against the seat. Her face was against the back of the seat, hidden from him. Her buttocks pointed up at his face. He crawled on top of her, pushing inside roughly. He pounded against her, waiting to hear her moans, waiting to see her abandon herself to him at last.

He continued to sit behind the wheel, still watching her. She had finished fastening her sari. She turned toward him, a tentative smile formed on her face. *I've never reached you, Moira,* he thought. At last he pulled her to him, and she lay there, head on his shoulder, her body stiff, her muscles tight. He was alone once again.

Al stumbled onto the porch, picked up his towel from the chair next to him, and massaged his head and shoulders vigorously. "Am I out of shape," Al said. "I'm going over to the gym tomorrow. I have to go to the library anyway, so I might as well work out."

"Yeah," Jim said.

"Want to come along? We can play some handball."

"No," Jim looked up at his brother. "I don't think so." He looked away, sensing what Al was probably thinking: *Is it that girl, Jim? You've been sitting around for months, no interest in much else. You haven't even written any poetry for a while.*

"Well, if you change your mind," Al said. He turned and went inside the house, towel draped over his shoulders.

"Catch," shouted Mike. He threw the football to Jim as he followed Al through the front door.

Jim tucked the football under his chair and continued to watch the rain. Again he felt separated from his brothers, seeing them as others might: identical people, clones of the same man, undifferentiated and interchangeable. Some had thought that they and their sister Kira would be identical in interests and achievements, as well as exactly like their father, Paul Swenson. But Paul, who had raised them and lived with them until his death in a monorail accident two years before, had different ideas. He had encouraged the five clones to develop individual interests. Al had become a student of astrophysics, Mike was studying physics, Ed was interested in both mathematics and music, and Kira, the only female clone, was a student of the biological sciences that had brought them into existence. Jim, however, had decided to study literature. Although he had been interested in the sciences and had studied them to some extent, it was to literature that he responded most deeply. He had often thought that he was the most emotional of the clones, that he had inherited somehow, or at least empathized with, a part of Paul's personality that had not been apparent to most of those who had known his father.

No, they had not been exactly like Paul. Instead, they were fragments of him. Paul Swenson had made his mark in astrophysics, his achievements culminating in the theoretical groundwork for a star drive that would take humanity beyond the solar system. But he had also studied other sciences, and was an accomplished violinist. In his later life Paul had written several books on the sciences, hoping to communicate what he had learned to others, and had even tried his hand at poetry. He had been honored and respected by the world until, at the very beginning of the century, he had allowed his friend Hidehiko Takamura to make an attempt to produce clones using Paul's genetic material. The scientific community throughout the world had placed a moratorium on cloning during the early 1980s, delaying any application of the procedure to human beings. The moratorium had been part of an automatic twenty-year delay period placed on the application of new scientific innovations. When that time had run out, Takamura had urged Paul Swenson to donate himself for duplication. Then Takamura and other biologists had taken nucleus materials from Paul and introduced them into eggs from which they had removed the nucleus, in order to insure that each potential child should inherit all of its genes from Paul Swenson.

The attempt had succeeded, and the world had been horrified. Legislation had been passed in the United States and Europe outlawing the application of cloning to human beings, and the artificial wombs used to nurture the clones before birth could no longer be used except to aid prematurely born infants. Newsfax sheets had made Paul Swenson out to be an egotist and megalomaniac, although in fact he had been gentle and self-effacing. The clones themselves were the subjects of stories claiming that they had telepathic powers or a communal mind. The stories had been discredited, but some people still believed them.

Jim sighed. His sister Kira, echoing Paul, often said that they all had a responsibility to use their talents as constructively as possible, to show the world that they were, after all, fellow human beings. Al, feeling the pressure of his father's reputation, did little but study. Ed had become shy, retreating from social contact. *And I*, Jim thought, *have done almost nothing except sit around feeling sorry for myself. But don't I have the right to, if I'm like everyone else? Why do I have to do anything noteworthy? Is it up to me to prove something about clones to everyone?*

He had, after all, tried to make Moira understand, and he had failed completely at that. The thought of Moira suddenly saddened him. He had been numb for most of the day and now her absence hit him at last. *I would have been with her now*, he thought, *we would have been running through the rain together.* He felt purposeless, empty, and alone.

A car was coming along the narrow road, a light green Lear model. It stopped in front of the Swenson house, and he saw his sister and a short stocky figure get out. The two raced through the downpour to the porch. Kira was laughing as she shook the water from her hair. The short stocky person turned out to be Hidehiko Takamura.

Jim wanted to disappear, but he sat and nodded to Dr. Takamura.

"What a downpour!" Kira said, "Can I get you something—a beer maybe?"

"Better make it tea," Dr. Takamura replied. "And I think I'll sit out here. I've been inside all day."

Kira looked at Jim. "I'll have some too," he said. She hurried into the house.

Jim looked over at Dr. Takamura as the older man seated himself. The man was still here at the university, still working at the same research center that had produced the clones, and now Kira was studying with him. Jim shuddered. He usually felt uneasy around the original participants in the experiment. He could never be sure whether they regarded him as a subject or were trying to recapture their friendship with Paul.

"How's everything, Jim?" The older man still retained a youthful appearance and was active, in spite of being in his seventies. "I haven't seen you for a while."

"I haven't been around the house much."

"I have seen you from a distance, wandering around the university with a very attractive young woman."

"Oh. Moira," Jim said. He paused, thinking he should say more. "I met her last winter. I was at home here, tuned in to a lit discussion, and we got into a debate. Then after the discussion was over, we stayed on the screen, just talking, so finally I asked her where she lived, and I went over to her dormitory. She's gone home until August," he finished lamely.

Kira returned and sat down next to Dr. Takamura. "Ed'll bring the tea out," she said. Jim looked at her face—his face, only more feminine—high cheekbones, large green eyes. She looked back, eyes questioning him: *Everything all right, Jim?* He tried to smile back at her.

"We were just discussing the young woman I've seen Jim with." Kira appeared startled. She brushed some of her thick brown hair off her face and leaned forward. "You know," Dr. Takamura went on, "she resembles a girl Paul was seeing when he was about your age, when we were both at Chicago. Rhoda something, her name was. She left for Israel a couple of years later. He was very serious about her for a while."

Jim began to feel uneasy. Kira sensed his mood. "It sure is raining," she said. "Must be about three inches by now."

Jim leaned toward Dr. Takamura. "What was she like?" he asked. His hands felt sweaty. Kira was still watching him.

"I didn't really know her that well," the older man

said. "She seemed, well, distant somehow. She was always friendly, sometimes very talkative, but she always seemed to be holding something back somehow, never really telling you anything about herself. Paul was always with her. He practically lived at her apartment, and they were thinking of getting one of their own."

The weather seemed to be colder. Kira coughed softly. "Certainly took me back," said Dr. Takamura. "I haven't thought of that whole business in years."

"What happened?" Jim mumbled. "What happened?" he said more clearly.

Dr. Takamura was gazing out at the lawn. "She broke it off. I don't think she ever told him why. Paul was pretty depressed for a while, apathetic about everything, but he pulled together. Jon Aschenbach and I managed to get him through his finals."

Jim shivered. "That was a long time ago," said Dr. Takamura.

Ed came out on the porch carrying a tray with three mugs of tea. Jim took one of the mugs and looked on as his brother exchanged greetings with the older man. Ed was the most austere of the clones; he was clean-shaven and wore his hair cropped close to his skull. He spent most of his time on his mathematical studies or his music, and his only close friends were the clones themselves.

Jim heard their voices but not their words. He saw Paul and Rhoda on the Chicago streets, Paul and Moira. . . . He had thought Moira could not bring herself to accept him because he was a clone. Perhaps it was not that at all, but something else. *That should console me*, he thought.

No.

This was worse.

I'm living Paul's life, he thought. He felt paralyzed.

He saw himself as a puppet walking through an ever-repeating cycle. *I'll go through it again*, his mind murmured. *I'll go on feeling the way I do, acting the way I do, and I won't have any choice. It's all happened before and I have no way of changing it.*

Moira was gone. He knew it. Moira was gone from him for good. Rhoda had not come back to Paul. Paul had eventually forgotten Rhoda, and Jim supposed he would forget Moira too. The thought, instead of cheering him, simply sat there in his mind, cold and damp, with no power to move him at all.

* * *

The early July weather was hot. The grass was beginning to look scorched, the flowers were wilted. The sun glared down at the earth, only occasionally disappearing behind a cloud and then emerging once again to mock at the stifled world below. Jim sat on his heels removing weeds that threatened the bushes alongside the house. His hair was tied back on his head. He had debated with himself about shaving his beard, and decided against it, knowing he would regret it when winter returned. There was another reason for not shaving it, he knew. The beard was his way of differentiating himself from his brothers.

He put this trowel down, sat back, and looked over at Kira. She was seated under one of the trees reading a book. She held the small microfiche projector to her eyes with one hand, turned a small knob on the projector with the other. Jim still preferred the feel of a book in his hands, enjoyed turning the pages, liked the smell of print and old paper. He had insisted on keeping the books in Paul's library, even though they took up more space than the tiny bits of tape he could have purchased to replace them.

He was like Paul in his attachment to old things. Paul had remained in his old slightly run-down house in the area surrounding the university while other researchers and professors had moved to living units inside one of the new pyramidal structures only a few minutes away from the campus by train. Paul had remained on earth while many of his colleagues in astrophysics had gone to the moon, and he had decided he was too old to go. He had raised the clones in the peaceful, almost timeless atmosphere of the university, feeling that this would best prepare them for the complex, almost chaotic world outside. He had wanted them to have a quiet place where they could discover themselves and gain intellectual tools. The universities, so disorganized during Paul's youth, were once again oases of liberal education. Those who had wished for activism had set up their own colleges in the disorderly cities of the continent; and specialists in many fields had their own research centers on ocean floors, in wilderness areas, and on the surface of the moon and Mars. The university had been, in a sense, a retreat for the clones, and Jim wondered if they might have become too easily adjusted to it and afraid to look beyond.

"Why don't you go inside?" he said to Kira. "It's a lot cooler there."

"It's too cool," she replied. "I don't think the regulator's working. I shiver all the time and I had to put blankets on my bed last night."

"I guess I better check it one of these days." He wiped sweat off his forehead with the back of his arm. He continued to watch Kira as she resumed reading. She had pinned her hair up on her head and wore a sleeveless blue-green tunic that barely reached the tops of her thighs. To Jim she suggested a woodland sprite who at any moment might disappear among the trees.

In spite of the heat and some painful blisters on his hands, Jim felt content, more at peace than he had been in a long time. He and Kira had been busy since the day Moira had gone home, making repairs on the house, painting the kitchen, putting some new shingles on the roof. He had buried himself in physical work, tiring himself so he could sleep soundly, hoping to keep the thought of Moira at a distance. Kira, too, had time on her hands. Dr. Takamura had gone to Kenya to aid in training scientists there who wished to clone needed animals for wildlife preserves. He and Kira had worked together, laughing and joking most of the time, exhausting themselves. One day Jim had realized that his sorrow had receded a little, only returning in force during the night, just before fatigue pushed him into deep sleep.

Yesterday had been different. They had been sitting with Ed on the front porch, talking about one of Jim's poems, listening to Ed play his violin, discussing some of the work Kira had done with Takamura. They talked for a long time, their minds drawing together, communicating ideas and feelings with perfect understanding. Then Al and Mike had joined them and they sat there until very late, finally giving in reluctantly to sleepiness, and Jim realized as he lay in his bed that he had not thought of Moira all day.

"Hey," he said to Kira, "how about driving up to the lake for a swim? It's too hot to do anything else."

Kira put down her projector. "I'd love to," she said, "but you know there'll be a mob there. I went up with Jonis last month, you could hardly find a place to put a towel down, so we went over to the nude beach and it was worse there. And there were picnickers all over the woods, and empty containers just thrown all around." Kira sighed and pulled up her legs, wrapping her arms around them. "They think the containers'll just disappear, they don't stop to think it takes months for them to dissolve completely. Jonis said she heard that guys go up and take pot shots at the eagles. They don't care—after all, we can always clone more. It makes me so damned mad. I wish they'd kept it closed after reclamation."

We can always clone more. He looked over at Kira and suddenly felt sorry for the cloned eagles. "We could drive to the park. It's always pretty empty," he said. "It'll be cooler there than here, and we could take some supper for later."

"Great," she said. "At least we'll get away from the house for a while." She stood up, brushed some grass from her tunic, picked up her projector by the handle, and walked toward the house, tanned arms swinging loosely at her sides.

Jim watched her until she disappeared around the corner of the house. She had inherited Paul's gentleness and concern for others. When one of the clones was depressed or worried about something, it was always Kira who was willing to listen or offer moral support. Her creation had been the result of curiosity about how Paul's qualities might manifest themselves in a female. As it happened, she was essentially no different from the brothers, and the concern she expressed for them was probably the product of her studies. She spent as much of her time in seminars discussing ethical problems raised by the biological sciences as in the laboratory. Perhaps she was more mature than he or the others, and there were often times when he thought she was more like Paul than any of them.

He picked up his trowel and followed her inside.

* * *

The night air was still warm, but pleasantly so. They had jogged around the perimeter of the park until the heat had subdued them. Then they had climbed up the hill to the stone wall overlooking the automated highway. They sat on the wall, legs dangling over the side, as they drank beer and finished the remnants of supper.

It had been a pleasant afternoon, but Jim had grown more silent as the sun set. He sat quietly, ignored the highway below, and watched the rising moon. Al had often spoken of going to the moon, joining the people there who were carrying on Paul Swenson's work. Jim tried to concentrate on the lunar disk, tried to ignore the tendrils of thought brushing at the edges of his consciousness. A warm breeze stirred the trees behind him.

He sat with Moira on the wall, held her hand lightly. He gestured toward the moon as he told her of his father's hopes and tried to communicate the reasons behind Paul's dreams. He looked at Moira as she sat listening quietly, seemingly interested, then heard her soft sigh of impatience.

He looked at Kira. She, too, was watching the moon. He wondered what Moira was doing now. He had managed to keep from calling her since she had left, afraid that she would misinterpret his motives. He should not have come to the park. It had only deepened his pain, bringing it to the surface once again. Kira turned slightly and her eyes met his.

"I never," he said, "really told you much about Moira, did I? Not even that time . . ." He looked away in embarrassment. *He was standing on the wall, ready to hurl himself toward the brightly lit highway. Kira clung to his arm, silvery tears glistened on her face. "Jump," she shouted, "jump, but you'll have to take me with you."* "Very melodramatic performance," he mumbled, and felt her hand on his arm.

"Don't degrade your pain, Jim," she said softly.

"She didn't just go home for the summer, you know. I don't think she wants to see me when she returns."

"I know," said Kira. "I could tell. You don't have to talk about it, Jim."

"I don't know what's wrong with me," he went on. "It's funny I should care so much about Moira when, if I were honest about it, I'd have to admit I never really knew her. I know she didn't understand me. She never really tried to, she just withdrew." He looked at Kira. "That sounds so cold," he said.

"Don't dwell on it," said Kira softly. "You can't analyze a thing like that, and you'll just feel worse if you try." She swung her legs over the wall and stood up. "Want to take a walk? My legs feel a little stiff."

"Sure." He picked up the small picnic basket and followed her.

They walked along the narrow path that wound through the woods. The path was lighted by the moon. The trees on either side of them were a dark and impenetrable forest. There was a smell of pine and wildflowers. Above him he could hear the movement of a small creature along the limbs of a tree. An owl hooted and was answered by crickets.

Moira stopped, leaned against one of the trees, and smiled at him. He moved to her side, put his arms around her slender waist, and she rested her head contentedly on his shoulder.

Jim halted to rest against a tree. His stomach was a closed fist inside him, his face was hot and his mouth dry. He struggled to restrain a moan. The picnic basket slipped from his fingers and hit the ground with a muffled thud. The handles clattered loudly against the sides of the basket.

"Jim." Kira stood in front of him, clutching his shoulders. "Jim." She released his shoulders and embraced him, cradling his head with one hand. "I know," she said softly.

He was a child again, curled on Paul's lap. "I know," Paul whispered, stroking his hair. "Let it out, Jimmy. Don't ever be ashamed to cry." He squeezed his eyelids together, but the tears would not come. She brushed his hair from his forehead.

She seemed to understand his pain almost instinctively. He rested against her and felt some of the loneliness subside. "I guess," he said finally, "this place must have brought it all back." The tightness of his stomach began to ease.

He stood up straight, arms still around her, and looked into her green eyes, level with his own. She was a dryad, a part of the forest in her tunic and sandaled feet, and it seemed that she might suddenly release him and vanish. He held her more tightly.

He felt his penis stiffen. Startled, he let go of Kira and stood awkwardly in front of her, arms dangling at his sides. She did not move away but continued to stand with her arms around his shoulders. Her face was pale in the moonlight. She tilted her head to one side. *Don't move away,* her eyes seemed to say. *Don't retreat.* She moved closer to him and kissed his lips gently.

The park had grown silent. He was paralyzed, rooted to the ground as surely as the tree against his back. He strained to hear the sounds of the forest, but there was only a thundering in his ears.

She released him and they faced each other, silent

and still. He tried to raise his arms. They trembled slightly as he reached out to her.

She unfastened the sash around her waist and let it flutter to the ground. She grasped her tunic with both hands and pulled it over her head. Then she slipped off her pants, balancing first on one leg, then the other. She moved slowly and as precisely as a dancer. She stood in front of him, and at last she met his eyes again.

He saw apprehension and fear on her face, as well as love and concern. He moved toward her, taking one step, then a second one—and he was in her arms, holding her tightly. He was afraid to speak. Kira, too, was trembling. He began to stroked her hair.

He loosened his shorts with one hand and dropped them on top of Kira's rumpled tunic. He ran his hands along her smooth back to her buttocks, only slightly wider and rounder than his own. She was no longer trembling.

They knelt, then lay on the ground together. He reached out, held her breasts gently as she watched him. Her face looked like Ed's in the moonlight, ascetic and austere. Then she suddenly smiled, reminding him of Mike in one of his playful moods. She touched his penis, running her thumb lightly over its tip, then grasped him firmly.

His fear faded. She thrust her hips up, pulled him to her. He thought of the uncertainty he had always felt with Moira, the lonely climaxes. There was no uncertainty with Kira. She was his female self, reaching for him now with the same urgency and impatience he felt. Her hand held him and guided him inside her.

She drew up her knees and they lay on their sides, facing each other. Still gazing into his own green eyes, he thrust with his hips, ran his hand along her thigh. Her lips parted and he heard a soft sigh. He continued to move and was conscious of her response; she was moaning now, clutching his shoulders tightly. He saw himself as a woman, receiving a man, opening to the hardness that plunged inside her, and knew that she was seeing herself as a man, moving inside the wet and welcoming orifice. They moved together, grinding their hips in perfect rhythm, and he felt the core of his excitement increasing, threatening at any moment to hurl him outside himself for a few timeless seconds.

This has never happened before. He suddenly realized that as he moved inside her, sighing his responses to her moans. *Never before.* He saw generation after generation evolve, become more differentiated, genetic structures changing and mutating. He saw millions of men and women seeking mates, trying to find those who would complete them, make them whole again, yet always separated from them by the differences passed on to them by eons of change. He saw Kira and himself, reflections of each other, able to move along their individual paths and yet meet in perfect communication. She was no longer his sister, but his other self, closer to him than a sister could have been, merging with him so completely and perfectly that they were one being.

He moved with her, breathed with her, sensitive to every movement of her hands on his body. Then he stopped, held his body absolutely still, prepared himself for the final thrust. She was still also, waiting, watching him with wide eyes. Her lips were parted and swollen, the warmth inside her body had grown even more intense.

At last, unable to bear it any longer, he thrust again, and she moved to meet him, gasping quietly at first, then crying out, shattering the night silence. He felt himself spurt inside her, and he trembled, moving with her, suspended in a pocket of timelessness. He was adrift with her in a universe contained by the skin of their bodies, and he called out as his pleasure compressed itself in his groin, then erupted throughout his body. He cried out again, could no longer tell which cries were his and which were Kira's.

Then it was over and he realized with a tinge of sadness how short a time it had actually been. He withdrew from her slowly but remained beside her, resting his head in her arms. He became aware of the sweat that covered their bodies, the warmth of the night. Now he kept his eyes from meeting hers.

Kira, as if responding to his fears, held him more closely. "Don't, Jim," she whispered. "Don't feel ashamed. I love you. I've known it for a while. How could I help it?" She was right, of course, the old codes and ancient prohibitions could not apply to them, had not even allowed for their existence.

He looked at her face. She lay at his side stroking his hair. It was Paul's face that watched him, smiling, gently reassuring him with love. He curled up next to her.

* * *

The thunderstorm had passed by morning, leaving behind it cool air and large fluffy clouds. The sun, previously a malevolent eye peering balefully at the earth, was now a friendly presence, occasionally hiding behind one of the white clouds as if ashamed of its former fit of temper. Jim had carried the light plastic chairs off the porch and placed them on top of old newsfax sheets and computer print-outs in the front yard. Aiming his spray can at one, he began to cover it with a surface of gray paint.

He glanced at Ed and Kira. They had moved two of

the three cars out into the road and were washing them down with the hose. Their shorts and shirts were plastered against their bodies. Kira hooted as she aimed the hose at Ed, drenching him completely. He grabbed the hose from her and began to spray her with water. Kira danced on her toes, laughing loudly.

Jim moved to spray the next chair. He had been trying to accept and understand his new relationship with Kira. He turned it over in his mind, trying to view it objectively: It wasn't harming them, it affected no one else, it gave them pleasure. It seemed cold and somehow negative to think of it that way.

"Is it so strange, Jim?" Kira had asked. They were sitting on her bed, legs folded in front of them, elbows on knees, heads in hands, perfectly matched. "It would be stranger if we didn't feel this way, weren't drawn to each other."

He continued to spray the chairs. *How do I feel about it?* he asked himself. *I'm able to reach someone else, able to love and communicate without rejection.* He thought of Moira. His love for her had been nervous and feverish, an uneasiness that was always with him, occupying his entire mind, refusing to let go. With Kira he was at peace, except for the occasional guilty doubts that nudged him from time to time, then retreated under the onslaught of his rationalizations. With Kira, he could work at his poetry or talk, easily sharing his thoughts and feelings and understanding hers as well.

Kira and Ed were walking toward the house, leaving the hose on the lawn. They seemed to be discussing something. Ed gestured with his right arm as they climbed the steps to the front porch and disappeared into the house. Jim finished spraying the last chair, then glared at the hose. All the clones had inherited an almost

obsessive tidiness from Paul, and he was annoyed that Ed
and Kira had not rewound the hose. It was not like them.

The chairs would need a little time to dry before he
moved them back to the porch. He ambled to the front
door, depositing the can on the porch, and went inside.

The house was silent. Al and Mike had gone to the
university earlier to do some lab work. Jim wandered
through the living room, which was furnished with old
overstuffed chairs and sofas. Two learning booths stood
in the corner. They resembled large transparent eggs;
their screens were blank and their earphones were lying
idly on the writing surfaces next to the chairs. Paul had
installed two more booths upstairs in the room he had
once used as a study. Few people had that many booths in
their homes, but Jim knew that few people used the one
booth they usually had, preferring to watch the large
vidscreens on their walls. Al had left several print-outs on
the writing surface of one booth. He was the "pack rat" of
the clones and would gather piles of neatly folded print-
outs until someone, usually Mike, threw them out. He
continued through the living room to the kitchen.

The kitchen was empty. Jim was surprised, having
assumed Kira and Ed had come in for a sandwich. He left
the kitchen, went back through the living room and up
the stairs, and decided he would ask them if they wanted
help with the hose and if they wanted to have some lunch
with him. He walked past Ed's room. The door was open
and there was no one inside. He went past Mike's room,
then his own, stopped at Kira's door.

It was closed. He knocked, heard the sounds of
someone moving in the room. "Kira?" he said. He
knocked again, then opened the door.

Kira and Ed were sprawled on the bed. Both were

naked. Ed turned and looked at Jim and appeared startled. Kira seemed calm. "Oh, no," said Jim. He clenched his hands into fists, "Oh, no." He felt himself shaking. The twin faces on the bed were watching him.

He wanted to pound his fist into the wall. He turned and fled down the hall to his own room. He stood there, alone, trying to sort out the thoughts that tumbled through his mind. He heard soft footsteps coming down the hall. They stopped at his door. "Jim," He did not move. "Jim." He turned and saw Kira standing in the door, a long red robe draped over her shoulders.

He gestured at the robe. "Your one concession to modesty," he said bitterly. She came into the room and closed the door.

"Why are you so angry, Jim?"

He turned from her and sat on the chair at his desk. "There's no reason to be angry," he muttered. "I found out that we're interchangeable to you too, that's all."

"No, Jim," she said softly, leaning against the door. "That's not what you found out. Do you think for one moment I confuse Ed with you? Forget about yourself for one minute and think about him. He's just about given up trying to reach out to anyone, including us. He's so quiet about his problems, it's easy to pretend he's just shy or not that interested in people. You know how you felt, how lonely you were, but at least you kept trying with Moira, and you could reach me. Ed gave up trying, and about all you've accomplished today is reinforcing the way he feels. Now he's sitting in my room feeling guilty."

Jim looked over at Kira. She was looking at the floor, folding her arms across her chest. "Oh, Jim, I don't know. Maybe I have my own problems too. Don't I have a right to solve them, or at least try? Or am I supposed to limit myself to you, or ignore Ed? Has this business really changed anything you might have found out through me?" She sighed. "Maybe it'll be harder for us, Jim. We have to find our own answers in our own way, and we don't even have the rough guidelines everybody else has. Some people would look at us and talk about incest taboos, and others would probably find it strange if we loved anyone else but the other clones. The point is, we have to try, and maybe we'll make mistakes, but ..."

She turned and opened the door. "I still love you, Jim, just as much as I did before. Maybe none of us will ever feel the same way about anyone else. Maybe we really can't, being the way we are, and that means that Ed needs me too, and maybe Al and Mike will if they ever look beyond each other."

She left the room but did not close the door. He sat at the desk trying to sort out his thoughts. He considered himself and the other clones, turned over their problems and relationships in his mind, and wondered what he should do now.

He was with Kira, hands on her belly. She looked up at him as he hovered over her, guided his hand between her legs. He felt her wetness with his finger, moved forward and embraced her, embraced himself, and sighed as they merged.

* * *

Jim lifted the suitcase and put it in the back seat of the car. Al leaned against the open car door. "We'll miss you," he said.

"I won't be gone long," he replied. He turned to Kira. Her brow was wrinkled with worry. He reached over to her, grasped her shoulders. "Come on, cheer up," he said. "I'll be back in a month or so. I'm not running away. I know what I'm doing, and I know why."

She smiled at him tentatively, and he kissed her

lightly on the forehead. Then he climbed into the car, waving his arm at the porch where Ed and Mike sat.

He had explained himself to them as best he could, and he was satisfied that they understood him as well as could be expected. He would drive up to Moira's home first. He would not make demands of her, would not force himself on her. He would not give up if she drew away from him. He would leave and go to a poetry workshop in Minnesota he had heard about, meet people there, be like anyone else.

Kira had come to his room the night before. They lay on his bed, arms and legs entwined, as he told her about his hopes and his plans.

It would be easy to stay with Kira, easy to give up on other people. He would not let himself do it yet, not until he had tried and failed many times.

He started the car and drove away from the house slowly. When he got to the end of the narrow road, he turned his head and saw Kira and Al walking to the front porch. Suddenly he felt doubtful about his actions, wondered if he should leave, asked himself if he really wanted to go.

He continued to drive until the house was out of sight and he was on the road leading to the automated highway. He thought of Kira again, saw her head resting on his shoulder, and wondered if he were making a mistake. *Will I love anyone else as completely?* The image of Kira faded from his mind. She had given him as many questions as answers.

The world out there was just as worthy of his attention as his own personal problems. It was a world very different from the sheltered enclave of the university, a world of neatly organized cities inside pyramids and under domes, and disorganized cities that sprawled across the landscape. It was a world of people who looked beyond the earth to the stars, and people who sought to preserve old customs and ancient ways. It was a world of abundance for many and starvation for some, of green and fertile reclaimed wildernesses and eroded deserts. It was time that he tried to understand his own place in this world.

He drove the car onto the bypass, punched out his destination, and leaned back as the highway control took over, guided his car around the curved bypass, and shot him forward into the stream of cars on the highway.

(1973)

If Ever I Should Leave You

When Yuri walked away from the Time Station for the last time, his face was pale marble, his body only bones barely held together by skin and the weak muscles he had left. I hurried to him and grasped his arm, oblivious to the people who passed us in the street. He resisted my touch at first, embarrassed in front of the others; then he gave in and leaned against me as we began to walk home.

I knew that he was too weak to go to the Time Station again. His body, resting against mine, seemed almost weightless. I guided him through the park toward our home. Halfway there, he tugged at my arm and we rested against one of the crystalline trees surrounding the small lake in the center of the park.

Yuri had aged rapidly in the last six months, transformed from a young man into an aged creature hardly able to walk by himself. I had expected it. One cannot hold off old age indefinitely, even now. But I could not accept it. I knew that his death could be no more than days away.

You can't leave me now, not after all this time, I wanted to scream. Instead, I helped him sit on the ground next to the tree, then sat at his side.

His blue eyes, once clear and bright, now watery with age and surrounded by tiny lines, watched me. He reached inside his shirt and fumbled for something. I had always teased Yuri about his shirts; sooner or later he would tear them along the shoulder seams while flexing the muscles of his broad back and sturdy arms. Now the shirt, like his skin, hung on his bones in wrinkles and folds. At last he pulled out a piece of paper and pressed it into my hand with trembling fingers.

"Take care of this," he whispered to me. "Copy it down in several places so you won't lose it. All the coordinates are there, all the places and times I went to these past months. When you're lonely, when you need me, go to the Time Station and I'll be waiting on the other side." He was trying to comfort me. Because of his concern, he had gone to the Time Station every day for the past six months and had traveled to various points in the past. I could travel to any of those points and be with him at those times. It suddenly struck me as a mad idea, an insane and desperate thing.

"What happens to me?" I asked, clutching the paper. "What am I like when I see you? You've already seen me at all those times. What do I do, what happens to me?"

"I can't tell you, you know that. You have to decide yourself, of your own free will. Anything I say might affect what you do."

I looked away from him and toward the lake. Two golden swans glided by, the water barely rippling in their wake. Their shapes blurred and I realized I was crying silently. Yuri's blue-veined hand rested on my shoulder.

"Don't cry. Please. You make it harder for me."

At last the tears stopped. I reached over and stroked his hair, once thick and blond, now thin and white. Only a year before we had come to this same tree, our bodies shiny with lake water after a moonlight swim, and made love in the darkness. We were as young as everyone else, confident that we would live forever, forgetting that our bodies could not be rejuvenated indefinitely.

"I'm not really leaving you," Yuri said. His arms held me firmly and for a moment I thought his strength had returned. "I'll be at the other side of the Time Station, any time you need me. Think of it that way."

"All right," I said, trying to smile. "All right." I nestled against him, my head on his chest, listening to his once-strong heart as it thumped against my ear.

Yuri died that night, only a few hours after we returned home.

* * *

The relationships among our friends had been an elaborate web, always changing, couples breaking up and recombining in a new pattern. We were all eternally young and time seemed to stretch ahead of us with no end. Throughout all of this, Yuri and I stayed together, the strands of our love becoming stronger instead of more tenuous. I was a shy, frightened girl when I met Yuri and was attracted in part by his boldness; he had appeared at my door one day, introduced himself and told me a friend of his had made him promise he would meet me. I could not have looked very appealing with my slouched, bony body, the thick black hair that would not stay out of my face, my long legs marked with bruises by my clumsiness. But Yuri had loved me almost on sight and I discovered, in time, that his boldness was the protective covering of a serious and intense young man.

Our lives became intertwined so tightly that, after a while, they were one life. It was inconceivable that anything could separate us. Our relationship may have lacked the excitement of others' lives. With almost three centuries to live at the full height of our physical and mental powers, and the freedom to live several different kinds of lives, changing our professions and pursuits every twenty or thirty years, we know how rarely anyone chooses to stay with the same person throughout. Yet Yuri and I had, even through our changes, fallen in love with each other over and over again. We were lucky, I thought.

We were fools, I told myself when Yuri was gone. I had half a life after his death. I was a ghost myself, wandering from friend to friend seeking consolation, then isolating myself in my house for days, unwilling to see anyone.

But Yuri had not really left me. I had only to walk down to the Time Station, give them the coordinates he had given me, and I would be with him again, at least for a little while. Yet during those first days alone I could not bring myself to go there. He's gone, I told myself angrily; you must learn to live without him. And then I would whisper, Why? You have no life alone, you are an empty shell. Go to him.

I began to wander past the Time Station, testing my resolve. I would walk almost to the door, within sight of the technicians, then retreat, racing home, my hands shaking. *Yuri*.

I would make the time and trouble he took useless. He had wanted to be with me when I needed him, but he had also wanted to see my future self, what I would become after his death. The Time Station could not penetrate the future, that unformed mass of possibilities. I would be denying Yuri the chance to see it through my eyes, and the chance to see what became of me.

At last I walked to the Time Station and through its glassy door into the empty hall. Time Portals surrounded me on all sides, silvery cubicles into which people would step, then disappear. A technician approached me, silently offering assistance. I motioned her away and went over to one of the unoccupied cubicles. I fumbled for the piece of paper in my robe, then pulled it out and stared at the first set of coordinates. I stepped inside the cubicle, reciting the coordinates aloud—time, place, duration of my stay.

Suddenly I felt as though my body were being thrown through space, that my limbs were being torn from my torso. The walls around me had vanished. The feeling lasted only an instant. I was now standing next to a small, clear pool of water shadowed by palm trees.

I turned from the pool. In front of me stretched a desolate waste, a rocky desert bleached almost white by the sun. I retreated farther into the shade of the oasis where I stood, and knelt by the pool.

"Yuri," I whispered as I dipped my hand into the coolness of the water. A pebble suddenly danced across the silvery surface before me, and the ripples it made mingled with those my hand had created.

I looked around. Yuri stood only a few feet away. He had barely begun to age. His face was still young, his skin drawn tightly across high cheekbones, and his hair was only lightly speckled with silver.

"Yuri," I whispered again, and then I was running to him.

* * *

After we swam, we sat next to each other by the small pool with our feet in the water. I was intoxicated, my mind whirling from one thing to another with nothing needing to be said. Yuri smiled at me and skipped pebbles across the pool. Some of my thoughts seemed to skip with them, while another part of me whispered, He's alive, he's here with you, and he'll be with you at a hundred other places in a hundred other times.

Yuri started to whistle a simple tune, one that I had heard for as long as I knew him. I pursed my lips and tried to whistle along but failed, as I always had.

"You'll never learn to whistle now," he said. "You've

had two and a half centuries to learn and you still haven't figured it out."

"I will," I replied. "I've done everything else I ever wanted to do and I can't believe that a simple thing like whistling is going to defeat me."

"You'll never learn."

"I will."

"You won't."

I raised my feet, then lowered them forcefully, splashing us both. Yuri let out a yell, and I scrambled to my feet, stumbled and tried to run. He grabbed me by the arm.

"You *still* won't learn how," he said again, laughing. I looked into his eyes, level with my own.

I pursed my lips again, and Yuri disappeared. My time was up and I was being thrown and torn at again.

I was in the cubicle once more.

I left the Time Station and walked home alone.

* * *

I became a spendthrift, visiting the Time Station several times a week, seeing Yuri as often as I wanted. We met on the steps of a deserted Mayan pyramid and argued about the mathematical theories of his friend Alney, while jungle birds shrieked around us. I packed a few of his favorite foods and wines and found him in Hawaii, still awaiting the arrival of its first inhabitants. We sat together on a high rocky cliff in Africa, while far below us apelike creatures with primitive weapons hunted for food.

I became busy again, and began work with a group who were designing dwelling places inside the huge trees that surrounded the city. The biologists who had created the trees hundreds of years before had left the trunks hollow. I would hurry to the Time Station with my sketches of various designs, anxious to ask Yuri for advice or suggestions.

Yet during this time I had to watch Yuri grow old again. Each time I saw him he was a little older, a little weaker. I began to realize that I was watching him die all over again, and our visits took on a tone of panic and desperation. He grew more cautious in his choice of times and sites, and I was soon meeting him on deserted island beaches or inside the empty summer homes of the twentieth century. Our talks with each other grew more muted, as I was afraid of arguing too vigorously with him and thus wasting the little time we had left. Yuri noticed this and understood what it meant.

"Maybe I was wrong," he said to me after I showed him the final plans for the tree dwellings. I had been overly animated, trying to be cheerful, ignoring the signs of age that reminded me of his death. I couldn't fool him. "I wanted to make it easier for you to live without me, but I might have made things worse. If I hadn't planned these visits, maybe you would have recovered by now, maybe—"

"Don't," I whispered. We were sitting near a sunny stretch of beach in southern France, hiding ourselves behind a large rock from the family picnicking below us. "Don't worry about me, please."

"You've got to face it. I can't make too many more of these journeys. I'm growing weaker."

I tried to say something but my vocal cords were locked, frozen inside my throat. The voices of the family on the beach were piercing. I wondered, idly, how many of them would die in their coming world war.

Yuri held my hand, opened his lips to say something else, then vanished. I clutched at the empty air in desperation. "No!" I screamed. "Not yet! Come back!"

I found myself, once again, at the Time Station.

* * *

I had been a spendthrift. Now I became a miser, going to the Time Station only two or three times a month, trying not to waste the few remaining visits I had with Yuri. I was no longer working on the tree dwellings. We had finished our designs and now those who enjoyed working with their hands had begun construction.

A paralysis seized me. I spent days alone in my house, unable even to clothe myself, wandering from room to room. I would sleep fitfully, then rise and, after sitting for a few hours alone, would sleep again.

Once I forced myself to walk to the Slumber House and asked them to put me to sleep for a month. I felt the same after awakening, but at least I had been able to pass that lonely month in unconsciousness. I went to the Time Station, visited Yuri, and went back to the Slumber House to ask for another month of oblivion. When I awoke the second time, two men were standing over me, shaking their heads. They told me I would have to see a Counselor before they would put me to sleep again.

I had been a Counselor once myself, and I knew all their tricks. Instead, I went home and waited out the time between my visits there.

It could not go on indefinitely. The list of remaining coordinates grew shorter until there was only one set left, and I knew I would see Yuri for the last time.

* * *

We met by a large wooden summer home that overlooked a small lake. It was autumn there and Yuri began to shiver in the cool air. I managed to open the back door of the house and we went inside, careful not to disturb anything.

Yuri lay on one of the couches, his head on my lap.

Outside, the thick wooded area that surrounded the house was bright with colors, orange, red, yellow. A half-grown fawn with white spots on his back peered in the window at the other end of the room, then disappeared among the trees.

"Do you regret anything?" Yuri suddenly asked. I stroked his white hair and managed a smile.

"No, nothing."

"You're sure."

"Yes," I said, trying to keep my voice from quavering.

"I have one regret, that I didn't meet you sooner. But I wouldn't have met you at all, except for that promise I made."

"I know," I said. We had talked about our meeting at least a thousand times. The conversation had become a ritual, yet I wanted to go over it again. "You were so blatant, Yuri, coming to my door like that, out of nowhere. I thought you were a little crazy."

He smiled up at me and repeated what he had said then. "Hello, I'm Yuri Malenkov. I know this is a little strange, but I promised a friend of mine I met today I'd see you. Do you mind if I come in for a little while?"

"And I was so surprised I let you in."

"And I never left."

"I know, and you're still around." Tears stung my eyes.

"You were the only person aside from that friend that I could talk to honestly right away."

By then tears were running down my cheeks. "You never told me anything about your friend," I said abruptly, breaking the ritual.

"An acquaintance, really. I never found that person again after that."

"Oh, Yuri, what will I do now? You can't leave me. I can't let you die again."

"Don't," he murmured. "You don't have much longer. Can't you see what's happening to you?"

"No."

"Get up and look in the mirror over the fireplace."

I rose, wandered over to the mirror, and looked. The signs were unmistakable. My once-jet-black hair was lightly sprinkled with silver and tiny lines were etched into the skin around my eyes.

"I'm dying," I said. "My body isn't rejuvenating itself any more." I felt a sudden rush of panic; then the fear vanished as quickly as it came, replaced by calm. I hurried back to Yuri's side.

"It won't be long," he said. "Try to do something meaningful with those last months. We'll be together again soon, just keep thinking of that."

"All right, Yuri," I whispered. Then I kissed him for the last time.

* * *

I did not fear death and do not fear it now. I became calmer, consoled by the fact that I would not be alone much longer.

How ironic it would be if my many recent uses of the Time Station had caused my sudden aging, if Yuri's gift to me had condemned me instead. Yet I knew this was not so. We all imagine that we'll have our full three centuries; most of us do, after all. But not everyone, and not I. The irony is part of life itself. It was the work not of any Time Station, but of the final timekeeper, Death, who had decided to come for me a few decades early.

What was I to do with the time left to me? I had trained as a Counselor many years ago and had worked as one before choosing a new profession. I decided to use my old experience in helping those who, like me, had to face death.

The dying began to come to me, unable to accept their fate. They were used to their youthfulness and their full lives, feeling invulnerable to anything except an accident. The suddenness with which old age had descended on them drove some to hysteria, and they would concoct wild schemes to bring about the return of their youth. One man, a biologist, spoke to me and then decided to spend his last months involved in the elusive search for immortality. Another man, who had recently fallen in love with a young girl, cried on my shoulder and I didn't know whether to weep for him or for the young woman he was leaving behind. A woman came to me, only seventy and already aging, deprived of what should have been her normal life span.

I began to forget about myself in talking with these people. Occasionally I would walk through the city and visit old friends. My mind was aging too, and on these walks I found myself lost in memories of the past, clearer to me than more recent events. As I passed the Time Station, I would contemplate a visit to my past and then shake my head, knowing that was impossible.

I might have gone on that way if I had not passed the Time Station one warm evening while sorting through my thoughts. As I walked by, I saw Onel Lialla, dressed as a technician, looking almost exactly the same as when I had known him.

An idea occurred to me. Within seconds it had formed itself in my mind and become an obsession. I can do it, I thought. Onel will help me.

Onel had been a mathematician. He had left the city some time before and I had heard nothing about him. I hurried over to his side.

"Onel," I said, and waited. His large black eyes watched me uncertainly and anxiety crossed his classically handsome face. Then he recognized me.

He clasped my arms. He said nothing at first, perhaps embarrassed by the overt signs of my approaching death. "Your eyes haven't changed," he said finally.

We walked toward the park, talking of old times. I was surprised at how little he had changed. He was still courtly, still fancied himself the young knight in shining armor. His dark eyes still paid me homage, in spite of my being an old gray-haired woman. Blinded perhaps by his innate romanticism, Onel saw only what he wished to see.

Twenty years before, while barely more than a boy, Onel had fallen in love with me. It had not taken me long to realize that Onel, being a romantic, did not really wish to obtain the object of his affections and had probably unconsciously settled on me because I was so deeply involved with Yuri. He would follow me almost everywhere, pouring out his heart. I tried to be kind, not wanting to make him bitter, and spent as much time as I could in conversation with him about his feelings. Onel had finally left the city, and I let him go, knowing he would forget and realizing that this, too, was part of his romantic game.

Onel remembered all this. We sat in the park under one of the crystalline willows and he paid court again. "I never forgot your kindness," he said to me. "I swore I would repay it someday. If there's anything I can do for you now, I will." He sighed dramatically at this point.

"There is," I replied.

"What is it?"

The opportunity had fallen into my lap with no

effort. "I want you," I went on, "to come to the Time Station with me and send me back to this park two hundred and forty years in the past. I want to see the scenes of my youth one last time."

Onel seemed stunned. "You know I can't," he said. "The Portal can't send you to any time you've already lived through. We'd have people bumping into themselves, or going back to give their earlier selves advice. It's impossible."

"The Portal can be overridden for emergencies," I said. "You can override it, you know how. Send me through."

"I can't."

"Onel, I don't want to change anything. I don't even want to talk to anybody."

"If you changed the past—"

"I won't. It would already have happened then, wouldn't it? Besides, why should I? I had a happy life, Onel. I'll go back to a day when I wasn't in the park. It would just give me a little pleasure before I die to see things as they were. Is that asking too much?"

"I can't," he said. "Don't ask this of me."

In the end he gave in, as I knew he would. We went to the Station. Onel, his hands shaking, adjusted a Portal for me and sent me through.

* * *

Onel had given me four hours. I appeared in the park behind a large refreshment tent. Inside the tent, people sat at small round tables enjoying delicacies and occasionally rising to sample the pink wine that flowed from a fountain in the center. As a girl I had worked as a cook in that tent, removing raw foodstuffs from the transformer in the back and spending hours in the small kitchen making desserts, which were my specialty. I had almost forgotten the tents, which had been replaced later on by more elaborate structures.

I walked past the red tent toward the lake. It too was as I remembered it, surrounded by oaks and a few weeping willows. Biologists had not yet developed the silvery vines and glittering crystal trees that would be planted later. A peacock strutted past me as I headed for a nearby bench. I wanted only to sit for a while near the lake, then perhaps visit one of the tents before I had to return to my own time.

I watched my feet as I walked, being careful not to stumble. Most of those in the park ignored me rather pointedly, perhaps annoyed by an old woman who reminded them of their eventual fate. I had been the same, I thought, avoiding those who would so obviously be dead soon, uncomfortable around those who were dying when I had everything ahead of me.

Suddenly a blurred face was in front of me and I collided with a muscular young body. Unable to retain my balance, I fell.

A hand was held out to me and I grasped it as I struggled to my feet. "I'm terribly sorry," said a voice, a voice I had come to know so well, and I looked up at the face with its wide cheekbones and clear blue eyes.

"Yuri," I said.

He was startled. "Yuri Malenkov," I said, trying to recover.

"Do I know you?" he asked.

"I attended one of your lectures," I said quickly, "on holographic art."

He seemed to relax a bit. "I've only given one," he said. "Last week. I'm surprised you remembered my name."

"Do you think," I said, anxious now to hang on to him for at least a few minutes, "you could help me over to that bench?"

"Certainly."

I hobbled over to it, clinging to his arm. By the time we sat down, he was already expanding on points he had covered in the lecture. He was apparently unconcerned about my obvious aging and seemed happy to talk to me.

A thought struck me forcefully. I suddenly realized that Yuri had not yet met my past self. I had never attended that first lecture, having met him just before he was to do his second. Desperately, I tried to recall the date I had given Onel, what day it was in the past.

I had not counted on this. I was jumpy, worried that I *would* change something, that by meeting Yuri in the park like this I might somehow prevent his meeting me. I shuddered. I knew little of the circumstances that had brought him to my door. I could somehow be interfering with them.

Yuri finished what he had to say and waited for my reaction. "You certainly have some interesting insights," I said. "I'm looking forward to your next lecture." I smiled and nodded, hoping that he would now leave and go about his business.

Instead he looked at me thoughtfully. "I don't know if I'll give any more lectures."

My stomach turned over. I knew he had given ten more. "Why not?" I asked as calmly as I could.

He shrugged. "A lot of reasons."

"Maybe," I said in desperation, "you should talk about it with somebody, it might help." Hurriedly I dredged up all the techniques I had learned as a Counselor, carefully questioning him, until at last he opened up and flooded me with his sorrows and worries.

He became the Yuri I remembered, an intense person who concealed his emotions under a cold, businesslike exterior. He had grown tired of the city's superficiality, uncomfortable with those who grew annoyed at his seriousness and penetration. He was unsuited to the gaiety and playfulness that surrounded him, wanting to pursue whatever he did with singleminded devotion.

He looked embarrassed after telling me all this and began once more to withdraw behind his shield. "I have some tentative plans," he said calmly, regaining control. "I may be leaving here in a couple of days with one of the scientific expeditions for Mars. I prefer the company of serious people and have been offered a place on the ship."

My hands trembled. Neither of us had gone with an expedition until five years after our meeting. "I'm sorry for bothering you with my problems," he went on. "I don't usually do that to strangers, or anyone else for that matter. I'd better be on my way."

"You're not bothering me."

"Anyway, I have a lot of things to do. I appreciate the time you took to listen to me."

He stood up and prepared to walk away. No, I thought, you can't, I can't lose you like this. But then I realized something and was shocked that I hadn't thought of it before. I knew what I had to do.

"Wait!" I said. "Wait a minute. Do you think you could humor an old lady, maybe take some advice? It'll only be an hour or so of your time."

"It depends," he said stiffly.

"Before you go on that expedition, do you think you could visit a person I think might enjoy talking to you?"

He smiled. "I suppose," he said. "But I don't see what difference it makes."

"She's a lot like you. I think you'd find her sympathetic." And I told him where I lived and gave him my name. "But don't tell her an old woman sent you, she'll think I'm meddling. Don't mention me. Just tell her it was a friend."

"I promise." He turned to leave. "Thank you, friend." I watched him as he ambled down the pebbled path that would lead him to my home.

(1974)

Bond and Free

I can't remember anything that happened to me before I came here, and neither can the others, or if they can
they're not saying. Tamu says he can, but he's lying, as
he lies about everything else. He is squatting on the
balustrade now, peering at the green meadow that sur-
rounds us on all sides. He sits on his heels and balances
on his toes. His brown skin seems to gleam in the sunlight. He is mocking me, waiting to see how long I can
stand it before I get up and rush across the balcony to
him, afraid that he might slip and fall to the ground a
hundred feet below. But I no longer care. I realize at last
that Tamu with his almost perfect reflexes will not fall
and will not do anything that will actually endanger him
in any way. His balancing act is a lie, his precariousness
on the edge of the balustrade a falsity. He turns his head
toward me, and I smile.

"Stop moving your face," Tomas says. Tomas is
busy applying my make-up, and he gets upset if I ruin his
handiwork. It takes him at least an hour to do it every
day, and that doesn't include the time he spends on my
hair. Then he expects me to spend the rest of the day
doing nothing that would endanger his creation. That
usually means doing nothing at all except reading or talking with the other patients. Last week I defied him and
went down to swim in the pool. When I came out of the
water with my hair plastered flat against my head and my
make-up ruined, poor Tomas almost cried; he had spent
three hours on me that day. He sulked for two days
afterward, and I was able to roam around outside letting

the wind whip my hair, able to eat without worrying about my lip paint. Then Tomas stopped sulking and my holiday was over.

Tamu is standing on his head now, hands in front of him, knees on his elbows. "There," says Tomas. "I think you're done." He holds his hand mirror in front of me. I am black and gold today, black lines over eyelids and brows, gold dust heavy on my lids and sprinkled on my cheekbones. My hair too is thick with gold dust, my lips painted gold, my eyes made black by lenses. Tomas has dressed me in a black velvet dress, and golden earrings hang like chains to my shoulders. Even my skin is golden today; my tan has begun to fade. "Please don't," he says, "move unnecessarily."

"I can't," I say, "move at all." The heavy velvet dress, stiff with stays that push my breasts up and pinch my waist in, is a cage. I can feel sweat under my arms and between my breasts. "I don't know why you couldn't find something more comfortable; I can hardly breathe." I am taking short, shallow breaths, unable to inhale deeply, and I am afraid that if I stand at all, I may faint.

"You were comfortable yesterday; you don't have to be today." Yesterday was a green leotard, green eyes, green spray on my hair. Tomas didn't like that effect and he didn't like the leotard. My thighs were too thin; my stomach was a bit too round. He had told me not to eat any supper because I was getting fat, and so I ate twice as much as I usually do. He is retaliating. It will be a miracle if I can eat at all now with the stays pinching at my waist.

"Perfect," Tomas murmurs, "perfect. I love you, Alia; that's why I make you beautiful. And I love you even more today; you're more beautiful than I've ever made you." I glance at him and notice the bulge in his crotch, under his shabby pants.

"Why are you such a slob, then?" I ask. Tomas is heavy around the waist and his dirty brown hair hangs down to his chest. He is wearing what he always wears, brown pants and a torn white vest. The vest is unbuttoned and spotted with stains. "Why don't you use some of your expertise on your own ugly self?" I look at his paunch and make a face. He seems upset now, not because of what I've said, but because he is afraid I'll disturb my make-up by showing any expression at all.

"I'm making *you* beautiful," Tomas protests. "Why should I waste the time on myself when it's obvious that nothing will come of it anyway." He pats his stomach. "I suppose I could diet. I love you, Alia. You're perfection today, a vision. . . ."

"A vision!" says Tamu, who has given up on his balancing act for now. "A vision I would prefer to see naked and on the bed inside."

"You had enough last night," I say. Tamu leers at me. I stick out my tongue at him.

"Stop that," says Tomas, "you're going to ruin your make-up."

"I'm dying," says Tamu. He sits on the arm of my chair. "Dr. Ehlah said I was dying. My insides are rotting away. I'm going to suffer terribly."

"Why don't you jump off the balcony, then?" I reply. Tamu is unable to keep from lying.

"Because then I couldn't see you any more, Alia," he says. "Because then I couldn't spend all that time ploughing your furrow. I don't mind suffering when I think of all the happy hours that await me in your presence, hours that will take my mind off my suffering if only for a little while." Tamu stands and begins to turn on his toes, stretching his arms toward the sun.

"Let's go downstairs," Tomas says. "Let's go and sit

in the ballroom so that everyone else can see you."

"I can't move. I can't even get through our room in this thing, let alone down the stairs." I feel perspiration on my face. Tomas begins to dab at it with a handkerchief.

"I don't want to die," Tamu suddenly shouts. "I want to live long enough to see my parents again, they were such fine people. They lived in a beautiful house in a large city. We had purple carpets on the floor, velvet carpets, and I would stand on them for hours, rubbing my feet on them, and sometimes I would even roll across them naked. They used to bring me little girls to play with."

"I thought they had a fine ranch with horses," I say, "and that they used to bring you little boys."

Tamu is pouting now. I am not supposed to notice his lies and have hurt his feelings by mentioning an old story. He sulks for a few seconds, then brightens. "They had the ranch too," he goes on, "and a cottage near a woodland glade. I used to watch my mother there while she was taking on the gardener."

I have to admire Tamu, in a way. At least he can invent a past. He and Tomas are much more intelligent than I am, and they can always find something to say about anything. I can do nothing but respond to their talk, rarely having anything of my own to offer. I expect this with Tomas; he is older and has been here for ten years or more. But Tamu is only fourteen. I should be cleverer than he. I have been here three years and am almost seventeen. Tamu has been here three months. I introduced him to Tomas, I let him move his bed into our room, and he doesn't show me proper deference. He is only the intermediary between Tomas and me, the tool through which Tomas expresses his love for me physically, and yet he insists on acting as if he is autonomous. But he is only a tool which pounds away in my open orifice while I cry out my love for Tomas, and afterward presents his ass to Tomas while Tomas cries out to me. It is I who lie in the big bed with Tomas during the night while he gazes down at my ruined make-up and speaks to me about how short-lived his art is, how soon beauty dies. Tamu has to lie in the small bed. Let him prance around with his pretty ass! He is only a tool.

"Why are we here," Tomas says, "and why can't we remember? I must have asked myself that a million times."

"I don't know why you do," I say. "The doctors told us. We're prone to certain illnesses and have to be kept in a restricted environment."

"I don't think that's true. I didn't believe it when I first came here, and I don't believe it now."

"What difference does it make?"

"Aren't you curious, Alia?"

"Sure," I say. "But I'm not going to sit around thinking about it. One day, I'll just get up and walk out of here, and I'll keep going until I see what's outside. You can come along if you want."

"But you can't just walk out of here," he says, looking worried.

"Why not? No one will stop me. I can just keep going, as far as I want to. I walked out once and stayed away for the whole day; I didn't come back until after supper; you remember, you were really upset. But the doctors didn't care."

Tomas is agitated. "You can't," he says. "You're susceptible to certain diseases; that's why you're here."

"But I thought you didn't believe that."

"Well, I don't entirely, but I haven't disproved it

either. If I'm going to find out anything, I'll find it out here."

"Suit yourself," I say. "You should come along, though; it might be a real adventure. This place is so boring I'd think you'd welcome the chance."

"I don't think it's boring. There's a library, plenty of people to talk to, and you, Alia. Why should I be bored?"

I begin to shrug my shoulders, then feel the pinch of my stays. Tamu is turning cartwheels now. "I'm dying," he shouts to us. "My bones will rot away until I can only flow across the floor." He begins to dance across the balcony, whirling faster and faster, his arms straight out from his shoulders, until I am almost dizzy watching him. I reach for Tomas's hand. He holds it, then kisses my golden-nailed fingers.

"You are beautiful," he says.

* * *

The fire of sunrise blazed beyond the balcony. Awakening, Alia sat up in her large brass-railed bed and gazed across the room.

Tomas had betrayed her again, creeping out of bed in the middle of the night to Tamu. She could see their bodies huddled together under Tamu's sheets, moles burrowing under the bedclothes.

Tamu was only an intermediary. Alia had never made love to him unless Tomas was present and able to witness the act. Yet Tomas had gone to Tamu while assuming that she still slept. She had heard their moans and remembered that it was Tamu's name he called out and not hers.

Well, thought Alia, it hardly matters now. She was leaving this morning. If the others were content to sit around here, that was their business. She had wanted Tomas to accompany her, but he, along with everyone else, preferred to huddle in the hospital even though he, and almost everyone else, did not really believe what the doctors had told them. No one had forbidden them to leave; none of them really wanted to go.

She put on her walking boots, straightened her slacks and checked her small knapsack. It was filled with food packets stolen from the kitchen and a canteen of water. She had a knife and could sleep on the ground using the knapsack as a pillow.

Alia hoisted the knapsack onto her back, then turned toward Tamu's bed. The two were still sleeping. She opened the door and walked out into the red-carpeted hallway.

No one else was up yet. She walked down the hallway to the elevator and pushed the down button. Tomas was afraid of the elevator and never let her use it; Tamu laughed at Tomas for his fear but wouldn't ride it either. The doors opened and she stepped aboard.

The elevator hummed down to the first floor lobby and stopped with a jolt. Alia paced through the lobby. Her booted footsteps echoed on the smooth white surface of the floor. Other Alias marched on either side of the large room, reflected from the mirrors that lined the walls. All of the Alias moved toward the arched doorway, then disappeared, leaving only one to pass through the doorway and outside the hospital.

The morning air was cool and the grass around the building still dewy. As she walked, Alia saw the tips of her boots darken with moisture. She pivoted and looked back.

The hospital seemed to tower above her. It was an ugly building, tall and square with baroque balustrades surrounding balconies on every floor of the thirty-story structure. The heavy wooden doors, propped open, which led into the lobby seemed out of place, an after-thought. She turned away from the hospital. Grasslands surrounded the building on all sides; the only tree she had ever seen was the weeping willow near the back entrance.

Alia set out across the green field in front of her. She hoped Tomas wouldn't worry, remembered seeing him under Tamu's sheets, then began to wish that he would worry a little. He would have to dress someone else to-day, if anyone would sit still that long. She laughed to herself.

* * *

The knapsack had grown heavier. Alia stopped, re-moved it and sat down. She was still surrounded by green meadows, and she could still see the hospital. It was small and close to the horizon, a grey block against the blue sky.

She couldn't have made much progress if she could still see the hospital. Annoyed, she stood up and began to drag her knapsack behind her. The cursed thing seemed to be made of lead.

Alia trudged on, dragging the knapsack. Occasional-ly she turned and, seeing the grey block, would keep going. The weather had grown warmer, and her clothes were sticking to her. She pushed on, dragging the knap-sack up a small hill and down the other side, through a field of dandelions and up another small hill. She moved on until she was exhausted and had to stop once more.

She fell next to the knapsack and stretched out on the ground, catching her breath. At last she sat up and climbed to her feet.

The hospital had vanished.

She sat down again, facing her long afternoon shad-ow. At last she was free of the place. If Tomas had been with her, he would be trying to guess what was beyond the meadow, if indeed there was anything beyond the meadow. Alia was content to wait. She shivered, suddenly apprehensive.

* * *

Alia had found some trees by nightfall and decided to sleep under them, feeling, somehow, that she would be safer there. By morning, she regretted the decision. The ground under the trees had been harder than the soft meadowland.

She began to walk around the trees, feeling numb in the cool morning air. Her jacket was damp with dew. "This is ridiculous," she said aloud, "walking all this way to see five trees." Her voice sounded hollow. She shuddered and decided not to talk to herself again.

She hoisted the knapsack onto her back and set off. Occasionally she looked back. The trees moved closer to the horizon and finally disappeared. A song Tamu had taught her ran through her mind, repeating itself monotonously.

At noon she sat down to rest. The silence of the grasslands had grown oppressive. She pulled out her canteen and drank noisily, smacking her lips between swallows. She opened a packet and gnawed at the rubbery chicken inside, then let out a loud belch.

Ahead of her was a very high hill, higher at least than any she had seen so far. She noticed a small structure on the side of the hill, squinted at it near-sightedly, but couldn't see what it was.

She hurried toward the hill, curious now. She moved quickly, ignoring the warmth of the sunlight and the increasing heaviness of the knapsack she was dragging.

Reaching the hill, she began to climb toward the

structure. It was a well. She had seen a painting of a well in the library; in fact, this looked like the same one, brown stones, wooden bucket parked on the edge, wild violets growing nearby.

There was one difference. She could see a wooden plank resting against the well. Someone had painted white letters on the plank. She read the message:

WATER—FILL UP
YOU'RE GOING TO NEED IT

Alia sat down and stared at the plank. Tomas, she thought, would have been terrified by now. She reached over and touched one of the white letters with her finger.

The paint was still wet.

She jumped up quickly and looked around. She saw nothing but grassy fields on all sides. Her hands were trembling. Someone had painted the sign very recently.

Whoever it was might be just over the hill.

Alia paced near the well, clenching her hands, trying to calm herself. Someone is telling me I need water, she thought, that's all; I'll fill my canteen and the empty packets and reseal them, and then I'll see what's over the hill.

She lowered the bucket into the well, then filled her canteen and empty food packets. She resumed her climb. The hill was steeper than it looked, and her legs ached from the exertion. The weather had grown extremely warm, and the air seemed dryer. The knapsack was pushing her toward the ground, and her calf muscles tightened.

At last, panting, she reached the top of the hill and looked around.

The green grass continued to the bottom of the hill, then stopped abruptly. In front of her, Alia could see only dry, flat desert land. The desert stretched to high mountains far in the distance, at least a day's walk away. There was no sign of life anywhere on the desert wastes except at one point midway to the mountains. There, she could see what looked like a small group of buildings. They seemed to shimmer before her eyes.

People. There might be people there.

A wave of panic swept over her. I should go back, she thought wildly, and shuddered at the thought of the diseases to which she might be exposing herself.

She turned quickly, tripped, and began to roll back down the hill, finally sliding to a stop.

"Stop it," she said aloud, "if you panic now, you've come all this way for nothing." Her voice was harsh, and she whispered her next words. "I'll stay near the well, and I'll sleep there, and rest, and decide tomorrow."

She walked back down to the well where, after a hasty look around, she stripped off her clothes and then lowered the bucket for water. She poured it over her body, welcoming the coolness. The water was a silver stream, refreshing and calming her. She threw herself to the ground, feeling the warm rays of the sun on her back, and sniffed at the wild violets.

* * *

She set out across the desert before dawn. It was cold at first, but after walking for a while, she peeled off her jacket and put it into the knapsack.

The sun was burning her face, and she could feel the desert heat through her boots. Alia began to whistle, marching in time to the tune. The desert blurred around her, and the thin layer of sand over rock seemed almost white. She kept marching, pausing only long enough to drink from one of the food packets.

Ahead of her, the buildings in the center of the desert shimmered. As she came closer, she noticed something odd about them. The ones at the edge of the town were not buildings at all, but only facades supported by wooden rails, as if the entire town were nothing more than a stage set. Moving nearer, she saw that in fact there was only one real building in the town, in the center of the facade.

She suddenly felt foolish, trudging across the desert to meet this display. She walked over to the building in the center, an old rickety wooden structure three stories high, feeling more alone than ever. It would at least shade her from the desert heat for a while. She peered inside the front window and saw an unlighted room with round tables, chairs, and a long bar on one side near the wall. She tried the door. It opened easily and she walked inside.

Everything in the room was coated with a layer of grey dust. Alia walked to a table near the bar and took the knapsack off her back, placing it next to a chair. Rummaging in the sack, she pulled out her jacket and dusted off the table. Then she sat down, resting her head on the tabletop.

She had come on a fool's errand. She should have turned back at the well, but she had come too far to turn back now. She sighed and closed her eyes.

"My God, honey, don't look so sad. What you need is a cold beer." Alia sat up quickly.

A tall busty red-headed woman was standing near her, arms resting on the dusty bar. She smiled at Alia.

"Who are you?" shouted Alia, almost rising to her feet.

"Don't look so worried, honey. My name's Eta. I own this establishment." The woman walked toward her, carrying a bottle. She wore a long purple dress which trailed behind her, picking up dust and leaving a streak on the floor. She put the bottle in front of Alia and sat down across from her, placing her elbows on the table. "Go ahead, it's on me. Business is so lousy lately, I can't lose much more giving it away." Eta smiled and fluttered her thick black eyelashes.

Alia picked up the beer. It was cold and wet with beads of condensation. She sipped at it tentatively, then began to gulp it down.

"You know," said Eta, "everyone used to come here. Why, you couldn't hardly find a place to rest your ass. But you know how people are; they go to a place, and before you know it they're moving on to a new place because it's got a band or hot horsy dervs or some other fool thing. I don't have all that, but I run an honest bar, and I don't care if people get boisterous or the girls want to make some spare money on the side or somebody wants to throw some chairs around, but I guess Eta's place just isn't good enough any more."

Alia stared at the woman. She could not understand what Eta was talking about and was afraid to ask. "This whole damn town used to come here," Eta went on. "I remember when Gar Tuli got so mad he threw a whole table through that window over there, and his woman— she was big, honey—sent him through the window when she found out about him and Neela. What a night!"

Alia looked down at her beer bottle. The woman must be mad. This could never have been a town, not unless everyone had moved and taken the buildings with them. "Maybe they'll all come back someday," she said, trying to smile sympathetically, "when they get tired of the other place." She finished her beer. Eta's eyes seemed to flicker a bit as she watched Alia. The woman was silent for a few seconds; then she slapped her thigh and laughed loudly.

"You're all right, honey. You know the right thing to say. I feel better already." Eta got to her feet. "You want another beer?"

Alia shrugged. Eta sailed over to the bar, making another trail in the dust with her train. She bent over behind the bar, then stood up. Alia could see silver beads on the bottle Eta was holding and wondered how the woman kept the beer cold.

"Where you headed for?" asked Eta.

"I thought I'd take a look at the mountains," Alia muttered. Eta came back with the beer and sat down again.

"There's nothing over there, honey," the woman said.

"How long does it take to get there?"

"A few hours. But I'd advise you to head back where you came from. Or you can stay here and maybe we can figure out how to get some customers. We oughta think of something between the two of us."

Alia stood up. "You're insane," she said quietly. Eta didn't respond. "You are really demented. There aren't any people here; there aren't even any buildings except this one. I've got better things to do than spend time with a madwoman." She picked up the knapsack, watching Eta. The woman was silent. Alia moved toward the door.

Suddenly Eta chuckled. "You sound like Gar Tuli," she said. "You know what he used to say? He used to say, 'Eta, you got cobwebs in the attic.' I think you better go back where you came from."

"Thank you for the drink," said Alia. "If I see anybody, I'll be sure to recommend your hospitality." She left Eta sitting at the table and stepped into the hot dry air outside. As she walked away from the building and past the facades on either side of her, she began to feel a bit more energetic in spite of the heat. Tendrils of guilt brushed at her mind, and she speculated about Eta, thinking that perhaps she should have stayed with her for a day, talked to her, and offered some help. She pushed Eta out of her mind. The woman was demented, after all; she could have done nothing for her. It was a wonder she had lasted in the middle of the desert; the woman must be more resourceful than she seemed.

Alia burped, then began to whistle again as she marched toward the mountains.

* * *

Alia had reached the mountains during the night and slept on the hard desert ground with her jacket wrapped around her. By morning she was shivering from the cold, and she welcomed the sight of the blood-red sun as it began to climb above the now-orange wilderness.

She looked up at the mountain above her. It was rocky and not quite as high as she had thought, although it would take some time to get to the summit. She opened her knapsack and removed some food.

"Mind if I join you?" said a voice. Alia turned her head quickly. A skinny old man sat on the rocks above her.

"Come on down." The old man clambered over the rocky slopes and was soon sitting next to her. He had an untrimmed grey beard which seemed to wobble on his face, and his shabby brown shirt, black slacks and boots showed signs of wear.

"I sure am hungry," the man said, eying her dried beef.

"I can only give you one packet." She rummaged in the sack and took out one of the apricot bars, which tasted sour anyway, and tossed it to him.

"I can take you up the mountain," said the man,

tearing open the food packet. "You can go up yourself, but it'll take you a lot longer; you don't know the mountain. I can take you up in three, four hours maybe."

Alia looked around at the mountain, then back at the man. "Halfway up it gets hard," he went on. "But I know a quick way."

"All right," said Alia. It would be safer going up with someone anyway, whether the old man could take her up more quickly or not. "All right, old man."

"I could use some more food first and water too." She took out another apricot bar and a packet filled with water.

"Where are you from, old man?"

He squinted at her. "None of your business."

"You wouldn't happen to be acquainted with Eta's place?"

"I'm not acquainted with anybody. I keep to myself and you should do the same." The old man finished his food and got to his feet. "Come on," he said. He began to climb over the rocks. Alia followed him, then noticed that there was a clearly defined path through the rocky slopes.

"I could have found this path myself, you old fraud," she shouted at the figure ahead of her.

"I told you," he shouted back, "it's halfway up you run into trouble." Alia sighed and kept going. Her muscles soon began to knot painfully.

"I don't suppose you could help carry this knapsack for a while," she shouted.

"Why the hell should I? It isn't mine."

"What's over the mountain?"

"You'll find out." His voice was faint. He was getting ahead of her.

She kept climbing, trying to ignore the hot sun. She

could go on for another two days before heading back to the hospital, maybe longer on short rations. She should have brought more. She wiped the sweat from her face and wished for a bath. Tamu's mindless song circled her mind once more as she climbed, stopped to rest, then climbed some more. The old man had disappeared.

At last she came to the end of the path. A smaller path forked to the right between two boulders. Alia looked up and saw only sheer cliff surface above her.

The old man had apparently been waiting. He sat on the ground, smiling complacently.

"What now?" she asked. The old man groaned and got up.

"And I just got comfortable too," he grumbled. He turned and she followed him along the small path until they reached a cave in the side of the mountain.

"Here we are." said the man. Above the cave in large letters someone had painted:

ENTER CAVE
CLIMB STAIRS TO TOP

"You old fraud," said Alia. She grabbed the man by the shoulders and pushed him against a boulder. "I could have found this cave myself." He twisted loose and ran past her back along the path. "Come back here," she shouted after him. "Aren't you going to the top?"

"Why bother?" The old man's voice floated back to her. "There's nothing up there."

She stood beside the cave, feeling angry and foolish, then walked inside. Someone had carved a flight of stairs in the rock; the steps curved around the cave walls in a spiral. She looked up and saw a speck of light above her.

She chuckled, then began to laugh. This is too easy, she thought; they're not making it hard enough; anyone can just walk out of the hospital and keep going. It wasn't consistent with the doctors' desire to prevent the exposure of susceptible people to disease.

On the other hand, she thought as she began to climb the stone steps, I haven't really seen anybody I could get a disease from except a couple of lunatics. Suddenly she felt cold. Maybe they *were* sick; maybe they, like her, had left the hospital and become ill, losing their minds in the process. Her stomach turned. She should go back.

She kept going up the steps. She would at least see what was over the mountain first. The stairway was dark and only intermittently lighted by phosphorescent green bars attached to the walls. She kept close to the wall, not wanting to lose her balance too close to the edge of the steps, which had no rail.

Alia climbed, stopping frequently to rest. She began to count steps and lost track of the number. She started to sing and lost track of the time. She was almost hypnotized by the time she reached the top of the stairs and could at last see the sky clearly. It looked like late afternoon.

Above her was a small metal ladder. It was attached to the wall and would take her out of the mountain. She hurried up the ladder. As she climbed out, a breeze wafted past her, and she smelled salty air.

She stood at the summit and looked around. A path had apparently been carved in this side of the mountain also; she could see its clearly defined boundaries among the rocks and boulders. At the bottom of the mountain there was a large expanse of white sand and beyond that a body of water stretching to the horizon. Even at this distance, she could hear the thunder of breakers as waves rolled toward the shore. An ocean, she thought. Tomas had shown her a picture of one in the library and had told her that it was thousands of miles wide, with salty water unfit to drink.

Alia sat down and stared at the grey sea. There was nowhere to go from this point. The mountains extended along the shore for as far as she could see. She could not get across the ocean. She would have to go back, get more supplies, try a different route. But maybe the doctors, who hadn't had to restrict anyone up to now, wouldn't let her leave again. They might be searching for her.

She considered the hospital. Perhaps there was nothing outside the hospital, and no one except a few demented individuals such as Eta or the old man. The doctors themselves might be susceptible to disease. But that wouldn't explain why some doctors disappeared for weeks at a time, or how supplies got to the hospital. No, there had to be other people somewhere.

If I've been exposed to disease, she thought, I'm already dead. I might as well go on, or the whole trip is for nothing. I'll walk till I drop, I'll stretch the food and water, I have to know. The image of Tomas flickered across her mind, and she felt a pang of regret, then shrugged it off.

Alia started down the mountain.

* * *

Four more sunrises, four sunsets; on the fifth day she was still walking, seeing nothing but white sand and ocean on her left, white sand and mountains on her right. The arc of the red sun marked time for her now; she no longer divided her days with meals, eating only when she grew weak. She was almost out of food and water. She could not turn back; she would not even get to the desert.

A crab scuttled past her. She stared at it as it scurried beneath a wave, then heard a cry above her. She looked up. Three gulls circled overhead. She turned to the mountains and saw trees and bushes growing on the slopes. The landscape around her had changed. She had left the barren mountains and arid desert behind.

Her tired feet carried her on. Two days before, she had washed her feet in the ocean, crying out in pain as the salty water washed over the bleeding blisters. She glanced at the ocean. It was receding from her as if it had postponed its apology until now. It withdrew from her and began to creep toward the horizon, leaving behind beached crabs and fish.

Food. It would be simple to gather up some of the fish and store it in empty food packets. With luck, she might be able to start a fire with some wood from the mountain slopes. If necessary, she would eat the fish raw. The ocean kept retreating, leaving behind an almost unnatural silence. Alia began to walk toward some beached fish, squashing the wet soft sand under her feet.

"Hey!" a voice shouted. She turned and saw a figure running across the beach toward her. It was a young man with black hair; he was well-tanned, clad only in a pair of ragged blue shorts. He waved his arms frantically as he ran.

He stopped near her, panting for breath. "Run!" he shouted. "Run for the mountains, run!"

"Why?"

"Don't ask, run!" The young man took off. She looked toward the ocean.

A wall of water was on the horizon. It was coming toward the shore, threatening to smash her and everything on the beach. She ran after the young man, her terror making it easy for her to catch up with him. She ran, pounding through the sand, ignoring the knapsack on her back, not even looking over her shoulder at the wave. She could hear it now, a low distant rumble coming ever closer to them. They reached the mountain, and she followed the man up the slope, ignoring the tree branches and bushes which clawed at her arms and legs. They stopped on a small ledge, and the young man turned to the sea. He stared at it intently. His jaw muscles tightened.

Alia saw the wave sweeping across the shore toward the mountain. "Come on!" she screamed at the man, "we've got to climb higher, come on!" He ignored her and continued to stare at the wave. It began to slow down, diminishing in size. By the time it reached the foot of the mountain it was a feeble sight, lapping gently at the trees there and then retreating, until the ocean was again where it should be.

The man relaxed, leaning against a tree behind him. "I'm tired," he said. "It's hard to stop them by yourself."

She was puzzled. She remembered reading something about tidal waves and knew that this one had not behaved normally.

"Don't worry about it," the man went on. "Someone was just fooling around." He smiled at her, showing even white teeth. "It happens sometimes."

Alia loosened the straps on her knapsack, letting it fall to the ground. "You're going to get awfully sick, wandering around like this," said the young man. "Don't you think you should go back?"

"Go back to where?" she asked warily.

"You know where. Whatever institution you wandered out of. Didn't they tell you that you might get sick?"

"Yes. I don't know if I believe it any more." She watched the young man carefully. "I've walked a long way. I don't think I want to turn back just yet."

"But I'll take you back. I'm sure it's much nicer there than here. Wouldn't you agree?"

Alia thought of Tomas and Tamu and her life at the hospital, free from any demands. The older patients had been there for fifty years or more and seemed content; in fact, one old man had grown terrified of the thought that a vaccine might be found for the patients and they would be forced to leave. The doctors had to tell him that no one would be forced out, and everyone else had been as relieved as the old man.

"I suppose it is nicer," she said to the young man. "It's easier at least."

"Don't you miss all your friends? They'll be so happy to see you again."

"How would we get there?"

"Oh, it's easy, and it would be fun too. I'll show you." The young man started to climb the mountain. Alia followed him, dragging the knapsack. As she scrambled over some rocks, she noticed a huge red globe hovering above some trees on a ledge just above her. The young man reached out a hand, she grabbed it, and he pulled her up. She saw a huge balloon, bright red and attached to a large basketlike bottom. The young man had apparently tied it to one of the trees.

"We can go back in my balloon," the young man said, walking toward it.

"How?"

"It's simple. When we want to descend, all I have to do is pull this—" he pointed to a rope attached to the balloon—"and we land; it lets some air out. To go up, I just pour some sand out of one of those bags there." He grinned at her. "Doesn't that sound like fun?"

"Sure does."

"We can have a great time on the way back," said the young man. "Come on, let's go." He turned toward the balloon. Alia raised her arm quickly and chopped him on the back of the neck. He toppled forward with a soft moan and lay silent.

She quickly climbed into the basket, cut the rope holding the balloon down with her knife, and poured sand out of one of the bags. The balloon rose, grazing some treetops on the way. She was soon above the mountains and could see the desert on her right. The balloon hovered above the mountains, and she waited for it to start drifting.

"What now," she muttered. The vehicle was of no use to her if it stayed here. She felt a warm breeze on her face; then she began to move. The balloon drifted to the north. At least, she thought, it won't go back to the hospital.

Ahead, she noticed that the mountains had started to curve to her right, surrounding the desert. She moved further away from the sea and was soon over a thick green forest. She had left the desert behind.

Deer were leaping through the underbrush below her, waving their small white tails at the balloon. A slender river wound through the trees, and she could see two horses, black and chestnut, on its banks. A flock of crystalline birds, with feathers that were prisms, swam in the river. Alia, clinging to the side of the basket, gazed happily at the forest. It was worth it, she told herself, it was worth it for this.

Then she glimpsed something on the edge of the forest. She squinted as the balloon floated on, and was able to discern large crystalline structures just beyond the wooded land. The crystals were green, gold, silver, blue and pink; some were spirals; others were slender towers.

They glittered in the sunlight. As she came closer, she saw large golden insects buzzing softly in the sky over the crystal buildings. A city, she thought, and something jarred her mind.

Home, her mind whispered. *She was a child again. She stood in a garden while her mother made the roses grow.* She was over the city now and could see people moving through the streets on silver bands. A few people were floating over the city, apparently unsupported by anything. *Her father was giving a concert with his mind, and people gathered near the house to listen. Alia heard only silence and the rustle of leaves.* Silvery vines formed patterns on the sides of some of the crystals, wrapping themselves around the buildings, then unwinding and forming new patterns. There were parks scattered throughout the city with trees and ponds, and she could see children playing in them. *The other children wouldn't play with her. She could not float up to the treetops or make the thunder roar.* One of the golden insects passed near her, and she saw people inside it. They gazed at her through the transparent golden walls of the craft and waved.

Home. Bits and pieces cluttered her mind, traces of the memories she had lost. *I have a brother, with red-gold hair like mine, and he sometimes dances with me in the garden. My home is sapphire-blue. Once he made a cloud for me, and it rained on the flowers.* She tugged at the rope attached to the balloon and began her descent. *Father is composing. He listens to the universe, the stars and winds, and adds his own notes. They tell me it is beautiful. I can't hear it. He listens to other times. I can't hear them. He travels. I cannot follow.* The balloon fell slowly toward a sapphire spiral, then landed with a bump in a small garden behind it.

A tall blonde woman was in the garden gathering pink flowers. Near her stood a man with silver hair. They wore white robes and stared at her as she clambered over the side of the basket. The balloon bobbed uncertainly next to her.

The woman let go of the flowers and they fell in a pink mass at her feet. "Mother," Alia said softly. "Father."

Alia. The name was unspoken as it entered her mind. "Let me stay," she said, "don't send me away again, let me stay." She began to run to them, arms outstretched. The woman turned away. The man still watched her, but did not hold out his arms.

She was surrounded by a blue cloud, frozen, unable to move. *I'm sorry, Alia,* something in her mind whispered, *I'm sorry, please believe that.* Then, very slowly, she fell forward, almost floating, until the blue cloud turned black.

* * *

Alia could hear a loud humming sound. She opened her eyes. She was rushing through an underground tunnel aboard a conveyance with transparent sides. The garden had disappeared. Around her, Alia could see only rock and an occasional flashing light. Someone had put her in a chair, and she struggled vainly at the straps which bound her to it.

Eta, the woman of the desert, sat in front of her, but she wore only a green robe and had removed her makeup. Next to Eta sat the young man from the beach and the old man who had guided her up the mountain. The young man was slouching in his chair, staring at the floor. The old man, also in a green robe, had trimmed his beard.

"What are you going to do with me?" asked Alia.

"You have to realize," said the young man, still looking at the floor, "that we are civilized. None of us has entered your mind; no one has since the time you were first taken to the hospital. It was necessary then, as you must know, but we haven't entered it since. If we had, you would be back at the hospital now and would never want to leave again. If I had, you could never have surprised me and stolen my balloon."

"We didn't think you'd get this far," said Eta. "You were timid when we placed you at that hospital. It seemed perfect for you. I didn't think you would become so adventurous."

"Take me home," she said. "Haven't I earned it? I know my mind is weak, but there must be a place for me. Ask my parents, they'll keep me, they have to."

The old man shook his head. "Would you want your parents to bear that?" he said softly. "They made the same decision everyone in their place has made."

"We tried to spare you all this," said the young man. "We tried to discourage you on your journey. We could have terrified you, driven you back with our minds, but that would have been wrong, using our minds like that against a helpless creature."

"Please take me home," she said. Her words seemed feeble. *On her last night at home, she sat sleepless in her room, trying desperately to raise her table with her mind, sobbing with frustration.*

"What would you have us do?" said the old man. "Structure our society around misfits and atavisms? Would you want to live with us, knowing that there was really nothing your poor mind could contribute? You can't shake the mountains or move the sea or bring meteors close to earth in showers of fire. You can't sail the clouds across the sky or make the spring come early out of the ground. You will never be free of the tyranny of time and space." The old man stood up and placed a hand on her shoulder. "I tell you this, even though you will forget. We do the best we can; we place you in environments that will make you happy. We prevent your suffering by removing memories of the past. Would it make you any happier if I told you that there are fewer of you now, that soon there will probably not be any?"

"Don't tell me all that," Alia said bitterly. She glared at the old man. "You have your own reasons for sending me away, I know that."

The old man sighed. "Yes, we do," he said. "Do you have any idea of the control we must exercise over ourselves in order to be certain that a momentary impulse isn't expressed outwardly by our minds? Helpless people such as you would be a constant temptation. You would be pawns which we could dominate, and you would make us cruel and decadent."

"That tidal wave," the young man muttered. "I couldn't resist the temptation. I was glad when I saw how terrified you were. Do you understand that? I never want to feel that way again."

"You'll be in a very nice place," said Eta.

"You'll be happy there," said the old man. "It's all arranged." Alia turned from him and looked out at the rocky walls rushing by them. They seemed to blur slightly as she watched.

* * *

I can't remember anything that happened to me before I came here, and neither can the others, or if they can they're not saying. The doctors tend to be a bit restrictive, but that's probably understandable. They don't want us traipsing around picking up all kinds of germs that might make us really sick. They wouldn't be too happy to know that Moro and I are on our way to the village.

Moro is skiing ahead of me. He slaloms along, then stops for a bit so I can catch up. I'm not as good a skier as Moro, and I have to go slowly. Moro has sneaked out of the hospital several times, and so has everyone else, I guess. The doctors don't make it too difficult, although they usually get annoyed if they find out.

It'll be my first time in the village. Already I can see it, just over the next slope, cottage roofs covered with inches of snow. Moro knows a tavern where they'll serve you without asking questions. The bartender there used to be at the hospital; I think most of the people in the village were once, but they're old now and were given permission to move.

Moro says that there's a city down at the bottom of the mountain, if you can call it a city. It's not much larger than the village up here. A few patients have been down there, but it's impossible to get to it in winter; you could never make it back up the mountain even if you got there. But Moro will take me in the spring, he's promised, and I'm looking forward to the trip. I don't like staying in the hospital all the time, but as long as I know I can go somewhere, I can stand it.

I manage to come to a stop near Moro without falling over. He is laughing, and there are crinkles on either side of his eyes. He kisses me on the cheek, and I begin to laugh too, stopping only to inhale some of the cold mountain air. I am falling in love with Moro, with his laughter and his talk and his sapphire-blue eyes. We will go to the tavern, and if I manage to acquire some courage with my beer, I may ask him to move into my room.

I think he will accept the offer.

(1974)

Shadows

The sun hid its face behind the clouds, a gray layered curtain which hung close to the Earth. Defeated, the city's inhabitants trudged along the highway, crowding the four lanes. Suzanne Molitieri could hear the droning of murmurs punctuated by an occasional wail. *Don't look back.* She kept her eyes resolutely focused on the asphalt at her feet as she walked. Her hand clutched Joel's, both palms dry. Around her, people twisted their necks as they glanced back at the empty city.

Above them silver insects hovered, humming softly and casting faint shadows over the people below. They were passing the suburbs now and more people joined the stream, trickling down the highway entrances, creating small eddies before becoming part of the river. *Herded like animals.* Suzanne glanced at Joel, saw his brown eyes focused on her, and grasped his hand more tightly.

Resistance had been futile. A few invaders had been slaughtered by gunfire in Buenos Aires as they left their ship, and Buenos Aires had vanished, people and all. When the same thing happened in Canton and Washington, the will to resist had subsided. Suzanne doubted that it had completely vanished.

The Earth was an anthill to the Aadae. They had descended on it from the skies, stepping on it here and there when it was necessary. Yet Suzanne had seen an Aada in the city streets weeping over the dead burned bodies of some who had resisted. Then she and the others had been herded from the city, allowed to take nothing with them but the clothes they wore and a few personal possessions. Suzanne carried more clothes in a knapsack. She had left everything else behind; the past would be of no use to her now. Joel carried a pound of marijuana and some bottles of liquor in his knapsack; he was already planning for the future.

Suzanne adjusted the burden on her back. Around her the murmuring died and she heard only the sound of feet marching, treading the pavement with soft thuds. The conquered people moved past the rows of suburban houses which were silent witnesses to the procession.

Suzanne thought of empty turtle shells. The gunmetal gray domes surrounded her, covering the countryside in uneven rows. Groups of people huddled in front of each dome, waiting passively. She thought of burial mounds.

"How they get them up so fast?" A stocky black man standing near her was looking at a dome. He began to rub his hand across its gray surface. Suzanne could hear the sound of weeping. A plump pale woman next to Joel was whimpering, clinging to a barrel-chested man who was probably her husband.

"They took her kids away," a voice said. Suzanne found herself facing a slender black woman with hazel eyes. The woman's hair was coiled tightly around her head in cornrow braids. "She had six of them," the black woman went on. "They took them all to some other domes."

Suzanne, not knowing what to say, looked down at her feet, then back at the woman. "Did you have kids too?" she asked lamely.

"No, I always wanted to, but I'm glad now I didn't." The woman smiled bitterly and Suzanne felt that the subject was being dismissed. The stocky black man had wandered to the dome's triangular entrance. "I'm Felice

Harrison," the woman muttered. "That's my husband Oscar." She waved at the man in the entrance.

"I'm Suzanne Molitieri." The introduction hung in the air between them. Suzanne wanted to giggle suddenly. Felice raised her eyebrows slightly.

"Are you all right?"

"I'm fine," said Suzanne, almost squeaking the words. Oscar joined his wife and placed his arm gently over her shoulders.

"This is Suzanne Molitieri," Felice said to Oscar, and Suzanne felt reassured by the steady smile on the man's broad face.

"I'm Joel Feldstein," Joel said quickly, and she felt his hand close around her waist. She had almost forgotten he was there. His hand seemed as heavy as a chain, binding her to him.

Joel smiled. His too-perfect teeth seemed to glitter; his brown eyes danced. With his free hand, he brushed back a lock of thick brown hair. *He's too beautiful—I had to love him.* "I guess we're going to live in these things," Joel continued. "I can't figure it out, I don't understand these people. That's quite an admission for me; I've studied psychology for years. In fact, I was finishing my doctoral studies." *You haven't been near a classroom in years.* "I wanted to go into research, then marry Suzanne, give her a chance to finish school; she's been working much too hard helping me out." He smiled down at her regretfully. *Somebody had to pay the bills.* "The thing I regret most is not getting the chance to help Suzie." She winced at the nickname. The chainlike pressure on her waist tightened. "What about you two, what did you do?"

"It hardly matters now," Felice said dryly. Her hazel eyes and Oscar's black ones were expressionless.

"I guess you're right," said Joel. "You know, I even

had a couple of papers published last year—I was really proud of that—but I guess that doesn't matter now either." *Why are you lying now?*

"I was a bus driver," said Oscar coldly. Suzanne suddenly felt that she was looking at the Harrisons across an abyss. Her mind began to clutch at words in desperation.

"What's it like inside the dome?" she said to Oscar. The black man seemed to relax slightly.

"Just a big room, with low tables and no chairs," Oscar answered. "Then there's these metal stairways winding around, and some rooms without doors, and the ceiling's glowing, don't ask me how. No lights, just this glow."

"Hey," Felice muttered. The people around them had formed a line. Suzanne turned. One of the Aadae stood in front of them, holding a small metal device.

Suzanne sniffed at the air. She hadn't realized how smelly the Aadae actually were. She watched the alien and wondered again how the military must have felt when they first saw the conquerors.

The Aada appeared human, a small female not more than five feet tall and slender, with large violet eyes and pale golden skin. Her blue-black hair, uncombed and apparently unwashed, hung to her waist. She wore a dirty pair of bikini bottoms, spotted with stains. The alien scratched her stomach, and Suzanne almost snickered.

"Give nameh, go inside," said the Aada. She waved the metal rod she held at the dome. Then she pointed it at Joel. "Give nameh, go inside." The Aada's violet eyes stared past them, as if perceiving something else besides the line of people.

"Joel Feldstein." The rod was pointed at Suzanne.

"Suzanne Molitieri."

"Oscar Harrison."

"Felice Harrison." They began to move toward the dome.

"Are my children all right, please tell me, are they all right?" The plump mother of six was pleading with the alien.

"Nameh," the Aada repeated. Suzanne looked into the alien's violet eyes and was startled to see sadness there. The Aada's small golden hand patted the plump woman reassuringly. "Nameh," and the word this time seemed tinged by grief.

Puzzled, Suzanne turned away and entered the dome.

* * *

"You tell me," said Joel, "how a technologically advanced culture can produce such sloppy, dirty people. I can't get within two feet of one." He grimaced.

"Cleanliness and technological advancement aren't necessarily related," said Gabe Cardozo, shifting his plump body around on the floor. "Besides, from their point of view, they might be very neat. It depends on your perspective."

Suzanne, huddled against the wall near the doorless entrance to their room, suddenly felt dizzy. They had been drinking from one of Joel's bottles since early that evening. She tried to focus on the wall opposite the entrance.

The room was bare of furnishings except for two mats on the floor. A small closet near the door held their possessions. There was little space to move around in and she knew they were lucky to have the room to themselves. Gabe, two domes down, was sharing his room with three other people. She had asked Joel if they could have Gabe move in with them; he was, after all, Joel's best friend. But Joel had dismissed the idea, saying he had little enough privacy as it was. *No, you have to hide, Joel, that's it, Gabe might find out what you really are.*

"What do they want, anyway?" said Joel. "They took the trouble to put up these domes, I don't know how, moved us in, and we've been sitting around for three days with nothing to do." Joel suddenly laughed. "Whoever thought an alien invasion would be so god-damn boring."

"Well, they obviously don't need slave labor," Gabe said. "They put up these domes with no help and they are technologically advanced. And if they'd wanted the planet for themselves, I suppose they could have executed us. They want us for something, and they probably moved us out here so they could watch us more carefully. People could hide in the city."

"What difference does it make?" Suzanne said loudly, irritated by Gabe's professorial manner. "We'll find out sooner or later; what good does it do talking about it?" She stood up, wobbling a bit on weak-kneed legs. Gabe's walruslike moustache seemed to droop slightly; Joel shrugged his shoulders.

* * *

She found herself outside the room on the metal stairway, leaning forward, clutching the rail. The large room below her was empty and someone had pushed the low tables closer to the walls. She began to move down the stairs, still holding the rail. When she reached the bottom, she sat down abruptly on the floor, clutching her knees. "God," she whispered. The floor shifted under her.

A hand was on her shoulder. Startled, she looked up into Felice's hazel eyes. "Are you all right?"

"I'm fine," said Suzanne. "I don't know. I think I'm going to vomit."

"You need some air, come on." Suzanne stumbled to her feet. Holding on to Felice, she managed to get to the triangular doorway and outside.

A cool breeze bathed her face. "You better now?" asked Felice.

"I think so." She looked at the rows of lighted doorways in front of her. "You're up pretty late, Felice."

"I'm up pretty early. It's almost morning." Suzanne sighed and leaned against the dome. "You feel like taking a walk, honey?"

"Can we?" asked Suzanne. "Will they let us?"

"They haven't stopped me yet. No wonder you look so bad, staying inside for three days. Come on, we can walk to the highway; do you good."

"All right." Her head felt clearer already. She began to walk past the rows of domes with Felice. Occasionally, shadows moved across the triangular doorways they passed, transforming themselves into loose-limbed dancing scarecrows on the path in front of Suzanne.

"What's going to happen to us?" Suzanne muttered, expecting no answer. An apathetic calm had embraced her; her feet seemed to drag her behind them.

"Who knows, Suzanne? We wait, we find out about these Aadae chicks, what their weak points are. That's all we can do. If we tried anything now, we got no chance. But we might later."

They reached the highway and stopped. Felice gestured at the domes across the road. "They live in those things, too," she said to Suzanne. "I found out yesterday. I looked inside one of their doorways. Exactly like ours."

Suzanne looked toward the city. She could barely see the tall rectangles and spires of its skyline. To the left of the city, the early morning sky was beginning to glow. Felice clutched her arm and she noticed the Aadae for the first time. They were sitting on the highway in a semicircle, soundlessly gazing east.

"Suzanne." She swung around and saw Gabe, his face almost white. His dark frizzy hair was a cloud around his head. "Are you all right? I followed you just to be sure; you didn't look too well."

"I'm fine. Where's Joel?"

"He fell asleep. Or passed out. I'm not sure which." Gabe looked apologetic.

She shrugged, then looked uncertainly at Felice. "Oh, Gabe, this is—"

"I know Felice, she was in my evening lit class." Gabe smiled. "She was the best student in it."

Felice was appearing uncharacteristically shy. She grinned and looked down at her feet. "Come on," she said. "You were a good teacher, that's all." Suzanne shuddered at the mention of the past. *She watched Joel as he slept beside her. His slim, muscled chest rose and fell with each breath. I love you anyway, Joel; there's been more good than bad. We just need time, that's all; you'll find yourself.*

Suddenly she hated the Aadae. She closed her fists, hoping for an Aada's neck around which to squeeze them. Tears stung her eyes, blurring the image of the Aadae in the road.

"What are they doing?" Gabe whispered. She ignored him and began to walk along the highway toward the aliens. A soft sigh rose from the semicircle of Aadae and drifted to her. They were swaying now, back and forth from the waist.

The sun's edge appeared on the horizon, lighting up the road. The Aadae leaned forward. Suzanne, hearing footsteps behind her, stepped forward and turned.

Five pairs of blind violet eyes stared through her. Startled, she moved away from the five Aadae and let them pass. The five, dressed in dirty robes, stumbled onto the road, arms stretched in front of them. They wandered to the edge of the semicircle and stood there, holding their arms out toward the sun. Suzanne followed them and stood with them. They didn't seem to realize she was there.

She waved an arm in front of the nearest Aada. The alien showed no reaction. *They're truly blind*, she thought as she gazed into the empty eyes. The five Aadae continued to stare directly into the rising sun. They began to sway on their feet, burned-out retinas unable to focus. She stepped back from them, moving again to the side of the road.

Gabe and Felice were with her, pulling at her arms. "Come on," said Gabe, "we'd better get out of here, come on." She pulled her arms free and continued to watch the Aadae.

Something was drawing her toward the aliens, something that hovered over her, tugging at her mind. She was at peace, wanting only to join the group on the road. She found her head turning to the sun.

A shadow rose in front of her. "Suzanne!" It was Gabe, holding her by the shoulders. Suddenly she was frightened. She stumbled backward, grabbing at Gabe's arms. The sighs of the Aadae were louder now, driving her away.

"Run!" Suzanne screamed. "Run!" Her feet, pounding along the side of the road, were carrying her back to the domes. She ran, soon losing herself among the domes. At last she stopped, exhausted, in front of one. She turned to the triangular doorway.

Two Aadae were there, one with stiff orange hair

like a flame and shiny copper-colored skin. The dark-haired golden-skinned one was coming toward her. She threw up her arms, trying to ward her off.

The alien took her by the arm and tugged gently. Suzanne followed the Aada passively, led like a child along the path between the domes. Then they stopped and she realized that she was in front of her own dome.

She sighed and leaned against the doorway. Her fear had disappeared, and she was feeling a bit foolish. *I must have been really drunk.* The Aada released her, then bowed from the waist in an Oriental farewell before disappearing among the domes.

* * *

The air was heavy and the sky overcast. People were sitting or standing around aimlessly; occasionally small groups of people, scarcely speaking to each other, would pass by. Suzanne sat with her back to her dome, watching Felice mend a shirt. That morning, at breakfast, one of the men had stood up and thrown his bowl, still filled with greenish mush, at the wall. All of them had been growing tired of the food, which was always the same. But until today, they had simply gone to the slots on the wall, pushed the buttons, and passively accepted the green mush and milky blue liquid which were all the slots ever yielded besides glasses of water.

The green mush had stuck to the wall, resembling a fungoid growth. Rivulets ran from it, trickling to the floor. Then a tiny gray-haired woman hurled her bowl. Within seconds, everyone in the large room was throwing bowls and following the bowls with the glasses of blue liquid, shrieking with laughter as the liquid mingled with the mush on the walls. Several people hurried to the food slots and punched buttons wildly, pulled out more food and threw it at the walls. The orgy of food throwing had lasted almost half an hour until the walls were thickly coated and the Aadae had arrived.

The two aliens had ignored the mess. They brought a cart with them filled with oddly shaped metal objects of different sizes. One of the Aadae rummaged among the objects and removed a small cylinder. Then she held it over her head, showing it to everyone in the room. Her companion handed her a silvery block and the Aada attached it to the cylinder, then fastened a blue block to the cylinder's other end.

"Put together," the alien said, pointing with the object to the cart. The two Aadae turned and left the dome.

"What the hell," Suzanne heard Oscar mutter.

"We better do it," said the tiny old woman. "Who knows what they'll do if we don't."

The room was beginning to stink. A few flies buzzed near the mush-covered walls. "I'd better get Joel his breakfast," Suzanne said absently to Felice. She wandered over to the food slots, punched the buttons and removed a bowl and glass. People had already begun work on the objects by the time she was climbing the stairs to her room, where Joel still lay sleeping. *At least it's something to do.*

It had taken only a couple of hours to put the objects together. Once again, they were left with time on their hands, long hours that were chains on their minds, minutes through which they swam, pushed underwater, unable to come up for air. Felice was mending the shirt on her lap slowly and carefully; the sewing of each stitch became an entire project.

"They'll come back," said Suzanne. "And give us more pointless stuff to do."

"You know what I think," said the small woman. "I think they're crazy. They don't need us to put that stuff together." Felice hunched herself over the shirt and continued sewing. "You can't even tell what the things are *for*."

Suzanne began to poke at a loose thread on her jeans. The humid air was making her sweat and her crotch was starting to itch. She had managed to wash her underwear by using several glasses of water from the food slots, but there was nowhere she could bathe except by one of the sinks in the bathroom where the water was always cold and anyone could wander in at any time. Suzanne was afraid to go to the bathroom alone anyway. A woman in one of the nearby domes had been raped in a bathroom; although her husband had beaten the man who had done it, the fear of rape had spread among many women. Now Suzanne went to the bathroom only with Joel or Felice or some of the other women in the dome. A couple of times Gabe would accompany her, looking modestly away from her at the wall while she squatted on the floor over the hole which would suck her wastes away down a large tube. There were no partitions between the holes; squatting over them had become ritualized, with everyone courteously avoiding a look at the others present in the bathroom. Occasionally there was moisture around the holes; someone had taken a piss and missed. One fastidious young couple tried to keep the bathroom clean, mopping the floor and walls with an old undershirt, but they were not always successful.

Suzanne was growing uneasy. She was used to seeing an occasional pair of Aadae stroll along the pathway in front of her, but the aliens seemed to have disappeared. Suddenly her muscles tightened involuntarily. Something was in the air, hovering over her.

She heard a scream, a high-pitched, ululating sound, and then a roar, a bellowing from hundreds of throats.

"Felice!" she cried, grabbing at the woman next to her. Felice dropped her shirt and they both stood up.

We should go inside. Suzanne looked down the pathway and saw a large group of men moving toward the highway. She began to run toward them with Felice close behind her. Again she heard the scream, which had taken on the cadences of a mournful song. It was closer to her now. A small group of people had gathered in front of a dome up ahead. She ran to them and pushed her way through the crowd. Then she shrank back, moaning softly, slapping a hand over her mouth.

An Aada hung in the doorway by her feet. Someone had tied a rope around her ankles. The alien had been stabbed several times; brown clots covered her body. Her long orange hair brushed the ground as she turned in the doorway, her violet eyes stared sightlessly at the crowd. They were all that was left of her face, smashed by fists. Bone fragments protruded from her jaw; her copper-colored skin was covered by greenish bruises. On the ground beneath her lay another Aada, dying from wounds which covered her body. The alien on the ground drew her black hair over her chest, lifted her head slightly, and opened her mouth, and Suzanne again heard the song-like scream. Then she turned from them and was silent.

The people around Suzanne said nothing. She heard only their breathing, the sound of a giant bellows near a flame. She turned away from the alien bodies and stumbled back to Felice.

"We have to get out of here, Suzanne," she heard Felice whisper. Another roar reached her ears. She could see the crowd of men crossing the highway. Some of them had their arms raised. Knives glittered in their fists. An elongated shadow fell across the mob on the highway and she became conscious of a faint humming sound. An alien air vehicle was in the sky, a slender silver torpedo waiting to strike.

A bright light flashed across the highway soundlessly. She threw an arm across her eyes and staggered backward. The people in front of the dome were running past her. An arm swung out and hit her, knocking her onto the path. She climbed to her feet, looking aimlessly around. The air vehicle was moving away to the north.

"Felice!" she cried out. Her voice shook. Then she saw that there were no longer any men on the highway, only burned, blackened bodies strewn about on the asphalt. The smell of charred flesh was carried to her nostrils and she bent over, vomiting quietly, arms wrapped around her shaking body.

"The fools." It was Felice's voice, harsh and bitter. "Too soon." A hand was on her shoulder, pulling at her gently. She looked over at Felice, then back at the highway.

A group of Aadae were there, looking down at the bodies. *Happy, aren't you? It wasn't even a contest.* There was no way now to tell who lay in the road, if anyone she knew was there. She would have to wait, find out who was missing, and that would take days. Any mourning would be general and unfocused. The Aadae began to circle around the bodies.

Then she heard the sobbing, deep and uncontrolled weeping. Three Aadae threw themselves down on the pavement, beating against it with their fists. The aliens were crying, not for the two Aadae who had been murdered, but for the men on the highway.

Felice was pulling her back along the pathway toward their own dome. As they retreated, Suzanne caught one last glimpse of the Aadae as they flung their arms open to the sun and heard once again their musical scream.

* * *

She heard Joel as he crept toward his mat in the darkness. She turned over and reached for him, brushing against his leg. He jumped back. "Jesus! Don't scare me like that."

"Joel, where have you been?"

"Where I was the night before."

"Where?"

"None of your goddamn business, Suzanne." He pulled off his clothes and sprawled on the mat next to hers.

"I just want to know, Joel."

"I can tell you're back to normal; you're going to revive the Inquisition. I'm tired. I'm going to sleep."

"You haven't gotten up one morning this week, Joel, ever since they started giving us that stuff to put together."

"I should care. You don't even know what the fuckers are *for*, you just sit there putting them together, you think it's really important, don't you, just like that dumb job at the warehouse you used to have."

"It's not that, Joel. They're going to find out you're not doing your share, and God knows what they'll do then."

"I could give a shit." She could hear him turn over on his mat and knew the conversation was finished. Suzanne had heard rumors about a group of men and a few women who would meet late at night to discuss what to do about the Aadae. She knew nothing more and was afraid to know even that much. She remembered the burned bodies on the highway and decided it was best simply to go about her business and wait.

She was pretty sure that Oscar Harrison was in the group and that Felice knew about it, although she doubted that the protective Oscar would allow his wife to go to the meetings. It wouldn't be hard for her to get involved if she wanted, but she preferred to wait and see if anything happened. She could act then.

"It's a perfectly good job, Joel; why are you always putting it down?" She put down her beer and glared at him across the kitchen table.

"It's a dead end and you know it. That's all life is for you, getting by. You could do more and you know it, but it's easier this way—you don't have to think or try. It's even easier to put up with me; it's better than being alone. At least I know what I am; you don't even look at yourself."

I was practical, at least. Not that it mattered now. There had been no more money for her training in music, so she had left school and taken the job in the warehouse office, telling herself it was only temporary, she could still have her voice lessons, go to the local opera company's rehearsals at night. But she stopped going to the rehearsals—she was usually too tired—and then she had stopped going to the voice lessons. *I wouldn't have been much good anyway.* Occasionally she sang for her friends at parties, smiling when they told her she should become a professional; *it's just a hobby.* Then Gabe had rushed over one day to tell her that the opera was holding auditions, they needed a new soprano, she would be perfect, the pay wasn't much, but she could at least quit that office job. And she promised to go to the audition, but by then she was out of training, her voice roughened by cigarettes, so she didn't go after all. There was no point to it. She had just gotten a raise; no sense in throwing it away.

It doesn't matter. The Aadae were here and had no use for singers, nor for office workers. Her past was a meaningless memory, her possible future in that other world only a shadow of the wishes that had once crossed her mind. Better that she had had no great ambitions when the Aadae came; she would not have been able to stand it. Her dreams had already died.

It's just as well.

* * *

The orange-haired alien was named Neir-let. Felice had mentioned that to her a couple of days before. Neir-let and her dark-haired companion were the Aadae who had instructed them in how to put together the metal objects which were now beginning to clutter the large downstairs room of the dome. Neir-let wore a blue gem on her forehead, a stone seemingly embedded in her skin, as did all the other Aadae. Suzanne hadn't even noticed this until Oscar had pointed it out; most of the aliens' foreheads were covered by their untidy hair. The gem was tiny, smaller than a Hindu's caste mark; it glittered, and Suzanne shivered involuntarily.

Neir-let had become more fluent in English, although no one could be sure about how she had learned it. Her companion never said anything. Neir-let had just demonstrated how to attach a silver globe to the apparatus they had been building, then she gave them a cartful of silver globes, several of which went rolling out of the cart over the floor, stopping their travels under the food slots. The metal objects on the floor were entwined in metallic tubing; the blocks and cylinders they had started out with were already hidden. The silver globes were to be attached to some of the loose ends of tubing.

Suzanne, sitting with Felice and a red-headed woman named Asenath Berry at one of the tables, reached for her bowl of mush. She was losing weight. Suzanne had already been thin before the Aadae came. On the diet of mush, she estimated, from the looseness of her clothing, that she had lost another ten pounds. *A scarecrow*. Her brown hair, always unruly, stood out around her head like a nimbus; there was no way to straighten it here.

No one made any move toward the objects they were supposed to be putting together. They had all learned that Neir-let was fairly easy-going and didn't seem to care what they did as long as the work was completed by the evening. Neir-let was sitting on the floor near the doorway, picking what looked like small insects out of her hair. Her companion leaned against the wall, scratching her crotch.

Suddenly Oscar stood up and walked over to Neir-let. Suzanne glanced at Felice. The chatter in the large room died down. No one had dared to approach an alien directly up to now. Asenath Berry poked Suzanne in the ribs. "What the hell is he up to?" the redhead asked. Suzanne shrugged. Asenath had lost little weight on the mush diet; her round, braless breasts were an edifice under her sleeveless blue top and Suzanne wondered if Asenath had used silicone. Her long tanned legs were set off by her white shorts. How she kept them shaved was a mystery. Felice had said that Asenath was a prostitute, that she had come out of the city with a closetful of clothes and cosmetics carried by three of her most faithful customers. Asenath shared her room with a lean black man named Warren, who, like Joel, usually slept late. "A mack," Felice had told her, sneering at the word. *What do I care*. Suzanne had met Asenath one night in the hallway. The redhead had taken one look at her frail figure and pulled out two cans of beef stew hidden in her purse. "You need them more than me, honey." She had hurried back to her room to share them with Joel, who opened them with his knife, and they had eaten them slowly, relishing each bite. Since then, she found it difficult not to be friendly to Asenath, although at the same time she was a bit frightened of her.

"I just want to ask a question," Oscar said to Neir-let. The room was silent. Neir-let looked up at Oscar and smiled. "I just want to know what that blue thing in your head is."

The alien was still smiling. "Through it I am with those above," she replied, and shrugged as if that were self-explanatory.

"The others of your kind?" Oscar said slowly.

"No, except . . ." Neir-let paused. "I have no words." She smiled at Oscar and raised her hands, palms up. Oscar nodded and returned to Felice's side, looking thoughtful.

A few people got up and began to attach the globes to some of the metal objects strewn across the floor. "I think they still have spaceships overhead," Oscar said to Felice, "and she means they can contact them with those blue stones. That's all it could mean. At any sign of trouble, they could wipe us all out." He clenched his fists. Asenath was smiling at a burly man seated at the next table. Suzanne ate her mush, licking it off her fingers, forcing herself. Asenath stood up, motioned to the burly man, and left the room with him. The Aadae were paying no attention.

Somebody should do something. She finished the mush and looked around. Everyone was devoting full attention either to the breakfast mush or to the metal objects. Neir-let and her friend had moved outside and were staring up at the sky. Suzanne's arms seemed to freeze on the table near her empty bowl. She was unable to move, eyes fixed on her fingertips. Thoughts were chasing each other through her mind; she could grasp none of them. A heavy weight was pushing her against the table, preventing her from standing up and going to work on the metal devices.

Someone nudged her. "That ho's lookin' for you," Felice drawled contemptuously. She forced herself to look up and saw Asenath on the metal stairway, motioning to her. The burly man had disappeared. "Don't go," Felice went on. "You don't want to be with the likes of her." Then Oscar put a restraining hand on his wife's shoulder.

"Don't tell Suzanne what to do," he said quietly. "You go ahead," he said to Suzanne. She hesitated for a moment, then got up and walked to the stairway.

"Come on up," she called to Suzanne. She climbed the stairs.

"What is it?"

"I got two packs of cigarettes off my friend," Asenath whispered. She winked at Suzanne and her black eyelashes seemed to crawl over her eye like an insect. "Want a couple?"

"That was fast work," Suzanne said, trying to smile. Asenath's cold blue eyes showed no reaction.

"You better come to my room, or else everybody's going to want one." The redhead turned and Suzanne followed her past the first level of rooms and up the next flight of stairs. Asenath finally stopped in front of a doorway. "Come on in." Suzanne entered the room. Warren was sprawled across his mat, clothed in a pink shirt and velvety purple slacks. He held a small hand mirror and was fiddling with his moustache. "Have a seat," said Asenath, motioning to her mat. Suzanne sat, feeling uneasy.

Asenath didn't sit down. She peered out into the hallway, then strode over to Suzanne. "There aren't any cigarettes, kid, just some questions."

Suzanne opened her mouth. Her vocal chords locked and nothing emerged except a sharp gasp. She swallowed and pulled her legs closer to her chest.

"What's that man of yours been up to?" Asenath asked.

"I don't know," she managed to say. "I don't know what you mean." Her voice sounded weak, ineffectual.

"Stop being stupid. He's been out every night this week, we know that, and we know where he is for some of the time. Now you tell us where he goes."

"I don't know."

"You're saying that a little too often; I don't want to hear it again. We've tried following him. We know he doesn't come back here right away. You must know something, he must have hinted at what he does."

Suzanne looked away from Asenath to Warren, who had put down his hand mirror and was staring blankly at the wall. "I don't know where he goes," she said, pronouncing the words carefully. "I don't know anything about his activities. Joel tells me nothing. He rarely told me anything, even before we all came here. Our relationship is not exactly what you would call open." She felt defeated and exposed before the red-headed woman and her dark silent partner.

"Christ," Asenath muttered.

"Let her go," said Warren. Suzanne stood up and began to move toward the door. A hand seized her shoulder and she found herself facing Asenath's blue eyes again.

"If you do find out anything," the prostitute whispered, "if he does decide to confide in you, you better let me know, I'm telling you, and right away. And you just keep quiet about this little talk."

She retreated from the room angry and frightened,

afraid to stop now in her own room to wake up Joel. *I have to warn him. I have to find out. I have to talk to somebody.* She paused at the top of the stairway, apprehensive about joining the people in the large room below. But they were ignoring her, busy working on their alien devices.

She continued down the steps, avoiding a glance at Felice and Oscar. She sat down in a corner and began fitting metal pieces together under the casual, almost reassuring gaze of Neir-let.

* * *

"I have to talk to you, Gabe."

"Sure."

"Not here." Suzanne eyed the people sitting in front of Gabe's dome nervously and felt that they were all watching her. She forced herself to look at them directly and realized that they were paying her little attention. "I mean, I feel like walking around."

"Okay." Gabe hoisted himself off the ground and brushed off his dirty rumpled trousers. Oddly enough, he seemed to be maintaining his girth on the Aadaen diet. He took her arm gently. "Back to your room?"

"Joel's there. I mean, I think he's still asleep." She recognized a face in front of one of the domes and waved at it while nodding her head. "Let's walk on the highway."

The weather was warm but not humid. White clouds danced across the blue sky under the benevolent gaze of the sun. A group of adolescent boys had somehow gotten hold of a baseball and bat and were playing a game on the highway. Farther down the road, Suzanne could see a group of children with some Aadae. They too were playing a game, chasing what looked like cylinders on wheels across the safety islands. Suzanne and Gabe walked toward the city, past the baseball players.

"I have to talk about Joel," she said. "I'm worried."

"What's the problem this time?"

"It isn't just a personal thing, Gabe. I'm scared. Joel's been out nights, I don't know where he goes. Maybe it's none of my business, I guess I should be used to it by now. But the thing is . . ." She lowered her voice. "A couple of other people want to know where he goes, too, Gabe; they were asking me about it this morning. They weren't being gentle. I think they would have beaten it out of me if they thought I knew."

Gabe scratched at his beard. In the absence of razor blades he, like most of the men, was looking shaggier than usual. "You don't know where he goes?"

"For God's sake, Gabe. No, I don't. I thought you might. I thought you could tell me what's going on."

"I think you should tell me who wanted to know about Joel, Suzanne."

"Asenath Berry. You've seen her, the good-looking redhead, the whore. She and her friend Warren wanted to know. I was dumb enough to think Asenath wanted to be my friend."

Gabe sighed and was silent for a few seconds. She could hear the shouts of the baseball-playing boys in back of them. "I'll talk to her," Gabe said at last. "She won't bother you again."

"Then you do know something." She stopped walking and faced him. "Tell me. What is it?"

"I shouldn't tell you. I tried not to; I thought it was best that you stay out of it. But I guess you have a right to know. A group of us have been making some plans; that's all I can say. Joel's part of the group. So is Asenath. Some of us have been a little suspicious of Joel lately. It seems he doesn't go directly home from our little get-togethers.

Asenath must have taken it upon herself to find out why."

She turned away from Gabe, bewildered. "Now I've just upset you," he muttered. "It's probably nothing. We're all a little paranoid; we have to be. We'll probably find out he's just visiting a friend or something. Don't worry, he's not that involved with us anyway; we've been holding meetings without him once in a while. I don't think he wants to get tangled up in anything too dangerous. You know Joel."

Gabe was leaving something out. Suddenly she didn't want to hear any more, didn't want to know what Gabe or Joel or anyone else might be planning. "He's seeing someone else," she said. "He's seeing another girl. It's happened before." *That must be it.* The thought left her empty, almost relieved.

"Why do you stay with him, Suzanne?"

"I don't know. What difference does it make now?" She turned to the city. "Let's just keep walking, Gabe, let's go back to the city; they'll never find us there, we'll get Joel and go back and we can sit around drinking at Mojo's like we used to."

"You know we can't."

"Why not?"

"They'll find us. We should go back, Suzanne. Come on, I'll walk you to your dome."

"I'd rather not go back there right now," she said wearily. She went to the side of the road and sat down on some grass. "You can leave if you want, Gabe, I think I'd rather be alone right now anyway."

"You're sure, Suzanne? You'll be okay?"

"I'll be fine."

"You won't do anything silly?"

"No."

"Well, if you want to talk to me later or anything, feel free." She watched him shuffle back down the highway, shoulders slumped forward.

She pulled at the grass near her foot. Things were slipping away from her again as they always had. Her relationship with Joel had always seemed fortuitous. He had drifted into her life at a party she almost didn't attend; he could very well drift out again and there was nothing she could do about it. At worst he would get involved in some foolhardy scheme with Gabe and the others, resulting in disaster; she was convinced that the Aadae could not be defeated. At best, he would stay with her and they would continue living in the dome as they had with no purpose other than constructing alien objects for the Aadae. The thought made her shudder. It was useless to look ahead; the best thing to do was to get through each day, forfeiting any hopes. She had practice at that already.

A cloud danced in front of the sun, shadowing the road in front of her. She shivered in the cooler air.

* * *

Joel had disappeared again. In the morning, his mat was empty. Suzanne, awake at dawn, was outside the dome, shivering slightly in the wet air.

A heavy fog hung over the domed settlement, its gray masses almost indistinguishable from the metal domes. Its tendrils wound along the pathway and wrapped themselves around her feet. Suzanne stepped away from the doorway into the fog and was soon lost in its billowing masses, unable to see more than dim shapes. She was hidden and protected.

She was not looking for Joel. She didn't really want to know where he was and didn't want to risk confronting him in the presence of someone else. She tried to think about him objectively in the gray silence. It was foolish to think she could be everything to him, that she could fulfill all his needs, particularly in the present situation. He had always come back before. She demanded little sexually, content to satisfy Joel's needs with few of her own. She thought of Paul, whom she had loved while still in school. After two months, she had finally allowed Paul to share her cot in the dormitory room, twisting against him frantically during the night. She had satisfied him, but not herself. She avoided Paul after that. There was another, a boy whose name she couldn't remember, at a party, and with him there were only spasms and a drained, nauseous feeling afterward. With Joel she acted, going through the motions but always distant, her mind drifting off as he entered her. At times she would feel a twinge or an occasional spasm. She knew she loved him, or at least had loved him once; yet if he had remained with her, never touching her except for a kiss or a few hugs, she would have been content. *I can't expect him to be satisfied with that; no one would be. Why shouldn't he see someone else? It's surprising he stays with me at all.* Her heart twisted at the thought. Her mind throbbed, recoiling from the image of Joel with a vague female shape, and tears stung her eyes. She hated her body, a piece of perambulating dead meat, an anesthetized machine. *No, not anesthetized.* She could, after all, feel pain.

She was lost in the fog. She no longer knew where her own dome was. She kept walking, thinking that if she could find the highway, she could reorient herself.

"Hey." She turned. "Hey." Two young black men stood in the doorway of a dome, watching her. They were smiling, and one of them gestured to her. She fled into the fog, turning down another path and almost running until she was sure the two men were far behind. Then she suddenly felt shame. *They probably just wanted to ask me something.* She shook off the thought. *I have to be careful.* But she wondered if she would have hurried away if the men had been white. Her cheeks burned.

She was more lost than before. She stopped in front of a dome and tried to figure out where she was. She should have come to the highway by now.

She peered inside the dome tentatively, then stepped back. It was guarded by two Aadae. Inside, she could see aliens sleeping on the floor in the large central room. She had not seen the inside of one of their dwellings before, afraid of approaching one. The guards looked at her inquisitively. She backed away farther, trying to smile harmlessly, then continued on the path.

She collided with someone. She opened her mouth to apologize, then threw her hands in front of her face and managed to suppress a scream. A bald, wizened figure stood there, clad only in a dirty robe. It was no more than five feet tall and its greenish-yellow skin was stretched tightly over bones. It stared at her blankly and she recognized the violet eyes of the Aadae. Its robe hung open, revealing a penis no thicker than a finger. The blue stone on its forehead seemed to wink at her.

One of the males. She felt nauseated. The figure tried to reach for her, his lips drawing back across his teeth in an imitation of a smile. She moved back, trying to ward him off with her arms.

Then another Aada was beside him, holding his arm. She recognized Neir-let. The Aada was whispering to the male in her own language. The male, still grinning, sat down.

"He frightens you?" Neir-let asked. Suzanne sighed with relief. "He is harmless."

"I didn't know . . . I haven't seen a male Aada before."

Neir-let looked puzzled for a second, then nodded. "Male. We have few, enough for children. We always have few. This one is old and no longer wise." The male was drooling and picking at his toenails. "Soon his mind will join the others above. In his travels, he may see our home again." Neir-let sat down with the male, her arm across his shoulders.

"Do you miss your home?" Suzanne said impulsively. She was suddenly curious about the Aadae, who as far as she knew rarely talked to anyone. Neir-let seemed to sigh.

"To you, Suzanne, I will talk," said the alien. She was shocked, not realizing that Neir-let knew her name. "You have a gift, I know. You have brushed those above once in the dawn. Do you remember? You fled from us."

Suzanne struggled with her memories, then recalled the morning she had seen the Aadae seated on the highway, staring into the sun. She nodded silently.

"Yes, I miss my home. I will not see it again as I am. But I could not stay there knowing that other minds would die. Your world is much like ours, but the small differences bring me sadness. Yet I could live here with my daughters and be pleased." Neir-let paused. Suzanne sat down near her, for once unafraid. "But we must leave here and the home of my daughters must be the ship."

Leave here. If we wait long enough . . . "Why are you here?" she asked.

"So that you will not die."

"You've killed so many of us, though. Why?"

Tears glistened in the alien's eyes. "If we had not, others would have joined them. Then all of you would die. It is a painful thing, Suzanne." Neir-let patted the male alien on the head and trilled to him. He nestled against her. Suzanne was at peace, strangely, not wanting to leave Neir-let's side. The fog had lifted slightly. *I should get back to the dome*, she thought, unwilling to move.

From the corner of her eye, she saw a shape leave the doorway of the dome where the Aadae slept. She turned to face it. *Joel.* The shape disappeared in the fog and she could not be sure.

Neir-let was still singing to the male Aada. Suzanne rose and began to thread her way through the maze of paths. She could see more clearly now and soon managed to find her own dome.

She hurried inside and up the stairway. In her room, Joel lay on his mat, seemingly asleep. Yet his breathing was shallow and his hair and face were dotted with small beads of moisture. She wanted to speak to him, to question him. She clamped her lips shut and curled up on her own mat, nursing her pain and her fear.

* * *

She had to talk to Gabe. She had to tell him what Neir-let had said.

She went looking for him as soon as she was through with her work for the day. The bright sunlight had burned away the fog of that morning and by noon the weather was hot and humid. A group of people, among them Oscar Harrison and Asenath Berry, had gathered in front of the dome when she left, speaking to each other in low, angry tones. One man reached out and grabbed her as she passed and she tried to pull away.

"Let her go," said Oscar. The man released her. Suzanne retreated, then looked back. Everyone in the area seemed to be leaving the vicinity as if expecting trouble. Joel was still asleep upstairs and for a moment she wondered if she should go back and wake him up.

Better to let him sleep; he'll miss the trouble. She went on to Gabe's dome.

Gabe was not in his room. One of his roommates, a frail-looking Chinese man named Soong, looked up as she entered.

"Do you know where Gabe is?" she asked him. "I have to talk to him." She felt impatient, on edge. "It's pretty important."

Mr. Soong smiled. "He is being entertained by a young lady, I believe, a few domes down. He has been away all night. You can find him there, but I do not know if he wishes to be disturbed."

The old windbag. "Which dome?"

"I am not sure. If you wish to wait here, you are welcome. Please be seated." The man nodded toward one of the mats which crowded the floor. "Gabe was indeed overwhelmed by good fortune. He was surprised when the young lady appeared last night and invited him to share her company. Usually he is back by morning, but she was a very attractive woman."

And he's always complaining about his lousy luck. "Thank you," said Suzanne, trying to be as dignified as Mr. Soong. "I'll come back later. Please tell him Suzanne's looking for him; he'll know who I am."

She went back out the door and down the stairway. She paused in the downstairs room, wondering if she should talk to Felice. Then she remembered the angry crowd in front of her dome. *I can't go back there.*

For the first time, it occurred to her that Neir-let might have spoken to her in confidence. Perhaps she didn't want Suzanne speaking to anyone else about their talk; maybe she would be angry if she found out she had. She shrugged off the idea. It couldn't hurt to tell someone and it might prevent them from acting rashly. She remembered the burned bodies on the highway. They could afford to wait, knowing that the Aadae planned to leave.

"Suzanne." Gabe was standing in the doorway. She hurried toward him. He was smiling contentedly. "I finally had some luck, this girl I hardly know . . ."

"Mr. Soong told me." She tried to smile back.

"Don't look so irritated. I'll start flattering myself by thinking you're jealous."

"Gabe, I have to talk to you. I was talking to one of the Aadae last night and she told me they were going to leave eventually, I don't know when, but that's what she said."

"Where did you see her?"

"I just happened to run into her, I was wandering around. Gabe, if we can just wait . . ."

"Suzanne, they won't leave until they've accomplished their purpose, whatever that is. It could be pretty hideous, you know."

"Neir-let said they want to keep us from dying."

Gabe wiped his forehead with the back of his hand. "No doubt she was speaking figuratively."

Someone outside was shouting. Suzanne shook her head and began to move toward the doorway. "What's going on," she said listlessly. Something seemed to be keeping her from looking outside.

Gabe was pulling at her hand. "Don't talk to Neir-let any more," he muttered. "In fact, I wouldn't advise talking to any of the Aadae unless you can't help it. Some people don't like it; you could get into trouble."

She was suddenly annoyed by Gabe. She withdrew her hand and went outside. A small group of people were standing in front of her dome. She wandered toward them. Something was in the doorway of the dome. She moved closer.

She saw Joel. A shock seemed to strike her body, paralyzing her. Blood rushed to her head and face. Her skin crawled over her stiff muscles, a cold piece of iron was resting in her belly.

Joel was hanging by his neck in the doorway. He had been stabbed several times. Someone had ripped off his shirt, revealing long scratches on his chest. His feet dangled loosely from his legs. Above him, someone had posted a sign: COLLABORATOR. His eyes were closed, the long lashes shadowing his cheekbones.

She began to push people aside as she walked to the doorway. She stumbled near a knife carelessly abandoned under the slowly rotating body. She picked up the bloodstained weapon and began to hack at the rope that held Joel by the neck.

"Suzanne." Gabe was near her. His voice seemed to reach her ears from a distance. "Come away from here." She continued to cut the rope until the body fell at her feet, a flesh-covered sack of bones. One hand draped itself across her left ankle, then slipped away.

She stepped over the body into the large central room. No one was there. Unfinished metal devices were strewn across the floor. She heard footsteps clatter near her and turned around.

Asenath Berry crouched on the stairway. Her blue eyes were hidden behind dark glasses. The redhead had a large knapsack on her back. Suzanne moved toward her, still holding the knife.

"Wait!" shouted Asenath, holding up her arms. "He told us everything before he died—he admitted it—we made sure of that. He told them everything he knew about our group, about our plans. They promised him a reward." Asenath continued to creep down the stairs. "He was a traitor, do you understand? He was looking out for himself."

The redhead was only a few feet away from her. Suzanne lunged toward Asenath, knocking her on her side. She lifted the knife. Asenath's foot hit her hand, knocking the knife across the room. The redhead tried to climb to her feet. Suzanne grabbed the curly red hair and began to pull at it silently.

Hands clawed at Suzanne's legs. "Stop it!" Asenath was screaming. Holding the prostitute's head with one hand, she started to punch her in the breasts.

"For God's sake!" Gabe's big arms were around her, pulling her away from Asenath. She sagged against him, suddenly exhausted, staring at the clump of red hair in her left hand. Asenath got up and scrambled out the door.

Gabe was shaking her by the shoulders. She managed to get free and saw the knife against the wall near the stairway. She picked it up and tucked it under her belt. Then she walked outside.

The small crowd was still there. Ignoring them, she grabbed Joel's feet and began to drag him along the pathway behind her. The people moved away from her, receding until she could see no faces, only blurs. She dragged Joel past the gray domes until she reached the side of the highway. She collapsed next to him, one arm across his chest.

I should have been with you. She drew his head near her chest. *I should have helped you. I didn't even talk to you. I didn't even try to find out what was wrong.*

She waited, watching the body, thinking that he would start to breathe again, that he would speak and hold out his arms to her. *You once told me you were a survivor, you would live forever.* He would hold on to her and she would take him back to the dome and help him recover.

She waited. A few people hurried past her and on down the highway, toward the city. They were leaving, ready to make plans and take their chances away from the domed settlement.

She waited. Joel did not move, did not speak. She began to dig his grave in the dirt, scratching at the soil with her knife and hands. She continued to dig until her hands were bleeding and her shoulders were stiff and sore.

She looked up. The sun had drifted to the west. Joel was covered by evening shadows. Overhead, the silvery aircraft of the Aadae hummed past, heading for the city. She stood up, staggering a little, and watched them.

The towers of the city gleamed. Several aircraft were hovering over them, insects over a crown. The sudden flash of light almost blinded her. She stumbled backward, closing her eyes.

When she opened them, she saw only blackened ruins where the city had been. Then the charred hulks collapsed before her eyes and she saw only a burned-out pit. Nearby, she could hear the strange mourning cry of the Aadae.

She dropped to her knees and began once more to dig.

* * *

Suzanne lay in her room. Now and then, she heard footsteps pass the door. Bits of conversation would drift from the main room up the stairs to her. She lay on her mat, her arms and legs held down by invisible bonds. Occasionally she slept.

Time became waves washing over her gently. She

floated, occasionally focusing her eyes on the ceiling. A dark shape with flaming hair leaned over her and she saw it was Neir-let. "We must finish our task," the alien whispered. "Please help." She closed her eyes and when she opened them again, the Aada had disappeared.

Joel was near. She could tell that he was trying to be silent so he wouldn't disturb her. He was rummaging in the kitchen, trying to cook the blueberry waffles he had surprised her with one Sunday morning. She turned on her side and saw Gabe sitting against the wall.

"I didn't know what they were going to do," he said. "It was a trick, that girl taking me to her room; they knew I was his friend; they didn't want me around." She opened her mouth, trying to speak. Her lips were cracked and dry. *Don't worry*, she wanted to say, *you can stay for breakfast; Joel doesn't mind*. She closed her eyes and felt a wet cloth on her face.

When she woke up again, she was lying under a long coat. Someone had removed her clothes. "I washed you off," said Gabe. He was holding a glass of blue liquid. He lifted her head and helped her sip some of it.

"How long have I been here?" she managed to ask.

"Days. I thought you were going to die." He put her head back on the mat.

"No, I won't die." She looked at her arm on top of the coat. Her hands had become bony claws, the blue veins which covered her arm were a web. "I won't die," she said again, in despair.

"I'll stay with you if you want me," said Gabe. "I moved into the room next door, but if you want me here, I'll stay. Just tell me."

She shook her head, rolling it from side to side on the mat. "No."

"Think it over, at least." He patted her hand. She withdrew it from him slowly and placed it under the coat.

"No." She was floating now. The room grew darker and the walls seemed to shimmer. Again she felt a wet cloth on her face.

When she woke up once more, Gabe was gone.

* * *

Suzanne wandered through the large downstairs room and took a seat next to the wall. She gazed at the people sitting around the tables. The tiny gray-haired woman was absent. Warren, Asenath, Oscar, and Felice were gone, as were others she had known only by sight: a big red-haired fellow, a bony middle-aged blonde, an acne-scarred Puerto Rican. She remembered the burned city, and then Joel.

She picked up one of the metal devices near her. Three cylinders, woven together with metallic tubing, were joined to three globes. The cylinders rested on golden rectangular bases. The whole apparatus was about three feet in height. She wondered absently if they would ever be finished. She put the device down and waited for the Aadae to arrive with more components.

She resumed watching the people at the tables. It was possible that some of them, even now, were planning a way to resist or defeat the aliens, but she doubted it. The city was still too vivid an example in their minds, most likely. Most of the resisters, the determined and forceful ones, had probably died there. *This crowd's like me*, she thought bitterly. *We'll get by.* She noticed that some of the people appeared uneasy and realized that she was glaring at them. She looked away.

Gabe's heavy denimed legs were in front of her. She

waved him away, but he sat down in front of her anyway.

"You had any breakfast, Suzanne?"

"No."

"You should eat. If you want, I'll get you some."

"I ate last night; I don't want anything now." She didn't tell him she had vomited the meal in the bathroom, kneeling on the floor and holding her hair off her face with one hand. "Thanks anyway, Gabe," she said tonelessly. He seemed to expand visibly at that, as if taking her words as encouragement. He hovered over her like a beast of prey, his brown beard making her think of a grizzly bear. She hated him at that moment. *Always sniffing around; you wanted Joel to die, you son of a bitch.* She was quickly ashamed of herself. *He's just trying to help.* She grew conscious of the hairy legs concealed by her dungarees, and her halitosis; one of her teeth, with no dental care, was slowly, painfully, and aromatically rotting away. She almost chuckled at the thought of Gabe, or anyone else, desiring her sexually. She folded her arms across her breasts, *knobby little things*, and again thought of Joel and all the ways in which she had failed him. Yet part of her still knew that regret was her justification, enjoyable for those who were seasoned to it, a way of believing that things could have been different. *Give me a thousand chances, and I would be the same.* That thought too had its comforting aspects. Her mind curled up inside her and continued its self-flagellation with the willows of guilt, leaving its peculiarly painful and pleasurable scars.

Gabe jostled her elbow. Neir-let and her companion were at the doorway, but this time they brought no components, only two small leatherlike pouches. Neir-let surveyed the room, apparently waiting for everyone's full attention; then she began to speak in her musical voice.

"We have almost finished assembly of these tools," she said. Suzanne straightened her back at the words. "Only one thing remains." The alien leaned over and picked up one of the metal objects. "Each of you should select one now, and keep it with you at all times." Suzanne reached over for the one she had handled before and watched as everyone scrambled about. No one appeared angry or relieved; they clutched the objects passively and silently, then retreated to the walls, seating themselves on the floor.

Neir-let opened her pouch and took out a small blue gem. It winked in the light and was seemingly answered by the blue stone embedded in Neir-let's forehead. "You will place this in the small dent you will find in one of the globes. It will adhere to the surface by itself." Neir-let and the other Aada began to move around the room, handing a blue stone to each person. Suzanne accepted hers from Neir-let and soon found the dented globe. She pressed the stone into the dent and waited.

The task was completed by everyone in a few minutes. Neir-let walked back to the doorway and held up her arms. "What I tell you now will be the hardest thing to do," she said. "You must sit with these tools and wait, concentrating on them as much as you are able. You may go outside if you wish, or sit by the road. If you grow weary, rest, then try again."

The two Aadae left the dome. Suzanne got up and began to follow them with her device. Gabe caught her by the arm.

"Where are you going?"

"Outside to concentrate," she replied. "What else can I do?"

"Don't. I wouldn't be surprised if they were trying

to turn us into a group of zombies. Forget it. Let them try to force us; there's no way you can compel a person to concentrate."

She pulled away from him and went outside. She didn't care about the device. She wanted to get away from Gabe and the dome, sit alone with her thoughts. She walked toward the highway and seated herself next to the mound under which Joel lay. She would keep her vigil with him.

She put the metal object down at her side and found herself distracted by the blue gem. It seemed to tug at her mind, drawing her attention to itself. She continued to stare at the stone, secure in its blue gaze. Her mind was steady, hovering over her body, able to look at the grave near her with no sadness. She was at peace.

Somehow she managed to withdraw from the object. She rose unsteadily to her feet. It was almost noon. Her feet were asleep, her back stiff. She stomped around, trying to restore her circulation.

"Suzanne." Neir-let was standing by the mound. "You have seen?"

"What is this thing? What does it do, Neir-let?" It was the first time she had addressed the Aada by name and her tongue slid uncertainly over the words.

"It is a tool to build strength. It will aid you, but in a short time you will not need it, I think."

Suzanne turned from the alien, and noticed that a group of boys were playing baseball on the highway, while others sat on the side of the road in conversation. She saw only one woman, outside a dome, concentrating on her device. "No one else seems to be bothering."

"It does not matter," Neir-let said. "One, or a few, will lead and they must follow. You will see. A few are more receptive."

Suzanne sat down again, with her back to the device. "You will see," Neir-let's voice whispered.

* * *

Suzanne continued to concentrate, sometimes in the evenings, sometimes in the early mornings before the others were awake. Her days consisted of long periods in front of the device, punctuated only by the need to return to the dome for sleep and, less often, food.

Gabe came to her once, as she sat by the highway. He carried her and her device back to the dome and insisted upon forcing food down her throat. He hid the device in his room, saying he would give it back when she looked healthier. Suzanne shrugged at this, by now indifferent to her bony limbs and slightly swollen belly. She wondered vaguely if she was pregnant; her period had not yet arrived. She spent several days lying on her mat, passively bearing Gabe's ministrations and wondering what Joel's child would be like. But after a week, her womb bled once more and she knew that there was now nothing left of Joel except the decaying body under a mound.

She regained her strength and managed to steal her device from Gabe's room while he slept. She fled from her dome and resumed her vigil farther up the highway. She ate her meals in another dome and slept in its large main room, arms draped over the metal object.

She often began her meditations while a group of Aadae sat in the road greeting the dawn. Her mind became clearer, more conscious of the things around her. She focused on a series of sharp images: the shadows of the seated, swaying Aadae, slender and elongated, rippling along the bumps and crevices of the pavement—
    the blinded eyes of the robed aliens, violet irises

afloat on a sea of white, with pupils that became small dark tunnels into darkness—

a strand of blue-black hair on a golden cheek, caressed by the invisible fingers of a breeze, becoming a long moustache over a lip—

a blade of grass among its fellows, its roots deep in the ground, attempting to draw moisture from the dandelion that hovered over it menacingly.

Her mind uncoiled and floated above her, drifting over the seated Aadae. The domes beneath her grew smaller, becoming overturned bowls on a table and then the tops of mushrooms. She was soaring over the burned bones of the city, strewn in a black pit, an omen to be read by a giant seer. She felt no fear as her mind traveled over the Earth and did not attempt to draw it back. She circled over the city. The highways were asphalt runes, incomplete, leading only to the pit.

Her mind came closer to the ground and returned to her, rushing through the domes where people still slept, dolls thrown on the mats by a careless child. She was staring once again at the metal apparatus in front of her.

Almost ready. It was a whisper, in her mind but not of it. The Aadae rose and began to walk back to their dome, leading their blinded sisters by the hand. Suzanne blinked. There were black spots before her eyes and she realized that she must have been staring at the sun for part of the time.

Her body was a burden which she hoisted to its feet. She would rest, and feed herself, then let her mind roam again.

An Aada near her began to wail. Suzanne opened her mouth and sang with her; her soprano was a bird flying over, then alighting on, the alien's clear mellow contralto. She soared effortlessly, and her crystalline tones circled over the lower voice, then flew on over the clouds to the sun.

* * *

Suzanne sat by the highway, away from the late afternoon shadows cast on the ground by the domes. She set her device in front of her and prepared her mind for its work.

She was suddenly frightened, and remembered the morning, long ago, when she had fled from the Aadae in fear. *Throw it away.* She recoiled from the metal construct before her. *Someone, please, tell me what to do.* The world was silent, the road empty.

Once more. She watched the blue stone on the device. It began to grow larger, drawing her mind into a blue vortex. She swam in a shimmering dark sea and shafts of light, sharp as spears of glass, pierced her eyes.

She was hurtling over the Earth, following the sun to the west. She moved through the eye of a storm and danced on the pinwheel of clouds. The Earth shrank beneath her and she turned to the moon, brushing against its rocky lifeless surface. Its craters were empty, its mountain peaks sharp, its shadows cold. She fled from the moon and was lost in darkness, heavy black velvet draped over her, pressing at her.

She pushed the blackness away. Now she was falling, spiraling uncontrollably toward the sun. Its flaming surface was a battleground screaming across space, crying for death, reaching out to immolate her. Two flares erupted on the surface and became wispy appendages, the arms of a lover seeking an embrace. *No.* The star thundered at her. Another flare rose and flung her into the emptiness.

A whisper reached her, almost as insubstantial as the flare dissolving around her. *Not yet, you are not ready.*

Frightened, she flew from the conflagration, moving outward until the planets were round pebbles and the sun only a distant lantern.

An invisible web surrounded her, pulling her toward a far red ruby glittering among diamonds. She passed a young world, still boiling, streaked with red and yellow streams. The red star in front of her grew larger and she drifted through its diffuse strands, to be met on the other side by a shaft of blue-white light. A tiny white sun circled the red star, a fierce sentry ready to defend its tired companion. She was pulled on, past a large gaseous world where heavy tentacled beasts fought in green seas, past a blue star around which dead rocks revolved, past a yellow sun linking flare-arms with its twin. She struggled against the web around her. *Take me back.* The web traveled more rapidly and she could catch only a glimpse of the worlds she passed.

Ahead of her lay clusters of suns, crowded together in the galactic hub, revolving slowly with companions or shrieking in death, murdering servant worlds around them. She whirled over them and retreated into memory:

Herds of automobiles stampeded through the streets. Their motors were an omnipresent growl, a subliminal threat. Trucks, oblivious to the smaller beasts around them, rolled by majestically; smaller cars made up for their lack in size by the use of clever tactics and, occasionally, increased belligerence. Suzanne walked the streets on a summer evening, clinging to Joel. She gazed up at his face and his eyes were momentarily two suns winking at her. She jostled a red-nosed drunk, rubbed elbows fleetingly with a young blonde woman whose cold green eyes became a green gas giant surrounded by rings. Ahead, a well-dressed silver-haired man shimmered, brushing aside luminous wisps before disappearing into a bar. Two adolescent girls flirted with three muscular boys dressed in embroidered denim jackets twinkling with constellations. She sniffed at the summer air: acrid odor of sweat, exhaust fumes, a whiff of aftershave, a charcoal-broiled steak, sulfur, ammonia, dust. Voices shrieked, babbled, murmured, roared, giggled, and bellowed, underscored by the insistent rumbling of the vehicles around them. She and the others began to retreat from the sidewalks, yielding them to the night. From her window, she could see the lighted windows in the towers around her. A dog was baying below. She heard a thunderous roar, then saw light on the street beneath her. Men on motorcycles screamed by, night creatures in search of prey.

A comet streaked past, throwing her from the starry city. She whirled through the tendrils of a nebula, spinning aimlessly into space. The intangible web which had held her disappeared. She was alone. She had no tears to cry for Joel, for her lost city, for the Earth now impossibly distant from her. She spun through the darkness, away from the pinwheels and discs of galaxies.

Something nearby was tugging at her mind. She drifted toward it, unable to resist. She did not belong here with her small fearful mind and her passive ineptitude. She could not deal with anything out here; she could not understand the processes that produced this immense spectacle, nor could she deal with it emotionally except as a series of frightening visions. Her mind seemed to contract, pushing in upon itself. *You are less than nothing here.*

Stellar corpses. She could not see them, but she felt their presence. Heavy chains dragged at her, drawing her on. She was a prisoner and assented to her bonds passively. It seemed somehow right that she should remain here, punished for having ventured too far.

Ahead, she saw a circle of blackness, darker even than the space around her, a deep well blotting out the nearer galaxies.

She was falling, tumbling forward into an endless pit. The black well grew wider. She cried out soundlessly and tried to crawl away with nonexistent limbs. *But I should wake up now.* The well surrounded her and she continued to fall.

The web was around her once more. *Pull away.* She tried to grasp the mind near her. The black pit was luring her on, teasing her with strands of light, whispering promises. *Resist.* The other mind touched her and she clung to it, struggling away from the hole in space.

Help me, she called to the other.

Help yourself. She pushed and the hole became a distant blot, then faded from sight. Streaks of blue and red light raced past her and she was ripped into a thousand pieces, beads on the thread of time. A thousand cries echoed in the vault of space and became one scream.

She was in the web, hovering over the Earth. She flew closer and rested above a pink cloud over her domed settlement. It was already morning below and she could see tiny specks huddled together on the highway.

You will grow stronger, the other mind whispered to her. *You will travel with the other minds of space, streaking among the stars with tachyonic beings who have transformed their physical shapes ages ago. You will meet those who abandoned their bodies but lurk near their worlds, afraid to venture further. And if you are very strong, you may approach a star where the strongest dwell, ready to fight you if you intrude. They will try to fling you far away, but if you contend with them long enough, they will reveal their secrets and allow you to join them. Your mind will grow stronger with each journey, and when your body can no longer hold it, you will leave it behind, a garment which you have outgrown, and journey among the stars. You will learn all one can learn here and then move on to where there is only unending reflection. Do you understand?*

Yes. She was sitting by the highway once again, held by the receptacle of her body. Neir-let was with her, clasping her hand.

"There is one more thing to do," the Aada murmured. "Are you strong enough, or must you rest?"

"Now," said Suzanne. Her mind floated up, brushed against Neir-let's, then leapt from her across the Earth. She was a spark, a burst of lightning striking every human brain she found, leaping from one to the next. She seized a group of minds and flung them away, watching them leap to other minds. Then she gathered them all to her and wove them into her net, four billion strands, and flung them from the Earth. They cried out to her, some in fear, others in awe, still others in delight. She drew them back and wound the fabric around her, caressing each thread.

She was once more at Neir-let's side. Exhausted, she rested her head on the Aada's shoulder. Neir-let's hand brushed her hair gently. Trapped in her body, Suzanne could still feel the bonds that linked her mind with all of humanity, and knew that they were now linked for all time. They would never be alone again, isolated and apart, shadows lingering in separate caves. However distant they might be, in thought or space, whatever they might do by themselves, they would all be joined as closely as lovers.

Neir-let stood up and removed the blue stone from the metal device. "You no longer need this," she said, gesturing at the apparatus. The Aada pulled a pointed knife from the belt over her briefs, reached over and pricked Suzanne's forehead, then pressed the stone against it. Suzanne bore the slight pain silently, wincing a bit, becoming calm as the stone pulsed between her temples. "This will help you to focus your mind, but soon you will not need it either."

Suzanne lifted her hand to her head, touching the stone. Other aliens nearby were already at work, embedding the small stones in the foreheads of people seated by the road. She stood up. A group of boys, stones glittering on their brows, approached her, palms open in thankfulness. She reached out to them with her mind and embraced them, crying out silently in joy.

* * *

Suzanne, clothed only in a tattered robe, stood in the doorway of a dome. The Aadae would teach humanity all that they knew before leaving for another world. Then mankind would have to ready its own ships and prepare to save another race from the oblivion of death. She knew her body would not last long enough to undertake the journey, but she would be with the ships, helping them to locate beings that still huddled together in fear.

She looked around her. The body of Gabe Cardozo was nearby, propped up against a wall, face empty of expression. Rivulets of saliva ran down his beard and she smiled, knowing that his mind was out among the stars. Other people sat in small groups with Aadae, trying to learn what was necessary for their future voyage.

She had done her share, and knew no more would be asked of her. She left the dome and walked to the highway, wanting only to roam through space again. She joined the group of Aadae seated in the road, blind eyes staring upward. A naked child ran past her, heedless of the festering sores on his arms and belly.

She sat down next to the Aadae and lifted her eyes to the flaming disc overhead. Her mind floated up effortlessly, drifting through the clouds.

The turbulent yellow star ahead seemed to beckon her. *I'll be ready for you, I'll take your wisdom with me before you fling me away.* She unfurled her wings and flew toward the sun.

(1974)

The Novella Race

Anyone who wants to be a contender has to start training at an early age. Because competitions are always in Standard, my parents insisted that I speak Standard instead of our local dialect. I couldn't use an autocompositor. We never owned a dictator either. "You'll only have a typewriter during the race," my mother would say. "You'd better get used to it now."

I had few friends as a child. You can't have friends while training in writing, or any other sport for that matter. The other kids plugged in, swallowed RNA doses, or were hypnotized in order to learn the skills they would need as adults. I had to master the difficult arts of reading and writing. At times I hated my typewriter, the endless sentence-long exercises, and the juvenile competitions. I envied other kids and wished that I too could romp carelessly through life.

Some people think being an athlete keeps you in shape. Everyone *should* take a few minutes each day to sit down and think. But competitive sports usually damage the body and torment the mind. A champion is almost always distorted in some way.

As I grew older, I noticed that others simply marked time. They were good spectators, consumers, and socializers, but they went to their graves without attempting anything extraordinary. I wanted a gold medal, honor, and fame. Even when I wanted to quit, I knew I'd gone too far to turn back.

* * *

By the time I was sixteen I knew I was neither a sprinter nor a distance runner. My short stories were incomplete and I did not have the endurance for the novel competition. Poetry was beyond me, although my grandmother had taken a bronze medal in the poetry race of 2024. I would have to train in the novella.

My parents wanted me to train with Phaedon Karath, who had won four Olympic gold medals before turning professional, thus disqualifying himself from further competition. Karath was hard on his trainees, but they did well in contests. I would have preferred going to Lalia Grasso, whose students were devoted to her. But those accustomed to her gentle ways often messed up during races; they did not develop the necessary streak of cruelty nor the essential quality of egotism.

Everyone knew about Eli Shankquist, her most talented trainee and a three-time Pan-American gold medalist as well. During the Olympic race, the only one that matters, he became involved with the notoriously insecure Maliah Senbok. Touched by her misery, he spent a lot of time encouraging her. And what did he get? He didn't finish his own novella and Senbok took a bronze. A lot of spectators sympathized with Shankquist, but most writers thought he was a fool.

None of Karath's students would have been in such a fix. So I sent off my file of fiction and waited long months for an answer. Just before my seventeenth birthday, a reply arrived on the telex. Karath wanted a personal interview. I left on the shuttle the next day.

Karath lived in a large villa overlooking the Adriatic. As I entered, I looked around the hallway. Several green beanbag chairs stood next to heavy Victorian tables covered with illuminated manuscripts. Colorful tapestries depicting minstrels and scribes hung on the walls. The servo, a friendly silver ball with cylindrical limbs, ushered me to the study.

The study was clean and Spartan. To my right, a computer console stood next to the wall. To the left, a large window overlooked the blue sea. Karath sat at his glass-topped desk, typing. He looked up and motioned to a straight-backed wood chair. I sat down.

As I fidgeted, he got up and paced to the window. I had seen him on the screen a few times but in person he seemed shorter. He was wiry, with thick dark hair and a small hard face. He looked, I thought apprehensively, like a young tough, in spite of his age. I waited, trying to picture myself in this house, typing away, making friends, workshopping stories, getting drunk, having an affair and doing all the things a writer does.

Karath turned and paced to the desk. As he picked up a folder, which I recognized as my file, he muttered, "You're Alena Dorenmatté."

I tried to smile. "That's me."

"What makes you think you belong here?"

"I want the best training in the novella I can get."

"That's a crock of shit. You want to fuck and get drunk and sit around thinking artistic thoughts and congratulating yourself on your sensitivity. You won't sweat blood over a typewriter. You want to be coddled."

He threw my file across the desk. It landed on the floor with a *plop*. I picked it up, clutching it to my chest.

"Let me fill you in, Dorenmatté. There's nothing but cow pies in that file. Understand? I don't think you could win a local."

"I won a local last year, I placed first in the Bos-Wash." He couldn't have reviewed my citations very carefully. "Why'd you ask me here anyway? You could have insulted me over the relay."

"Maybe the truth wouldn't sink in over the relay. I like to say what I think face to face. You're not a writer. Your stories are nothing but clichés and adolescent trage- dy. You can't plot and you can't create characters. You have nothing to say. You'd make a fool of yourself in Olympic competition. Cow pies, that's what you write. Go home and learn how to socialize so you don't ruin your life."

My face was burning. "I don't know why anybody trains with you. If the other trainers were that mean, no one would ever write again."

He flew at me, seized the file, and tore it in half, scattering papers over the floor. Terrified, I shrank back.

"Let me tell you something, Dorenmatté. A writer doesn't give up. He takes punishment, listens to criti- cism, and keeps writing. If he doesn't make it, it's be- cause he wasn't any good. I don't run a nursery, I train writers. Now get out of here. I have work to do."

I stood up, realizing that I couldn't respond without bursting into tears. Grasping at my last threads of digni- ty, I turned and walked slowly out of the room.

* * *

I could have applied to another trainer. Instead I moped for months. At last my father issued an ultima- tum: I would have to move to a dormitory and learn to socialize or enter a competition.

Even my parents were deserting me. I moved out and rented an apartment in Montreal. I stayed inside for weeks, unable to move, barely able to eat. One night I tried to hang myself, but I could never tie knots properly and only fell to the floor, acquiring a nasty bruise on my thigh. Fate had given me another chance.

I had forgotten that the PanAmerican Games were being held in Montreal that year. Somehow, even in my hopeless state, they drew me. I found myself entering the qualifying meet in paragraphs. I lugged my typewriter to the amphitheater and sat with a thousand others at desks under hot lights while the spectators came and went, cheering for their favorites. Several writers made use of the always-popular "creative anguish" ploy, slapping their foreheads in frustration while throwing away wads of paper. Ramon Hogarth, winner of the West Coast local, danced around his desk after completing each sentence. My style was standard. I smoked heavily and gulped coffee while slouching over my machine. Occasionally I clutched my gut in agony, drawing some applause.

I qualified for the semifinals and was given a small room filled with monitoring devices. The judges, of course, had to watch for cheating, and spectators all over the hemisphere would be viewing us. I tried to preserve my poise at the typewriter, but gradually I forgot everything except my novella. I wrote and rewrote, rarely taking breaks, knowing that I was up against trained contenders. Whenever I became discouraged, I remembered the mocking voice of Phaedon Karath.

I made it to the finals. I recall that I envied the short-story writers, who had a four-month deadline, and pitied the novelists, who had to suffer for a year. I can remember the times when my words flowed freely, but there were moments when I was ready to disqualify myself. I agonized while awaiting the decision and wondered if I could ever face another race.

I placed sixth. Delighted, I got drunk and daringly sent off my sixth-place novella to Phaedon Karath. A few days later, his reply appeared on my telex: STILL COW PIES BUT IMPROVEMENT STOP COME TO ITALY STOP SEE IF YOU CAN TAKE REAL WORKOUT STOP.

*   *   *

At the villa I had to work on sentences for months before I was allowed to go on to paragraphs. Karath insisted on extensive rewriting, although constant rewriting could kill you off in competition as easily as sloppy unreworked first drafts. He rarely praised anyone.

We workshopped a lot, tearing each other's work apart. Reina Takake, a small golden-skinned woman who became my closest friend, used to run from the room in tears. The more she cried, the more Karath picked on her. We would spend hours together planning tortures for him and occasionally writing about the tortures in vivid detail.

At last Reina packed and left, saying good-bye to no one. Karath told us of her departure during a workshop, watching us with his gray eyes as he said that Reina couldn't cut it, that she had no talent, and that it was useless to waste time on someone who couldn't take criticism.

I hated him for that. I stood up and screamed that he was a petty tyrant and a sadist. I told him he had no understanding of gentle souls. I said a few other things.

He waited until I finished. Then he looked around the room and said, "The rest of you can continue. Dorenmatté, step outside."

Trembling, I followed him out. He led me down the hall and stopped in front of my room. He turned, grabbed me by the arms, and shoved me inside. I stumbled and almost fell.

"Stay in there," he said. "You're not coming out until you finish a specific assignment."

"What assignment?" I asked, puzzled.

"The novella you're going to write, and rewrite if necessary. You'll write about Takake and about me if you like. Do it any way you please, but you have to write about Takake. Now get to work."

He slammed the door quickly. I heard him turn the lock. I screamed, bellowed, and cursed until I was hoarse. Karath did not respond.

* * *

I spent a few hours in futile weeping and a few days in plotting an escape. Food was brought to me, occasionally with wine; the upper door panel would open and the amiable servo would lower the food into my room. At first I refused it but after a few days I was too hungry to resist.

I soon realized I'd never get out of my windowless room until I wrote the novella. I took a bath, then bitterly went to work. At first I rambled, noting every passing thought, incorporating some of the paragraphs Reina and I had written about torturing Karath. But soon a particular plot suggested itself. I outlined the story and began again.

I worked at least a month, maybe more, before I had a draft to show Karath. Oddly enough, I could not sustain my anger at him nor my grief at Reina's departure. I understood what had happened and what I had felt, but these events and feelings were simply material to be shaped and structured.

I gave my final draft to the servo and waited. At last the door opened. I made my way downstairs to Karath's study.

He sat behind his desk perusing my novella. I cleared my throat. His cold eyes surveyed me as he said, "It isn't bad, Dorenmatté. It wouldn't make it in a race, but there might be some hope for you." As I basked in this high praise, he threw the manuscript at me. "Now go back to work and clean up some of your sentences."

A year later I took the gold medal in the PanAmerican Games.

* * *

But it was Olympic gold I wanted, the high point for a champion. There would be publicity, perhaps other competitions if my health held out. But contests were for the young. Eventually I would become a trainer or sign contracts with the entertainment industry; gold-medal winners can get a lot for senso plots or dream construction. Maybe novelists can do serialized week-long dreams and short-story writers are better at commercials, but you can't beat a novella writer for an evening's sustained entertainment. Since practically no one reads now, except of course the critics, most of them failed writers who write comments on our work for one another and serve as judges during competitions, there isn't much else a champion can do when the contest years are over.

The Olympics! Karath rode us mercilessly in preparation for them. He presented countless distractions: robots outside with jackhammers, emotional crises, dirty tricks meant to disorient us, impossible deadlines.

Two years before the Games, which like the ancient Olympics are held only every four years, I had to enter preliminaries. I got through them easily. The night before I left for Rome, Karath and the others workshopped a story of mine and tore it to shreds. I recall the hatred I saw in the faces of my fellow trainees. None had qualified this time, although all had won locals or regionals. They would undoubtedly gossip maliciously about me when I left and point out to each other how inferior my work really was.

I arrived in Rome the day before the opening ceremonies. The part of the Olympic Village set aside for writers was a scenic spot. The small stone houses were surrounded on three sides by flower gardens and wooded areas. Below us lay all of Rome; the dome of St. Peter's, the crowded streets, the teeming arcologies. I wanted to explore it all, but I had to start sizing up the competition.

I sought out Jules Pepperman, who had been assigned a house near mine. I had met him at the Pan American Games. Jules was tied into the grapevine and always volunteered information readily.

He was a tall slender fellow with an open, friendly personality and a habit of trying to write excessively ambitious works during competition, a practice I regarded as courting disaster. It had messed him up before, but it had also won him a gold in the Anglo-American Games and a silver in the PEN Stakes. I couldn't afford to ignore him.

His house smelled of herb tea and patent medicines. Jules had arrived with every medication the judges would allow. I wondered how he endured competition, with his migraines and stomach ailments. But endure it he did, while complaining loudly about his health to everyone.

I sat in his kitchen while he poured tea. "Did you hear, Alena? I'm ready to go home, I'm sick of working all the time, the prelims almost wiped me out. There's this migraine I can't get rid of and the judges won't let me take the only thing that helps. And when I heard . . . you want honey in that?"

"Sure." He dropped a dollop in my tea. "What did you hear?"

"Ansoni. He's so brilliant and I'm so dumb. I can't take any more."

"What about Ansoni?"

"He's here. He's competing. Haven't you heard? You must have been living in a cave. He's competing. In novella."

"Shit," I said. "What's the matter with him? He must be almost sixty. Isn't he ineligible?"

"No. Don't you keep up with anything? He never worked professionally and he wasn't a trainer."

I tried to digest this unsavory morsel. I hadn't even known that Michael Ansoni was still among the living. He had taken a gold medal in short-story competition long ago and gone on to win a gold eight years later in novella, the only writer to change categories successfully. I couldn't even remember all his other awards.

"I can't beat him," Jules wailed. "I should have been a programmer. All that work to get here, and now this."

I had to calm Jules down. I didn't like his writing, which was a bit dense for my taste, but I liked him. "Listen," I said, "Ansoni's old. He might fold up at his age. Maybe he'll die and be disqualified."

"Don't say that."

"I wouldn't be sorry. Well, maybe I would. Who else looks good?"

"Nionus Gorff." Gorff was always masked; no one had ever seen his face. He had quite a cultish following.

"*Naah*," I responded. "Gorff hates publicity too much, he'll be miserable in a big race like this."

"There's Jan Wolowski. But I don't think he can beat Ansoni."

"Wolowski's too heavyhanded. He might as well do propaganda."

"There's Arnold Dankmeyer."

I was worried about Dankmeyer myself. He was popular with the judges, although that might not mean much. APOLLO, the Olympic computer, actually picked the winners, but the judges' assessments were fed in and considered in the final decisions. No one could be sure how much weight they carried. And Dankmeyer was appealingly facile. But he was often distracted by his admirers, who followed him everywhere and even lived in his house during races. He might fold.

"Anyway," I said, "you can't worry about it now." I was a bit insulted that Jules wasn't worried about me.

"I know. But the judges don't like me, they never have."

"Well, they don't like me either." I had, in accordance with Karath's advice, cultivated a public image with which to impress the judges. My stock-in-trade was unobtrusiveness and self-doubt. I would have preferred being a colorful character like Karath, but I could never have carried that off. Being quiet might not win many points, but there was always a chance the judges would react unfavorably to histrionics and give points to a shy writer.

"At least they don't hate you," Jules mumbled. "I need a vacation. I can't take it."

"You're a champion, act like one," I said loftily. I got up and made my departure, wanting to rest up for the opening ceremonies.

* * *

We looked terrific in the stadium, holding our quill pens, clothed in azure jumpsuits with the flags of our countries over our chests. The only ones who looked better were the astrophysicists, who wore black silk jumpsuits studded with rhinestone constellations. They were only there for the opening ceremonies; their contests would be held on the Moon. At any rate, the science games didn't draw much of an audience. Hardly anyone

knew enough to follow them. And mathematicians—
they were dressed in black robes and held slates and
chalk—were ignored, even if they were gold medalists.
The social sciences drew the crowds, probably because
anyone could, in a way, feel he was participating in them.
But we writers didn't do so badly. No one read what we
wrote, but a lot of people enjoyed our public displays. At
least one writer was sure to crack up before the Games
were over, and occasionally there was a suicide.

We marched around, the flame was lit, and I smiled
at Jules. At least we were contenders. No one could take
that away.

* * *

The race began. I worked methodically, meaning
that I used my own method. During the first two weeks I
wrote nothing. I saw a lot of Rome. A wisp of an idea was
forming in my mind, but I wasn't ready to work on it.

Jules was slaving away. He would creep along slowly and finish a draft, then take a week off during which he
would feel guilty about not working. He had to rewrite a
lot. "Otherwise," he had told me, "I'd be incomprehensible."

During the second month, I met Jan Wolowski while
taking a walk. He was too intense for my taste. He was
always serious, even at parties, and he had no tolerance
for the foibles of writers. He was also dogmatic and
snobbish. But he *was* competition.

I said hello and we continued walking together.
"How are you doing?" I asked, not really wanting to
know.

"Still taking notes and working out my plot."

"I hate making notes. I like to write it as it comes.
But I don't have a chance anyway." That last line was

part of my self-depreciation routine, but on some level I believed it. If I really thought I was good, some part of me was sure, I would lose.

"I wrote a good paragraph this morning," he said. "I have my notebook with me. Want to hear it?"

"No." Wolowski liked to read to other competitors. It would bore, exasperate, or demoralize them. He read me his paragraph anyway. Unfortunately, it was good.

We passed Dankmeyer's house. He was holding court at a picnic table with his admirers, some fettucini, and plenty of wine. Dankmeyer could turn out a novella in a week, so he was able to spend most of his time garnering publicity.

"Did you ever meet Lee Huong?" Wolowski asked as I waved to Dankmeyer, hating his courtier's guts.

"No."

"You should. She may be the best writer here."

"I never heard of her. What's she won?"

"Nothing, except a bronze in the Sino-Soviet Games years ago. She's close to forty."

"Then she can't be that great. At that age, she ought to quit." We passed Ansoni's house. All the shutters were closed. I had heard he slept during the day and worked at night.

"I mean," Wolowski continued, "that she's the best *writer*. If people still read, they'd read her. I've read her best stuff and it wasn't what she wrote in contests."

We stopped by a café and sat down at a roadside table. I signaled to a servo for a beer. The man was trying to disorient me. I knew these tricks. "Better than Ansoni?" I asked.

"Better than him."

"Bullshit. I don't believe it." I looked around and saw some spectators. They grinned and waved. A boy shouted, "Go get it, Dorenmatté!" It was nice to have admirers.

* * *

I spoke to Lee Huong only once, two months before the end of our race, at a party for the short-story medalists.

The party was held in an old villa. The dining room was filled with long tables covered with platters of caviar, various fruits, suckling pigs, standing rib roasts, and bowls of pasta. I settled on a couch and dug in. Across from me, Jules was flirting with the silver medalist in short stories, a buxom red-haired woman.

Benjamin MacStiofain sat next to me and grimly devoured a pear. "These Olympics are disgusting," he muttered. "What's the use? We come here, we agonize, we break our hearts, then someone wins and everybody forgets about it. I hate it all. This is my last competition." MacStiofain always said every meet was his last.

"I heard Dankmeyer finished his novella already."

MacStiofain's mustache twitched. "Did you have to tell me that?" He got up and wandered away morosely.

Then I saw Lee Huong. She drifted past, dressed in what appeared to be white pajamas. Her small light-brown face was composed; her almond eyes surveyed the room benevolently. It was eerie. This late in the race a writer might be depressed, anxious, fatalistic, or hysterical, but not calm. It had to be a tactic.

She nodded to me, then sat down on the couch. I nodded back. "Is this your first Olympic contest?" she asked.

I said it was.

"It means little."

"You're absolutely right," I replied. "It means nothing . . . if you're a loser." I was being crude. But Lee

Huong only smiled as she got up and walked away. Maybe she knew something I didn't know.

I remembered what Wolowski had said. What if he was right about Huong? If she was the best, it meant that inferior writers defeated her regularly. And if that was true, it might mean that inferior writers beat better ones in all contests. MacStiofain, I recalled uncomfortably, believed that APOLLO picked the winners at random, although the human judges might give you an edge. The Olympic committee had denied this, but we all knew that MacStiofain's sister had taken a gold in cybernetics. She might have told him something.

I had lost my appetite during these ruminations, so I got up and made a show of leaving, waving to Jules and telling him that I was heading back to work. This obvious maneuver almost always succeeded in making the writers who remained feel guilty. Karath's classic move, bringing his typewriter to parties and working in the midst of them, was one I greatly admired but could never emulate with conviction.

On my way back, I saw Effie Mae Hublinger sitting on a stone wall with a few spectators. Her game was being just folks, nothin' special 'bout me, jes' throwin' the ol' words around, but at heart Ah'm jes' a li'l ol' socializer. Anyone who believed that about a writer deserved to be fooled, or worse yet, put into a story as a character.

* * *

The last month was pressurized. Anyone who could spare the time was playing dirty tricks. Wolowski, who admittedly was erudite, lectured to anyone he saw on the subject of our ignorance and lack of real ability. This upset a few writers, but only encouraged Jules, for some strange reason.

MacStiofain finally cracked. In a show of poor

sportsmanship, he duked it out with a novelist. The day after that brawl, he was disqualified for taking unauthorized drugs.

They had to drag him away. The robopols put him in a straitjacket while he screamed that someone had planted the drugs, but we knew that wasn't true. At any rate, we all calmed down a bit, since a formidable contender was now out of the race.

Lee Huong kept her equilibrium. That drove Effie Mae Hublinger crazy. With a few of her friends, she camped out on Huong's front step for three days, creating a ruckus. This infantile tactic only lost Hublinger time she could have spent on her own novella.

Someone visited Jules and managed to swipe his medicines, unnoticed by the monitors. Even Jules, angry as he was, had to admire such skill and daring. But it was Dankmeyer who created a classic new ploy. Two weeks before the end of competition he handed in his novella.

Jules, hysterical by then, relayed this news to me. He was having trouble with his ending. He stomped around my workroom, talked himself into utter panic, talked himself out of it, then went back to his house. Even Ansoni had been thrown off balance by that trick. Everyone had always waited for the deadline, revising and polishing. Dankmeyer would be famous. He topped off his stunt with a nervous collapse, which would help with the judges.

The day before the deadline, Rigel Jehan left without finishing his novella and was disqualified. Poor Rigel, I thought, glad he was gone. He could never finish anything during the big contests.

And then the deadline arrived. We handed in our manuscripts and carefully avoided each other while awaiting judgment. I went on a drunk in Rome. I came to in an alley with a large bump on my head, no money, and a hangover. I suppose it's all grist for the mill.

* * *

The closing ceremonies were held two years after the start of the Games. It took that long for some of the races to be completed. The economists, in gold lamé, sashayed around the arena, drawing a few cheers. The anthropologists topped them, weaving in and out, then dancing a nifty two-step in their robes and feathers. I wore my bronze medal proudly as I strutted with the others, our quill pens held high. There was, after all, no shame in being defeated by Ansoni, although it irked me that Dankmeyer had taken the silver. He had recovered nicely from his nervous breakdown and was casting friendly glances at me with his sensitive brown eyes. I ignored him.

I returned to Karath's villa after that. He congratulated me but got down to essentials quickly. I had only a couple of months to train for the next Olympic prelims.

Then disaster struck. I had no words left. At first I thought it was only exhaustion. I grew listless. I put the cover over my typewriter, then hid it under my desk, where it reproached me silently. The other trainees whispered about me. I had to face the truth: I had a writer's block. I might never write again. No one ever discussed writer's block, considering it indelicate, but I knew others had gone mute.

Karath was kind and sympathetic, although he knew I could not remain at the villa; he had to worry about contagion. He was too courteous to ask me to leave. I left by myself, one cold cloudy morning, not wanting to see the other trainees gloat, and took a shuttle to New Zealand.

* * *

Blocked and miserable, I shut myself off from all news. I received a few kind notes, which I did not answer; nothing is worse than the pity of other writers. Yet even in that state I had to view the next Olympics.

Reina Takake took the gold; I found out she had gone back to Karath after I left. I watched her receive it, hating her, hating my former best friend more than I had ever hated anyone.

That did it. Hate and envy always do. Something jogged loose in my brain and I started writing again. Let's face it, I'm not fit for anything else. I only hope I can be a contender once more.

(1978)

The Summer's Dust

Andrew was hiding. He sat on the roof, his back to the gabled windows. He had been there for only a few minutes, and knew he would be found; that was the point.

He heard a door open below. "Andrew?" The door snapped shut. His mother was on the porch; her feet thumped against the wood. "Andrew?" She would go back inside and find that he was still near the house; tracing the signal, she would locate him. He glanced at his left wrist. The small blue stone of the Bond winked at him. The silver bracelet was a tattletale chain; it would give him away.

He looked down at the gutter edging the roof. The porch's front steps creaked, and his mother's blonde head emerged. A warm breeze feathered her hair as she glided along the path leading down the hill. From the roof, Andrew could see the nearby houses. At the foot of the hill, two kobolds tended the rose garden that nestled near a low stone house. The owner of the house had lived in the south for years, but her small android servants still clipped the hedges and trimmed the lawn. Each kobold was one meter tall, and human in appearance. On pleasant evenings, he had seen the little people lay a linen tablecloth over the table in the garden and set out the silverware, taking their positions behind the chairs. They would wait silently, small hands crossed over their chests, until it was night, when they would clear the table once more. A troll stood by the hedge; this creature was half a meter taller than the kobolds. The troll's misshapen body was bent forward slightly; its long arms hung to the ground, fingertips touching grass. At night, the troll would guard the house. The being's ugly bearded face and scowl were a warning to anyone who approached; the small silver patch on its forehead revealed the cybernetic link that enabled it to summon aid.

Farther down the road, the facets of a glassy dome caught the sun, and tiny beings of light danced. Andrew's friend Silas lived there with his father Ben and several Siamese cats. Andrew frowned as he thought of Silas and of what his friend wanted to do.

Andrew's own house was old. His mother had told him it had been built before the Transition. Even with extensive repairs and additions to the house, the homeostat could not run it properly. The rooms were usually a bit warm or too cold; the doors made noises; the windows were spotted with dirt.

He watched his mother wander aimlessly along the path. Joan had forgotten him, as she often did. They could be in the same room and she would become silent, then suddenly glance at him, her eyes widening, as if she were surprised to find him still there.

His father, Dao, was different; completely attentive whenever Andrew was around, but content to ignore him the rest of the time. He wondered if Dao would ever speak to him at all if Andrew didn't speak first.

He moved a little. His right foot shot out and brushed against a loose shingle. Andrew slid; he grabbed for the window sill and held on. The shingle fell, slapping against the cement of the path.

Joan looked up. She raised her hands slowly. "Andrew." Her voice was loud but steady. He pulled himself up; he would not fall now. Joan moved closer to the house. "What are you doing up there?"

"I'm all right."

She held her arms up. "Don't move."

"I've got my lifesuit on."

"I don't care. Don't move, stay where you are." Her feet pounded on the steps and over the porch. The front door slammed. In a few moments, he heard her enter his room. Her arms reached through the open window and pulled him inside.

Andrew sighed as she closed the window, feeling vaguely disappointed. "Don't ever do that again."

"I'm wearing my lifesuit." He opened his shirt to show her the protective garment underneath.

"I don't care. It's supposed to protect you, not make you reckless. You still could have been hurt."

"Not at that distance. Bruises, that's all."

"Why did you do it?"

Andrew shrugged. He went over to his bed and sat down. The bed undulated; Joan seemed to rise and fall before him.

"Why did you do it?"

"I don't know."

"Do I have to have a kobold follow you around? I thought you were too old for that."

"I'm all right." I wouldn't have died or anything, he thought.

Joan watched him silently for a few moments. She was drifting again; he knew the signs. Her blue eyes stared through him, as if she were seeing something else. She shook her head. "I keep forgetting how old you are." She paused. "Don't go out there again."

"I won't."

She left the room. He rose and crossed to the windows, staring out at the houses below and the forested hills beyond. His room suddenly seemed cramped and small; his hands tapped restlessly against the sill.

* * *

Andrew was sitting on the porch with Dao and Joan when Silas arrived. The other boy got off his bicycle and wheeled it up the hill to the porch. He parked it and waved at Andrew's parents. Joan's thin lips were tight as she smiled. Dao showed his teeth; his tilted brown eyes became slits.

Andrew sat on the steps next to Silas. His friend was thirteen, a year older than Andrew. He was the only child Andrew had met in the flesh; the others were only holo images. Silas was big and muscular, taller than Joan and Dao; he made Andrew feel even smaller and slighter than he was. Andrew moved up a step and looked down at the other boy.

Silas rose abruptly. Brown hair fell across his forehead, masking his eyes. He motioned to Andrew, then began to walk down the hill. Andrew followed. They halted by the hedge in front of the empty stone house. The troll waved them away, shaking its head; its long tangled hair swayed against its green tunic.

"How about it?" Silas said as they backed away from the hedge.

"What?"

"You know. Our journey, our adventure. You coming with me? Or are you just going to stay here?"

Andrew held out his arm, looking at his Bond. "We can't go. They'll find us."

"I said I'd figure out a way. I have a plan."

"How?"

"You'll see," Silas said. He shook his head. "Aren't you sick of it here? Don't you get tired of it?"

Andrew shrugged. "I guess."

Silas began to kick a stone along the road. Andrew glanced up the hill; Joan and Dao were still on the porch. They had lived in that house even before bringing him home, making one journey to the center to conceive him and another when he was removed from the artwomb. They had gone to some trouble to have him; they were always telling him so. "More people should have children," Dao would say. "It keeps us from getting too set in our ways." Joan would nod. "You're very precious to us," Joan would murmur, and Dao would smile. Yet, most of the time, his parents would be with their books or speaking to distant friends on the holo or lost in their own thoughts.

Joan could remember the beginnings of things. Dao was even older. He could remember the Transition, when the world had realized that people no longer had to die. Dao was filled with stories of those days—the disorder, the fear, the desperate attempts to reach as many people as possible with the treatments that would give them youth and immortality. He always spoke of those days as if they had been the prelude to great adventure and achievement. Gradually, Andrew had realized that those times had been the adventure, that nothing important was likely to happen to Joan and Dao again. Dao was almost four hundred years old; Joan was only slightly younger. Once, Andrew had asked his mother what she had been like when she was his age. She had laughed, seeming more alive for a moment. "Afraid," she had answered, laughing again.

Silas kicked the stone toward the hill. "Listen," he said as they climbed. "I'm ready. I've got two knapsacks and a route worked out. We'd better leave this week before my father gets suspicious."

"I don't know."

The taller boy turned and took Andrew by the shoulder. "If you don't go, I'll go by myself. Then I'll come back and tell you all about it, and you'll be sorry you didn't come along."

Andrew pulled away. Silas's face was indistinct in the dusk. Andrew felt anxious. He knew that he should be concerned about how his parents would feel if he ran away, but he wasn't; he was thinking only of how unfair it had been for them to assume that he would want to hide in this isolated spot, shunning the outside world. They had told him enough about death cults and accidents to make him frightened of anything beyond this narrow road. He knew what Silas was thinking, that Andrew was a coward.

Why should I care what he thinks, Andrew thought, but there was no one else against whom he could measure himself. He wondered if he would have liked Silas at all if there had been other friends. He pushed the thought away; he could not afford to lose his one friend.

As they came toward the house, Andrew saw his parents go inside. A kobold was on the porch, preparing for its nightly surveillance; behind it, a troll was clothed in shadows. Silas got on his bicycle.

"See you," he mumbled and coasted down the hill recklessly, slowing down as he reached the bottom, speeding up as he rode toward his home.

The kobold danced over to Andrew as he went up the steps. It smiled; the golden curls around its pretty face bobbed. A tiny hand touched his arm. "Good night, Andrew," it sang.

"Good night, Ala."

"Good night, good night, good night," the tiny voice trilled. "Sleep well, sweet dreams, sweet dreams." The troll growled affectionately. The kobold pranced away, its gauzy blue skirt lifting around its perfect legs.

Andrew went inside. The door snapped shut behind him, locking itself. He walked toward the curving staircase, then paused, lingering in the darkened hallway. He would have to say good night.

He found his parents in the living room. He knocked on the door, interrupting the sound of conversation, then opened it. Dao had stripped to his briefs; Joan was unbuttoning her shirt. On the holo, Andrew saw the nude images of a blond man and a red-haired woman; a dark-haired kobold giggled as it peered around the woman's bare shoulder. The flat wall-sized screen had become the doorway into a bright, sunny bedroom.

"Five minutes," Dao said to the images. "We'll call you back." The people and the room disappeared. "What is it, son?"

Joan smiled. Andrew looked down at the floor, pushing his toe against a small wrinkle in the Persian rug. "Nothing. I came to say good night."

He left, feeling their impatience. As he climbed the stairs, he heard the door below slide open.

"Andrew," Joan said. She swayed, holding the ends of her open shirt. "I'll come up later and tuck you in. All right?"

I'm too old for that, he wanted to say. "I'll be asleep," he said as he looked down at her.

"I'll check on you anyway. Maybe I'll tell you a story."

He was sure that she would forget.

* * *

In the end, he went with Silas, as he had known he would. They left two days later, in the morning, stopping at Silas's house to pick up the knapsacks. Silas's father was out in the back, digging in his garden with the aid of a troll; he did not see them leave.

They avoided the road, keeping near the trees. When they were out of sight of Andrew's house, they returned to the road. Andrew was not frightened now. He wondered what his parents would say when he returned to tell them of his journey.

Silas stopped and turned around, gazing over Andrew's head. "A kobold's following us." Andrew looked back. A little figure in blue was walking toward them; it lifted one hand in greeting.

"What'll we do?"

"Nothing, for the moment." Silas resumed walking.

"But it's following us." Andrew walked more quickly, trying to keep up with his friend's strides. "We could outrun it, couldn't we? It won't be able to keep up."

"That's just what we can't do. If we do that, it'll tell the others, and we'll have your parents and my father on our trail."

They came to a bend in the road. Silas darted to one side and hurried through the brush. Andrew ran after him, thrashing through the green growth. It had rained the night before; the ground was soft and muddy, and leaves stuck to his boots. Silas reached for his arm and pulled him behind a tree.

"Wait," Silas said. He glanced at Andrew, then peered at him more closely. Andrew stepped back. Silas was looking at his chest. Andrew looked down. One of his shirt buttons was undone, revealing the silver fabric underneath.

"You're wearing a lifesuit."

"Aren't you?"

"Of course not. You're stupid, Andrew. Don't you know you can be tracked with that on?"

"Not as easily as with a Bond." He wondered again what Silas was going to do about their Bonds.

"Take it off right now."

"You can't hurt me, not while I'm wearing it."

"I'll leave you here, then."

"I don't care." But he did. He took off his knapsack and unbuttoned his shirt. Twigs cracked in the distance; the kobold had tracked them. Andrew removed his life-suit, and handed it to Silas.

As he dressed, Andrew felt exposed and vulnerable. His clothing seemed too light, too fragile. He watched as Silas dug in the mud, burying the lifesuit with his hands. He looked up at Andrew and grinned, his hands caked with wet earth.

"Get behind that tree," Silas said as he picked up a rock. Andrew obeyed, flattening himself against the bark. A bush shook. He could see the kobold now. For a moment, the android looked like a man; then it moved closer to another bush and was small again. Its dark beard twitched.

"Silas," the kobold called. "Silas." It shaded its eyes with one hand. "Silas, where are you bound? You should not come so far without protection." The creature had a man's voice, a tenor, but it had no resonance, no power; it was a man's voice calling from far away. The kobold came closer until it was only a meter from Andrew, its back to him as it surveyed the area.

Silas moved quickly, brushing against Andrew as he rushed toward the kobold. He raised the rock and Andrew saw him strike the android's head. The little creature toppled forward, hands out. Andrew walked toward it slowly. Silas dropped the red-smeared rock. The small skull was dented; bits of bone and slender silver threads gleamed in the wound. The silver patch on its forehead was loose.

"You killed it."

"I didn't mean to hit it so hard. I just wanted to knock it out." Silas brushed back his hair with one dirty hand. "It's only a kobold. Come on, we have to go. Now that its link is out, another one'll come looking for it."

Andrew stared at the body.

"Come on." He turned and followed his friend. They came to a muddy clearing and went around it. Silas led him to a nearby grove of trees.

Two cages rested against a tree trunk. Two cats, trapped inside, scratched at the screening. "I told you I had a plan," Silas said. "Now we take care of our Bonds."

"I don't understand."

The other boy exhaled loudly. "Messing up the signal's too complicated, and we can't take them off and leave them because the alarm would go out after a minute or so. So there's only one thing left. We put them on somebody else. Or something else. The system can't tell if it's us or not; it only knows that the Bonds are on some living thing. And it'll assume it's still us, because these Bonds are ours. Everyone'll look for us around here. By the time anyone figures it out, we'll be far away."

Andrew stared at his friend. It seemed obvious and simple, now that he had explained. "They might just wander back to your house," he murmured as he shifted his gaze to the cages.

"Not these cats. They're kind of wild. They'll stay out here for at least a day or two." He opened one cage and removed a Siamese. The cat meowed and tried to scratch. Silas stroked it tenderly. "Hold him." Andrew held the animal as Silas removed his Bond and put it around the cat's neck, adjusting it. The cat jumped from Andrew's arms and scampered away. "Now yours."

Andrew backed away. "I can't," he said. "I can't do it." His mouth was dry. He would be cut off from the world without his Bond; he had never removed it except when it was being readjusted.

"Coward. I know what's going to happen to you. You're going to run home, and your mother and father'll make sure their little precious doesn't run away again. And you'll stay there forever. You'll be a hundred years old, and you'll still be there, and you'll never do anything. And you'll always be afraid, just like them."

Andrew swallowed. He took off the Bond while Silas held the other cat. He fumbled with the bracelet and dropped it. "Here, hold the cat," Silas said, sighing. He picked up the Bond and attached it himself, then put the cat on the ground. The creature began to lick a paw.

Andrew was numb. He blinked. Silas pushed him, and he almost fell. "We have to go, Andrew. Another kobold'll be here soon."

* * *

Late that afternoon, they reached a deserted town. Weeds had grown through the cracks in the road. The wooden structures were wrecks. A few had become only piles of lumber; others still stood, brown boards showing through the worn-away paint. Broken windows revealed empty rooms.

They walked slowly through the town. A sudden gust of wind swayed a weeping willow, and Andrew thought he heard a sigh. He shivered and walked more quickly.

A stone house stood at the edge of the town. A low wall surrounded it; the metal gate was open. Silas lingered at the gate, then went through it. The broken pavement leading to the front door was a narrow trail through weeds and tall grass. Andrew followed his friend up the steps. Silas tried the door knob, pushing at the dark wood with his other hand until the door creaked open.

The hallway was empty; dust covered the floor. Andrew sneezed. The floorboards creaked under their feet. Cobwebs shimmered in the corners. They turned to the right and crept into the next room.

Andrew sniffed. "Are we going to stay here? We'll choke." His voice was small and hollow.

Silas glanced around the empty room, then walked over to a tall window facing the front yard. "We can sleep here. If we open the window, we'll have air."

"Maybe we'd better leave it closed." Andrew wondered whether he would prefer a closed window and a dusty room to an open window in the dark. Silas did not seem to hear him; he stared through the filmy window-pane for a moment, then pushed at the window, straining against it until it squeaked open.

"Come here," he said to Andrew. He wandered to the window and peered out over Silas's shoulder. "Look."

"At what?"

Silas pushed his arm. "Don't you see anything, Andrew? Look at the town. It's like it's still alive."

He saw it. The tall grass hid the piles of lumber; only the standing houses were visible, colored by the orange glow of the setting sun. He could walk back to the town and find people preparing supper or gathering in the street. He sighed and backed away, making tracks in the dust as he slid his feet along the floor.

Silas took a shirt out of his knapsack and swept a spot clean. When he was finished, Andrew sat down. Now that he was safe, Andrew felt a little better. He had seen none of the terrible things his parents had warned him against, only old roads, forest, and a deserted town. He said, "I thought it would be worse."

"What?" Silas removed food and water from his knapsack.

"I thought it would be more—I don't know—more dangerous." He shrugged out of his knapsack and stretched.

Silas shook his head. "You listen to your parents too much. Besides, there aren't that many people around here; it's too far north."

"What's that got to do with it?"

"You know. Maybe you don't, because you never went anywhere. They don't like seasons, most of them. They like places where it's always the same. Here, the fall comes, and plants die." Silas said the word *die* harshly, defiantly at Andrew. "They don't like to see that."

Andrew accepted food from his friend, opening his package of stew and letting it heat up for a few moments. Silas smacked his lips as he ate. "Sometimes I hate them," he went on. "They don't do anything. I don't want to be like that." He paused. "Once my father had this party, when we were living in Antigua, and this guy came, I forget his name. Everybody was just sitting around, showing off what languages they knew or flirting. And some of them were making fun of this man in a real quiet way, but he knew they were doing it, he wasn't that dumb."

"Why were they making fun of him?"

"Because he couldn't play their stupid little word games. This one woman started saying that there were people who just weren't very smart, and you could tell who they were because they couldn't learn very much even with a long life and plenty of time, that they just couldn't keep up. She was saying it to this other man, but she knew that other guy heard her, she said it right in front of him."

"What did he do?" Andrew asked.

"Nothing." Silas shrugged. "He looked sad. He left a little later, and I had to go to bed anyway. Know what happened?" He leaned forward. "He went up in this little plane a couple of days later, and he went into a dive and smacked into this house down the road. You should have seen it blow up."

Andrew was too shocked to speak.

"Luckily, nobody was home. The man died, though. Some people said it was an accident, but I don't think most of them believed it. That man knew how to fly. He went diving right in there." Silas slapped his right hand against his left palm.

Andrew shook his head. "That's awful." He looked enviously at his friend, wishing that he too had witnessed such an event.

"At least he did something."

Andrew lifted his head. "But that's terrible." He thought guiltily about his own foray onto the roof outside his window.

"So what? It's terrible. Everybody said so, but it was almost all they ever talked about afterwards. I know for a fact that a lot of them watched the whole thing on their screens later on. A woman was out with her holo equipment just by luck, and she got the whole thing and put it in the system. That's the point, Andrew. He did something, and everybody knew it, and for a while he was the most important guy around."

"And he was so important you forgot his name."

"I was little. Anyway, that's why my father came here. He decided he didn't want to be around a lot of people after that. He kept saying it could have been our house." Silas threw his empty container into the corner and leaned back against the wall, smiling. "That would have been something, if it had been our house. Old Ben wouldn't have ever gotten over it. I'll bet he would have moved us underground."

Andrew pulled up his legs and wrapped his arms around them, imagining a plane streaking through the sky. The room seemed cozy now; the thought of danger beyond made it seem even cozier. Antigua, of course, was safely distant. He looked admiringly at his friend. Silas had seen danger, and nothing had happened to him; Andrew would be safe with his friend.

* * *

Andrew was awake in the darkness. The knapsack under his head was bumpy, and the floor was hard. His muscles ached. He thought of his bed at home.

He supposed he must have slept a little. It had still been light outside when he had gone to sleep. He listened; Silas was breathing unevenly. He felt a movement near him and realized his friend was awake. He was about to speak when he heard a click.

The front door was opening. He stiffened and held his breath. The door creaked. He heard footsteps in the hall, and his ears began to pound.

He wanted to make for the window and get outside, but he could not move. Silas had stopped breathing. The footsteps were coming toward them. He tried to press his back against the floor, as if he could sink between the boards and hide.

A beam of light shot through the darkness, sweeping toward them in an arc. Andrew sat up. The light struck him, and he threw up an arm. He tried to cry out, but let out only a sigh. Silas shouted.

Someone laughed. Andrew blinked, blinded by the light. The footsteps came closer and the light dimmed. The shadowy figure holding it leaned over, set the slender pocket light on the floor, and sat down.

The intruder's face was now illuminated by the light. It was a girl with curly shoulder-length hair. She said, "Who are you?"

Andrew glanced at Silas. "I'm Silas, this is Andrew. We aren't doing anything."

"I can see that. Hold out your arms."

Andrew hesitated.

"Hold them out." Her voice was hard. The boys extended their arms. "You're not wearing Bonds. Good. I don't want a signal going out." She had one hand at her waist; Andrew wondered if she was hurt. Then she withdrew it, and he saw a metal wand. She was armed. He lowered his arms slowly and clutched his elbows.

"We're exploring," Silas said.

"You mean you're running away. I'm running away, too. My name's Thérèse. Who are you running away from?"

"Our parents."

"Why?"

"I told you, we just want to look around."

"Then they're looking for you."

Silas shook his head. "We threw them off the track. If they're looking, they won't look here." Andrew was hoping that his friend was wrong. "Do your parents live around here?"

"I'm not running away from parents." The girl brushed a curl from her forehead. "Where are you from?"

"Oh, a long way from here," Silas answered. "It

took us all day to get here. There's only three houses where we're from; there's just Andrew's parents and my father and one woman who's practically never there. So you don't have to worry." Andrew suspected that the other boy was as frightened as he was.

"I'm not worried." Thérèse reached for the light, then stood up. "I'm going to sleep in the hall. I'll talk to you tomorrow."

The boards groaned under her feet as she left; Andrew heard her close the door. He moved closer to Silas. "We can still go out the window," he whispered.

"What if she comes after us?"

"We can wait until she's asleep."

Silas was silent for a few moments. "Why bother? She's running away, too. We might be safer with her anyway. She has a weapon."

"She might be dangerous."

"I don't know. She's just another kid. If she was really dangerous, she could have lased us right here."

Andrew shuddered. "Maybe we should go home."

"That's all you can think about, isn't it, running home to Joan and Dao." Silas paused. "Something interesting's going on, and you want to hide. Look, if we have to, we can always get away later. All we have to do is go to the nearest house and send out a message, and somebody'll come. Let's go to sleep."

Andrew stretched out on the floor. Silas might be scared, but he would never admit it. He considered escaping by himself, but the thought of traveling alone in the night kept him at Silas's side.

* * *

They shared some dried fruit and water with Thérèse in the morning. Andrew realized that they would run out of food sooner if they divided it three ways. They would have to go home then. That notion cheered him a bit as they set out from town.

In the early morning light, Thérèse did not seem as frightening. He guessed that she was about twelve. She was taller than he was, but her long legs and thin arms were gangly and her chest was flat. Her cheeks were round and pink; strands of reddish-brown hair kept drifting across her face, causing her to shake her head periodically. She carried nothing except her weapon and her light, both tucked in her belt. Her shirt and slacks were dirty, and there were holes in her pants near her knees.

Andrew was on the girl's left; Silas walked at her right. Silas also seemed more at ease. He had joked with Thérèse as they ate, finally eliciting a smile. Thérèse was reserved; Andrew wondered if all girls were like that or only this one. He remembered the girls he had spoken with over the holo and the way a couple of them often looked at him scornfully, as if he were still a little child.

"Why did you run away?" she asked abruptly.

"I told you," Silas answered.

"I mean the real reason. Are your parents cruel, or is it just that they don't seem to care?"

"My father's all right."

"What about your mother?"

"I don't have one, they used stored ova for me."

"What about you?" she said to Andrew.

"I don't know," he replied. "Silas was going, so I went with him."

"That's not a good reason. Don't you like your home?"

"I like it fine."

"You shouldn't have left it, then."

Andrew wanted to ask Thérèse why she had run away.

"Maybe you ought to go back," she went on.

"We'll stick with you," Silas said. "You don't mind, do you?"

"If I minded, I wouldn't be walking with you, now would I?" The girl slowed, peering down the cracked and potholed asphalt. "We shouldn't stay on this road." She turned her head, surveying the area. A bridge was ahead. She pointed. "Maybe we should follow the river."

"Fine with me," Silas said. They left the road, scampering down the hill to the bank. The river flowed west; they climbed over rocks and strolled along the grassy bank.

"How long have you been traveling?" Silas asked.

"Long enough," Thérèse replied. "Since spring. A couple of months."

Silas whistled. The girl tumbled, waving her arms in an attempt to regain her balance. Pebbles rolled down the bank. Andrew reached for her, grabbing her arm. She jerked away violently, almost falling.

The slap stung his cheek. He stepped back. "Don't touch me," Thérèse shouted. "Keep away from me." Her arm was up, as if she was about to hit him again.

"I was trying to help." He crouched, holding out a hand. Thérèse was breathing heavily; her cheeks were flushed. Silas moved away from her and came closer to Andrew. The girl lowered her hands.

"I'm sorry," she said at last. "Don't touch me. Don't get too close to me. I can't stand it. All right?"

Andrew nodded. She turned and marched ahead, not looking back. Silas raised his eyebrows, then followed her. Andrew trailed behind. The look in Thérèse's brown eyes had chilled him; he had not seen the heat of anger or the wide eyes of fear, only a cold look of malice and hatred. He stuffed his hands in his pockets as he walked and kept back, afraid to get too close to Thérèse.

* * *

By noon they had left the river and found a dirt road that wound through wooded hills. Thérèse had remained silent, but she had also managed to smile at a couple of Silas's remarks. Andrew began to whistle a tune, then turned it into the *1812 Overture*. Silas added sound effects, shouting "Boom" at the appropriate moments. Thérèse laughed, but her mouth twisted, as if she found the whole thing silly as well.

Then she stopped, and pointed. Below them, the road dipped. A woman was walking along the road, her back to them, a kobold behind her. Apparently she had not heard them. She was moving toward a clearing; a small house, surrounded by a trimmed lawn, stood back from the road. A maple tree was in front of the house; near it, several flat stones formed a circle on the ground.

Andrew went as close to Thérèse as he dared. "What now?" he said softly.

She frowned. "We can catch up with her."

"But she'll—"

"Come on." She moved ahead quickly, and both boys followed. The woman stopped walking and lifted a slender white cylinder to her lips, lighting it; she was smoking a cigarette. Then she turned and saw them.

Her dark eyes were wide. She dropped the cigarette quickly, as if ashamed that they had seen it, grinding it out with her foot. The kobold drew near her protectively. Its white hair was short, and its eyebrows bushy; it scowled.

Thérèse, approaching, lifted a hand. "Hello."

"Hello?" the woman answered. Her greeting seemed

tentative. She plucked nervously at her long black hair.

The girl moved closer, glancing at the kobold. It drew itself up, adjusting its red cape. Andrew and Silas kept behind Thérèse. Andrew was not afraid of the woman, only of the android, which might move quickly if it thought its mistress was being threatened. He kept his hands at his sides, palms open, in sight of the small creature.

"What do you want?" the woman asked.

Thérèse said, "We need food, and a place to rest. Please help us. We won't bother you, or anything." The girl's voice was higher, gentler than the tone Andrew had heard on the road. The woman gazed at Thérèse's outstretched hands, and her eyelids fluttered; Andrew was sure she had noticed the weapon at the girl's waist.

The woman straightened. She lifted her head and stuck out her chin, as if ready for a confrontation, but her hands trembled. "What are you doing out here?" Her voice was high and weak.

"We're running away," Thérèse said. "We're experiments." Andrew tried not to look surprised; Silas was keeping a straight face. "These biologists were testing us. I know they didn't think they were doing anything mean, but you know how they are. This one man said he'd help us if we got away. So we're on our way to his place."

The woman frowned. "I never heard of such a thing."

"They do a lot they don't talk about. They can do anything they want, because everybody depends on them. Please don't give us away." Thérèse blinked her eyes, as if about to cry.

The woman pressed her hands together. "You poor things. You'd better follow me."

She led them toward her house. Andrew noticed that she was keeping near her kobold.

* * *

The woman's name was Josepha. The inside of her home smelled musty, as if she had been away and only recently returned. She had questioned them, and Thérèse had mumbled vaguely, avoiding answering.

Now the woman sat under her maple tree with a pad, sketching, while the children sat near the house, finishing the food she had given them. Josepha, although seemingly sympathetic, still kept her kobold at her side. The android faced them, hands at its waist.

"Was that true?" Andrew asked Thérèse.

"Was what true?"

"That story about the biologists."

"Of course not." With Josepha in the distance, the girl's voice was once again low and clipped. "It could be true. They made those things, didn't they?" She gestured at the kobold; it lifted its head.

"That isn't the same as experiments with people."

"What would you know about it?" Thérèse replied. "They made them, they made us, they used the same genetic material. They just make different modifications. What's the difference?"

"There's a lot of difference," Andrew protested, thinking of the dead kobold in the woods near his home. "They're limited, they can't do much without direction."

"I had to tell her something," Thérèse murmured. "It doesn't matter whether she believes it or not."

"Why not?"

"Because she won't do anything. First of all, we're kids, so she feels protective. Second, she's afraid. She won't do anything that might put her in danger, and that's why she won't alert anyone. The older people get, the fewer risks they take. Why do you think she's hiding away here? She's afraid. She'll do what we want. By the time she gets around to checking, and finding out we lied, we'll be long gone. It takes them ages to make up their minds to do something anyway."

Silas finished his roll and leaned back. "Why take the chance?" he asked.

"I just finished telling you, it isn't a chance. She doesn't want to be threatened. I could wing her with this laser before that kobold stopped me, all it's got is a tranquilizer gun. They'd rather have their life than anything, those people, they beg for mercy, they do anything to avoid death."

Andrew felt sick. Thérèse's words were coarse and disgusting.

"Anyway, she's one of the scared ones," Thérèse continued. "I saw that right away. I've been running longer than you have. I need real food and a good night's sleep. Don't worry, I've done this before, and no one's caught me yet." Her voice was calmer.

"Why'd you run away, Thérèse?" Andrew asked.

She was staring past him, curling her lip. She was very quiet; he could not even hear her breathe. "I had my reasons," she said at last. She pressed her lips together and said no more.

* * *

They slept in Josepha's living room. That was where the woman had her holo screen and computer. The girl shook them awake at dawn. She had slept on a mat spread out on the carpet, leaving the large sofa to the boys. Andrew picked up his knapsack and hoisted it to his back while Silas yawned and stretched.

"We'd better get going," Thérèse whispered. She

propped Josepha's drawing pad against the back of the sofa. She had written a message on it:

Dear Josepha,

Thank you for the food, and especially for the bath. We really are grateful. We're going to head west now to find our friend. Maybe he'll call and thank you himself when we're settled. We'll be thinking of you.

Terry, Simon, and Drew

Andrew had thought they'd been clever with their aliases; now, seeing them written out, they seemed a poor disguise. The words had been scrawled in a large, childish hand. Thérèse had transformed herself for Josepha, becoming a victimized and gentle child; she had played the role so well that even he had almost believed it. He and Silas had been merely the supporting players in the performance.

Thérèse signaled to them. They crept from the house, passing the kobold at the front door. The android looked up. "May I help you?" it asked.

The girl stopped. She seemed sad as she looked at the kobold. She raised one hand slowly and patted the kobold on the head. It smiled. "Is she good to you?" Thérèse asked. "Are you treated well?"

"May I help you? I can guide you to the road."

The girl drew back. "No; we're all right. Goodbye."

"Good-bye. It was nice to see you." It waved with one small hand.

The three headed across the lawn to the road. "Are we really going west?" Andrew asked.

"Of course not," the girl answered. "We're going north. Fewer people." She paused. "Maybe you two ought to go back. Josepha could get you home." She said the words stiffly, as if she did not mean them.

Silas said, "We'll stick with you."

She seemed relieved. They hiked along the road silently. The morning air was damp and cool; Andrew shivered. He wondered if his parents were looking for him now, if they had found out about the cats. Then he realized that they would probably search south first, because Silas had always talked about how things were better there.

Silas had fallen under Thérèse's spell. His friend followed her contentedly, as if happy to have found a leader. The ease of his surrender had surprised Andrew. He had thought of Silas as decisive; now he wondered if his friend had ever decided much of anything. His past actions now seemed to be only a surrender to his feelings.

He glanced at the girl as they walked. What would she do if they were found? She seemed desperate. He thought of how she had pulled away and slapped him, of how she had talked about death. She knew about him and Silas, but they knew nothing about her. Would she have hurt Josepha if the woman had tried to summon others? The girl had sounded as if she would, yet she had treated Josepha's android with kindness.

They left the road and began to climb a hill. It was dark under the trees; leaves rustled as they climbed. Thérèse's pockets bulged with cheese and dried fruit which she had taken from Josepha; she swayed as she moved. Andrew ached, though not as much as the day before.

Silas moved closer to him. "I keep thinking about my father," he said between breaths. "He must be worried. I think about it now, and it seems awful. I keep wondering why I didn't think of it before. I mean, I thought about it, but in a way I didn't."

"Does it bother you?" Andrew asked. Thérèse had moved farther ahead of them, setting her feet down heavily and awkwardly as if trying to flatten the earth. Her knees were thrust out; the upper part of her body was bent forward.

"I don't know," Silas said. "As long as I don't have to see it, it's like it isn't there. It's hard to explain. If I went home, I'd see how upset he is, and then I'd feel rotten, but here I don't see it. I know the sooner I go back, the better it'll be for him, but I'm afraid to go back, because then I'll have to see him getting mad and upset, and I don't want to."

"We have to go back sooner or later," Andrew murmured.

"I know." Silas sighed. "I didn't think of that, either. All I thought about was getting away and wandering around." He glanced up at Thérèse. Then he looked at Andrew for a moment. His eyes pleaded silently.

Andrew thought: He wants me to decide. Thérèse stopped and turned around, folding her arms across her chest as she waited for them to reach her. For a moment, she looked older. Her eyes were aged and knowing; her face was set in a bitter smile. The wind stirred the tree limbs above, and shadows dappled her face, forming a mask over her eyes.

* * *

In the evening, it began to rain. They found shelter under an outcropping of rock. The rain applauded them as it hit the ground.

Andrew and Silas relieved themselves, pointing their penises at the rain beyond, then sat down. The ground was hard and stony, but dry. They ate their cheese and fruit in silence, then curled up to sleep.

Andrew dozed fitfully. His legs were cramped; if he stretched them, his feet would be in the rain. He stirred, trying to get comfortable. Something pressed against him in the dark.

"It's me," Thérèse whispered. He stiffened, afraid. Silas was asleep; he could hear his slight snort as he inhaled. "Just don't grab at me, that's all. All right?"

"Sure," he whispered back.

She pressed her chest against his spine, draping an arm over him. Her body shook slightly and she sniffed. He heard her swallow.

"Thérèse. Are you all right?"

"I'm fine."

"You're crying."

"No, I'm not." Her body was still. He turned over on his back, raising his knees, careful not to touch her with his hands, and settled his head against the knapsack. He was growing hard; he covered his groin with one hand, confused, afraid she would notice.

"Listen," he said softly, "maybe you should go home." Her hand clutched his abdomen absent-mindedly; he froze and went limp. "You could stay at my house first, if you want, or with Silas. They wouldn't mind."

"I can't go home." He felt her breath on his ear. "Do you understand? Not ever. This isn't some adventure for me. I'll always have to hide."

"But you can't stay out here."

"I can. It's better than what I had. They'll stop looking when I'm—"

Andrew waited for her to finish. He heard her sigh. She removed her arm. "I won't give you away," he whispered. "I promise."

She was silent. The rain was not as heavy now; the stream of water rushing down from the outcropping had become a trickle. I'm your friend, Thérèse. He mouthed the words silently in the dark.

* * *

They stood at the top of a hill, facing north. The pine trees were thick around them; Andrew could catch only glimpses of the rolling land below.

Thérèse said, "Give me a boost." Silas cupped his hands; she raised a foot, and he boosted her to a tree limb. She scrambled up and gazed out at the landscape. Andrew watched her, afraid she might fall, and wondering if he should get out of the way. She crouched, hung by the limb with her hands, and dropped to the ground.

"There's a house down there," she said. "We can stop there, or go around it." She bowed her head.

"What do you want to do?" Andrew asked.

"I'm asking you." She did not look at him. "I'm going to have to move on sooner or later by myself, you know that. I don't want to get too attached to you."

Silas looked at Andrew. Andrew did not reply. The girl turned and started down the hill, motioning for them to follow. Andrew thought about Thérèse continuing on her lonely journey. She had traveled alone before meeting them. She could handle herself, but the idea still bothered him.

Why did she have to hide, living on the edge of the world? Maybe she hadn't lied about being part of an experiment. Once Dao had told him that some people were afraid of the biologists because they were dependent, all of them, on the scientists' skill. They were kept immortal by them; they were afraid to have the few children they did without the biologists' help. The dependency engendered fear. Thérèse must have made up the story after all.

There were, however, the kobolds and the trolls. He

had never thought much about them. He recalled the way Thérèse had looked at Josepha's kobold, as if she were speaking to a person rather than to a being of limited intelligence. Were the androids aware of what had been done to them? Did dim notions cross their minds before being drowned out by their cybernetic links or the commands of their masters?

Andrew went down the hillside cautiously, avoiding the uneven ground and loose stones. He could now see the house. It was a two-story wooden structure, painted white; it stood a few meters from a dirt road overgrown with weeds and wildflowers. The land immediately around the house was dusty and barren, as if plants refused to take root there. A smaller building, with peeling paint, stood in back of the house.

They came to the bottom of the hill and walked up the road. "I don't think there's anyone there," Andrew said.

The girl glanced at him. "Do you think you could find your way home?" she asked.

"I guess we could. We could always go back to Josepha's house."

"You'd have to tell her we lied. It doesn't matter. I'd have a head start." They walked over the dusty ground toward the house. The lifelessness of the land around the structure was disturbing. Andrew suddenly wanted to flee.

The front door opened. Something fluttered in the darkness beyond the outer screen door. Andrew moved behind Thérèse. The screen door swung open and a kobold emerged, followed by a woman. She wore a long white dress with a high collar; she crossed the porch and stood on the top step, watching them.

Thérèse held her arms out; the boys did the same. "Hello," the girl called out.

"Why, hello." The woman waved. "Come on up here, let me take a look at you."

Thérèse hesitated. She balanced on the balls of her feet, as if ready to run. She moved a little closer to the steps. "Come on up," the woman said again. "Sit here, on the porch. I haven't had visitors in quite a while."

They went up the steps and seated themselves on the wicker chairs. The woman rested against the railing in front of them. The kobold stood near her protectively; it carried a silver wand. Andrew frowned; he noticed that Thérèse had also seen the weapon. The android's blue shirt and pants were wrinkled; its face was marred by a large nose and wide mouth. The woman beamed, unafraid.

"You poor things," the woman said. "You look as though you've had quite a trip."

"We have," Thérèse said. Now that Andrew was closer to the woman, he could see her face. There was something wrong with it; deep lines were etched around her mouth and eyes, and her jowls shook slightly as she spoke. Her skin was rough and yellowish. Even her hair was strange. She had pulled it back from her face, showing the grey streaks around her forehead and ears.

"Your face," Andrew blurted out before he could stop himself.

The woman glared at him for a moment, then smiled again. "You think it's ugly," she said slowly. "You think it's odd. Not all of us want to look twentyish. I like to look my age." She chuckled, as if she had made a joke. "What are all of you doing way out here?"

Thérèse licked her lips. "We're running away."

"Running away. How sad. I suppose you must have a reason." She held up her hand. "You needn't tell me what it is. People are so thoughtless. I wouldn't let any children of mine run away. You look as though you could use a good meal. Come on inside."

She led them into the house. The front room was small, but clean. Lace doilies covered the arms of the worn blue sofa and chairs; two heavy brass lamps stood on end tables. The desk computer and holo screen were against the wall.

"You just sit down and take it easy. My name's Emily. I'll go get you something from the kitchen." She squinted. "You're not wearing your Bonds."

"Of course not," Thérèse said. "We're running away."

"I'll be right back."

"We'll come with you." They followed the woman to the kitchen and sat at the small wooden table while Emily punched buttons on her console.

"I know what you're thinking," Emily said, turning to face them while the food was materializing. "You thought I might have a communicator here. You thought I'd send for someone. Well, I won't. I didn't move out here so that I could have people dropping in all the time. I don't like people." She grinned. "I like children, though. If you want to go running around the countryside, that's fine with me, but you can stay here as long as you like."

She removed the food, took out bowls, and spooned vegetable soup into them, putting them on the table with glasses of milk and a small loaf of bread. She sat down and watched them as they ate. Andrew forgot his worries, eating the soup rapidly, slurping as he ate.

Emily nodded at them approvingly when they were done. Something in the gesture reminded him of Joan.

He tried not to think of his return home. He would get through it somehow, and then it would be over. For now, he was safe.

* * *

They slept in the front room. Thérèse had claimed the sofa; Emily had provided two cots.

The girl was awake early. She bumped against Andrew's cot as she rose; he opened his eyes and sat up. He watched as she took food and water from one knapsack and put it in the other.

He said, "You're leaving."

"I left you some stuff in the other sack, enough to get you by."

"You're leaving."

"You knew I was going to sooner or later."

Silas was still sleeping, arm over his eyes. "Listen to me, Andrew," she went on quietly. "I think you should wake him up and get going yourselves."

"Emily'll help us."

"There's something funny about her. I don't think you should stay here. I have to go." She moved toward the door, then looked back at him. "Andrew, if anybody tells you anything about me someday, just remember that it isn't how it seems. I mean, I wouldn't have hurt you two, I really wouldn't have."

"I know that."

"Good-bye. Say good-bye to Silas for me, will you? And get out of here yourselves." She opened the screen door and went out.

He got out of bed and followed. The kobold was outside the door. It let Thérèse pass, trailing her to the steps. A troll sat in front of the house, its long arms folded on the ground. Thérèse bounded down the steps and walked toward the road.

The troll rose and moved rapidly, scampering in front of the girl. She hopped to one side; it blocked her. She stood still for a few seconds, swaying, then hurried to her left. The troll ran, blocking her again.

"Let me pass," he heard her say to the creature. She stepped forward, and it hit her. She backed toward the porch.

Andrew watched, confused and apprehensive. Thérèse turned and faced him. Her chest rose and fell; her pink cheeks were becoming rosier. She squinted and shook her head. She spun around suddenly and danced to her right. The troll blocked her again; it was too fast for her.

Her hand fluttered at her waist. She removed her wand, pointing it at her antagonist. Andrew saw a flash of light; Thérèse cried out. For a moment, he did not know what had happened. The girl swayed helplessly, holding her right arm. The kobold darted past her and swept up the rod on the ground.

Andrew hurried back to Silas and shook him awake. The other boy moaned.

"Silas. Get up."

"What?" He shook his head and stared blankly at Andrew.

"Thérèse. The kobold shot at her."

Silas was awake. He jumped from the cot, following Andrew to the door. Thérèse had retreated to the porch, still holding her hand.

"Are you hurt?" Andrew asked as he opened the door.

"No. Just my fingers. I'm all right."

"Listen, there's three of us. If we can distract the androids, maybe you can get away."

She shook her head. "I can't do that. I don't have my

weapon now. This is my fault, I got careless. We should have left as soon as I saw she wasn't afraid."

"We'll be all right," Andrew said. "She probably just told them to guard us. As soon as she wakes up—"

"How do you know that?" Thérèse interrupted. "How do you know she isn't trying to keep us here?"

He didn't know. He went back inside and crossed the room to the console. He pressed a button.

"Code, please," the computer responded.

The machine was locked. Andrew shivered, backing away. Thérèse and Silas had come back inside.

"It won't work," he muttered. Thérèse was staring past him.

"How are my young visitors this morning?"

Andrew turned. Emily stood at the entrance to the room. She wore a gingham gown; her greying hair was loose around her shoulders. Another small kobold stood at her side; it too was armed.

Thérèse drew herself up, eying the woman belligerently. "We appreciate your hospitality," she said slowly. "We'd like to be on our way."

"Not so soon. I haven't had visitors in ever so long. Do take off that knapsack, and I'll get breakfast ready."

"We'd like to leave now," Thérèse said.

"But you can't."

"Why not?" Silas said loudly. His voice was high, breaking on the second word.

"Because I'm not ready to let you go." Emily smiled as she spoke. "Now sit down. What would you like? Let's have pancakes. That would be tasty, now wouldn't it?"

Thérèse moved toward the woman, stopping when the kobold extended an arm, pointing at her with its weapon. Its black eyes narrowed. "You'd better be careful," Emily went on. "They're very protective of me, and

I wouldn't want you hurt because of a silly mistake. Now sit down and stop being naughty. I'll get breakfast."

* * *

They spent the day in the living room, guarded by the kobolds. Andrew had been unable to eat breakfast or lunch; Silas had lapsed into a sullen silence. Thérèse kept wandering over to the window, as if searching for a way to escape. Occasionally Emily would come to the door, smiling in at them solicitously. In the afternoon, she brought them a Chain of Life puzzle. Silas applied himself to it, assembling the pieces until he had part of the helix put together, then abandoned the puzzle to Andrew.

Andrew worked silently, trying to lose himself in concentration. The kobolds, standing nearby, watched without speaking. Once in a while, he looked up. The black-eyed android held its weapon with one hand while stroking its dark beard with the other. The blond one near the screen door was still. They were both ugly, the ugliest kobolds he had ever seen; it was as if Emily, with her own lack of beauty, wanted nothing beautiful around her. He wondered if she had made the creatures mute as well.

Andrew broke down at suppertime. Food had been laid out on the coffee table next to the helix. He stuffed himself, not tasting anything; Silas picked at his chicken while Emily hovered, beaming at them. Then she settled herself in a chair and sipped wine. She wore her white dress, but the setting sun in the window made the dress seem pink.

Thérèse was not eating. She scowled at the woman and drummed her fingers on the arm of the sofa. A finger caught in the doily. Thérèse tore at the lace, and it fluttered to the floor.

Thérèse said, "Give me some wine."

"Aren't you a little young for that, dear?"

"Give me some wine."

Emily poured more of the pale liquid into her glass and handed it to the girl. Thérèse downed it in two gulps and held out the glass. The woman poured more wine. Thérèse leaned back. Her face was drawn.

Andrew's stomach felt heavy and too full. Silas, seated cross-legged on the floor, had stopped eating. Emily said, "Would you like to hear a story?"

"No," Andrew replied.

"I'll tell you one, and then maybe you can tell me one."

Thérèse raised her glass, peering over it at the woman. She said, "Go ahead, tell it. It better be good."

"Oh, it is." Emily sat up. "It's very good. It's about a lovely young woman, like a princess in a fairy tale."

The young people were silent. Emily stared at the helix for a moment. "Once, there was a lovely young woman," she began. "She lived in a beautiful house on the edge of a great city, but she was very sad, because the world beyond was cruel and hard. Even in her citadel, the evil of the world outside could reach her. It was as if everyone was under an evil spell; a dark spirit would come upon them, and they would go to war. Do you know what a war is?"

No one replied.

"That's when people take all their talent and organize themselves to kill other people. Well, one day, something wonderful happened. The wars stopped. They stopped because some people had found a way to keep from dying. Now, before that, they had already found a way to stop people from aging as rapidly; they had a substance that cleared out all the protein cross-linkages."

"We know about that," Andrew said impatiently.

Emily shot him a glance. "Hush, child. Let me finish. These people had found a way to make everyone younger. You see, they were trying to find out about cancer, and they learned a lot about cells, and they found that they could stimulate the body to rejuvenate itself and become younger. No longer did our genetic structure condemn us. When people realized that they could live forever, the world changed. It was made beautiful by those who knew that now they would have to remain in it forever. We call that time the Transition."

Andrew fidgeted. Thérèse sipped her wine. Emily's long fingers stroked the arms of her chair; her pale hands had small brown spots around the blue veins.

"The young woman was happy. She opened her house to others, and they all spoke of the new age, their escape from death. But then the young woman began to grow weak. Soon she discovered that evil was still in her body. A malignancy was growing within her, her cells were out of control." Emily paused. "It didn't matter. The growth was soon inhibited by another substance, which enabled her immune system to control the disease. But later, when she received her rejuvenation treatments once more, the cancer returned. Her body was a battleground; her own cells were at war."

Emily's voice was trembling. Andrew moved a bit closer to Thérèse.

"Do you understand?" The woman's voice was firm again. "It was as if the woman had been cursed. When she received the treatment that would allow her to live, the disease returned, because the same process that caused her body to renew itself allowed those cells to grow. When she took interferon—that is what controlled the disease—she would be well, but growing older. Do you understand now? Each time, she grew a bit older physically than she had been; she was aging—very slowly, to be sure, but aging nonetheless. There were others who had the same problem, but she did not care about them."

The woman tilted her head. "She became a project," she went on. "Biologists studied her. They discovered that she had a defective gene. The substance that enabled her body to rejuvenate itself triggered a response, and cancerous cells would multiply along with those that made her younger. Now these scientists were able to keep this gene from being passed on to others, but they could do little for the woman. They tried but nothing worked."

Andrew sat very still, almost afraid to breathe. Thérèse threw her head back and finished her second glass of wine. Silas cleared his throat uneasily.

"The young woman left the world," Emily said. "She didn't want to be where she could see the youthful bodies and cheerful spirits of others. When she had clung to hope, she had drifted into depression and deep sorrow. Now she released her hopes and accepted her situation and found a freedom in so doing. Denied life—denied, at least, a full life—she would accept death, and find peace in the acceptance. So, you see, the story has a happy ending after all."

Emily's green eyes glittered. For a moment, her face seemed younger in the evening light.

Thérèse spoke. "The woman can still stay alive. She can still be helped. It's her own fault if she gives up. More is known now, isn't it?"

Emily smiled. "You don't understand. Hope was too painful. Even healthy ones sometimes seek death, even now, you know that. The evil hasn't disappeared, but it too has its consolations, even its own beauty. Flowers are beautiful because they die, aren't they? And isn't there a special poignancy in thinking of something you've lost? It's a mercy. That's what people used to say about death sometimes, it's a mercy. It was a good death. He didn't linger, he isn't suffering now, he's gone to meet his Maker, he's cashed in his chips, he's gone to his reward. Many of the old expressions were quite cheerful." She lowered her chin. "There is little new knowledge now, only tinkering, little workshops where they play with genes and make things like those." She waved a hand at one of the kobolds. "Something else died when we decided to live, and that was great change. There is no hope for the woman, but it doesn't matter. There is a happy ending, you see. There, I've told you a story. Now you can tell me one."

Silas looked up at Andrew apprehensively. Andrew lifted his head, unable to gaze directly at Emily. "We don't have a story," he mumbled.

"Come now. Of course you do, all alone in the middle of nowhere without your Bonds."

"No, we don't."

"Maybe your girl friend has one, then. Don't you, Terry? Why don't you tell it?"

Thérèse held out her glass. "Give me a drink first."

"You've had quite enough," Emily said, but she poured more wine anyway. Thérèse rose and walked over to the window; the dark-haired kobold moved closer to the woman. Thérèse turned around.

"All right. I'll tell you a story." She took a breath. "A girl was living with a man. She'd lived with him all her life. He wasn't her biological father, but he was the only parent she had ever known. He'd brought her home and cared for her ever since she'd been born." Her voice shook a bit as she spoke.

"A rather abrupt preface," Emily said. "But do go on."

"At first, he was kind. Then he changed. He began to come to her room at night. He'd make her do things, and sometimes he hurt her. It got to where she sometimes even liked the pain, because he'd be sorry for a while afterwards, and he'd be nicer when he was sorry, and do what she wanted. But then it would start again. She tried to run away, but he hurt her badly, and she was afraid to try again. It was all her fault. That's what he made her think. Everything he did was her fault, because something in her led him to do it."

Thérèse's voice did not tremble now; it was flat and toneless. She perched on the window sill; her face was shadowed.

"She was still growing. She began to change. The man didn't like that, because he didn't like women, only girls. So he began to give her the same thing that kept him young. It was tricky, but he managed. No one found out. They lived alone, and not many people saw her. He was only doing what the biologists do, wasn't he? He was shaping a body to be what he wanted, that's all, that's how he looked at it. The years went by, and the girl grew older, while still remaining a child. The man began to forget that she wasn't what she seemed."

Thérèse gulped the rest of her wine and set the glass on the sill. "The girl was careful. She watched the man and bided her time. One day, she was able to escape, and she did. My story has a happy ending, too."

Andrew realized that he was digging his fingers into his thighs. He tried to relax. Emily was watching the girl out of the sides of her eyes.

"You didn't tell the whole story," the woman said at last. Thérèse shook her head. "Tell the rest. The girl didn't just run, did she? She killed the man while making her escape, didn't she?"

Thérèse did not reply.

"They're looking for her. She's still missing. She killed someone. You know what they'll do when she's found? They'll send her up." Emily pointed at the sky. "They'll exile her, they'll send her to a prison asteroid, with all the other murderers. She'll have to stay there. After a year of low gravity, she'll need an exoskeleton to live on Earth again. There won't be a happy ending if she's caught."

Thérèse moved her arm, hitting the glass. It fell to the floor, shattering. Andrew started. Emily rose. "Enough stories for tonight, don't you think? It's time to rest now."

She left. The bearded kobold remained; the blond one went out on the porch and stood in front of the screen door. Andrew got up and went to Thérèse. "It isn't true."

She said nothing.

"It isn't true, Thérèse. They won't send you away, they can't."

She pushed him aside and threw herself across one of the cots. He hovered at her side, wanting to touch her, but afraid to do so. She hid her face. Her body was very still.

The kobold made a sound. "Others," it said and Andrew started. "Others, before. Other visitors. Gone now. Go to sleep."

The raspy voice made Andrew shiver. Silas stood. He picked up a plate and smashed it on the floor. Thérèse turned her head. Silas broke another plate. "Stop," the kobold said.

Andrew went to his friend. "Silas." He reached for

the shadowy shape and held the other boy by the shoulders.

Silas shook his head and pushed Andrew away. "I'm all right now." He sat down on the sofa. Thérèse was lying on her side, her hip a dark hyperbola obscuring part of the window.

Silas lifted his chin. "Did you really do it?"

"Do what?" Her voice was flat.

"What she said."

"I didn't mean to. I was trying to get away. He tried to stop me. He should have let me go. When it was over, I was glad. I'm glad he's dead." The cot squeaked as she settled herself. "Go to sleep."

"Go to sleep," the kobold echoed.

Silas said, "We have to get out of here."

Thérèse did not answer. Andrew stretched out on the other cot. The girl seemed resigned. He realized that Thérèse had only exile to anticipate, more wandering or a prison world. He heard footsteps in the hall; they faded, and the back door slammed. The house was quiet; outside, crickets chirped. There was light just beyond the window; the moon had risen.

Silas got up and went around the cots to the window. He put his elbows on the sill. The small shape outside the screen door disappeared; a small head appeared near Silas, making him look, for a moment, like a two-headed creature. Silas stood up.

"Come out," the blond kobold on the porch said. It was a black shadow with a silver nimbus around its head. "Come outside."

Silas backed away. The bearded kobold crossed to the screen door. "Go on," it whispered, as if conspiring with them.

Silas came closer to Andrew. "They want to help us."

Andrew shook his head. "No, they don't. They don't want to do anything. Emily tells them what to do. Don't listen to them."

"If I could get away, I could get help. It's worth a try, isn't it?"

"Don't go outside, Silas." He looked toward Thérèse. "You tell him. Tell him not to go."

"Andrew's right," Thérèse said from the cot.

"They said there were others," Silas replied. "Maybe they helped them get away."

"You're wrong. Kobolds can only do what they're told; they have to be directed. They don't have minds." But Andrew heard the doubt in the girl's voice.

"It's worth a chance, isn't it?" Silas said. "Maybe you don't want to go because you know what's going to happen to you when you're caught. You don't want help to come. You don't care what happens to us."

"Don't go," Andrew said.

Silas leaned over him; Andrew could feel his breath. "It's your fault, too." Andrew shrank back, puzzled. "You should have stopped me before, if you hadn't come along, I wouldn't be on this trip. And it's her fault for having us stop here. I'm not going to stay because of what you tell me." He walked to the door; the bearded kobold let him pass. The screen door slammed behind Silas.

Thérèse slid off her cot and stood up. The kobold made a circle with its wand. She moved closer to the creature and it pointed the wand at her. Andrew rolled off his cot toward the sofa, trying to decide what to do. Thérèse backed to the window. The android's head turned.

Andrew's hand was reaching for the brass lamp near

him. He pulled out the cord. He seemed to be moving very slowly. Thérèse lifted a hand to her face. He picked up the lamp. The kobold was pivoting on one foot. He saw its face as he leaped, bringing the base of the lamp down on its head.

It squeaked. The wand flew from its hand, clattering across the floor. Andrew hit it again and it was still as it fell, its limbs stiff. He dropped the lamp and began to shake.

Thérèse was breathing heavily. "You took a chance," she said. "You really took a chance." She knelt and began to crawl over the floor. "I have to find that weapon."

"Use your light."

"I lost my light."

Andrew remembered Silas. He went to the door. Thérèse was slapping the floor. He breathed the night air and smelled dirt and pollen. Opening the door cautiously, he went out on the porch; his skin prickled as a cool breeze touched him.

The blond kobold was below, in front of the porch. Silas was running across the barren yard, kicking up dust. The troll was blocking him, leaping from side to side and waving its long arms as if playing with the boy. Silas darted to the left, but the creature was too quick for him. It herded him, driving him back toward the house. The boy hopped and danced, coming closer to Andrew.

Andrew came down the steps, pausing on the bottom one. The kobold saw him. He could hear Silas panting; there were shiny streaks on his friend's face. The troll put its hands on the ground and swung between them on its arms, lifting its knees to its chest. It grinned, showing its crooked teeth. Then Andrew saw Emily.

The woman had come around the side of the house and now stood to Andrew's left, watching the pursuit.

Her white dress shone in the moonlight and fluttered in the breeze. She raised her hands as if casting a spell, and Andrew saw that she was holding a wand.

He opened his mouth to cry out. His throat locked; he rasped as breath left him. The woman pointed her wand. The beam struck Silas in the chest. He fell. Andrew heard a scream.

He stared numbly at his friend. A black spot was covering Silas, flowing over his chest; his eyes gazed heavenward. "Silas?" Andrew murmured. He swayed on the steps. "Silas?" The troll stood up; the kobold stood near Silas's head. Dust had settled in the boy's thick hair.

Emily was walking toward him, still holding the wand. She was smiling; the blue stone of her Bond seemed to wink. Andrew faced her, unable to move. His limbs were heavy; invisible hands pressed against him. He saw one white arm rise.

A beam brightened the night. Andrew gasped. Emily was falling. Andrew clutched at his abdomen and spun around, almost falling from the step. Thérèse was climbing through the window; her feet hit the porch. She came to the railing and leaned over it, firing at Emily with her weapon. The white dress was stained. The kobold raised its wand. Andrew dived for it as it fired, and heard a cry. He wrested the weapon from it and knocked the creature aside.

Thérèse was screaming. She continued to fire at Emily. One beam struck the woman in the leg; another burned through her head. One arm jerked. The stone on Emily's Bond was black. Thérèse kept shooting, striking the ground near the body.

His vision blurred for a moment. He found himself next to the girl. "Thérèse, stop." She cried out as he reached for her and held out her left arm. Her hand was a burned, bloody claw; he gasped and touched her right shoulder. She tore herself from him and went down the steps to Silas. She knelt in the dirt, patting his face with her right hand.

"I was too late," she said. She was crying. The kobold sat up, rubbing its head. Andrew gripped his wand, aimed it at the android, then let his arm drop. The troll scampered to the side of its dead mistress. It lifted her in its arms and held her. A sudden gust whipped Andrew's hair; he caught the metallic smell of blood in the summer's dust.

* * *

Joan tried to stop Andrew at the door.

"Where are you going?"

"I want to say good-bye to Thérèse."

Joan frowned. "I don't think you should."

"She's my friend."

"She killed two people." Joan's voice tripped over the word *kill*. "She's very ill."

"She's not. She did what she had to do. She had to kill Emily."

Joan stepped back. "That woman was very disturbed, Andrew. She needed help, reconditioning. She was ill."

"She wasn't ill. She was going to die, and so she wanted other people to die, too, that's all." He thought of Emily's body in the dirt, and his throat tightened; Thérèse had cursed their rescuers when they destroyed Emily's kobold and troll. The troll had looked at Andrew before it died, and he had thought he saw awareness in its eyes.

Joan took him by the shoulders. Her eyes were narrowed; her lips were pulled back over her teeth. "You'll forget all this. The psychologist will be here tomorrow, and that will be that. You'll think differently about this incident."

He twisted away and went out the door. Dao was outside. He let Andrew pass.

A tent had been put up at the bottom of the hill, a temporary shelter for Thérèse and the two psychologists who were now with her. They had questioned the girl and interrogated him; they had set up a tent because Joan had been afraid to have the girl in her house. Now they would take Thérèse away. The evil in his world would be smoothed over, explained and rationalized. Thérèse would not be sent to an asteroid; only people who were hopelessly death-loving were sent there, and even they could change, given enough time. That was what the female psychologist had told him. They had high hopes for Thérèse; she was young enough to heal. They would help her construct a new personality. The mental scars would disappear; the cruelty would be forgotten. Andrew thought of it, and it seemed like death; the Thérèse he knew would no longer exist.

Thérèse came out of the tent as he approached. The brown-skinned woman followed her; the red-haired man was near their hovercraft, putting things away. Thérèse reached for Andrew's hand and held it for a moment before releasing it. The psychologist lingered near them.

"I want to talk to him alone," Thérèse said. "Don't worry, you'll find out all my secrets soon enough." The woman withdrew. Thérèse led Andrew inside the tent.

They sat down on an air mattress. The girl looked down at the Bond on her right wrist. "Can't get this one off so easily," she muttered. Her mouth twisted. She gestured with her bandaged left hand. "They're going to fix my hand first," she went on. "It'll be just the way it was, no scars."

He said, "I don't want you to go."

"It won't be so bad. They told me I'd be happier. It's probably true. They're nice people."

Andrew glanced at her. "Ben might clone Silas. That's what he told Dao. He's thinking about it. He's going to go away."

"It won't be Silas."

"I know."

Thérèse shook back her hair. "I guess I won't remember much of this. It'll be like a dream."

"I don't want you to forget. I won't. I promise. I don't want to forget you. Thérèse. I don't care. You're the only friend I have now."

She frowned. "Make some new friends. Don't just wait around for someone else to tell you what to do." She paused. "I could have just aimed at her arm, you know. Then she would have still been alive."

"She was dying anyway."

"They could have helped her eventually. She was dying very slowly. I didn't have to kill Rani, either." Her eyes were wide; she stared past him. "I didn't. He was down, he begged me to stop. I kept hitting him with the poker until his skull caved in. I wanted to be sure he wouldn't come after me. I was glad, too. I was glad he was dead and I was still alive."

"No," Andrew said.

"Stop it." She dug her fingers into his shoulder. "You said you didn't want to forget me. If you don't see me the way I am, you've forgotten me already. Do you understand?"

He nodded, and she released him. His eyes stung; he blinked. "Listen, Andrew. We'll be all right. We'll grow up, and we'll be alive forever. When everyone lives forever, then sooner or later they have to meet everyone else, don't they? If we live long enough, we're bound to see each other again, it'll be like starting all over."

He did not reply.

"It's true, you know it's true. Stop looking like that." She jabbed him with her elbow. "Say good-bye, Andrew. I don't want you hanging around when we leave. I won't be able to stand it."

"Good-bye, Thérèse."

"Good-bye." She touched his arm. He got up and lifted the tent flap. He wanted to look back at her; instead, he let the flap drop behind him.

He climbed the hill, trying to imagine endless life. Joan and Dao were on the porch, waiting for him. He thought of Silas. You'll always be afraid, just like them; that was what his friend had said. No, Andrew told himself; not any more. His friend's face was suddenly before him, vivid; Joan and Dao were only distant, ghostly shapes, trying to face up to forever.

(1981)

Out of Place

> "For something is amiss or out of place
> When mice with wings can wear a human face."
> —Theodore Roethke,
> "The Bat"

Marcia was washing the breakfast dishes when she first heard her cat thinking. "I'm thirsty, why doesn't she give me more water, there's dried food on the sides of my bowl." There was a pause. "I wonder how she catches the food. She can't stalk anything, she always scares the birds away. She never catches any when I'm nearby. Why does she put it into those squares and round things when she just has to take it out again? What is food, anyway? What is water?"

Very slowly, Marcia put down the cup she was washing, turned off the water, and faced the cat. Pearl, a slim Siamese, was sitting by her plastic bowls. She swatted the newspaper under them with one paw, then stretched out on her side. "I want to be combed, I want my stomach scratched. Why isn't he here? He always goes away. They should both be here, they're supposed to serve me." Pearl's mouth did not move, but Marcia knew the words were hers. For one thing, there was no one else in the house. For another, the disembodied voice had a feline whine to it, as if the words were almost, but not quite, meows.

Oh, God, Marcia thought, I'm going crazy. Still eyeing the cat, she crept to the back door and opened it. She inhaled some fresh air and felt better. A robin was pecking at the grass. "Earth, yield your treasures to me. I hunger, my young cry out for food." This voice had a musical lilt. Marcia leaned against the door frame.

"I create space." The next voice was deep and sluggish. "The universe parts before me. It is solid and dark and damp, it covers all, but I create space. I approach the infinite. Who has created it? A giant of massive dimensions must have moved through the world, leaving the infinite. It is before me now. The warmth—ah!"

The voice broke off. The robin had caught a worm.

Marcia slammed the door shut. Help, she thought, and then: I wonder what Dr. Leroy would say. A year of transactional analysis and weekly group-therapy sessions had assured her that she was only a mildly depressed neurotic; though she had never been able to scream and pound her pillow in front of others in her group and could not bring herself to call Dr. Leroy Bill, as his other clients did, the therapy had at least diminished the frequency of her migraines, and the psychiatrist had been pleased with her progress. Now she was sure that she was becoming psychotic; only psychotics heard voices. There was some satisfaction in knowing Dr. Leroy had been wrong.

Pearl had wandered away. Marcia struggled to stay calm. If I can hear her thoughts, she reasoned, can she hear mine? She shivered. "Pearl," she called out in a wavering voice. "Here, kitty. Nice Pearl." She walked into the hall and toward the stairs.

The cat was on the top step, crouching. Her tail twitched. Marcia concentrated, trying to transmit a message to Pearl. If you come to the kitchen right now, she thought, I'll give you a whole can of Super Supper.

The cat did not move.

If you don't come down immediately, Marcia went on, I won't feed you at all.

Pearl was still.

She doesn't hear me, Marcia thought, relieved. She was now beginning to feel a bit silly. She had imagined it all; she would have to ask Dr. Leroy what it meant.

"I could leap from here," Pearl thought, "and land on my feet. I could leap and sink my claws in flesh, but then I'd be punished." Marcia backed away.

The telephone rang. Marcia hurried to the kitchen to answer it, huddling against the wall as she clung to the receiver. "Hello."

"Marcia?"

"Hi, Paula."

"Marcia, I don't know what to do, you're going to think I'm crazy."

"Are you at work?"

"I called in sick. I think I'm having a nervous breakdown. I heard the Baron this morning, I mean I heard what he was thinking. I heard him very clearly. He was thinking, 'They're stealing everything again, they're stealing it,' and then he said, 'But the other man will catch them and bring some of it back, and I'll bark at him and he'll be afraid even though I'm only being friendly.' I finally figured it out. He thinks the garbage men are thieves and the mailman catches them later."

"Does he think in German?"

"What?"

"German shepherds should know German, shouldn't they?" Marcia laughed nervously. "I'm sorry, Paula. I heard Pearl, too. I also overheard a bird and a worm."

"I was afraid the Baron could hear my thoughts, too.

But he doesn't seem to." Paula paused. "Jesus. The Baron just came in. He thinks my perfume ruins my smell. His idea of a good time is sniffing around to see which dogs pissed on his favorite telephone poles. What are we going to do?"

"I don't know." Marcia looked down. Pearl was rubbing against her legs. "Why doesn't she comb me," the cat thought. "Why doesn't she pay attention to me? She's always talking to that thing. I'm much prettier."

Marcia said, "I'll call you back later."

* * *

Doug was sitting at the kitchen table when Marcia came up from the laundry room.

"You're home early."

Doug looked up, frowning under his beard. "Jimmy Barzini brought his hamster to Show and Tell, and the damn thing started to talk. We all heard it. That was the end of any order in the classroom. The kids started crowding around and asking it questions, but it just kept babbling, as if it couldn't understand them. Its mouth wasn't moving, though. I thought at first that Jimmy was throwing his voice, but he wasn't. Then I figured out that we must be hearing the hamster's thoughts somehow, and then Mrs. Price came in and told me the white rats in her class's science project were talking, too, and after that Tallman got on the P.A. system and said school would close early."

"Then I'm not crazy," Marcia said. "Or else we all are. I heard Pearl. Then Paula called up and said Baron von Ribbentrop was doing it."

They were both silent for a few moments. Then Marcia asked, "What did it say? The hamster, I mean."

"It said, 'I want to get out of this cage.'"

* * *

Did cats owned by Russians speak Russian? Marcia had wondered. Did dogs in France transmit in French? Either animals were multilingual or one heard their thoughts in one's native tongue; she had gathered this much from the news.

Press coverage and television news programs were now given over almost entirely to this phenomenon. Did it mean that animals had in fact become intelligent, or were people simply hearing, for the first time, the thoughts that had always been there? Or was the world in the midst of a mass psychosis?

It was now almost impossible to take a walk without hearing birds and other people's pets expressing themselves at length. Marcia had discovered that the cocker spaniel down the street thought she had a nice body odor, while Mr. Sampson's poodle next door longed to take a nip out of her leg. Cries of "Invader approaching!" had kept her from stepping on an anthill. She was afraid to spend time in her yard since listening to a small snake: "I slither. The sun is warm. I coil. I strike. Strike or be struck. That is the way of it. My fangs are ready."

Marcia found herself hiding from this cacophony by staying indoors, listening instead to the babble on the radio and television as animal behaviorists, zoo officials, dog breeders, farmers, psychiatrists, and a few cranks offered their views. A Presidential commission was to study the matter; an advisor to the President had spoken of training migratory birds as observers to assure arms control. Marcia had heard many theories. People were picking up the thoughts of animals and somehow translating them into terms they could understand. They were picking up their own thoughts and projecting them onto the nearest creatures. The animals' thoughts were a manifestation of humankind's guilt over having treated other living, sentient beings as slaves and objects. They were all racists—or "speciesists," as one philosopher had put it on "Good Morning, America"; the word had gained wide currency.

Marcia had begun to follow Pearl around the house, hoping for some insight into the cat's character; it had occurred to her that understanding a cat's point of view might yield some wisdom. Pearl, however, had disappointed her. The cat's mind was almost purely associative; she thought of food, of being scratched behind the ears, of sex, of sharpening her claws on the furniture. "I want to stalk those birds in the yard," she would think. "I like to feel the grass on my paws but it tickles my nose, when I scratched that dog next door on the nose, he yipped, I hate him, why did my people scream at me when I caught a mouse and put it on their pillow for them, I'm thirsty, why don't they ever give me any tuna fish instead of keeping it all to themselves?" Pearl reminded Marcia, more than anything, of her mother-in-law, whose conversations were a weakly linked chain.

Yet she supposed she still loved the cat, in spite of it. In the evening, Pearl would hop on her lap as she watched television with Doug, and Marcia would stroke her fur, and Pearl would say, "That feels good," and begin to purr. At night, before going to bed, Marcia had always closed the bedroom door, feeling that sex should be private, even from cats. Now she was glad she had done so. She was not sure she wanted to know what Pearl would have had to say about that subject.

* * *

The President had gone on television to urge the nation to return to its daily tasks, and Doug's school had reopened. Marcia, alone again for the day, vacuumed the living room while thinking guiltily that she had to start looking for another job. The months at home had made her lazy; she had too easily settled into a homemaker's routine and wondered if this meant she was unintelligent. Persisting in her dull-wittedness, she decided to do some grocery shopping instead of making a trip to the employment agency.

Doug had taken the bus to work, leaving her the car. She felt foolish as she drove down the street. Anton's Market was only a block away and she could have taken her shopping cart, but she could not face the neighborhood's animals. It was all too evident that Mr. Sampson's poodle and a mixed-breed down the road bore her ill will because she was Pearl's owner. She had heard a report from India on the morning news. Few people there were disturbed by recent events, since audible animal contemplation had only confirmed what many had already believed; that animals had souls. Several people there had in fact identified certain creatures as dead relatives or ancestors.

As she parked behind Anton's Market and got out of the car, she noticed a collie pawing at Mr. Anton's garbage cans. "Bones," the dog was thinking. "I know there are bones in there. I want to gnaw on one. What a wonderful day! I smell a bitch close by." The collie barked. "Why do they make it so hard for me to get the bones?" The dog's mood was growing darker. It turned toward Marcia's car. "I hate them, I hate those shiny rolling carapaces, I saw it, one rolled and growled as it went down the street and it didn't even see her, she barked and whined and then she died, and the thing's side opened and a man got out, and the thing just sat there on its wheels and purred. I hate them." The dog barked again.

When Marcia entered the store, she saw Mr. Anton behind the cash register. "Where's Jeannie?" she asked.

Mr. Anton usually seemed cheerful, as if three decades of waiting on his customers had set his round face in a perpetual smile. But today his brown eyes stared at her morosely. "I had to let her go, Mrs. Bochner," he replied. "I had to let the other butchers go, too. Thirty years, and I don't know how long I can keep going. My supplier won't be able to get me any more meat. There's a run on it now in the big cities, but after that—" He shrugged. "May I help you?" he went on, and smiled, as if old habits were reasserting themselves.

Marcia, peering down the aisle of canned goods, noticed that the meat counter was almost empty. Another customer, a big-shouldered, gray-haired man, wandered over with a six-pack of beer. "I don't know what things are coming to," the man said as he fumbled for his wallet. "I was out in the country with my buddy last weekend. You can't hardly sleep with all the noise. I heard one of them coyotes out there. You know what it said? It said, 'I must beware the two-legged stalker.' And you know who it meant. Then it howled."

"You should have seen '60 Minutes,'" Mr. Anton said. "They did a story about the tuna fishermen, and how they're going out of business. They showed one of the last runs. They shouldn't have stuff like that on when kids are watching. My grandson was crying all night." He draped an arm over the register. "A guy has a farm," he said. "How does he know it's actually a concentration camp? All the cows are bitching, that's what they say. You can't go into a barn now without hearing their complaints." He sighed. "At least we can still get milk—the cows can't wander around with swollen udders. But what the hell happens later? They want bigger stalls, they want better feed, they want more pasture. What if they want to keep all the milk for their calves?"

"I don't know," Marcia said, at a loss.

"The government should do something," the gray-haired man muttered.

"The chickens. They're all crazy from being crowded. It's like a nuthouse, a chicken farm. The pigs—they're the worst, because they're the smartest. You know what I feel like? I feel like a murderer—I've got blood on my hands. I feel like a cannibal."

Marcia had left the house with thoughts of hamburgers and slices of baked Virginia ham. Now she had lost her appetite. "What are you going to do?"

"I don't know," Mr. Anton replied. "I'm trying to get into legumes, vegetables, fresh produce, but that puts me in competition with John Ramey's fruit and vegetable market. I'm going to have to get a vegetarian advisor, so I'll know what to stock. There's this vegetarian college kid down the street from me. She's thinking of setting up a consulting firm."

"Well," Marcia said, looking down at the floor.

"I can give you some potato salad, my wife made it up fresh. At least potatoes don't talk. Not yet."

* * *

Doug nibbled at his dinner of bean curd and vegetables. "Have you noticed? People are getting thinner."

"Not everybody. Some people are eating more starch."

"I guess so," Doug said. "Still, it's probably better for us in the long run. We'll live longer. I know I feel better."

"I suppose. I don't know what we're going to do when Pearl's cat food runs out." Marcia lowered her voice when she spoke of Pearl.

After supper, they watched the evening news. Normality, of a sort, had returned to the network broadcast;

the first part of the program consisted of the usual assort-
ment of international crises, Congressional hearings, and
press conferences. Halfway through the broadcast, it was
announced that the President's Labrador retriever had
died; the *Washington Post* was claiming that the Secret
Service had disposed of the dog as a security risk.

"My God," Marcia said.

There was more animal news toward the end of the
program. Family therapists in California were asking
their clients to bring their pets to sessions. Animal shel-
ters all over the country were crowded with dogs and cats
that workers refused to put to sleep. Medical researchers
were abandoning animal studies and turning to computer
models. Race tracks were closing because too many
horseplayers were getting inside information from the
horses. There were rumors in Moscow that the Kremlin
had been secretly and extensively fumigated, and that
there were thousands of dead mice in the city's sewers.
There was a story about a man named MacDonald,
whose column, "MacDonald's Farm," was made up of
sayings and aphorisms he picked up from his barnyard
animals. His column had been syndicated and was being
published in several major newspapers, putting him in
direct competition with Farmer Bob, a "Today" show
commentator who also had a column. Marcia suspected
editorial tampering on the part of both men, since Mac-
Donald's animals sounded like Will Rogers, while Farmer Bob's reminded her of Oscar Wilde.

Pearl entered the room as the news was ending and
began to claw at the rug. "I saw an interesting cat on Phil
Donahue this morning," Marcia said. "A Persian. Kind
of a philosopher. His owner said that he has a theory of
life after death and thinks cats live on in a parallel world.
The cat thinks that all those strange sounds you some-

times hear in the night are actually the spirits of cats. What's interesting is that he doesn't think birds or mice have souls."

"Why don't you look for a job instead of watching the tube all day?"

"I don't watch it all day. I have to spend a lot of time on meals, you know. Vegetarian cooking is very time-consuming when you're not used to it."

"That's no excuse. You know I'll do my share when you're working."

"I'm afraid to leave Pearl alone all day."

"That never bothered you before."

"I never heard what she was thinking before."

Pearl was stretching, front legs straight out, back arched. "I want to sleep on the bed tonight," the cat was thinking. "Why can't I sleep on it at night, I sleep there during the day. They keep it all to themselves. They let that woman with the red fur on her head sleep there at night, but not me."

Doug sucked in his breath. Marcia sat up. "He pushed her on it," the cat went on, "and they shed their outer skins, and he rolled around and rubbed her, but when I jumped up on the bed, he shooed me away."

Marcia said, "You bastard." Doug was pulling at his beard. "When did this happen?" He did not answer. "It must have been when I was visiting my sister, wasn't it? You son of a bitch." She got to her feet, feeling as though someone had punched her in the stomach. "Red fur on her head. It must have been Emma. I always thought she was after you. Jesus Christ, you couldn't even go to a motel."

"I went out with some friends for a few beers," Doug said in a low voice. "She drove me home. I didn't expect anything to happen. It didn't mean anything. I would have told you if I thought it was important, but it wasn't, so why bother you with it? I don't even like Emma that much." He was silent for a moment. "You haven't exactly been showing a lot of interest in sex, you know. And ever since you stopped working, you don't seem to care about anything. At least Emma talks about something besides housework and gossip and Phil Donahue."

"You didn't even close the door," Marcia said, making fists of her hands. "You didn't even think of Pearl."

"For God's sake, Marcia, do you think normal people care if a cat sees them?"

"They do now."

"I'm thirsty," Pearl said. "I want some food. Why doesn't anybody clean my box? It stinks all the time. I wish I could piss where I like."

Doug said, "I'm going to kill that cat." He started to lunge across the room.

"No, you're not." Marcia stepped in front of him, blocking his way. Pearl scurried off.

"Let me by."

"No."

She struggled with him. He knocked her aside and she screamed, swung at him, and began to cry. They both sat down on the floor. Marcia cursed at him between sobs while he kept saying he was sorry. The television set blared at them until Doug turned it off and got out some wine. They drank for a while and Marcia thought of throwing him out, then remembered that she didn't have a job and would be alone with Pearl.

Doug went to bed early, exhausted by his apologizing. Marcia glared at the sofa resentfully; it was Doug who should sleep there, not she.

Before she went to sleep, she called Pearl. The cat crept up from the cellar while Marcia took out some cat food. "Your favorite," she whispered to the cat. "Chicken livers. Your reward. Good kitty."

* * *

Marcia had heard a sharp crack early that morning. The poodle next door was dead, lying in the road. When Mr. Sampson found out, he strode across the street and started shouting at Mr. Hornig's door.

"Come out, you murderer," he hollered. "You come out here and tell me why you shot my dog. You bastard, get out here!"

Marcia stood in her front yard, watching; Doug was staring out the bay window at the scene. The Novaks' cocker spaniel sat on the edge of Marcia's lawn. "I smell death," the spaniel thought. "I smell rage. What is the matter? We are the friends of man, but must we die to prove our loyalty? We are not friends, we are slaves. We die licking our masters' hands."

Mr. Hornig opened his door; he was holding a rifle. "Get the hell off my lawn, Sampson."

"You shot my dog." Mr. Sampson was still wearing his pajamas; his bald pate gleamed in the sun. "I want to know why. I want an answer right now before I call the cops."

Mr. Hornig walked out on his porch and down the steps; Mrs. Hornig came to the door, gasped, and went after her husband, wresting the weapon from him. He pulled away from her and moved toward Mr. Sampson.

"Why?" Mr. Sampson cried. "Why did you do it?"

"I'll tell you why. I can live with your damn dog yapping all the time, even though I hate yappy dogs. I don't even care about him leaving turds all over my yard and running around loose. But I won't put up with his spying and his goddamn insults. That dog of yours has a dirty mind."

"Had," Mr. Sampson shouted. "He's dead now. You killed him and left him in the street."

"He insulted my wife. He was laughing at her tits. He was right outside our bedroom window, and he was making fun of her tits." Mrs. Hornig retreated with the rifle. "He says we stink. That's what he said. He said we smell like something that's been lying outside too long. I take a shower every day, and he says I stink. And he said some other things I won't repeat."

Mr. Sampson leaned forward. "You fool. He didn't understand. How the hell could he help what he thought? You didn't have to listen."

"I'll bet I know where he got his ideas. He wouldn't have thought them up all by himself. I shot him and I'm glad. What do you think of that, Sampson?"

Mr. Sampson answered with his fist. Soon the two pudgy men were rolling in the grass, trading punches. A few neighborhood children gathered to watch the display. A police car appeared; Marcia looked on as the officers pulled the two men away from each other.

"My God," Marcia said as she went inside. "The police came," she said to Doug, who was now stretched out on the sofa with the Sunday *New York Times*. She heard Pearl in the next room, scratching at the dining room table. "Good and sharp," Pearl was saying. "I have them good and sharp. My claws are so pretty. I'm shedding. Why doesn't somebody comb me?"

"I've let you down," Doug said suddenly. Marcia tensed. "I don't mean just with Emma, I mean generally." They had not spoken of that incident since the night of Pearl's revelation.

"No, you haven't," Marcia said.

"I have. Maybe we should have had a kid. I don't know."

"You know I don't want kids now. Anyway, we can't afford it yet."

"That isn't the only reason," Doug said, staring at the dining room entrance, where Pearl now sat, licking a paw, silent for once. "You know how possessive Siamese cats are. If we had a kid, Pearl would hate it. The kid would have to listen to mean remarks all day. He'd probably be neurotic."

Pearl gazed at them calmly. Her eyes seemed to glow.

"Maybe we should get rid of her," Doug went on.

"Oh, no. You're just mad at her still. Anyway, she loves you."

"No, she doesn't. She doesn't love anyone."

"Pet me," Pearl said. "Somebody better scratch me behind the ears, and do it nicely."

* * *

"We have chickens today," Mr. Anton said as Marcia entered the store. "I'll be getting beef in next week." He leaned against the counter, glancing at the clock on the wall; it was almost closing time. "Jeannie's coming back on Tuesday. Things'll be normal again."

"I suppose," Marcia said. "You'll probably be seeing me on Saturdays from now on. I finally found a job. Nothing special, just office work." She paused. "Doesn't it make you feel funny?" She waved a hand at the chickens.

"It did at first. But you have to look at it this way. First of all, chickens are stupid. I guess nobody really knew how stupid until they could hear them thinking. And cows—well, it's like my supplier said. No one's going to hurt some nice animal, but a lot of them don't have nice things to say about people, and some of them sound like real troublemakers. You know who's going to get the axe, so to speak. It's a good thing they don't know we can hear them." Mr. Anton lowered his voice. "And the pigs. Think they're better than we are, that's what they say. Sitting around in a pen all day, and thinking they're better. They'll be sorry."

* * *

As Marcia walked home with her chicken and eggs, the street seemed quieter that evening. The birds still babbled: "My eggs are warm." "The wind lifts me, and carries me to my love." "The wires hum under my feet." "I am strong, my nest is sound, I want a mate." A squirrel darted up a tree. "Tuck them away, tuck them away. I have many acorns in my secret place. Save, save, save. I am prepared."

She did not hear the neighborhood pets. Some were inside; others were all too evident. She passed the bodies of two gray cats, then detoured around a dead mutt. Her eyes stung. We've always killed animals, she thought. Why should this be different?

Louise Novak was standing by her dead cocker spaniel, crying. "Louise?" Marcia said as she approached the child. Louise looked up, sniffing. Marcia gazed at the spaniel, remembering that the dog had liked her.

"Dad killed her," the girl said. "Mrs. Jones overheard her and told everybody Dad hits Mom. Dad said she liked Mom and me best, he heard her think it. He said she hated him and chewed his slippers on purpose and she wanted to tear out his throat because he's mean. I wish she had. I hate him. I hope he dies."

When Marcia reached her own house, she saw the car in the driveway; Doug was home. She heard him moving around upstairs as she unpacked her groceries and put them away. Pearl came into the kitchen and meowed, then scampered to the door, still meowing. "I want to go outside. Why doesn't she let me out? I want to stalk birds, I want to play."

Pearl was so unaware, so insistent, so perfect in her otherness. You'd better be careful, Marcia thought violently. You'd better keep your mind quiet when our friends are here, if you know what's good for you, or you'll stay in the cellar. And you'd better watch what you think about me. Appalled, she suddenly realized that under the right circumstances, she could dash the cat's brains out against the wall.

"I want to go outside."

"Pearl," Marcia said, leaning over the cat. "Pearl, listen to me. Try to understand. I know you can't, but try anyway. You can't go outside, it's dangerous. You have to stay here. You have to stay inside for your own good. I know what's best. You have to stay inside from now on."

(1981)

The Broken Hoop

There are other worlds. Perhaps there is one in which my people rule the forests of the northeast, and there may even be one in which white men and red men walk together as friends.

I am too old now to make my way to the hill. When I was younger and stronger, I would walk there often and strain my ears trying to hear the sounds of warriors on the plains or the stomping of buffalo herds. But last night, as I slept, I saw Little Deer, a cloak of buffalo hide over his shoulders, his hair white; he did not speak. It was then that I knew his spirit had left his body.

Once, I believed that it was God's will that we remain in our own worlds in order to atone for the consequences of our actions. Now I know that He can show some of us His mercy.

* * *

I am a Mohawk, but I never knew my parents. Perhaps I would have died if the Lemaîtres had not taken me into their home.

I learned most of what I knew about my people from two women. One was Sister Jeanne at school, who taught me shame. From her I learned that my tribe had been murderers, pagans, eaters of human flesh. One of the tales she told was of Father Isaac Jogues, tortured to death by my people when he tried to tell them of Christ's teachings. The other woman was an old servant in the Lemaîtres' kitchen; Nawisga told me legends of a proud people who ruled the forests and called me little Manaho, after a princess who died for her lover. From her I learned something quite different.

Even as a child, I had visions. As I gazed out my window, the houses of Montreal would vanish, melting into the trees; a glowing hoop would beckon. I might have stepped through it then, but already I had learned to doubt. Such visions were delusions; to accept them meant losing reality. Maman and Père Lemaître had shown me that. Soon, I no longer saw the woodlands, and felt no loss. I was content to become what the Lemaîtres wanted me to be.

When I was eighteen, Père Lemaître died. Maman Lemaître had always been gentle; when her brother Henri arrived to manage her affairs, I saw that her gentleness was only passivity. There would no longer be a place for me; Henri had made that clear. She did not fight him.

I could stay in that house no longer. Late one night, I left, taking a few coins and small pieces of jewelry Père Lemaître had given me, and shed my last tears for the Lemaîtres and the life I had known during that journey.

* * *

I stayed in a small rooming house in Buffalo throughout the winter of 1889, trying to decide what to do. As the snow swirled outside, I heard voices in the wind, and imagined that they were calling to me. But I clung to my sanity; illusions could not help me.

In the early spring, a man named Gus Yeager came to the boarding house and took a room down the hall. He was in his forties and had a thick, gray-streaked beard. I suspected that he had things to hide; he was a yarn-spinner who could talk for hours and yet say little. He took a liking to me and finally confided that he was going west to sell patent medicines. He needed a partner. I was almost out of money by then and welcomed the chance he offered me.

I became Manaho, the Indian princess, whose arcane arts had supposedly created the medicine, a harmless mixture of alcohol and herbs. I wore a costume Gus had purchased from an old Seneca, and stood on the back of our wagon while Gus sold his bottles: "Look at Princess Manaho here, and what this miracle medicine has done for her—almost forty, but she drinks a bottle every day and looks like a girl, never been sick a day in her life." There were enough foolish people who believed him for us to make a little money.

We stopped in small towns, dusty places that had narrow roads covered with horse manure and wooden buildings that creaked as the wind whistled by. I remember only browns and grays in those towns; we had left the green trees and red brick of Pennsylvania and northern Ohio behind us. Occasionally we stopped at a farm; I remember men with hatchet faces, women with stooped shoulders and hands as gnarled and twisted as the leafless limbs of trees, children with eyes as empty and gray as the sky.

Sometimes, as we rode in our wagon, Gus would take out a bottle of Princess Manaho's Miracle Medicine and begin to sing songs between swallows He would get drunk quickly. He was happy only then; often, he was silent and morose. We slept in old rooming houses infested with insects, in barns, often under trees. Some towns would welcome us as a diversion; we would leave others hastily, knowing we were targets of suspicion.

Occasionally, as we went farther west, I would see other Indians. I had little to do with them, but would watch them from a distance, noting their shabby clothes and weather-worn faces. I had little in common with such people; I could read and speak both French and English. I could have been a lady. At times, the townsfolk would look from one of them to me, as if making a comparison of some sort, and I would feel uncomfortable, almost affronted.

* * *

We came to a town in Dakota. But instead of moving on, we stayed for several days. Gus began to change, and spent more time in saloons.

One night, he came to my room and pounded on the door. I let him in quickly, afraid he would wake everyone else in the boarding house. He closed the door, then threw himself at me, pushing me against the wall as he fumbled at my nightdress. I was repelled by the smell of sweat and whiskey, his harsh beard and warm breath. I struggled with him as quietly as I could, and at last pushed him away. Weakened by drink and the struggle, he collapsed across my bed; soon he was snoring. I sat with him all night, afraid to move.

Gus said nothing next morning as we prepared to leave. We rode for most of the day while he drank; this time, he did not sing. That afternoon, he threw me off the wagon. By the time I was able to get to my feet, Gus was riding off; dust billowed from the wheels. I ran after him, screaming; he did not stop.

* * *

I was alone on the plain. I had no money, no food and water. I could walk back to the town, but what would become of me there? My mind was slipping; as the sky darkened, I thought I saw a ring glow near me.

The wind died; the world became silent. In the distance, someone was walking along the road toward me. As the figure drew nearer, I saw that it was a woman. Her face was coppery, and her hair black; she wore a long yellow robe and a necklace of small blue feathers.

Approaching, she took my hand, but did not speak. Somehow I sensed that I was safe with her. We walked together for a while; the moon rose and lighted our way. "What shall I do?" I said at last. "Where is the nearest town? Can you help me?"

She did not answer, but instead held my arm more tightly; her eyes pleaded with me. I said, "I have no money, no place to go." She shook her head slowly, then released me and stepped back.

The sudden light almost blinded me. The sun was high overhead, but the woman's face was shadowed. She held out her hand, beckoning to me. A ring shone around her, and then she was gone.

I turned, trembling with fear. I was standing outside another drab, clapboard town; my clothes were covered with dust. I had imagined it all as I walked through the night; somehow my mind had conjured up a comforting vision. I had dreamed as I walked; that was the only possible explanation. I refused to believe that I was mad. In that way, I denied the woman.

* * *

I walked into the town and saw a man riding toward the stable in a wagon. He was dressed in a long black robe—a priest. I ran to him; he stopped and waited for me to speak.

"Father," I cried out. "Let me speak to you."

His kind brown eyes gazed down at me. He was a short, stocky man whose face had been darkened by the sun and lined by prairie winds. "What is it, my child?" He peered at me more closely. "Are you from the reservation here?"

"No. My name is Catherine Lemaître, I come from

the east. My companion abandoned me, and I have no money."

"I cannot help you, then. I have little money to give you."

"I do not ask for charity." I had sold enough worthless medicine with Gus to know what to say to this priest. I kept my hands on his seat so that he could not move without pushing me away. "I was sent to school, I can read and write and do figures. I want work, a place to stay. I am a Catholic, Father." I reached into my pocket and removed the rosary I had kept, but rarely used. "Surely there is something I can do."

He was silent for a few moments. "Get in, child," he said at last. I climbed up next to him.

* * *

His name was Father Morel and he had been sent by his superiors to help the Indians living in the area, most of whom were Sioux. He had a mission near the reservation and often traveled to the homes of the Indians to tell them about Christ. He had been promised an assistant who had never arrived. He could offer me little, but he needed a teacher, someone who could teach children to read and write.

I had arrived at Father Morel's mission in the autumn. My duties, besides teaching, were cooking meals and keeping the small wooden house next to the chapel clean. Father Morel taught catechism, but I was responsible for the other subjects. Winter arrived, a harsh, cold winter with winds that bit at my face. As the drifts grew higher, fewer of the Sioux children came to school. The ones who did sat silently on the benches, huddling in their heavy coverings, while I built a fire in the woodburner.

The children irritated me with their passivity, their lack of interest. They sat, uncomplaining, while I wrote words or figures on my slate board or read to them from one of Father Morel's books. A little girl named White Cow Sees, baptized Joan, was the only one who showed interest. She would ask to hear stories about the saints, and the other children, mostly boys, would nod mutely in agreement.

I was never sure how much any of them understood. Few of them spoke much English, although White Cow Sees and a little boy named Whirlwind Chaser, baptized Joseph, managed to become fairly fluent in it. Whirlwind Chaser was particularly fond of hearing about Saint Sebastian. At last I discovered that he saw Saint Sebastian as a great warrior, shot with arrows by an enemy tribe; he insisted on thinking that Sebastian had returned from the other world to avenge himself.

I lost most of them in the spring to the warmer days. White Cow Sees still came, and a few of the boys, but the rest had vanished. There was little food that spring and the Indians seemed to be waiting for something.

I went into town as often as possible to get supplies, and avoided the Indians on the reservation. They were silent people, never showing emotion; they seemed both hostile and indifferent. I was irritated by their mixture of pride and despair, saw them as unkempt and dirty, and did not understand why they refused to do anything that might better their lot.

I began to view the children in the same way. There was always an unpleasant odor about them, and their quiet refusal to learn was more irritating to me than pranks and childish foolishness would have been. I became less patient with them, subjecting them to spelling drills, to long columns of addition, to lectures on their ignorance. When they looked away from me in humiliation, I refused to see.

* * *

I met Little Deer at the beginning of summer. He had come to see Father Morel, arriving while the children and I were at Mass. He looked at me with suspicion as we left the chapel.

I let the children go early that day, watching as they walked toward their homes. White Cow Sees trailed behind the boys, trying to get their attention.

"You." I turned and saw the Indian who had come to see Father Morel. He was a tall man, somewhat paler than the Sioux I had seen. He wore a necklace of deer bones around his neck; his hair was in long, dark braids. His nose, instead of being large and prominent, was small and straight. "You are the teacher."

"Yes, I am Catherine Lemaître." I said it coldly.

"Some call me John Wells, some call me Little Deer. My mother's cousin has come here, a boy named Whirlwind Chaser."

"He stays away now. I have not seen him since winter."

"What can you teach him?"

"More than you can."

"You teach him Wasichu foolishness," he said. "I have heard of you and have seen you in the town talking to white men. You think you will make them forget who you are, but you are wrong."

"You have no right to speak to me that way." I began to walk away, but he followed me.

"My father was a Wasichu, a trader," Little Deer went on. "My mother is a Minneconjou. I lived with the Wasichu, I learned their speech and I can write my name and read some words. My mother returned here to her people when I was small. You wear the clothes of a Wasichu woman and stay with the Black Robe, but he tells me you are not his woman."

"Priests have no women. And you should tell Whirlwind Chaser to return to school. White men rule here now. Learning their ways is all that can help you."

"I have seen their ways. The Wasichus are mad. They hate the earth. A man cannot live that way."

I said, "They are stronger than you."

"You are only a foolish woman and know nothing. You teach our children to forget their fathers. You think you are a Wasichu, but to them you are only a silly woman they have deceived."

"Why do you come here and speak to Father Morel?"

"He is foolish, but a good man. I tell him of troubles, of those who wish to see him. It is too bad he is not a braver man. He would beat your madness out of you."

I strode away from Little Deer, refusing to look back, sure that I would see only scorn on his face. But when I glanced out my window, I saw that he was smiling as he rode away.

* * *

The children stayed away from school in the autumn. There were more soldiers in town and around the reservation and I discovered that few Indians had been seen at trading posts. I refused to worry. A young corporal I had met in town had visited me a few times, telling me of his home in Minnesota. Soon, I prayed, he would speak to me, and I could leave with him and forget the reservation.

Then Little Deer returned. I was sweeping dust from the porch, and directed him to the small room where Father Morel was reading. He shook his head. "It is you I wish to see."

"About what? Are you people planning another uprising? You will die for it—there are many soldiers here."

"The Christ has returned to us."

I clutched my broom. "You are mad."

"Two of our men have seen him. They traveled west to where the Fish Eaters—the Paiutes—live. The Christ appeared to them there. He is named Wovoka and he is not a white man as I have thought. He was killed by the Wasichus on the cross long ago, but now he has returned to save us."

"That is blasphemy."

"I hear it is true. He will give us back our land, he will raise all our dead and return our land to us. The Wasichus will be swept away."

"No!" I shouted.

Little Deer was looking past me, as if seeing something else beyond. "I have heard," he went on, "that Wovoka bears the scars of crucifixion. He has told us we must dance so that we are not forgotten when the resurrection takes place and the Wasichus disappear."

"If you believe that, Little Deer, you will believe anything."

"Listen to me!" Frightened, I stepped back. "A man named Eagle Wing Stretches told me he saw his dead father when he danced. I was dancing with him and in my mind I saw the sacred tree flower, I saw the hoop joined once again. I understood again nature's circle in which we are the earth's children, and are nourished by her until as old men we become like children again and return to the earth. Yet I knew that all I saw was in my thoughts, that my mind spoke to me, but I did not truly see. I danced until my feet were light, but I could not see. Eagle Wing Stretches was at my side and he gave a great cry and then fell to the ground as if dead. Later, he told me he had seen his father in the other world, and that his father had said they would soon be together."

"But you saw nothing yourself."

"But I have. I saw the other world when I was a boy."

I leaned against my broom, looking away from his wild eyes.

"I saw it long ago, in the Moon of Falling Leaves. My friends were talking of the Wasichus and how we would drive them off when we were men. I grew sad and climbed up a mountain near our camp to be alone. In my heart, I believed that we would never drive off the Wasichus, for they were many and I knew their madness well—I learned it from my father and his friends. It was that mountain there I climbed."

He pointed and I saw a small mountain on the horizon. "I was alone," Little Deer continued. "Then I heard the sound of buffalo hooves and I looked down the mountain, but I saw no buffalo there. Above me, a great circle glowed, brighter than the yellow metal called gold."

"No," I said softly.

He looked at me and read my face. "You have seen it, too."

"No," I said after a few moments.

"You have. I see that you have. You can step through the circle, and yet you deny it. I looked through the circle, and saw the buffalo, and warriors riding at their side. I wanted to step through and join them, but fear held me back. Then the vision vanished." He leaned forward and clutched my shoulders. "I will tell you what I think. There is another world near ours, where there are no Wasichus and my people are free. On that mountain, there is a pathway that leads to it. I will dance there, and I will find it again. I told my story to a medicine man named High Shirt and he says that we must dance on the mountain—he believes that I saw Wovoka's vision."

"You will find nothing." But I remembered the circle, and the robed woman, and the woods that had replaced Montreal. I wanted to believe Little Deer.

"Come with me, Catherine. I have been sick since I first saw you—my mind cannot leave you even when I dance. Your heart is bitter and you bear the seeds of the Wasichu madness and I know that I should choose another, but it is you I want."

I shrank from him, seeing myself in dirty hides inside a tepee as we pretended that our delusions were real. I would not tie my life to that of an ignorant half-breed. But before I could speak, he had left the porch, muttering, "I will wait," and was on his horse.

* * *

On a cold night in December, I stared at Little Deer's mountain from my window.

I was alone. Father Morel was with the Indians, trying again to tell them that their visions were false. The ghost dancing had spread and the soldiers would act soon.

Horses whinnied outside. Buttoning my dress, I hurried downstairs, wondering who could be visiting at this late hour. The door swung open; three dark shapes stood on the porch. I opened my mouth to scream and then saw that one of the men was Little Deer.

"Catherine, will you come with me now?" I managed to shake my head. "Then I must take you. I have little time." Before I could move, he grabbed me; one of his companions bound my arms quickly and threw a buffalo robe over my shoulders. As I struggled, Little Deer dragged me outside.

He got on his horse behind me and we rode through

the night. Snowflakes melted on my face. "You will be sorry for this," I said. "Someone will come after me."

"It will soon be snowing and there will be no tracks. And no one will follow an Indian woman who decided to run off and join her people."

"You are not my people." I pulled at my bonds. "Do you think this will make me care for you? I will only hate you more."

"You will see the other world, and travel to it. There is little time left—I feel it."

We rode on until we came to a small group of houses which were little more than tree branches slung together. We stopped and Little Deer murmured a few words to his companions before getting off his horse.

"High Shirt is here," he said. "A little girl is sick. We will wait for him." He helped me off the horse and I swung at him with my bound arms, striking him in the chest. He pulled out his knife and I thought he would kill me; instead, he cut the ropes, freeing my hands.

"You do not understand," he said. "I wish only to have you with me when we pass into the next world. I thought if I came for you, you would understand. Sometimes one must show a woman these things or she will think you are only filled with words." He sighed. "There is my horse. I will not force you to stay if your heart holds only hate for me."

I was about to leave. But before I could act, a cry came from the house nearest to us. Little Deer went to the entrance and I followed him. An old man came out and said, "The child is dead."

I looked inside the hovel. A fire was burning on the dirt floor and I saw a man and woman huddled over a small body. The light flickered over the child's face. It was White Cow Sees.

The best one was gone, the cleverest. She might have found her way out of this place. I wept bitterly. I do not know how long I stood there, weeping, before Little Deer led me away.

* * *

A few days after the death of White Cow Sees, we learned that the great chief Sitting Bull had been shot by soldiers. Little Deer had placed me in the keeping of one of his companions, Rattling Hawk. He lived with his wife, Red Eagle Woman, in a hovel not far from Little Deer's mountain. I spent most of my days helping their three children search for firewood; I was still mourning White Cow Sees and felt unable to act. Often Rattling Hawk and Red Eagle Woman would dance with others and I would watch them whirl through the snow.

After the death of Sitting Bull, I was afraid that there would be an uprising. Instead, the Indians only danced more, as if Wovoka's promise would be fulfilled. Little Deer withdrew to a sweat lodge with Rattling Hawk, and I did not see him for three days.

During this time, I began to see colored lights shine from the mountain, each light a spear thrown at heaven; the air around me would feel electric. But when daylight came, the lights would disappear. I had heard of magnetism while with the Lemaîtres. Little Deer had only mistaken natural forces for a sign; now he sat with men in an enclosure, pouring water over hot stones. I promised myself that I would tell him I wanted to go back to the mission.

But when Little Deer and High Shirt emerged from the lodge, they walked past me without a word and headed for the mountain. Little Deer was in a trance, his face gaunt from the days without food and his eyes already filled with visions. I went back to Rattling Hawk's home to wait. I had to leave soon; I had seen soldiers from a distance the day before, and did not want to die with these people.

Little Deer came to me that afternoon. Before I could speak, he motioned for silence. His eyes stared past me and I shivered in my blanket, waiting.

"High Shirt said that the spirits would be with us today. We climbed up and waited by the place where I saw the other world. High Shirt sang a song of the sacred tree and then the tree was before us and we both saw it."

"You thought you saw it," I said. "One would see anything after days without food in a sweat lodge."

He held up his hand, palm toward me. "We saw it inside the yellow circle. The circle grew larger and we saw four maidens near it dressed in fine dresses with eagle feathers on their brows, and with them four horses, one black, one chestnut, one white, and one gray, and on the horses four warriors painted with yellow streaks like lightning. Their tepees were around them in a circle and we saw their people, fat with good living and smiling as the maidens danced. Their chief came forward and I saw a yellow circle painted on his forehead. He lifted his arms, and then he spoke: Bring your people here, for I see you are lean and have sad faces. Bring them here, for I see your people traveling a black road of misery. Bring them here, and they will dance with us, but it must be soon, for our medicine men say the circle will soon be gone. He spoke with our speech. Then the circle vanished, and High Shirt leaped up and we saw that the snow where the circle had been was melted. He ran to tell our people. I came to you."

"So you will go and dance," I said, "and wait for the world which will never come. I have seen—" He took my arm, but I would say no more. He released me.

"It was a true vision," he said quietly. "It was not Wovoka's vision, but it was a true one. The Black Robe told me that God is merciful, but I thought He was merciful only to Wasichus. Now I think that He has given us a road to a good world and has smiled upon us at last."

"I am leaving, Little Deer. I will not freeze on that mountain with you or wait for the soldiers to kill me."

"No, Catherine—you will come. You will see this world with me." He led me to Rattling Hawk's home.

* * *

He climbed up that evening. Rattling Hawk and his family came, and High Shirt brought fifteen people. The rest had chosen to stay behind. "Your own people do not believe you," I said scornfully to Little Deer as we climbed. "See how few there are. The others will dance down there and wait for Wovoka to sweep away the white men. They are too lazy to climb up here."

He glanced at me; there was pain in his eyes. I regretted my harsh words. It came to me that out of all the men I had known, only Little Deer had looked into my mind and seen me as I was. At that moment, I knew that I could have been happy with him in a different world.

We climbed until High Shirt told us to stop. Two of the women built a fire and I sat near it as the others danced around us.

"Dance with us, Catherine," said Little Deer. I shook my head and he danced near me, feet pounding the ground, arms churning at his sides. I wondered how long they would dance, waiting for the vision. Little Deer seemed transformed; he was a chief, leading his people. My foot tapped as he danced. He had seen me as I was, but I had not truly seen him; I had looked at him with the eyes of a white woman, and my mind had clothed him in white words—" half-breed," "illiterate," "insane," "*sauvage*."

I fed some wood to the fire, then looked up at the sky. The forces of magnetism were at work again. A rainbow of lights flickered, while the stars shone on steadily in their places.

Suddenly the stars shifted.

I cried out. The stars moved again. New constellations appeared, a cluster of stars above me, a long loop on the horizon. Little Deer danced to me and I heard the voice of High Shirt chanting nearby.

I huddled closer to the fire. Little Deer pounded the ground, his arms cutting the air like scythes. He spun around and became an eagle, soaring over me, ready to seize me with his talons. The stars began to flash, disappearing and then reappearing. One of the women gave a cry. The dancers seemed to flicker.

I leaped up, terrified. Little Deer swirled around me, spinning faster and faster. Then he disappeared.

I spun around. He was on the other side of the fire, still dancing; then he was at my side again. I tried to run toward him; he was behind me. A group of dancers circled me, winking on and off.

"Catherine!" Little Deer's voice surrounded me, thundering through the night. His voice blended with the chants of High Shirt until my ears throbbed with pain.

I fled from the circle of dancers and fell across a snow-covered rock. "Catherine!" the voice cried again. The dark shapes dancing around the fire grew dimmer. A wind swept past me, and the dancers vanished.

I stood up quickly. And then I saw the vision.

A golden circle glowed in front of me; I saw green

grass and a circle of tepees. Children danced around a fire. Then I saw High Shirt and the others, dancing slowly with another group of Indians, weaving a pattern around a small tree. The circle grew larger; Little Deer stood inside it, holding his arms out to me.

I had only to step through the circle to be with him. My feet carried me forward; I held out my hand and whispered his name.

Then I hesitated. My mind chattered to me—I was sharing a delusion. The dancers would dance until they dropped, and then would freeze on the mountain, too exhausted to climb down. Their desperation had made them mad. If I stepped inside the circle, I would be lost to the irrationality that had always been dormant inside me. I had to save myself.

The circle wavered and dimmed. I saw the other world as if through water, and the circle vanished. I cried out in triumph; my reason had won. But as I looked around at the melted snow, I saw that I was alone.

* * *

I waited on the mountain until it grew too cold for me there, then climbed down to Rattling Hawk's empty home before going back up the mountain next day. I do not know for how many days I did this. At last I realized that the yellow circle I had seen would not reappear. In my sorrow, I felt that part of me had vanished with the circle, and imagined that my soul had joined Little Deer. I never saw the glowing hoop again.

I rode back to the mission a few days after Christmas through a blizzard, uncaring about whether I lived or died. There, Father Morel told me that the soldiers had acted at last, killing a band of dancing Indians near

Wounded Knee, and I knew that the dancing and any hope these people had were over.

I was back in the white man's world, a prisoner of the world to come.

(1982)

The Shrine

Christine heard the childish, high voice giggling out an indistinct sentence; the woman's voice was lower and huskier. She waited. A door squeaked open and then she heard her mother's rapid footsteps on the stairs.

Christine stepped into the hall and peered at the slightly open door. Her mother had been in Christine's old room again; she had been there last night when Christine first heard the voices and had recognized one as her mother's. She went to the door, pushed it all the way open, and gazed.

Her mother had done no redecorating here, as she had everywhere else. Christine entered, turning to look at the wall of framed photographs and documents above the slightly battered dresser. A young Christine with wavy blond hair and a wide smile stood with a group of other little girls in Brownie uniforms. A thirteen-year-old Christine wore a white dress and held a clarinet; an older Christine, slightly broad-shouldered but still slender, grinned up from a pool where she floated with other members of the Mapeno Valley High Aquanettes; a bare-shouldered Christine in a green formal stood at the side of a tall, handsome boy in a white dinner jacket. Her high school diploma was framed, along with other certificates; another photo showed her parents beaming proudly as they stood behind Christine and her luggage at the Titus County Airport, waiting for the plane that would take their daughter to Wellesley. There, as far as the room indicated, Christine's life ended. She had lasted less than one year at Wellesley.

She gazed at the top of the dresser, where her high school yearbook had been opened to her page. A pretty girl with flowing locks smiled up at her.

Matthews, Christine

"Onward and Upward!"

National Merit Scholar; National Honor Society, 3, 4; Student Council, 2, 3; Class Vice-President, 4; Aquanettes, 3, 4; Assistant Editor, Mapeno Valley *Clarion*, 3, 4; Dramatics Club, 3, 4; Orchestra, 2, 3, 4; Le Cercle Français, 2, 3, 4; Yearbook Staff, 4.

She closed the yearbook. The room was suddenly oppressive. She was surrounded by past glories; the room, with its embroidered pillows and watercolor paintings, was a shrine to what she had once been. Her mother could drive to her brother's house, only forty-five minutes away, to view his athletic trophies and his various certificates, but Christine's had remained here. She had been a good daughter, as Charles had been a good son. He was still a good son. Christine had not been a good daughter for a long time.

* * *

"Just coffee for me," Christine said as she entered the kitchen.

Her mother looked up from the stove. "Now, Chrissie, you know how important a good breakfast is."

"I never eat breakfast."

"You should."

Christine sat down at the small kitchen table while her mother served the food. "Well," she said, and sipped her coffee.

"Well," Mrs. Matthews replied. She poked at her eggs, took a bite of toast, then gazed at her daughter with calm gray eyes. "So it really is over between you and Jim."

"He moved all his stuff out."

"I was sorry to hear it. Maybe if you and Jim had gotten married—"

"Oh, Mom, that would have been great. The lawyers would have made everything even worse. I suppose you think a divorce would have been more respectable." Christine caught herself, too late. "I'm sorry."

"I meant that if you had been married, you would have had more of a commitment, and you both might have worked harder to stay together." Mrs. Matthews lowered her eyes. "Your father and I had almost thirty pretty good years. Maybe we wouldn't have had that much without a strong commitment. We had more than a lot of people have. Actually, I'm not alone—I think a third of my friends are divorced. Or widowed—that's probably worse."

Christine ate part of an egg, then nibbled at some sausage. "You haven't redone my room. You've redone every other room in the house. Every time I come here, the whole house is different."

"I only do a little, once in a while. If you came home more often, you'd see I don't redecorate that much."

"You know I don't have time." Christine's voice was harsh.

"I know, dear. I was only making a point, not an accusation."

Christine sighed, trying to think of what else to say.

"You never hung up my degree from State."

"I guess I never got around to it."

"You didn't put it up because you expected more from me."

"Now, Chrissie, you know that isn't true. I only wanted you to be happy."

Christine said, "I heard voices last night, in my old room."

Her mother's head shot up; Christine saw fear in her eyes. Mrs. Matthews's once-blond hair was nearly all gray. Her face was thinner, too, the hollows in her cheeks deeper; her long blue housedress seemed looser. One blue-veined hand pushed the plate of sausage and eggs aside; Mrs. Matthews had barely touched her breakfast.

"It was the radio," the older woman said at last. "One of those plays on the public station."

"It didn't sound like the radio. I heard your voice, and someone else's. A child's."

"It was the radio." Mrs. Matthews's voice was unusually firm.

"Maybe it was." Christine drummed on the table top with her fingers, then stood up. "I'm going for a walk."

"I'll clean up here. Your brother jogs now, you know. Three miles a day."

"I don't jog. I only walk."

* * *

Colonial houses stood on each side of the winding road. Christine searched the neighborhood for signs of change. Three houses now had solar panels; others had cords of wood stacked in yards under tarpaulins.

A young woman hurried down a driveway, juggling a box and a large purse. "Toni!" Christine shouted.

"Chris!" The woman opened her car door, threw in the box and the purse, and strode toward Christine. "God, I haven't seen you in ages. You haven't changed."

Christine smiled at the lie, grateful that her raincoat hid her heavy thighs. Toni was stockier, her dark hair shorter and frizzed by a permanent. "Mother told me you were back."

Toni hooted. "Back! What a nice way to put it. I guess she must have told you about my divorce."

"She mentioned it."

"My parents have really been great. Mom takes care of Mark when he gets home from school. I have a job at the mall now, with Macy's." Toni glanced at her watch. "How's that guy you're living with?"

"We broke up."

"God, I'm sorry to hear it."

"Don't be. I wasn't." Christine tried to sound hard and rational. "This place looks the same."

"It'll never change. It's stuck in a time warp or something. There's a couple down the street with *four kids*—can you imagine anyone having four kids nowadays? I don't know how they afford it. Mrs. Feinberg's running a day care thing in her house—you can't afford these houses without two incomes. Maybe a few things have changed." Toni paused. "How is your mother, by the way?"

"She's all right."

"I don't want to sound nosy. She looks kind of pale to me. She's in your old room a lot."

Christine looked up, startled.

"I can't help noticing," Toni went on. "I see the light at night. She's in there almost every day after she comes home."

"She likes to listen to the radio there while she does her sewing." Christine hoped that she sounded convincing.

Toni looked at her watch again. "Hey, why don't you come over tonight? We can talk after Mark goes to bed."

Christine saw two girls standing by a pool, giggling; they would swim through life as they had swum through the blue, chlorinated water. "I can't. We're going to Chuck's for supper."

"Maybe tomorrow."

"Mother has tickets for the symphony. And I'm leaving the day after."

"Well. Next time, maybe."

"Next time."

"See you, Chris."

* * *

As she approached her mother's house, Christine looked up at the window of her old room. The window was at the side of the house, overlooking the hedged-in yard.

A shape moved past the window; a small hand pressed against the pane. A little girl was looking at her through the glass; her long blond hair curled over her shoulders. The child smiled.

Except for the child's bright, golden hair, thicker and wavier than hers had ever been, she might have been looking at herself as a little girl. The child continued to smile, then reached for the curtains and pulled them shut.

Christine hurried around the yard to the back door and pushed it open, entering the kitchen. The house was still. At last she heard her mother's footfall in the hall above, and then the creak of the stairs.

"Chrissie," her mother said as she entered the kitchen. She still wore her long blue housedress; she had always dressed early in the morning before.

"Who's that little girl?"

"What little girl?"

"The one I saw in my room, looking out the window."

"You must be mistaken." Her mother's voice was flat. "There was no one in your room."

"I saw her."

"You're imagining it."

Christine passed her mother and pounded up the stairs. The door to her old room was still open; she hurried through it.

The little girl was not there. The room felt cold; Christine pulled her coat more tightly about her. Abruptly the floor shifted under her feet. She staggered, righted herself, and heard the sound of a child's laughter.

Christine covered her ears, then let her hands drop. The room was warm again; everything was as it had been. Her mother had said that there was no little girl; that meant she had imagined it all. She would have to put it out of her mind.

* * *

After Christine had greeted her sister-in-law, said hello to her nephew, and peeked into the baby's room, Charles led her to the basement. His bar sat in one corner in front of a stainless steel sink. He poured her a bourbon, then opened the refrigerator and took out a light beer. "My refuge," he said. He came around the bar and sat down next to her.

"Shouldn't we go upstairs?"

"It's all right. Jenny's got to nurse Trina again, and then she'll have to put Curt to bed, and then she and Mom'll watch the MacNeil-Lehrer Report before supper. We can go up then." He paused. "I heard about Jim."

"He moved all his stuff out finally."

"I thought you two would be together forever. I kept

expecting you to call and say you'd gotten married."

Christine sipped her bourbon, then gazed at the glass. "After he left, I came home one day and started fixing drinks. Jim always had a vodka and tonic and I always had a bourbon. Well, I fixed myself a drink and then I suddenly realized I'd fixed his, too. That was when I finally cried about it." She shook her head. "You seem to be doing all right."

"I guess so." Charles's ash blond hair was already thinning around his temples; his moustache was thicker, as if to compensate. "One thing about being a dentist—the customers can't talk back to you while you're working."

"You'll be all right. You always were. You were always the good child. I screwed up."

"Chris. Mom worries about you sometimes."

"No, she doesn't. She's never forgiven me, not since my breakdown. It was as if I was saying she was a lousy mother because I didn't turn out right. And I'm not married, and I don't have kids, and I don't have a lovely home and a fine husband. She hates me for it, but she won't say so." Christine gulped at her bourbon. "If she says she worries about me, it's only because she thinks she's supposed to say it."

"Oh, Chris, come on."

"She never came to see me when I was in that expensive bin. She never asked me why I broke down. After that, I was damaged goods as far as she was concerned. As long as I was perfect, she loved me. When I wasn't, she just turned herself off."

"What do you want her to do, say she's sorry?"

"That wouldn't change anything."

"Then forget it. It's your problem, Chris. You can't keep feeling sorry for yourself."

She glared at him. "It's easy for you to talk, Chuck. You didn't fail."

"You think so? Every time Dad visits, he asks me why I don't keep up my sports more, maybe coach Little League. I know he would have liked to see me pitch in the major leagues—hell, I wanted it, too. Nobody grows up thinking, 'Boy, I'm really into teeth.' But I'm not going to get depressed over it."

"Chuck, Mother's been spending a lot of time in my old room. It worries me. She—" Christine was about to mention the little girl, but changed her mind. "That room gives me the willies. I wish she'd put all my old crap away."

"You could take it with you when you drive back to the city."

"I don't have room. And I wouldn't care to be reminded of how wonderful I once was."

"Chris, you've got to stop it. You have the rest of your life—don't poison it. Grow up. Everyone fails in some way. You have to learn to live with that."

* * *

She heard the voices again.

Christine threw off her sheet and coverlet and tiptoed toward the door, opening it slowly. Creeping into the darkened hallway, she moved cautiously toward her old room.

A child's voice giggled. "Do you like it?"

"I think it's beautiful. But you always do everything well."

"I'm glad. I love you, Mommy."

"I love you, too."

Christine trembled as she recognized her mother's voice.

"Read to me, Mommy." Bedsprings squeaked.

"Which book?"

"*The House at Pooh Corner.*"

"You're such a good little girl. You won't disappoint me, will you, Chrissie?"

"Never."

Chrissie. Christine backed toward the guest room. How long had the child been living in this house, and what had enabled her to appear? She knew the answer to the second question—her own failure, and her mother's disappointment. She shook her head. It was a dream; it had to be.

She got back into bed and lay there, awake, for a long time.

*   *   *

Christine had slept uneasily and her eyes felt gritty in the morning. She got out of bed, pulled on her robe, and darted into the hall before she had time to change her mind. As she entered her old room, she closed the door behind her.

The bed had been made, or had never been slept in at all. The artifacts of her childhood and youth still hung on the walls in their usual places, and *The House at Pooh Corner* was back on the bookshelf between *Winnie-the-Pooh* and *Stuart Little*. The yearbook was open once again, this time to a picture of Christine and a boy named Lars Heldstrom under the caption "Most Likely To Succeed."

She gripped the dresser; her hands became claws. "Come out," she muttered. "Damn you, come out." The room was still. She was having another breakdown; the breakup with Jim and the visit home had unhinged her. But her mother had been in the room, and she had seen the child in the window.

"Who are you? If you don't come out, I'll take Mother away. You'll never see her again."

"No, you won't." The voice seemed to hover above her; she clutched at the dresser, afraid to move. "She's mine now. Go away."

Christine spun around. The little girl was standing in front of the closet door, dressed in a pair of blue overalls and a white turtleneck. Her small hands held a clarinet; her blue eyes were icy.

"Who are you?"

"I'm Chrissie. Don't you know that?" The girl's voice was low and harsh. "This isn't your room any more. Mommy comes to visit me every day."

"She's not your mommy."

"She is. I could feel her calling me, and I wanted to be with her so much. I found out I could come in here and stay for a while. I'll never let her go away."

"You will. I'll force you to."

"You won't. She loves me. She doesn't love you any more."

Christine strode toward the child. The little girl retreated to a corner, her back against the closet door. As Christine reached for the girl, the wall suddenly dropped away; she was standing at the edge of the floor, gazing down into a thick gray fog. She teetered on the edge, afraid she would fall and keep falling, and clawed at the gray mists, then staggered back and fell across the bed.

She sat up. The room was as it had been; the little girl was gone.

Christine pressed her hands to her face. She had never had delusions; even during the worst days of her illness, she had never seen things that weren't there. Depression had been her affliction, and despair, and guilt.

She rushed from the room and was halfway down the stairs before she had time to think. Her mother would only evade a confrontation, and there was no one else to help her.

* * *

Christine climbed the front steps, reached into her purse, and removed the key she had taken from the kitchen wall that morning; she had parked her car in front of a house farther down the street. Her mother would not be expecting her; Christine had said that she was going to the mall to see Toni.

Opening the storm door, she propped it against her back while inserting the key, turning it slowly so that the lock would not snap, then pushed the door open. After closing both doors, she took off her coat and put it on the entryway's wooden bench with her purse, then slipped off her shoes.

The living room was a beige desert, its modular furniture unstained, its only oases of color two potted plants and a Picasso print over the fireplace. Her stockinged toes curled against the thick, pale rug. She could hear nothing; she knew where her mother was.

She moved stealthily through the dining room and toward the back of the house, stopping when she reached the staircase. Her face was flushed; she pressed icy fingers to her cheeks. She had often sneaked up the stairs when she came home late from dates, always able to avoid the steps that creaked. She set her foot down on the first, skipping the second, holding on to the bannister.

When she reached the next floor, she could hear the voices; the door to her room was ajar. She moved toward the crack of light, the wood under her feet was hard and cold. The child said, "I'm going to be the best, Mommy.

I'm going to be the best at everything."

Christine thrust the door open violently; it bounced against the door stop. The little girl, still dressed in overalls, looked up; she was kneeling on the floor, her arms around Mrs. Matthews's legs. The older woman sat in a rocker; she gazed past Christine, her gray eyes empty.

"Mother," Christine said. The woman's face seemed even paler now, her hair more silvery. "Mother."

The child stood up slowly. "Leave her alone," the little girl said. "You can't have her. She's mine. She'll always be mine."

"Mother, listen to me." Mrs. Matthews stirred slightly at Christine's words. "You have to come away from here."

"She gave you everything," the child said. "She did everything for you, and you failed. But I won't."

"Mother, come out of this room."

"It's too late," the little girl said. "It's too late. You can't change anything now. You can't say you're sorry—it won't help." She grabbed the older woman's hand. "She's mine."

Christine looked around the room, the monument to her past. She strode to the wall, pulled off a framed photograph, and smashed it on the floor. "This isn't me now. You should have thrown all this out years ago." She pulled down another photo, then hurled the National Merit certificate against the wall.

"Chrissie." Her mother was standing now. Christine took a step toward her, then noticed that Mrs. Matthews was gazing down at the child. "May I go with you now?"

The little girl smiled. "Yes. We'll never come back, never."

"No," Christine cried.

"I need her now," the child said. "You don't." She tugged at Mrs. Matthews's hand, leading her toward the corner next to the closet door.

Christine darted after them, stepped off the floor, and was surrounded by fog. "Come back!" The gray formlessness swallowed her words; the thick masses pinned her arms to her side. She could feel nothing under her feet. "Mother, don't go." The mists parted for a moment, revealing a distant room, a tiny canopied bed, the small figures of a little girl and a woman in a blue housecoat. "I need you, too." The fog closed around her again, imprisoning her.

Hands gripped her shoulders; she was being pulled back. She flailed about, stumbled, and found herself leaning against the closet door, clinging to someone's arm.

"Chrissie. Chrissie, are you all right?"

Christine raised her head. A woman was with her. She wore a long housedress; her face was Mrs. Matthews's. But her blond hair was only lightly sprinkled with silver and her gray eyes were warm.

"I'm fine," she said, letting go of the woman's arms.

"I hope so. You look a little pale. I thought I'd find you here." The woman waved a hand at the wall. "Maybe I can help you decide what to take with you—I'll just store these old things in the attic otherwise." She poked at the broken glass on the floor with one toe, then tilted her head to one side. "Are you sure you're all right?"

Christine managed to nod her head.

"Good. I'd better get dressed so we can get started. I wish you could stay longer—I do so enjoy having you home."

Before she left the room, Christine leaned for a moment against her new mother, the one who, through some slip in possibility, would understand and forgive, the one she had always wanted.

(1982)

The Old Darkness

The kitchen window was white with light; a thousand invisible hands clapped in unison. Nina tensed. The kitchen was suddenly dark; outside, the wind howled as rain drummed against the window.

"What was that?" Andrew shouted from the living room.

"I don't know. It sounded like something hit the house."

"It had to happen now—bottom of the ninth, with a tie." She heard her husband shuffle through the hallway toward the kitchen. It was growing darker outside; evening's dim gray light was fading.

"I don't know what I'm going to do about supper," Nina said, staring at her now-useless food processor. "I was just going to chop the onions."

Andrew leaned against the refrigerator. "You used to chop them without that thing."

"I know, but it's made me lazy. I can't do anything without it." She crossed the room, crept into the hall and opened the door, peering into the dark corridor. "Everything's out."

"Nina?"

She recognized her neighbor's voice. "Rosalie?"

"Yeah, it's me. I looked outside a second ago. I can't see a light on the whole street."

"Damn it," Nina said. "I was fixing supper."

"Well, the gas is still on. Just be glad you don't have an electric stove."

Nina cleared her throat. The darkness was making

her uneasy; the air in the hallway seemed heavy and thick. She backed into her apartment, closing the door.

Andrew was still in the kitchen, dialing a number. "Who are you calling?" she asked.

"Power company. Hello? Yeah, I wanted to ask— O.K., I'll wait." He leaned against the wall. Thunder rolled overhead as Nina went to the window; the wind shrieked. The rain was a silver sheet nearly parallel to the ground, a curtain buffeted by the wind.

"Hello? Yeah, I just wanted to know—uh-huh. We're on the north side. Yeah." Andrew paused. "How soon? Uh-huh. O.K. Well, thanks." He hung up. "One of the main lines is down. They said they should have it fixed in an hour or two."

"I guess we can eat late. I can't make this dish without the Cuisinart."

"Oh, come on. You can get along without electricity."

"I can't even see what I'm doing."

"We've got candles. I'll set some up for you. We've got a flashlight." He rummaged in one drawer, pulling out a box of matches. "We can rough it for one evening."

* * *

Nina finished preparing dinner by the flickering yellow light of the candles. Andrew had set one on the stove, another on the counter top, and two more on the table, with a mirror behind them to catch the light.

She shivered. The air seemed unusually cold, in spite of the oven's heat. She felt oddly vulnerable without the familiar presence of electricity, unable to prepare food without it, unable to read—she couldn't even dry her long, thick hair without a hair dryer. The artifacts of technology had only made her more incompetent; she thought of the past, imagining families going about their tasks as the sun set, reading to one another by the light of a fire, drawing close against the night.

Her grandparents, believers in progress, had always told her things were better now. Human minds had been darker when people couldn't read late at night, their prejudices greater when they had lacked television's images of other places, their work harder without the appliances many took for granted. Nina was not so sure; technical civilization had isolated people from the basics of life, and had fooled them into believing that they controlled the world.

Andrew set the table, then put a portable radio and cassette player near the candles. "This isn't so bad. Kind of romantic, actually. We should do this more often."

"They still haven't repaired the line."

"They will."

"Everything in the freezer's going to get ruined."

"Forget about the freezer. It'll keep. Just don't open the door." He uncorked a bottle of wine while she served the stuffed peppers.

As she carried the plates to the table, the thunder rumbled again. Storms had always frightened her, and the darkness beyond the lighted room was filled with threatening shadows. She sat down, facing the mirror. The smell of melting wax mingled with the odor of tomato sauce and spices.

"We've got food. We've even got music." Andrew's voice sounded hollow and distant. A dark shadow loomed behind Nina, about to cloak her in black; she stared at the mirror, afraid to move. Andrew popped a cassette into the player, and the sound of Bach filled the room.

The music was soothing. Andrew began to conduct

with his fork. "Magnificat," he bellowed, along with the chorus.

A fist pounded on the door. Nina started. "Who is it?"

"Rosalie."

That surprised her; Rosalie usually had a gentle, tentative knock. As Nina left the light of the kitchen, the air pressed in around her; she was once again afraid. She opened the door. "Come on in."

The words were hardly out of her mouth before her neighbor was inside. Rosalie panted, then leaned against the wall, hands over her belly. Nina took her arm and led Rosalie into the kitchen, seating her across from Andrew.

"I'm all right now," Rosalie said. "It's the dark. I guess it got to me. I really got scared."

"It's O.K. Do you want a pepper?"

Rosalie shook her head, but accepted a glass of wine from Andrew. "I wouldn't have come over, but I couldn't stay there alone. I was going to go over to Jeff's, but the radio said people should stay off the roads—the wind's knocking down trees."

"Where's Lisanne?"

"At her father's for the weekend." Rosalie lifted her glass; her hand was shaking. She sipped some wine. "All I've got is a flashlight, so I wasn't very prepared."

Andrew turned down the music; a shadow in the corner seemed to darken. "I felt it, too," Nina said. "I got the creeps when I went to answer the door."

"You're too suggestible," Andrew said in a loud voice.

"It was cold," Rosalie said in a flat tone as the candlelight flickered on her face, adding a golden glow to her coppery hair. "I was in the living room, and I felt a cold spot, right in the center of the room. Then the O'Haras started screaming at each other—I could hear them through the floor."

"The O'Haras were fighting?" Nina said, surprised.

"You bet. I didn't know she knew that kind of language. The living room got colder. Something was breathing down my neck, and I thought I heard a sigh. Then I thought, if I don't get out of here, I'll be trapped—I won't be able to—"

"A draft." Andrew gestured with his knife. "There's always a draft in this building."

"It wasn't a draft. The air was just sitting there."

Nina tried to smile. "It's a good thing my grandparents aren't here. They'd be telling old stories by now. You know, there's a legend that the first people who settled in this valley disappeared—just vanished into the woods. And once—" Andrew was warning her with his eyes. "It's just a story. No one believes it."

"You grew up here, didn't you?" Rosalie asked.

Nina nodded. "Lived here all my life, except for college." The rest of her family had left, moving to places of warmth and light, while she had remained behind, afraid to live among strangers unilluminated by familiarity.

The Bach cantata came to an end; Andrew clicked off the cassette player.

"They *still* haven't repaired the line," Nina said.

"The storm's probably worse than they expected." Rosalie's voice echoed in the kitchen. The room was darker; the candle on the stove had gone out. The shadow in the corner was now a misshapen birdlike figure; its wing tips fluttered. "I hope," Rosalie went on, "that you've got more candles. These won't last much longer."

"There's a scented one in the living room." Andrew stood up. "I'd better go get it."

"Take the flashlight," Nina said.

"I can find my way."

Nina turned toward her neighbor as Andrew left the kitchen. She was about to speak when she saw Rosalie's lips draw back over her teeth; the woman was a predator, her jaws ready to bite, her hands claws. "That bastard," Rosalie said softly. "Ever since our divorce, he's been making Lisanne think he's the good guy. I'll bet he's telling her right now that it was all my fault."

Nina drew back. Rosalie had always been on good terms with her ex-husband; their divorce had been notable for its lack of rancor. "He was the one who wanted it," Rosalie continued. "He manipulated me into court, and I didn't even see it. I thought he was being nice, and so I got screwed on the settlement—he knew I wouldn't fight it."

Nina felt trapped. The kitchen seemed small, the walls too close. Then she heard a thud in the front of the apartment, and a cry.

She jumped up, grabbed the flashlight from the counter, and hurried into the living room. "Andy?"

He was lying on the floor, his face pale in the flashlight's beam. "Something hit me." He picked up a thick book and put it on the coffee table.

"Are you all right?" She knelt beside him. He nodded, rubbing his head. "You'd better put up another shelf."

"I haven't had time."

"Then get rid of some of that junk." Nina's voice was sharp. "It's taking over the place. Pretty soon, we'll have to get an apartment just for the books." She was shouting, longing to sweep the rows of hardcover mysteries from the shelves and hurl them into the rain. "And you never do your share of the dusting, either." She took a breath, feeling light-headed; the feeling of oppression had lifted.

A candle danced in the darkness, illuminating Rosalie's face. "Anything wrong?"

Nina sighed as Andrew climbed to his feet. "Book hit me in the head, that's all."

* * *

Andrew cleared the table and put the dirty dishes into the sink, then moved their remaining candles into the living room, along with the cassette player. He lighted only the scented candle, saving the others.

"We've got about three or four hours' worth of candles," he said. "They have to have the line repaired by then." Nina, listening to the whine of the wind, was not so sure.

Andrew turned on the cassette player. Voices singing God's praises wavered, missing a few notes. He hit the machine, then turned it off.

"Haven't you got anything else?" Rosalie asked.

"I've got Vivaldi, and Handel, and some—"

"I should have brought my tapes," Rosalie interrupted. "Unfortunately, I left them in my car." She glanced at the window. "And I'm not going out in that."

Andrew said, "I can't say I'm sorry."

Rosalie lifted her head. "What's that supposed to mean?"

"I can't stand that music you're always playing—if you can even call it music."

"And just what's wrong with it?"

"It's all screaming and percussion—a perfect example of human primitivism and banality."

"Really! I suppose you think that Tinkertoy music is better."

"Don't call it Tinkertoy music."

"It's boring," Rosalie said. "It's all the same."

"How can you say that?"

"Stop it!" Nina shouted. Rosalie sank back on the couch; Andrew, seated on the floor, draped one arm over the coffee table. "We don't have to argue about it." Nina's stomach was tight with tension; she wondered if the stuffed peppers were giving her indigestion. "It's a matter of taste."

Lightning brightened the room for an instant; Andrew's moustache was black against his face. "It's a matter of taste, all right," he said. "Good taste and bad."

Before Rosalie could respond, he had turned on the music again. Andrew shook his head. "I'm sorry, Rosalie."

"It's O.K. I'm sorry, too."

Nina heard footsteps on the stairs, then a knock on the door; a child squealed. "I'll get it," Andrew said.

As he made his way out of the room, Nina leaned toward Rosalie. "He didn't mean it."

"I know. I feel all right now. I just wanted to lash out at someone all of a sudden."

Andrew was speaking to their callers; Nina recognized the voices of Jill and Tony Levitas. Their daughter Melanie preceded them into the room, sat down at one end of the sofa, and began to suck her thumb. The music sounded sluggish; Nina turned off the cassette player.

"Sorry," Jill said as she sat in a chair. "We didn't want to come upstairs, but—I don't know how to put it."

"You were getting the creeps," Rosalie said. "That's why I came over."

Jill lowered her voice. "Our dining room table started to move—honest to God. Then Melanie got hysterical. She said there was something in her room, and she refused to go to bed. She's never been afraid of the dark before."

Rosalie said, "The O'Haras were fighting. Can you believe it?"

"I heard them. It sounded pretty grim."

"I brought a libation," Tony said, setting a jug of wine on the table. Andrew came in with more glasses and poured the wine, then retreated to a corner with Tony.

"We were going to go out tonight," Jill said. "Then the babysitter called, and said she couldn't make it—a tree fell in her driveway. Not that it matters—the theater's probably blacked out, too. So we're stuck."

"Steinbrenner should just leave them alone and let them play ball," Andrew was saying.

"He's paying them." Tony wrapped his arms around his long, thin legs.

"Of course, we have to have this storm on practically the first night in months we were going out," Jill said bitterly. "And it'll probably be ages before we go out again. Let that be a lesson to you, Nina." Two reflected flames fluttered on Jill's glasses. "Don't have a kid until you've done everything you want to do, because you don't get a chance later on. And don't expect your husband to help."

"I heard that," Tony said.

"It's true."

"Look, I have to work. I do my share on the weekends."

"You were the one who talked me into quitting my job."

"Because it would have cost us more for you to work."

"So what? Doesn't my peace of mind mean anything to you?"

"Jill! You *hated* that job."

"At least I was with adults. I'm regressing. The biggest intellectual effort I make now is comparing the merits of 'General Hospital' with 'The Young and The Restless.'"

"You wanted the kid, Jill."

"*You* wanted her!"

"You know what your trouble is?" Tony's voice was unusually high. "You never bothered to look for a job you liked, because you thought some man would take care of you. Now you're bitching because you don't like housework. Well, make up your mind."

Melanie curled up, covering her head with her hands. Nina rubbed her arms; the room felt cold. Something rustled; she heard a crack. Several books flew off the shelves, crashing to the floor; one struck her in the back.

She jumped up. Inside her, a snake uncoiled, creeping up to her throat. "Damn it, Andy! Do you have to get so many books?" She was shouting again. She rarely shouted, and she had done so twice in a few minutes. She strode to the window, peering out at the storm. Lights twinkled on a distant hill, reminding her of stars; at least the south side still had power.

Five men, barely visible, were on the sidewalk below. They were drinking, ignoring the rain that drenched them. Water streamed from their jackets and hair, making them look as though they were melting. One man held his beer bottle by its top, then pitched it over the fence into the front yard.

"Shit," Nina muttered. "Somebody just threw a bottle into the yard."

Andrew was at her side. He pushed up the window, then opened the storm window behind it. Rain sprayed Nina's face.

"Hey!" Andrew shouted above the wind as he shone his flashlight on the litterers. "Pick up your bottle!" The men were still. "Don't throw your crap in our yard."

Another man drew his arm back; a bottle flew, smashing against the side of the building. A second bottle followed it, landing in the branches of the pine tree.

Nina closed the storm window hastily. "Call the police."

"You can't," Tony responded. "The phones are out now. I tried to call you before we came upstairs."

Andrew turned off the flashlight. "I've seen those guys before. They never acted like that."

Melanie whimpered and began to cry. "Hush," Jill said. Melanie wailed. "Be quiet!"

Rosalie reached for the child, trying to soothe her. "Leave her alone."

"There's something to be said for divorce," Jill said. "At least you get to unload Lisanne once in a while. How's that sound, Tony? I'll even give you custody."

"Shut up, Jill."

"I'll even pay child support."

Tony lumbered across the room. "Shut up, damn it."

"I don't know what you're complaining about," Rosalie cried. "I wish I had more time with my kid. That goddamned Elliott made sure he had someone else lined up before he told me he wanted a divorce."

Nina leaned against the window sill. The bitter voices seemed far away, the harsh words dim. The room was warmer, as if her friends' anger had driven away the cold. She gazed at the fluttering shadows near the couch, surprised that the placid Jill and the cheerful Rosalie had such strong feelings.

Andrew gulped down his wine, reached for the jug, and poured another glass. A breath of air tickled Nina's ear. "He's had enough to drink." The voice was so low she could barely hear it; she looked around quickly. "He can't handle it. He never could hold his liquor." Before she could see where the voice was coming from, rage had taken hold of her; she clenched her fists.

Andrew knelt, hitting the cassette player. "Damn battery's dead. Go get some more."

Nina said, "There aren't any more."

"You mean you didn't pick any up?"

"I was going to get some tomorrow." She screamed the words. "You expect me to remember everything."

Andrew poured himself more wine. Nina reached for the bottle; he pulled it away.

"You've had enough, Andy."

"Get off my case." He gulped the wine defiantly.

"Andy, stop it. You know you can't drink that much."

"I'll do what I please. I don't need your permission."

"He'll be a drunk, just like his father," the voice sighed.

"You'll be like your father," Nina said. "You'll drink yourself right into the hospital."

"It's only wine, for Christ's sake." Andrew stood up. "I can't tell you how many times I've wanted to tie one on, and how many times I resisted. You and your nagging. Leave me alone. You'd like to see me drunk, wouldn't you, just to prove your point."

Nina heard a slap. "You son of a bitch!" Jill shouted. "Now you're turning into a wife beater. Go ahead, hit me again."

Tony said, "I'll give you more than a slap next time."

Nina wanted to scream. The voice was whispering again. "Jill always has her television set on too loud. And Tony forgets to mow the lawn. And Melanie leaves her toys on the stairs." She covered her ears, but could still hear the voice. "Admit it," the voice said. "You hate them."

"No!" Nina cried. Melanie had stopped weeping; the racking sobs she heard now were Rosalie's. "We've got to stop this." She felt a sharp pain in her chest, and gasped for air. The room was darker; the walls creaked as the wind outside gusted. "We've never had arguments before—what's the matter with us?" The pain was worse; she sat down, clutching her abdomen. She hated everyone in the room, and the only way she could get rid of the hate was to let it out.

"She's right," Tony said; his voice sounded hoarse. The coffee table rattled; the candle danced. Another book flew across the room, hitting the wall with a thud. The whispers were now so pronounced that Nina could barely hear anything else.

"You know what it is?" Tony said, cackling. "I didn't bless the wine. My parents always told me to bless my food or it would do bad things to me." His voice cracked as he sang a prayer in Hebrew.

Nina's pain was fading. She sniffed; the air, so heavy before, now smelled clean. "What's going on?"

"I don't know," Tony replied.

"Keep praying," Andrew said. Tony sang another prayer. "That's it. If we only had some batteries—we could play more Bach."

"What's that got to do with it?" Rosalie asked.

"It's sacred music. Didn't you notice? When the

cassette was on, we were O.K. Now Tony's praying, and I can't hear those voices anymore."

"You heard them, too?"

"I think we all did."

Nina reached for Andrew's hand. Tony paused for breath; Rosalie began to sing "Rock of Ages." "It's the power failure," Andrew went on. "It's as if electricity is some sort of white magic, keeping things in check. Now we have to use older magic."

Nina trembled. An unseen hand pressed against her head, waiting to crush her when the songs failed. She had always dismissed her grandparents' lore, and even they had not taken it all that seriously. Now she recalled their tales of objects flying across rooms, of occasional murders which usually happened at night, of people barring their doors against the darkness.

"I can't believe it," Tony said. "This is the twentieth century, for God's sake." Rosalie was now singing "Amazing Grace"; her voice faltered on the high notes.

Out in the kitchen, a dish smashed to the floor. The candle on the coffee table went out.

* * *

Nina felt as though she were at the center of a vortex; unseen beings whirled around her. Rosalie continued to sing as Andrew lit the candle. The walls, Nina felt, would cave in on her; whatever was with them would not be held off by a few simple songs and prayers.

"We have to get out of here," Andrew said. "The south side still has power. We ought to be safe there."

"We can't," Jill replied. "It's too risky. They told people to stay off the roads unless it's an emergency."

"This is an emergency. I think we should get into our cars and go."

"No," Rosalie said as Tony began to sing. "We're safer here."

"As long as you keep singing." Books hopped on the shelves. "And maybe not even then."

"Andy's right," Nina said. A cushion of cold air seemed to swallow her words. "Please come with us." She glanced at the sofa. "At least let us take Melanie."

"No," Jill said, moving toward the child and shielding her with one arm.

Nina retreated to the door with Andrew. At the end of the hall, the refrigerator rattled; more dishes fell. She reached for her purse, pulling it off a hook. "I'd better drive. You can't with all that wine in you." The words sounded harsher than she had intended; the pain was returning.

Andrew opened the door. Nina looked back at her neighbors, who were huddled around the candle; a misty barrier now separated her from them. She crept into the hall and down the darkened stairway, clinging to the railing. There was an ominous silence behind the O'Haras' door.

As she opened the front door, the wind nearly tore it from her grasp; she hung on. Andrew took her purse, fumbling for the car keys. She pushed the door shut.

He threw her the purse and sprinted toward the car, which was parked across the street. A large puddle had formed on the lawn, reaching to the sidewalk. Rain poured over her, plastering her clothes against her body. Next door, a man stood outside his house, screaming at the porch. Nina could not see the rest of the street: the sky, dark as it was, seemed lighter than the black earth below it.

Lightning lit her way. A shape was crouching near the building; it barked. "Oscar," she murmured, recognizing the O'Haras' dachshund and wondering what it was doing outside. "Poor thing."

The dog leaped at her, biting at her leg. Claws and teeth tore at her jeans. She swung her purse, hitting the animal in the head and knocking it against the door.

"Come on, Nina!" She ran for the car, climbing in next to Andrew, and started the engine. Windshield wipers fanned back and forth, but the rain was so heavy she could see nothing else.

She turned on the headlights. The car crawled down the road. A tree had fallen, blocking the left side of the street; a group of people were in the right lane. Some were grinning; the headlights caught the white of their teeth and made their eyes gleam.

Nina honked her horn. The crowd rushed the car. She braked. Fists beat against the windows; the car rocked.

"Get going!" Andrew shouted.

She gunned the motor. The car shot forward; the people dropped away. She made a right turn, toward the south. "We'll make it," Andrew said. "Not much farther to go."

The car stalled. Nina turned the key, pumping the pedal. "Damn." The motor turned over and died. "What's wrong with it?"

"I don't know."

"You forgot to take it to the garage. I told you, and you forgot."

"I didn't have time."

"Damn it, Andy!" She struck at him; he grabbed her fists, holding her back. She tried to kick.

"Nina!" He shook her. "We'll have to walk, that's all."

"Out there?"

"You're already soaked. Come on."

They got out of the car. As they ran to the sidewalk, the wind howled, nearly knocking Nina to the ground. She heard a sharp crack. A tree toppled over, smashing the abandoned car.

Andrew grabbed her arm, leading her down the darkened street.

* * *

A dark mass milled in front of the shopping center; Nina heard the sound of shattering glass. Two men brushed past her, carrying a case of bourbon; a boy hurried by with a portable television set.

A crowd had gathered in front of the blacked-out stores. Several people were inside, hurling clothes, small appliances, and bottles through the broken windows to those in the parking lot.

Andrew stopped. Nina tugged at his arm. "We'd better get going!" she shouted. "The police will be here pretty soon." Alarms powered by batteries whined and clanged; the crowd cheered as a microwave oven hurtled through one window. She looked around hastily, wondering where the police were.

Another mob was running toward them; Nina and Andrew were suddenly in the midst of the crowd, being pushed toward the stores. She reached for her husband and clutched air.

"Andy!" She struggled to stay on her feet, afraid she would be trampled if she fell. "Andy!"

A toaster flew past her, hitting another woman, who dropped out of sight. A few people were carrying flashlights, holding them as if they were torches. A young girl raced past, her arms filled with jeans. Nina reached out for a post and held on as the crowd surged toward the liquor store.

Several people were lying on the walkway; she heard groans. Lightning lit up the scene; Nina imagined that she saw a black pool of blood near one man's head. "Andy!"

"Nina."

Andrew was near her, sprawled on the ground. She leaned over, pulling at him. He moaned. "My leg—it's hurt."

She pulled him up; he leaned against her heavily. More people ran past them, joining the crowd looting the nearby hardware store. "I don't think I can make it. You'd better leave me."

"Save yourself," the voice whispered.

"I won't!" Nina shouted. She said a prayer as she hauled Andrew through the parking lot and toward the road.

* * *

The wind had died down; the rain was falling more slowly. Trees threatened Nina with their branches as she passed, swatting at her as she struggled along with the limping Andrew. She was muttering prayers almost automatically, surprised that she, who had not said them in years, could remember so many.

They passed a lawn littered with furniture, and heard a distant scream. A beam blinded her for a moment; pebbles struck her as children laughed. Nina flailed at the air with her free arm. The flashlight fled from her as the children retreated.

She peered through the rain, seeing a hazy golden glow. "Light," she said. "We're almost there." She could now make out streetlights and tried to move faster; Andrew was slowing her down. She said, "You won't get me." A lighted road wound up a hill; an electric company truck was blocking it. She moved toward the truck.

A police car was parked under a streetlight, near the truck. Leading Andrew toward it, she approached the boundary between darkness and light, then stopped.

She tried to step forward and could not; something was holding her back. She pushed; her knees locked.

"No!" she screamed.

A door opened on one side of the police car; a man in a slicker hurried toward her. "What are you doing out here?" he shouted.

"Help us," she said, stretching out an arm. She couldn't reach him. He grabbed at her, then fell back.

"We can't get in," the policeman said. "We've tried. We're still trying."

"And you can't get out," the voice whispered.

She tried to step forward again, and felt herself stumble back; Andrew slipped to the ground.

"I can't help you, lady." The policeman waved his arms helplessly. "I wish I could."

She sank to the ground, cradling Andrew in her arms. The night was suddenly brighter; she was having delusions, seeing the light she longed for. The wind howled its rage. Arms seized her; she held on to Andrew.

"Come on, lady!" The policeman was holding her; he had reached her somehow. He let go and pulled Andrew up. She stumbled to her feet and followed the two men to the car, where the policeman's partner was waiting.

"Look!" the partner shouted.

Nina turned. Her side of town was now starry with light. A solid blackness lifted from the ground, then began to roll back toward the hills in the north. "We're safe," she said to Andrew. "We're safe." The policeman was shaking his head as he gazed at the ebony fog.

Sparks danced along a power line overhead; the line

snapped, writhing down at them like a snake. They dragged Andrew to the car. The north side was once again dark, and growing darker; soon the impenetrable darkness was so thick that Nina, safe in the light, could not see through the blackness at all.

* * *

She had dozed off. Nina awoke with a start, shook herself, and got out of the police car.

The rain had stopped. In the dim light, she could see a medic wrapping a bandage around Andrew's leg. A crowd stood in the street, staring at the black veil before them.

"It's on!" a man's voice shouted. "Power's back!"

As the sun peeped over the hills to Nina's right, the black wall rolled away, defeated by the light. Someone cried out. Only blackened earth lay where the darkness had been; the gloom had taken everything away, leaving only a vast, scarred plain. Only the power lines, the town's humming sentries, remained on the ravaged north side.

Nina thought of her friends, trapped forever in the dark. Where, she wondered, would the darkness go? She knew. It would retreat to the edge of the world, and into the people she knew, and into her; she could feel it lurking there even now, hiding in her mind's shadows with her fears. It would wait for the white magic to fail.

(1983)

The Mountain Cage

Mewleen had found a broken mirror along the road. The shards glittered as she swiped at one with her paw, gazing intently at the glass. She meowed and hunched forward.

Hrurr licked one pale paw, wondering if Mewleen would manage to shatter the barrier, though he doubted that she could crawl through even if she did; the mirror fragments were too small. He shook himself, then padded over to her side.

Another cat, thick-furred, stared out at him from a jagged piece of glass. Hrurr tilted his head; the other cat did the same. He meowed; the other cat opened his mouth, but the barrier blocked the sound. A second cat, black and white, appeared near the pale stranger as Mewleen moved closer to Hrurr.

"She looks like you," Hrurr said to his companion. "She even has a white patch on her head."

"Of course. She is the Mewleen of that world."

Hrurr narrowed his eyes. He had seen such cats before, always behind barriers, always out of reach. They remained in their own world, while he was in this one; he wondered if theirs was better.

Mewleen sat on her haunches. "Do you know what I think, Hrurr? There are moments when we are all between worlds, when the sights before us vanish and we stand in the formless void of possibility. Take one path, and a fat mouse might be yours. Take another, and a two-legs gives you milk and a dark place to sleep. Take a third, and you spend a cold and hungry night. At the moment before choosing, all these possibilities have the same reality, but when you take one path—"

"When you take one path, that's that." Hrurr stepped to one side, then pounced on his piece of glass, thinking that he might catch his other self unaware, but the cat behind the barrier leaped up at him at the same instant. "It means that you weren't going to take the other paths at all, so they weren't really possibilities."

"But they were for that moment." Mewleen's tail curled. "I see a branching. I see other worlds in which all possibilities exist. I'll go back home today, but that cat there may make another choice."

Hrurr put a paw on the shard holding his twin. That cat might still have a home.

"Come with me," Mewleen said as she rolled in the road, showing her white belly. "My two-legged ones will feed you, and when they see that I want you with me, they'll honor you and let you stay. They must serve me, after all."

His tail twitched. He had grown restless even before losing his own two-legged creatures, before that night when others of their kind had come for them, dragging them from his house and throwing them inside the gaping mouth of a large, square metal beast. He had stayed away after that, lingering on the outskirts of town, pondering what might happen in a world where two-legged ones turned on one another and forgot their obligations to cats. He had gone back to his house only once; a banner with a black swastika in its center had been hung from one of the upper windows. He had seen such symbols often, on the upper limbs of people or fluttering over the streets; the wind had twisted the banner on his house, turning the swastika first into a soaring bird, then a malformed claw. A strange two-legs had chased him away.

"I want to roam," he replied as he gazed up the road, wondering if it might lead him to the top of the mountain. "I want to see far places. It's no use fighting it when I'm compelled to wander."

Mewleen bounded toward him. "Don't you know what this means?" She gestured at the broken mirror with her nose. "When a window to the other world is shattered, it's a sign. This place is a nexus of possibilities, a place where you might move from one world to the next and never realize that you are lost to your own world."

"Perhaps I'm meant to perform some task. That might be why I was drawn here."

"Come with me. I offer you a refuge."

"I can't accept, Mewleen." His ears twitched as he heard a distant purr, which rapidly grew into a roar.

Leaping from the road, Hrurr plunged into the grass; Mewleen bounded to the other side as a line of metal beasts passed them, creating a wind as they rolled by. Tiny flags bearing swastikas fluttered over the eyes of a few beasts; pale faces peered out from the shields covering the creatures' entrails.

As the herd moved on up the road, he saw that Mewleen had disappeared among the trees.

* * *

Hrurr followed the road, slinking up the slope until he caught sight of the metal beasts again. They had stopped in the middle of the road; a gate blocked their progress.

Several two-legged ones in gray skins stood by the gate; two of them walked over to the first metal beast and peered inside its openings, then stepped back, raising their right arms as others opened the gate and let the first beast pass. The two moved on to the next beast, looking in at the ones inside, then raised their arms again. The flapping arms reminded Hrurr of birds; he imagined the men lifting from the ground, arms flapping as they drifted up in lopsided flight.

He scurried away from the road. The gray pine needles, dappled by light, cushioned his feet; ahead of him, winding among the trees, he saw a barbed-wire fence. His whiskers twitched in amusement; such a barrier could hardly restrain him. He squeezed under the lowest wire, carefully avoiding the barbs.

The light shifted; patches of white appeared among the black and gray shadows. The trees overhead sighed as the wind sang. "Cat! Cat!" The birds above were calling out their warnings as Hrurr sidled along below. "Watch your nests! Guard your young! Cat! Cat!"

"Oh, be quiet," he muttered.

A blackbird alighted on a limb, out of reach. Hrurr clawed at the tree trunk, longing to taste blood. "Foolish cat," the bird cawed, "I've seen your kind in the cities, crawling through rubble, scratching for crumbs and cowering as the storms rage and buildings crumble. The two-legged ones gather, and the world grows darker as the shining eagles shriek and the metal turtles crawl over the land. You think you'll escape, but you won't. The soil is ready to receive the dead."

Hrurr clung to the trunk as the bird fluttered up to a higher limb. He had heard such chatter from other birds, but had paid it no mind. "That doesn't concern me," he snarled. "There's nothing like that here." But he was thinking of the shattered mirror, and of what Mewleen had said.

"Foolish cat. Do you know where you are? The two-legged ones have scarred the mountain to build themselves a cage, and you are now inside it."

"No cage can hold me," Hrurr cried as the bird flew

away. He jumped to the ground, clawing at the earth. I live, he thought, I live. He took a deep breath, filling his lungs with piney air.

The light was beginning to fade; it would soon be night. He hunkered down in the shadows; he would have to prowl for some food. Below ground, burrowing creatures mumbled sluggishly to one another as they prepared for sleep.

* * *

In the morning, a quick, darting movement caught Hrurr's attention. A small, grayish bird carelessly landed in front of him and began to peck at the ground.

He readied himself, then lunged, trapping the bird under his paws. She stared back at him, eyes wide with terror. He bared his teeth.

"Cruel creature," the bird said.

"Not cruel. I have to eat, you know." He had injured her; she fluttered helplessly. He swatted her gently with a paw.

"At least be quick about it. My poor heart will burst with despair. Why must you toy with me?"

"I'm giving you a chance to prepare yourself for death."

"Alas," the bird sang mournfully. "My mate will see me no more, and the winds will not sing to me again or lift me to the clouds."

"You will dwell in the realm of spirits," Hrurr replied, "where there are no predators or prey. Prepare yourself." He bit down; as the bird died, he thought he heard the flutter of ghostly wings. "I'm sorry," he whispered. "I have no choice in these matters. As I prey upon you, another will prey upon me. The world maintains its balance." He could not hear her soul's reply.

When he had eaten, he continued up the slope until

he came to a clearing. Above him, a path wound up the mountainside, leading from a round, stone tower with a pointed roof to a distant chalet. The chalet sprawled; he imagined that the two-legs inside it was either a large creature or one who needed a lot of space. Creeping up to the nearer stone structure, he turned and looked down the slope.

In the valley, the homes of the two-legged ones were now no bigger than his paw; the river running down the mountainside was a ribbon. This, he thought, was how birds saw the world. To them, a two-legs was only a tiny creature rooted to the ground; a town was an anthill, and even the gray, misty mountains before him were only mounds. He suddenly felt as if he were gazing into an abyss, about to be separated from the world that surrounded him.

He crouched, resting his head on his paws. Two-legged ones had built the edifices on this mountain; such creatures were already apart from the world, unable even to hear what animals said to one another, incapable of a last, regretful communion with their prey, eating only what was stone dead. He had always believed that the two-legged ones were simply soulless beings whose instincts drove them into strange, incomprehensible behavior; they built, tore down, and built again, moving through the world as if in a dream. But now, as he gazed at the valley below, he began to wonder if the two-legged ones had deliberately separated themselves from the world by an act of will. Those so apart from others might come to think that they ruled the world, and their constructions, instead of being instinctive, might be a deliberate attempt to mold what was around them. They might view all the world as he viewed the tiny town below.

This thought was so disturbing that he bounded up, racing along the path and glorying in his speed until he drew closer to the chalet. His tail twitched nervously as he stared at the wide, glassy expanse on this side of the house. Above the wide window was a veranda; from there, he would look no bigger than a mouse—if he could be seen at all. Farther up the slope, still other buildings were nestled among the trees.

His fur prickled; he longed for Mewleen. Her sharp hearing often provoked her to fancies, causing her to read omens in the simplest and most commonplace of sounds, but it also made her aware of approaching danger. He wanted her counsel; she might have been able to perceive something here to which he was deaf and blind.

Something moved in the grass. Hrurr stiffened. A small, gray cat was watching him. For an instant, he thought that his musings about Mewleen had caused the creature to appear. In the next instant, he leaped at the cat, snarling as he raised his hair.

"Ha!" the smaller cat cried, nipping his ear. Hrurr swatted him, narrowly missing his eyes. They rolled on the ground, claws digging into each other's fur. Hrurr meowed, longing for a fight.

The other cat suddenly released him, rolling out of reach, then hissing as he nursed his scratches. Hrurr licked his paw, hissing back. "You're no match for me, Kitten." He waited for a gesture of submission.

"You think not? I may be smaller, but you're older."

"True enough. You're only a kitten."

"Don't call me a kitten. My name is Ylawl. Kindly address me properly."

"You're a kitten."

The other cat raised his head haughtily. "What are you doing here?"

"I might ask the same question of you."

"I go where I please."

"So do I."

The younger cat sidled toward him, but kept his distance. "Did a two-legs bring you here?" he asked at last.

"No," Hrurr replied. "I came alone."

Ylawl tilted his head; Hrurr thought he saw a gleam of respect in his eyes. "Then you are one like me."

Ylawl was still. Hrurr, eyes unmoving for a moment, was trapped in timelessness; the world became a gray field, as it always did when he did not pay attention to it directly. Mewleen had said such visions came to all cats. He flicked his eyes from side to side, and the world returned.

"There is something of importance here," he said to Ylawl. "A friend of mine has told me that this might be a place where one can cross from one world into another." He was about to tell the other cat of the vision that had come to him while he was gazing at the valley, but checked himself.

"It is a cage," Ylawl responded, glancing up at the chalet. "Every day, the metal beasts crawl up there and disgorge the two-legged ones from their bellies, allowing them to gather around those inside, and then they crawl away, only to return. These two-legged ones are so prized that most of this mountain is their enclosure."

Hrurr stretched. "I would not want to be so prized that I was imprisoned."

"It's different for a two-legs. They live as the ants do, or the bees. Only those not prized are free to roam."

Hrurr thought of his two-legged creatures who had been taken from him; they might be roaming even now. He was suddenly irritated with Ylawl, who in spite of his youth was speaking as though he had acquired great wisdom. Hrurr raised his fur, trying to look fierce. "You are a foolish cat," he said, crouching, ready to pounce. Ylawl's tail thrust angrily from side to side.

A short, sharp sound broke the silence. Hrurr flattened his ears; Ylawl's tail curled against his body. The bark rang out once more.

Ylawl scrambled up and darted toward a group of trees, concealing himself in the shadows; Hrurr followed him, crouching low when he reached the other cat's side. "So there are dogs here," he muttered. "And you must hide, along with me."

"These dogs don't scare me," Ylawl said, but his fur was stiff and his ears were flat against his head.

A female two-legs was walking down the path, trailed by two others of her kind. A black terrier was connected to her by a leash; a second terrier was leashed to one of her companions. Hrurr's whiskers twitched with contempt at those badges of slavery.

As the group came nearer, one of the dogs yipped, "I smell a cat, I smell a cat." He tugged at his leash as the female two-legs held on, crooning softly.

"So do I," the second dog said as his female struggled to restrain him.

"Negus!" the two-legs in the lead cried out as she knelt, drawing the dog to her. She began to murmur to him, moving her lips in the manner such creatures used for speaking. "Is that dog loose again?"

"I am sure she isn't," one female replied.

"How she hates my darlings. I wish Bormann had never given her to Adolf." The two-legged one's mouth twisted.

"There's a cat nearby," the dog said. The two-legs, unable to hear his words, stood up again; she was taller than her companions, with fair head fur and a smiling face.

"He must listen to the generals today, Eva," one of the other females said. Hrurr narrowed his eyes. He had never been able to grasp their talk entirely, mastering only the sounds his two-legged ones had used to address him or to call him inside for food.

"Why talk of that here?" the fair-furred one replied. "I have nothing to say about it. I have no influence, as you well know."

Her terrier had wandered to the limit of his leash, farther down the path toward the hidden cats. Lifting a leg, he urinated on one of the wooden fence posts lining the walkway. "I know you're there," the dog said, sniffing.

"Ah, Negus," Ylawl answered. "I see you and Stasi are still imprisoned. Don't you ever want to be free?"

"Free to starve? Free to wander without a master's gentle hand? I think not." He sniffed again. "There is another with you, Ylawl."

"Another free soul."

Negus barked, straining at his leash, but his two-legs was already urging him back toward the chalet. Ylawl stretched out on his side. "Slavish beast." The gray cat closed his eyes. "He has even forgotten his true name, and knows only the one that the two-legs calls him." He yawned. "And the other one is even worse."

"His companion there?"

"No, a much larger dog who also lives in that enclosure." Ylawl rolled onto his stomach, looking up at the chalet. "That one is so besotted by her two-legs that she has begun to lose her ability to hear our speech."

"Is such a thing possible?"

"The two-legged ones have lost it, or never had it to

begin with," Ylawl said. "They cannot even hear our true names, much as we shout them, and in their ignorance must call us by other sounds. Those who draw too close to such beings may lose such a skill as well."

Hrurr dug his claws into the ground. He had never cared for dogs, clumsy creatures who would suffer almost any indignity, but the thought that a dog might lose powers of speech and hearing drew his pity. Mewleen was right, he thought. He had crossed into a world where such evil things could happen. A growl rose in his throat as he curled his tail.

"What's the matter with you?" Ylawl asked.

"I cannot believe it. A dog who cannot speak."

"You can't have seen much of the world, then. You're lucky you didn't run into a guard dog. Try to talk to one of them, and he'll go for your throat without so much as a how-de-do. All you'll hear are barks and grunts."

The worldly young cat was beginning to annoy him. Hrurr swatted him with a paw, Ylawl struck back, and they were soon tussling under the trees, meowing fiercely. He tried to sink his teeth into Ylawl's fur, only to be repulsed by a claw.

Hrurr withdrew. Ylawl glared at him with gleaming eyes. "Now I understand," Hrurr said softly. "I know why I was drawn here."

"And why is that?" the young cat said, flicking his tail.

"I must speak to this dog you mentioned. If she realizes what is happening to her, she'll want to escape. Not that I care for dogs, you understand, but there is more at stake here. The two-legged ones may draw more creatures into their ways, separating us one from another, and then the world will be for us as it is for them. Where there were voices, there will be only silence. The world will end for us."

"It is already ending," Ylawl said pensively. "I have heard the birds speak of burning cities and the broken bodies of two-legged ones amidst the stones. But it is ending for the two-legged ones, not for us. They'll sweep themselves away and the world will be ours again, as it was long ago."

"They will sweep us away with them," Hrurr cried, recalling the blackbird's words.

"Look around. Do you see anything to worry about here? There are the dogs, of course, but one can hardly avoid such animals no matter where one travels. Clearly the creatures who dwell here are valued and carefully caged. If we stay here, we ought to be safe enough."

"I won't live in a cage," Hrurr responded. "Even a dog deserves better. I must speak to her. If she heeds me, she will escape and may be better able to rouse her fellows to freedom than I would be."

Ylawl arched his back. "I see that you must do this thing before you discover how futile it is." He lay down in the shadows again, shielding himself from the bright summer sun.

Hrurr kept his eyes still, and the world vanished once more. Where did it go, he asked himself, and why did it fade away? When he moved his eyes, he found that Ylawl was still with him; the chalet remained on the hill. How many times had he crossed from one world to another without realizing he had done so? Was each world so like every other that no movement could lead him to a truly different place, or was he forever trapped in this one, able only to glimpse the others through windows of shiny glass?

"When will I see this dog?" he asked.

"Soon enough," Ylawl said. "You must wait for her two-legs to lead her outside."

* * *

More metal beasts had come to the chalet, leaving their gray-clothed two-legged ones near the door, where the house had swallowed them. The last to arrive had been a man in black; he entered the chalet while two companions, also in black, lingered near his beast, ignoring the group of two-legged ones in gray who were pacing restlessly.

Hrurr, settling on the grass nearby, waited, grooming himself with his tongue while Ylawl scampered about and inspected the beasts. Occasionally, he could discern the shapes of men behind the wide window above.

At last the other two-legged ones came back out of the house, shaking their heads as they walked toward their metal beasts. The waiting men stiffened and flapped their right arms before opening the beasts' bellies. One of the black-clothed creatures stared directly at Hrurr; the man reminded him of something, but the memory was just out of reach. He waited to hear a gentle croon or to receive a pat on the head, but the two-legs turned away, watching as the other beasts roared toward the road.

Someone had appeared on the veranda above the window; Hrurr widened his eyes. Two men were perching on the stone barrier surrounding the balcony; one turned and gazed out over the land. Hrurr continued to stare. Suddenly a head appeared next to the two-legs; it had the long muzzle of a large Alsatian dog.

"There she is," Ylawl said as he strutted over to Hrurr, tail held high. The two-legs had put his hand on the dog's head and was stroking her affectionately; she opened her mouth, showing her tongue.

"I must speak to you," Hrurr called out.

The dog rose, paws on the balustrade, and barked.

"I must speak to you," Hrurr repeated. "Can't you hear me?"

The Alsatian's ears twitched as she barked again. Her two-legs rubbed her back as she gazed at him happily. Hrurr, turning his attention to this creature, saw that his dark head fur hung over part of his forehead; a bit of dark fur over his lip marked his otherwise hairless lower face.

"What is she called?" Hrurr asked Ylawl.

"Blondi," the younger cat answered, tripping a bit over the odd sound. "It is what her two-legs calls her. She, too, has forgotten her name."

"Blondi!" Hrurr cried. The dog barked again. "Are you so lost to others that you can't even hear me?" Instead of replying, Blondi disappeared behind the balustrade. "She doesn't hear."

"I think she did," Ylawl said. "Either she doesn't want to talk to you, or she's afraid to speak in front of her two-legs."

"But he can't hear what she would say." Hrurr, disappointed, trotted down the hill toward the path leading away from the house. When he looked back, the two-legged creatures had vanished.

He groomed himself for a while, wondering what to do next when a band of two-legged ones rounded the corner of the house, marching toward the path. Blondi, unleashed, was among them. She lifted her nose, sniffing.

"Cats!" she cried as she began to bark. Ylawl was already running toward a tree. The dog raced after him, a blur of light and movement, still barking. Hrurr bounded after Ylawl, following him up the tree trunk toward a limb.

The two cats, trapped, hissed as Blondi danced beneath them. She reared up, putting her paws on the trunk. "Go away," she said. "Leave master alone. Nothing here for you."

Her words chilled Hrurr; they were slurred and ill-formed, the sounds of a creature who had hardly learned how to communicate, yet she seemed unaware of that.

"Blondi," Hrurr said, clinging to the limb, "can you understand what I am saying?"

The dog paused; her forelimbs dropped to the ground. "Too fast," she replied. "More slow."

His fur prickled. Ylawl, fur standing on end, showed his teeth, snarling. "You are losing your power of speech," Hrurr said slowly. "Don't you know what that means?"

The dog barked.

"You have lived among the two-legged ones for too long, and have given up part of your soul. You've drawn too close to them. Listen to me! You must save yourself before it's too late."

"I serve master."

"No, he's supposed to serve you. Let him feed you and keep you at his side if he must, but when you lose your power of speech, he asks too much. The world will become as silent for you as it is for him. Don't you understand?"

"Blondi!" The moustached two-legs had stepped away from his group and was calling to her. She hesitated, clearly wanting to harass the cats, then bounded back to him, rolling in the grass as she groveled at his feet. He barked at her and she stood on her hind legs. Picking up a stick, he held it at arm's length and barked again. The dog leaped over it, then sat on her haunches, tongue out as she panted.

Hrurr, sickened by the slavish display, could hardly bear to watch. Hope had risen in him when he saw the dog without a leash; now he knew that she did not need one, that her master enslaved her without it.

Blondi accepted a pat from her two-legs, then bounded ahead of the group as they began to descend the path, walking in two rows. Blondi's two-legs, walking next to the fair-furred female Hrurr had seen earlier, was in the lead. Behind him, the man in black offered his arm to another female; the others trailed behind, reminding the cat of a flock of geese.

"Blondi!" Hrurr called out once more, but the dog kept near her two-legs, leaping up whenever he gestured to her.

Ylawl hunkered down on the tree limb. "You just had to speak to her. You wouldn't listen to me. Now we're trapped. I don't know how we're going to get down."

Hrurr was already backing away toward the trunk. He clung to the bark with his claws, moving backward down the tree. His paws slipped. He tumbled, arching his body, and managed to land on his feet. "Come on down."

"I can't."

"Don't be such a kitten."

"I can't." The younger cat began to meow piteously as Hrurr fidgeted below.

They had drawn the attention of the two black-clothed creatures near the house, who were now approaching. Hrurr hissed as one of the strangers clucked at him, and retreated a bit, feeling threatened.

One two-legs held out his hands as he boosted his companion, who reached up, grabbed Ylawl by the scruff of the neck, then jumped down. The small cat suddenly dug his claws into his rescuer's arm; the man dropped him, kicking at him with one leather-clad leg. Ylawl dodged him, then ran, disappearing around the side of the house.

One two-legs knelt, holding out a hand to Hrurr as his lips moved. The cat tensed, transfixed by the man's pale eyes and the tiny, gleaming skull on his head covering. His memory stirred. Another man in such a head covering had towered over him as his black-clothed companions had dragged Hrurr's two-legged creatures from their house. He shivered.

"Where are my people?" he asked, forgetting that they could not hear him. The kneeling man bared his teeth; the other began to circle around the cat.

Hrurr leaped up and ran down the hill, the two creatures in pursuit. As he came to a tree, he turned and noticed that the pair had halted. One waved his arms. Giving up the chase, the two climbed back toward the chalet.

Hrurr settled himself under the tree. Had his people been taken to this place? If so, the black-clad men might only have wanted to return him to them. He licked his fur while pondering that possibility. One of his female two-legged ones had screamed, nearly deafening Hrurr as the black-clothed ones dragged her outside; another of his people had been kicked as he lay on the ground. Wherever they were now, he was sure that they would not have wanted him with them; they had not even called out the name they used for him. They must have known that he would be better off on his own.

He should never have come to this place, this cage. He now knew what the broken mirror in the road had meant; his world was shattering, and the black-clad men would rule it along with other creatures who could not hear or speak. He was lost unless he could find his way out of this world.

* * *

The two-legged ones were walking up the path, Blondi bounding ahead of them. Hrurr stretched. He had one last chance to speak. Summoning his courage, he sprang out into the dusky light and stood above the approaching people.

Blondi growled, about to leap up the slope toward the cat when her two-legs seized her by the collar, trying to restrain her. Hrurr struggled with himself, wanting to flee.

"Foolish dog," Hrurr said, raising his fur and arching his back. "Strike at me if you can. At least then I'll be free of this world, and become one of the spirits who stalk the night."

The dog hesitated at his words.

"Free yourself," Hrurr went on. "Leave your two-legs before it's too late. Go into the forest and restore yourself before you can no longer hear our words."

"Free?" Blondi replied. "Free now."

"You're a prisoner, like the one who holds you. You are both imprisoned on this mountain."

Blondi bounced on her front paws, then crouched. Her two-legs knelt next to her, still holding her while his companions murmured and gestured at the cat. "Brave, isn't it?" one man said. "What more could you ask of a German cat?"

The two-legs lifted his head, staring at Hrurr with pale eyes. The cat's tail dropped, pressing against his side. He suddenly felt as though the man had heard his words, could indeed see into his soul and rob him of it, as he had robbed Blondi of hers. Hrurr's ears flattened. The man's gaze seemed to turn inward then, almost as if he contained the world inside himself.

"Blondi!" Hrurr's heart thumped against his chest. "I see death. I see death in the pale face of your master. Save yourself. I see wild dreams in his eyes."

"Have food," the dog said. "Have shelter. No prisoner. Go where he goes, not stay here always. Black-clad ones and gray-clad ones serve him, as I do, as all do. I follow him all my life. Free. What is free?"

The two-legs reached inside his jacket, pulled out a leash, and attached it to Blondi's collar. The dog licked his hand.

The procession continued toward the house. Hrurr leaped out of their way, then trailed them at a distance, hearing Blondi's intermittent, senseless barks. Her two-legs turned around to glance down the mountain, waving a hand limply at the vista below.

"There is the mountain where Charlemagne is said to lie," the two-legs said, indicating another peak. "It is said he will rise again when he is needed. It is no accident that I have my residence opposite it."

"What does it mean?" Hrurr cried out, imagining that Blondi might know.

"That he rule everything," Blondi replied, "and that I serve, wherever he goes."

"We shall win this war," the two-legs said. Behind him, two other creatures were shaking their heads. The fair-furred woman touched his arm.

"Let us go inside, my Fuehrer," one man said.

* * *

The chalet's picture window was bright with light. Hrurr sat below, watching silhouetted shapes flutter across the panes. Earlier in the night, the fair-furred woman had appeared on the balcony above; she had kindly dropped a few bits of food, glancing around nervously as if afraid someone might see her.

"Well?"

Hrurr turned his head. Ylawl was slinking toward him, eyes gleaming in the dark. "I see that Blondi's still there." The dog, a shadow outlined by the light, was now gazing out the window.

"Her master still holds her," Hrurr said. "I think she would even die for him." He paused. "Come with me, Ylawl."

"Where will you go?"

"Down to the valley, I suppose." He thought of returning to Mewleen, wondering if he would ever find her again.

"It's a long way."

"I wish I could go to a place where there are no two-legged ones."

"They are everywhere. You'll never escape them. They'll swallow the world, at least for a time. Best to take what they offer and ignore them otherwise."

"They serve no one except themselves, Ylawl. They don't even realize how blind and deaf they are." Hrurr stretched. "I must leave."

The smaller cat lingered for a moment, then slipped away. "Goodbye, then," Ylawl whispered.

* * *

Hrurr made his way down the slope, keeping away from the roads, feeling his way through the night with his whiskers. The mindless bark of a guard dog in the distance occasionally echoed through the wood; the creature did not even bother to sound warnings in the animals' tongue. He thought of Blondi, who seemed to know her two-legs's language better than her own.

By morning, he had come to the barbed-wire fence;

slipping under it, he left the enclosure. The birds were singing, gossiping of the sights they had seen and the grubs they had caught and chirping warnings to intruders on their territory.

"Birds!" Hrurr called out. "You've flown far. You must know where I would be safe. Where should I go?"

"Cat! Cat!" the birds replied mockingly. No one answered his question.

* * *

He came to the road where he had left Mewleen and paced along it, seeking. At last he understood that the broken mirror was gone; the omen had vanished. He sat down, wondering what it meant.

Something purred in the distance. He started up as the procession of metal beasts passed him, moving in the direction of the distant town. For a moment, he was sure he had seen Blondi inside one beast's belly, her nose pressed against a transparent shield, death in her eyes.

When the herd had rolled past, he saw Mewleen gazing at him from across the road, bright eyes flickering. He ran to her, bounding over the road, legs stretching as he displayed his speed and grace. Rolling onto his back, he nipped at her fur as she held him with her paws; her purring and his became one sound.

"The fragments are gone," he said.

"I know."

"I'm in my own world again, and the dog has been taken from the cage."

"Whatever do you mean?" Mewleen asked.

He rolled away. "It's nothing," he replied, scrambling to his feet. He could not tell Mewleen what he had seen; better not to burden her with his dark vision.

"Look at you," she chided. "So ungroomed—I imagine you're hungry as well." She nuzzled at his fur.

"Do you want to come home with me now? They may shoo you away at first, but when they understand that you have no place to go, they'll let you stay."

He thought of food and dark, warm places, of laps and soft voices. Reluctantly, he was beginning to understand how Blondi felt.

"For a while," he said, clinging to his freedom. "Just for a while." As they left the road, several birds flew overhead, screaming of the distant war.

(1983)

Heavenly Flowers

The sun was too bright. Maisie tried to ignore the ache in her joints and the gnawing pain in her intestines. She sat in the back seat of an old Ford station wagon, her head resting on Gene's shoulder. Junior, sitting on Maisie's left, squealed as he caught sight of a thick, green bush and a patch of blue wildflowers, their colors bright against the desolate, pockmarked ground.

Lydia was driving, and the car began to lurch, jostling Maisie and making her ache even more. Talia began to bounce on the front seat and whined softly as her father Drew stared out the window, trying to ignore the girl.

"Need anything?" Gene asked Maisie.

"I can hold out."

He patted her shoulder. The car stalled. Lydia gunned the motor, then switched off the ignition.

Drew sighed. "Better get out and stretch," he said.

Everyone got out and stood by the side of the highway while Drew opened the hood and fiddled with the engine. Lydia tied Talia's bonnet firmly on the child's head, then said to Junior, "Put on your hat."

"Aw."

"Put it on right now."

Junior put on his oversized fedora. Maisie adjusted her widebrimmed hat and rolled down her sleeves. They had allowed themselves plenty of time, but she had hoped that they would arrive early; she did not want to miss any of the festivities. This ceremony was special, the thirtieth anniversary, and perhaps the last time a nationwide ceremony would be held. Radio broadcasts had alerted everyone; people from all over the country would be there. Maisie's family had been traveling for two days and would reach the fairground by the following evening if Drew did not have to spend too much time nursing the Ford. She suspected that this was the last long trip the car would ever make.

"I could use some now," Maisie said to Gene.

He grunted and reached inside his shirt pocket, took out a pouch, and tapped some weed into a cigarette paper while Lydia looked on, frowning her disapproval. Gene passed the lighted joint to Maisie, who toked on it, then handed it back.

The highway, pocked with potholes and partly covered by drifting sand, stretched out toward the horizon in the east and disappeared among brown hills in the west. Maisie squinted; another vehicle was approaching from the east, crawling along the road as it weaved its way around the potholes and broken asphalt. As it came nearer, she saw that it was a red Subaru, and wondered how its owner had kept it going; parts for Japanese cars had become hard to find lately.

The Subaru pulled up behind the Ford and a middle-aged man got out; his passenger stayed inside. The man rolled down his sleeves and adjusted his hat. Maisie took a last toke and handed the roach to Gene, who leaned over, stubbed it out, and tucked it into his pocket.

"Hey!" the stranger said as he walked over to them.

"Hey," Gene answered.

"You going to the fairground?"

"You bet," Maisie said, thinking it was a foolish question.

"So am I. Jim Fairbairn." He stuck out his gloved hand and Gene shook it. "That's my wife, Dora. She's not feeling so good at the moment."

"Gene Sakowitz."

"Mrs. Sakowitz?" Jim Fairbairn said as he shook Maisie's hand.

She shook her head. "Maisie Torrance. Gene's my man, but we aren't married. This is our daughter, Lydia Simpson—that's her husband, Drew, by the car. And this is Talia, and that's their boy Junior over there."

Junior was pissing at the side of the road. "Say hello to the man," Lydia shouted. Junior buttoned his trousers, wandered over, and mumbled a greeting while Talia stared. Maisie wiped her face with one sleeve; the sun was hot.

"How's your car holding up?" Jim asked.

"It's doing all right," Maisie said. "How far have you come, Jim?"

"From Ohio."

"Long way." Maisie cleared her throat, which was dry from the pot, and took a breath, feeling better; her pain had been dulled. "Been out before?"

"Not since I was a kid. This highway goes all the way to the fairground, doesn't it? I checked an old map before I left."

"Yeah. But I wouldn't follow it if I were you. About twenty miles from here, you run into a hot spot— you have to take the long way around if you don't want to get cooked."

Jim frowned. "Maybe I can follow you."

Gene shrugged. "If you want."

"I'd be obliged."

"Keep your hat on, young man," Lydia shouted at Junior, who was swinging it over his head.

Jim glanced at the boy. "Nice-looking kid. You must be proud of him."

Lydia nodded. Maisie tapped Gene's pocket. He took out his weed, rolled another joint, and handed it to Jim. "For your wife," Maisie said. "It helps the pain a little."

"Thanks."

Drew had finished with the engine and was filling the tank with alcohol. When he was done, he motioned to them. Lydia picked Talia up, lugging the girl's heavy body back to the car; Jim opened the door for her.

Drew took the wheel. They rode on, the Subaru trailing them. Lydia turned toward Maisie, resting her arm on the seat. "You didn't have to make a point of telling him you and Father aren't married."

Maisie was about to reply, but caught herself. Younger people set more store by such ceremonies, and she couldn't blame them for it; they longed for the signs of order and normality. But only one ceremony mattered to her, the one they were soon to witness, the one that reminded Maisie of how much she had lost and of how lucky she was to be alive.

* * *

The plain was covered by tents and pavilions, and Maisie's family had to set up camp on the edge of the grounds after arriving at the fairground. There was one consolation; a big truck carrying tanks of water had parked near them, so they would not have to go far for that commodity.

Maisie sat against the Ford while Drew and Lydia settled the children inside their tent. Gene, after pawing through his collection of items for barter, had taken out a tape cassette to swap for some water. A man on horseback rode by and waved; he was followed by a woman offering to trade flashlights and pencils for dried meat.

Gene returned with two large bottles and two men. The older man was stooped and wizened, but Maisie caught her breath as she stared at the younger one. Under his hat, his handsome face glowed with good health; she had not seen such a beautiful young man in a long time. As the young man sat down, he bowed his head, as though aware of Maisie's reaction.

Gene introduced Maisie, then gestured at the two men. "David Chung. And this is his son, Paul."

Paul brushed back a lock of black hair, smiled at Maisie, then looked down again. David grinned. "We've only been here a few hours, and Paul's had offers already."

Maisie said, "I'm not surprised."

"I have two grandchildren already," David went on. "One of them takes after Paul."

"We've got a strong grandson." Maisie did not mention poor Talia.

"I know—Gene told me."

"We met over by the water truck," Gene said. "David came all the way from California."

"I don't know if we should have come at all," Paul blurted out. "We dwell on it too much. Maybe it's better just to forget."

Maisie shook her head. "Even if we tried, we couldn't. And we shouldn't. People have to remember. It's important for you young folks to keep up the ceremony after we're gone."

"How?"

Paul had asked a good question, and Maisie did not have an answer. David pulled a pipe out of his pocket and tapped in some weed. "Sinsemilla," he said proudly.

Gene sighed. "I didn't think there was any left."

"We still grow some." David lit the pipe, puffed, and passed it to Maisie, who drew in the smoke deeply. She felt a rush as she handed the pipe to Gene. Paul did not smoke; like all young people, he guarded his health, avoiding such habits.

When they had finished David's marijuana, Gene got out a little of his homegrown, and they passed the pipe again. Lydia glared at them as she came over for one of the water jars; as she caught sight of Paul, she straightened up and stared at him. Maisie giggled as Lydia retreated to the tent.

"Your daughter?" David asked. "The one with the healthy boy?"

Maisie nodded; the pot made her want to laugh again.

"What do you think?" David said to Paul.

"Maybe we can bargain," the young man answered.

"What do you think?" David asked Maisie.

"You'll have to talk to Drew—that's her husband. And Lydia'll want to know Paul's history."

Paul got up and went to the tent. Drew and Lydia came outside and talked to him while the old people finished the pot. Maisie, noticing that the sun was almost down, took off her hat and fanned herself with it as she watched.

At last Drew went to the car, took out a pack, rummaged in it, and removed a vial, handing it to Paul. As Lydia approached, Drew took her hand, kissed her on the cheek, then gave her hand to the other man. That's Drew, Maisie thought, formal as always—never neglecting custom.

Paul led Lydia away. "Hope it works out," David said.

"Hope so." Maisie, stoned, was feeling optimistic.

Her own attempts with other men at past festivals had resulted in two miscarriages, but she had lost two of Gene's children as well. Lydia was stronger.

They sat, talking of old times until it was completely dark. David took out a pocket flashlight while Gene and Maisie showed him some of their treasures—a matchbox bearing the University of Wisconsin seal, a Phillips screwdriver, a Boy Scout handbook, a pair of scissors.

When Lydia returned, she went directly to the tent. David stood up. "Better get some rest. Things start early."

"See you tomorrow," Gene said. He helped Maisie to her feet. "Feeling all right?"

"I'm fine."

"I think Drew gave a lot of the medicine to Paul."

Maisie was suddenly resentful; Drew should have asked her first. but Lydia's chance at another healthy baby was more important, and she could get by without the pills for now.

* * *

The clear blue morning sky promised a good day for the ceremonies. Maisie sat on the hood of the Ford, estimating the crowd; there were close to three thousand people on the plain, and she supposed that almost every town had sent several of its citizens.

Two rivers of people were streaming toward the distant silos; for that extra thrill, they would miss much of the ceremony itself. Others were seating themselves near the raised platform of wood in the center of the field, putting up umbrellas and canopies to shade themselves.

Lydia strode toward her from the tent. "Mother? We're going over to Paul's tent with Junior, and then we're going to try to get a good seat. Need anything?"

"I'm fine." Maisie frowned. "Twice with Paul?"

"That was the bargain. And Drew thinks Junior ought to meet him."

"He would. He must have given Paul a lot of pills for two times."

"I know. I'm sorry. But you understand." Lydia lowered the veil on her floppy blue hat, hiding her face.

"Yes, I understand."

"We'll see you afterwards. Talia's in the tent—I gave her something, so she should sleep through everything, but you'd better look in on her once in a while."

"Sure."

Lydia walked off with Drew and Junior. Five young people passed Maisie on their way toward the platform; their faces were attractive, but she could not know what their loose, flowing garments hid. Two of the boys wore Panama hats, another had a sombrero, and the two girls were wearing large white bonnets. Maisie adjusted her hat, lowering the brim. She had put it on at dawn, out of habit, though she could not benefit from its protection now. Two veiled women passed, their long skirts swaying around their legs.

Jim Fairbairn got out of his car and came over to her. "Going to look for a seat?"

"We're staying here." She paused. "We've got binoculars."

Jim whistled. "Lucky you." He glanced toward the platform. Several old soldiers were on the stand, fiddling with the sound system; they would soon be on their way to the silos. "As I recall," Jim went on, "they don't get started until late afternoon."

"That's right. But if you want a good seat, you'd better go now."

"I'm staying here. Dora's pretty sick. I don't want to leave her alone." He lowered his voice. "She's the one who really wanted to come. I didn't think she'd make it this far. She just wanted to be here, even if she doesn't see anything."

"I can understand that."

Jim leaned against the car. "We were just little kids when it happened, so we don't really know what it was like before. It must be harder for you."

Maisie did not reply at first, wishing Jim had not spoken of that. "We're alive," she said. "We're thankful for that." She could say it now; she could not have said it thirty years ago, when she had longed for death and had cursed herself for surviving.

"Well, I'd better get back to Dora."

As Jim got back into his car, Gene returned with David Chung. "Dave's going to sit with us. Think we'll see well enough from here?"

Maisie lifted her binoculars and focused on the platform. "Sure."

"The Chinese envoy's here," David said. "And a Russian from the Council. They're really doing things up this year."

Maisie nodded. "I heard on the radio that we sent people to their ceremonies, too."

"I wonder what we'll do next year," Gene murmured.

Maisie thought, I won't be doing much of anything. She climbed down from the car. "I'm going to check on Talia, and then rest for a while." She hobbled away from the men, pressing her lips together, trying to ignore the pain.

* * *

The sky was still unclouded that afternoon as Maisie waited for the ceremony to begin. The crowd, noisy throughout the day, was settling down. People had positioned themselves near the platform on chairs and blankets and under protective umbrellas and veils while vendors circulated among them, trying to make a few last trades for food and drink before the ceremony started.

She glanced at Jim's car; he and Dora were still inside. Taking the binoculars from David, she gazed at the platform. Various dignitaries were already seated under the canopy; one old soldier, dressed in an officer's uniform, got up, crossed the platform, and knelt before a group of old people sitting near the edge. They gazed sightlessly past him. The old people, representing all of those who had been blinded thirty years before by glancing at the approaching destruction, had a special place of honor.

The officer beat his chest and wailed as the crowd grew silent. Then the president rose and approached the microphone.

"Testing," he said, and the ominous word rang out over the plain. "Testing." He adjusted his hat, a Stetson bearing the Stars and Stripes, then struck his chest with one fist. "I accuse myself." He was a lean young man with the scars of skin cancer surgery on his face, and could not have been more than a child thirty years ago, but the words were part of the ceremony. "I accuse myself of murder. I am guilty of genocide. Billions lie in graves because of me."

The Russian was at his side; he wore a fedora with an embroidered hammer and sickle. "I accuse myself," the Russian said as the president yielded the microphone. "I am a murderer, guilty of the worst crime in human history." The Chinese envoy, a small woman wearing a cap with a red star, then said the same words in a high-pitched singsong.

Maisie drew up her knees, resting her elbows on

them as she gazed through her binoculars. Gene and David took turns looking through the other pair. The three dignitaries on the platform lifted their eyes to the sky.

"We brought death on the world, and our guilt will never be washed away," the president cried. "Speak the names."

The crowd below uttered an indistinct barrage of names. Maisie put down her binoculars and whispered as many as she could remember; her father, her mother, her two brothers, her best friends. She blocked her memories of that day, thinking only of the names. Gene rocked as he spoke; David covered his eyes. Within an hour, a billion had died; within a month, another billion; within a year, most of the world. Maisie had found that out only later.

As the murmuring faded, the president spoke again. "Let the ceremony begin."

Maisie lifted her binoculars. The president knelt, and others on the stand approached, carrying long sticks, tapping them on the president's shoulder as they passed. This part of the ceremony depicted the death of the president who had launched the missiles, who had been beaten to death by an angry, dying mob when he had emerged from his shelter. Maisie muttered the name of that man, making it a curse. The Russian and the Chinese were also tapped with the sticks, though rumor had it that the Russian leader had been assassinated in his shelter by his successor, while the Chinese leader had committed suicide.

A woman stepped forward, stood near the president, and wailed as she clutched her belly, symbolizing the fear of mothers for their children and the birth of the maimed and deformed. Another woman was strewing dirt on the platform, a reminder of the poisoned earth.

Maisie lowered her arms. The pain was returning. She clenched her teeth, determined to get through the rest of the ceremony somehow. A few people on the edges of the crowd seemed restless. A couple of small children, obviously bored, were poking at each other; a group of young people whispered among themselves. The ceremony meant little to them. Maisie shook her head. They had to be made to remember.

"Never again," the president shouted, and the crowd took up the cry: "Never again." The young people Maisie was watching looked up; she saw their lips move. "Never again." At least they were saying the words.

"We have disarmed," the president went on. "Never again will so many die. Never again will men fight other men. Never again will the world know mass weapons of destruction. At last we have what so many sought— universal peace, a world council, and good will toward all our fellows."

"A little late," David muttered.

Maisie touched his arm. "At least you have Paul."

"I hope he and your daughter have a good, strong child."

"I hope so, too." .

"I think it's a mistake—not having any more national ceremonies after this one."

"Maybe. But there'd be nothing to hold them with. That's good, though. We'll be rid of them all after tonight."

"But the custom's important," David said.

"This is my last ceremony. I'll never see another one anyway."

"I don't think I will, either."

The sun was setting. The people on the platform

were now lifting tattered flags, holding them up before the spectators, then slapping them down on the planks, stamping on them with their feet. Stars and stripes fell next to a red flag bearing the hammer and sickle, followed by a red star, the Union Jack, a maple leaf, the Tricolor, the Sword and Crescent, the Star of David, and various other banners. Some of the flags were so ragged that it was impossible to tell which countries they had once represented.

A woman marched forward with the world flag, a phoenix rising from ashes against a black background, and the audience sighed, then was still. Maisie trembled at the silence, which reminded her of the quiet that had pressed in around her when she had emerged to find the world in ruins.

As the sun disappeared behind the distant mountains, she heard the rumble, and clutched at David's hand. Gene let out his breath. The rumble grew louder, thundering over the plain; the ground trembled. Maisie tensed, thinking for a moment that she would be thrown from the earth. She covered her ears, but her body still felt the thunder.

As the missiles were launched from the east, the car vibrated with the roar. Maisie lifted her head, following the trails as the missiles arced toward the purple sky. She gazed at the flickering flames and the threads of smoke until she heard the last clap of thunder, and could see the weapons no more.

She waited. A bloom of light, far above the atmosphere, dying in the darkness. She closed her eyes and turned her head away, even though she knew there was no danger. Far away, physics was different, like the silence under the sea or the warmth of the sun.

"We live," the president shouted.

"We live! We live!" the crowd answered.

The last weapons were gone; the world was disarmed.

"We live," Maisie whispered.

The people near the stand were dancing, shouting out the words. The celebration would last into the night; she supposed that many bargains would be made before morning.

The pain clawed at her then; she toppled forward, almost sliding off the car. David caught her while Gene hurried around to her side. "Maisie?"

"Gene," she said, slumping into his arms.

* * *

She awoke in the tent, and saw light through the flap; it was morning. Gene was at her side. He put a pill in her mouth and handed her a cup of water; she swallowed it.

"We have plenty of medicine now," he said. "I gave the binoculars to David, and he gave back the pills Drew gave to Paul. Paul doesn't mind, and we need the medicine more than an extra set of binoculars."

"Thanks." She tried to sit up, and could not. "I won't make it home."

"Yes, you will."

She shook her head. He lifted her up and carried her outside, setting her down on a pillow against the Ford, then put her hat on her head. Two cars, a truck, and a horse-drawn buckboard rattled by; people were heading home.

Jim Fairbairn's car was gone, a mound of earth in its place. Maisie pulled at Gene's sleeve.

"Dora died last night," he said. "I helped Jim dig the grave. I guess we're all experts at that."

Maisie sighed, wondering how long she and Dora might have lived without the war. Drew wandered over and peered at her, looking concerned. "You all right, Maisie?"

"I'm fine."

"Did Gene tell you? The president said that, next year, every town should hold its own ceremony—he announced it at dawn. He'll say something over the radio, and every town will have a festival, so this isn't the last one after all. Of course, they'll be smaller, and we'll have to use fireworks instead of missiles."

"We won't forget," Gene said. "It'll be like the Fourth of July used to be."

"No," Maisie said. "Not like the Fourth."

Drew went to help Lydia take down the tent. Maisie gazed at them, Drew with his slightly humped back and skin cancer scars, Lydia with her oversized head. They didn't look too bad—not as bad as some. Talia, lying next to Maisie, kicked her feet, twisting the shapeless garment that hid her armless body, then hummed tunelessly while Maisie stroked her granddaughter's head, wondering if the child would ever be able to speak.

Junior sat near the tent, pouting. Gene motioned to him. "You going to behave?" Junior did not answer. "He got into a fight with another boy this morning," Gene went on. "Called him a mutie. I had to break it up." He waved at the boy again. "Get over here, young man, before that tent falls on top of you."

Junior wandered over to them, clutching a toy made of wood. One end of the toy came to a point; two wings had been carved on its sides. The boy lifted it, swooped toward Maisie, then stabbed the toy into the ground at her feet.

"Boom," Junior shouted as he strewed dirt around with his hands. "Kaboom. Boom. Bang."

(1983)

Fears

I was on my way back to Sam's when a couple of boys tried to run me off the road, banging my fender a little before they sped on, looking for another target. My throat tightened and my chest heaved as I wiped my face with a handkerchief. The boys had clearly stripped their car to the minimum, ditching all their safety equipment, knowing that the highway patrol was unlikely to stop them; the police had other things to worry about.

The car's harness held me; its dashboard lights flickered. As I waited for it to steer me back onto the road, the engine hummed, choked, and died. I switched over to manual; the engine was silent.

I felt numb. I had prepared myself for my rare journeys into the world outside my refuge, working to perfect my disguise. My angular, coarse-featured face stared back at me from the mirror overhead as I wondered if I could still pass. I had cut my hair recently, my chest was still as flat as a boy's, and the slightly padded shoulders of my suit imparted a bit of extra bulk. I had always been taken for a man before, but I had never done more than visit a few out-of-the-way, dimly lighted stores where the proprietors looked closely only at cards or cash.

I couldn't wait there risking a meeting with the highway patrol. The police might look a bit too carefully at my papers and administer a body search on general principles. Stray women had been picked up before, and the rewards for such a discovery were great; I imagined uniformed men groping at my groin, and shuddered. My disguise would get a real test. I took a deep breath, released the harness, then got out of the car.

* * *

The garage was half a mile away. I made it there without enduring more than a few honks from passing cars.

The mechanic listened to my husky voice as I described my problem, glanced at my card, took my keys, then left in his tow truck, accompanied by a younger mechanic. I sat in his office, out of sight of the other men, trying not to let my fear push me into panic. The car might have to remain here for some time; I would have to find a place to stay. The mechanic might even offer me a lift home, and I didn't want to risk that. Sam might be a bit too talkative in the man's presence; the mechanic might wonder about someone who lived in such an inaccessible spot. My hands were shaking; I thrust them into my pockets.

I started when the mechanic returned to his office, then smiled nervously as he assured me that the car would be ready in a few hours; a component had failed, he had another like it in the shop, no problem. He named a price that seemed excessive; I was about to object, worried that argument might only provoke him, then worried still more that I would look odd if I didn't dicker with him. I settled for frowning as he slipped my card into his terminal, then handed it back to me.

"No sense hanging around here." He waved one beefy hand at the door. "You can pick up a shuttle to town out there, comes by every fifteen minutes or so."

I thanked him and went outside, trying to decide what to do. I had been successful so far; the other mechanics didn't even look at me as I walked toward the road. An entrance to the town's underground garage was just across the highway; a small, glassy building with a sign saying "Marcello's" stood next to the entrance. I knew what service Marcello sold; I had driven by the place before. I would be safer with one of his employees, and less conspicuous if I kept moving; curiosity overcame my fear for a moment. I had made my decision.

* * *

I walked into Marcello's. One man was at a desk; three big men sat on a sofa near one of the windows, staring at the small holo screen in front of them. I went to the desk and said, "I want to hire a bodyguard."

The man behind the desk looked up; his mustache twitched. "An escort. You want an escort."

"Call it whatever you like."

"For how long?"

"About three or four hours."

"For what purpose?"

"Just a walk through town, maybe a stop for a drink. I haven't been to town for a while, thought I might need some company."

His brown eyes narrowed. I had said too much; I didn't have to explain myself to him. "Card."

I got out my card. He slipped it into his outlet and peered at the screen while I tried to keep from fidgeting, expecting the machine to spit out the card even after all this time. He returned the card. "You'll get your receipt when you come back." He waved a hand at the men on the sofa. "I got three available. Take your pick."

The man on my right had a lean, mean face; the one on the left was sleepy-eyed. "The middle guy."

"Ellis."

The middle man stood up and walked over to us. He was a tall black man dressed in a brown suit; he looked me over, and I forced myself to gaze directly at him while the man at the desk rummaged in a drawer and took out a weapon and holster, handing them to my escort.

"Ellis Gerard," the black man said, thrusting out a hand.

"Joe Segor." I took his hand; he gripped mine just long enough to show his strength, then let go. The two men on the sofa watched us as we left, as if resenting my choice, then turned back to the screen.

* * *

We caught a shuttle into town. A few old men sat near the front of the bus under the watchful eyes of the guard; five boys got on behind us, laughing, but a look from the guard quieted them. I told myself again that I would be safe with Ellis.

"Where to?" Ellis said as we sat down. "A visit to a pretty boy? Guys sometimes want escorts for that."

"No, just around. It's a nice day—we could sit in the park for a while."

"I don't know if that's such a good idea, Mr. Segor."

"Joe."

"Those crossdressers hang out a lot there now. I don't like it. They go there with their friends and it just causes trouble—it's a bad element. You look at them wrong, and then you've got a fight. It ought to be against the law."

"What?"

"Dressing like a woman. Looking like what you're not." He glanced at me. I looked away, my jaw tightening.

We were in town now, moving toward the shuttle's first stop. "Hey!" one of the boys behind us shouted. "Look!" Feet shuffled along the aisle; the boys had rushed to the right side of the bus and were kneeling on the seats, hands pressed against the window; even the guard had turned. Ellis and I got up and changed seats, looking out at what had drawn the boys' attention.

A car was pulling into a spot in front of a store. Our driver put down his magazine and slowed the bus manually; he obviously knew his passengers wanted a look. Cars were not allowed in town unless a woman was riding in one; even I knew that. We waited. The bus stopped; a group of young men standing outside the store watched the car.

"Come on, get out," a boy behind me said. "Get out of the car."

Two men got out first. One of them yelled at the loiterers, who moved down the street before gathering under a lamppost. Another man opened the back door, then held out his hand.

She seemed to float out of the car; her long pink robe swirled around her ankles as she stood. Her hair was covered by a long, white scarf. My face grew warm with embarrassment and shame. I caught a glimpse of black eyebrows and white skin before her bodyguards surrounded her and led her into the store.

The driver pushed a button and picked up his magazine again; the bus moved on. "Think she was real?" one of the boys asked.

"I don't know," another replied.

"Bet she wasn't. Nobody would let a real woman go into a store like that. If I had a girl, I'd never let her go anywhere."

"If I had a trans, I'd never let her go anywhere."

"Those trans guys—they got it made." The boys scrambled toward the back of the bus.

"Definitely a trans," Ellis said to me. "I can tell. She's got a mannish kind of face."

I said, "You could hardly see her face."

"I saw enough. And she was too tall." He sighed. "That's the life. A little bit of cutting and trimming and some implants, and there you are—you don't have to lift a finger. You're legally female."

"It isn't just a little bit of cutting—it's major surgery."

"Yeah. Well, I couldn't have been a transsexual anyway, not with my body." Ellis glanced at me. "You could have been, though."

"Never wanted it."

"It's not a bad life in some ways."

"I like my freedom." My voice caught on the words.

"That's why I don't like crossdressers. They'll dress like a woman, but they won't turn into one. It just causes trouble—you get the wrong cues."

The conversation was making me uneasy; sitting so close to Ellis, hemmed in by his body and the bus's window, made me feel trapped. The man was too observant. I gritted my teeth and turned toward the window. More stores had been boarded up; we passed a brick school building with shattered windows and an empty playground. The town was declining.

* * *

We got off in the business district, where there was still a semblance of normal life. Men in suits came and went from their offices, hopped on buses, strolled toward bars for an early drink.

"It's pretty safe around here," Ellis said as we sat on a bench. The bench had been welded to the ground; it was covered with graffiti and one leg had been warped. Old newspapers lay on the sidewalk and in the gutter with other refuse. One bore a headline about the African war; another, more recent, the latest news about Bethesda's artifical womb program. The news was good; two more healthy children had been born to the project, a boy and a girl. I thought of endangered species and extinction.

A police car drove by, followed by another car with opaque windows. Ellis gazed after the car and sighed longingly, as if imagining the woman inside. "Wish I was gay," he said sadly, "but I'm not. I've tried the pretty boys, but that's not for me. I should have been a Catholic, and then I could have been a priest. I live like one anyway."

"Too many priests already. The church can't afford any more. Anyway, you'd really be frustrated then. They can't even hear a woman's confession unless her husband or a bodyguard is with her. It's just like being a doctor. You could go nuts that way."

"I'll never make enough to afford a woman, even a trans."

"There might be more women someday," I said. "That project at Bethesda's working out."

"Maybe I should have gone on one of those expeditions. There's one they let into the Philippines, and another one's in Alaska now."

I thought of a team of searchers coming for me. If they were not dead before they reached my door, I would be; I had made sure of that. "That's a shady business, Ellis."

"That group in the Amazon actually found a tribe—killed all the men. No one'll let them keep the women for themselves, but at least they have enough money to try for one at home." Ellis frowned. "I don't know. Trouble is, a lot of guys don't miss women. They say they do, but they really don't. Ever talk to a real old-timer, one that can remember what it was like?"

"Can't say I have."

Ellis leaned back. "A lot of those guys didn't really like girls all that much. They had places they'd go to get away from them, things they'd do together. Women didn't think the same way, didn't act the same—they never did as much as men did." He shaded his eyes for a moment. "I don't know—sometimes one of those old men'll tell you the world was gentler then, or prettier, but I don't know if that's true. Anyway, a lot of those women must have agreed with the men. Look what happened— as soon as you had that pill that could make you sure you had a boy if you wanted, or a girl, most of them started having boys, so they must have thought, deep down, that boys were better."

Another police car drove past; one of the officers inside looked us over before driving on. "Take a trans," Ellis said. "Oh, you might envy her a little, but no one really has any respect for her. And the only real reason for having any women around now is for insurance— somebody's got to have the kids, and we can't. But once that Bethesda project really gets going and spreads, we won't need them any more."

"I suppose you're right."

Four young men, dressed in work shirts and pants, approached us and stared down at us silently. I thought of the boys I had once played with before what I was had made a difference, before I had been locked away. One young man glanced quickly down the street; another took a step forward. I stared back and made a fist, trying to keep my hand from shaking; Ellis sat up slowly and let his right hand fall to his waist, near his holster. We kept staring until the group turned from us and walked away.

"Anyway, you've got to analyze it." Ellis crossed his

legs. "There's practical reasons for not having a lot of women around. We need more soldiers—everybody does now, with all the trouble in the world. And police, too, with crime the way it is. And women can't handle those jobs."

"Once people thought they could." My shoulder muscles were tight; I had almost said *we.*

"But they can't. Put a woman up against a man, and the man'll always win." Ellis draped an arm over the back of the bench. "And there's other reasons, too. Those guys in Washington like keeping women scarce, having their pick of the choice ones for themselves—it makes their women more valuable. And a lot of the kids'll be theirs, too, from now on. Oh, they might loan a woman out to a friend once in a while, and I suppose the womb project'll change things some, but it'll be their world eventually."

"And their genes," I said. I knew that I should change the subject, but Ellis had clearly accepted my pose. In his conversation, the ordinary talk of one man to another, the longest conversation I had had with a man for many years, I was looking for a sign, something to keep me from despairing. "How long can it go on?" I continued. "The population keeps shrinking every year—there won't be enough people soon."

"You're wrong, Joe. Machines do a lot of the work now anyway, and there used to be too many people. The only way we'll ever have more women is if someone finds out the Russians are having more, and that won't happen—they need soldiers, too. Besides, look at it this way—maybe we're doing women a favor if there aren't as many of them. Would you want to be a woman, having to be married by sixteen, not being able to go anywhere, no job until she's at least sixty-five?"

And no divorce without a husband's permission, no contraception, no higher education—all the special privileges and protections could not make up for that. "No," I said to Ellis. "I wouldn't want to be one." Yet I knew that many women had made their peace with the world as it was, extorting gifts and tokens from their men, glorying in their beauty and their pregnancies, lavishing their attention on their children and their homes, tormenting and manipulating their men with the sure knowledge that any woman could find another man—for if a woman could not get a divorce by herself, a man more powerful than her husband could force him to give her up if he wanted her himself.

I had dreamed of guerrillas, of fighting women too proud to give in, breeding strong daughters by a captive male to carry on the battle. But if there were such women, they, like me, had gone to ground. The world had been more merciful when it had drowned or strangled us at birth.

Once, when I was younger, someone had said it had been a conspiracy—develop a foolproof way to give a couple a child of the sex they wanted, and most of them would naturally choose boys. The population problem would be solved in time without having to resort to harsher methods, and a blow would be leveled at those old feminists who had demanded too much, trying to emasculate men in the process. But I didn't think it had been a conspiracy. It had simply happened, as it was bound to eventually, and the values of society had controlled behavior. After all, why shouldn't a species decide to become one sex, especially if reproduction could be severed from sexuality? People had believed men were better, and had acted on that belief. Perhaps women, given the power, would have done the same.

* * *

We retreated to a bar when the sunny weather grew cooler. Ellis steered me away from two taverns with "bad elements," and we found ourselves in the doorway of a darkened bar in which several old and middle-aged men had gathered and two pretty boys dressed in leather and silk were plying their trade.

I glanced at the newscreen as I entered; the pale letters flickered, telling me that Bob Arnoldi's last appeal had failed and that he would be executed at the end of the month. This was no surprise; Arnoldi had, after all, killed a woman, and was always under heavy guard. The letters danced on; the President's wife had given birth to her thirteenth child, a boy. The President's best friend, a California millionaire, had been at his side when the announcement was made; the millionaire's power could be gauged by the fact that he had been married three times, and that the prolific First Lady had been one of the former wives.

Ellis and I got drinks at the bar. I kept my distance from one of the pretty boys, who scowled at my short, wavy hair and nestled closer to his patron. We retreated to the shadows and sat down at one of the side tables. The table top was sticky; old cigar butts had been planted on a gray mound in the ashtray. I sipped my bourbon; Ellis, while on the job, was only allowed beer.

The men at the bar were watching the remaining minutes of a football game. Sports of some kind were always on holo screens in bars, according to Sam; he preferred the old pornographic films that were sometimes shown amid war coverage and an occasional boys' choir performance for the pederasts and the more culturally inclined. Ellis looked at the screen and noted that his team was losing; I commented on the team's weaknesses, as I knew I was expected to do.

Ellis rested his elbows on the table. "This all you came for? Just to walk around and then have a drink?"

"That's it. I'm just waiting for my car." I tried to sound nonchalant. "It should be fixed soon."

"Doesn't seem like enough reason to hire an escort."

"Come on, Ellis. Guys like me would have trouble without escorts, especially if we don't know the territory that well."

"True. You don't look that strong." He peered at me a little too intently. "Still, unless you were looking for action, or going to places with a bad element, or waiting for the gangs to come out at night, you could get along. It's in your attitude—you have to look like you can take care of yourself. I've seen guys smaller than you I wouldn't want to fight."

"I like to be safe."

He watched me, as if expecting me to say more.

"Actually, I don't need an escort as much as I like to have a companion—somebody to talk to. I don't see that many people."

"It's your money."

The game had ended and was being subjected to loud analysis by the men at the bar; their voices suddenly died. A man behind me sucked in his breath as the clear voice of a woman filled the room.

I looked at the holo. Rena Swanson was reciting the news, leading with the Arnoldi story, following that with the announcement of the President's new son. Her aged, wrinkled face hovered over us; her kind brown eyes promised us comfort. Her motherly presence had made her program one of the most popular on the holo. The men around me sat silently, faces upturned, worshipping her—the Woman, the Other, someone for whom part of them still yearned.

* * *

We got back to Marcello's just before dark. As we approached the door, Ellis suddenly clutched my shoulder. "Wait a minute, Joe."

I didn't move at first; then I reached out and carefully pushed his arm away. My shoulders hurt and a tension headache, building all day, had finally taken hold, its claws gripping my temples. "Don't touch me." I had been about to plead, but caught myself in time; attitude, as Ellis had told me himself, was important.

"There's something about you. I can't figure you out."

"Don't try." I kept my voice steady. "You wouldn't want me to complain to your boss, would you? He might not hire you again. Escorts have to be trusted."

He was very quiet. I couldn't see his dark face clearly in the fading light, but I could sense that he was weighing the worth of a confrontation with me against the chance of losing his job. My face was hot, my mouth dry. I had spent too much time with him, given him too many chances to notice subtly wrong gestures. I continued to stare directly at him, wondering if his greed would win out over practicality.

"Okay," he said at last, and opened the door.

I was charged more than I had expected to pay, but did not argue about the fee. I pressed a few coins on Ellis; he took them while refusing to look at me. He knows, I thought then; he knows and he's letting me go. But I might have imagined that, seeing kindness where there was none.

* * *

I took a roundabout route back to Sam's, checking to make sure no one had followed me, then pulled off the road to change the car's license plate, concealing my own under my shirt.

Sam's store stood at the end of the road, near the foot of my mountain. Near the store, a small log cabin had been built. I had staked my claim to most of the mountain, buying up the land to make sure it remained undeveloped, but the outside world was already moving closer.

Sam was sitting behind the counter, drumming his fingers as music blared. I cleared my throat and said hello.

"Joe?" His watery blue eyes squinted. "You're late, boy."

"Had to get your car fixed. Don't worry—I paid for it already. Thinks for letting me rent it again." I counted out my coins and pressed them into his dry, leathery hand.

"Any time, son." The old man held up the coins, peering at each one with his weak eyes. "Don't look like you'll get home tonight. You can use the sofa there—I'll get you a nightshirt."

"I'll sleep in my clothes." I gave him an extra coin.

He locked up, hobbled toward his bedroom door, then turned. "Get into town at all?"

"No." I paused. "Tell me something, Sam. You're old enough to remember. What was it really like before?" I had never asked him in all the years I had known him, avoiding intimacy of any kind, but suddenly I wanted to know.

"I'll tell you, Joe." He leaned against the doorway. "It wasn't all that different. A little softer around the edges, maybe, quieter, not as mean, but it wasn't all that different. Men always ran everything. Some say they didn't, but they had all the real power—sometimes they'd dole a little of it out to the girls, that's all. Now we don't have to any more."

* * *

I had been climbing up the mountain for most of the morning, and had left the trail, arriving at my decoy house before noon. Even Sam believed that the cabin in the clearing was my dwelling. I tried the door, saw that it was still locked, then continued on my way.

My home was farther up the slope, just out of sight of the cabin. I approached my front door, which was almost invisible near the ground; the rest of the house was concealed under slabs of rock and piles of deadwood. I stood still, letting a hidden camera lens get a good look at me. The door swung open.

"Thank God you're back," Julia said as she pulled me inside and closed the door. "I was so worried. I thought you'd been caught and they were coming for me."

"It's all right. I had some trouble with Sam's car, that's all."

She looked up at me; the lines around her mouth deepened. "I wish you wouldn't go." I took off the pack loaded with the tools and supplies unavailable at Sam's store. Julia glanced at the pack resentfully. "It isn't worth it."

"You're probably right." I was about to tell her of my

own trip into town, but decided to wait until later.

We went into the kitchen. Her hips were wide under her pants; her large breasts bounced as she walked. Her face was still pretty, even after all the years of hiding, her lashes thick and curly, her mouth delicate. Julia could not travel in the world as it was; no clothing, no disguise, could hide her.

I took off my jacket and sat down, taking out my card, and my papers. My father had given them to me—the false name, the misleading address, the identification of a male—after I had pleaded for my own life. He had built my hideaway; he had risked everything for me. Give the world a choice, he had said, and women will be the minority, maybe even die out completely; perhaps we can only love those like ourselves. He had looked hard as he said it, and then he had patted me on the head, sighing as though he regretted the choice. Maybe he had. He had chosen to have a daughter, after all.

I remembered his words. "Who knows?" he had asked. "What is it that made us two kinds who have to work together to get the next batch going? Oh, I know about evolution, but it didn't have to be that way, or any way. It's curious."

"It can't last," Julia said, and I did not know if she meant the world, or our escape from the world.

There would be no Eves in their Eden, I thought. The visit to town had brought it all home to me. We all die, but we go with a conviction about the future; my extinction would not be merely personal. Only traces of the feminine would linger—an occasional expression, a posture, a feeling—in the flat-breasted male form. Love would express itself in fruitless unions, divorced from reproduction; human affections are flexible.

I sat in my home, in my prison, treasuring the small freedom I had, the gift of a man, as it seemed such freedom had always been for those like me, and wondered again if it could have been otherwise.

(1984)